Gold and Black Diamonds

by

Paul H. Pazery

DORRANCE PUBLISHING CO., INC.
PITTSBURGH, PENNSYLVANIA 15222

ISBN # 0-8059-6192-5
Printed in the United States of America

First Printing

For information or to order additional books, please write:
Dorrance Publishing Co., Inc.
701 Smithfield Street
Third Floor
Pittsburgh, Pennsylvania 15222
U.S.A.
1-800-788-7654
Or visit our web site and on-line catalog at www.dorrancepublishing.com

Chapter 1

When Vice Consul Jacques de Thoranne entered the French Consulate in Philadelphia's Ledger Building on the morning of July 9,1940, he sensed at once that something was wrong. The door was latched, not locked, as he found it every morning, for he was always the first to arrive. He entered cautiously. Someone waited in the counsel's office. He walked across the employees' room and opened the door.

The consul himself was at his desk! That had never happened before. In all the time that Jacques had been there, he had never seen his boss arrive before 10:00 A.M.

"Jacques, what time do the employees get here in the morning?" the consul asked.

"Sir, they usually arrive between nine-fifteen and nine-thirty."

"You had better make sure that the two senior employees get here by nine-thirty," the consul said. "We are expecting an important visitor."

"Sir," said Jacques. "By now, they are probably on their way in, but I'll call their homes to make sure."

The two men arrived a few moments later. Both were French citizens and longtime employees of the consulate. Since the collapse of France the month before, they came to the office as a matter of course. There was nothing to do. There were no visitors, no phone calls, no communications. They did not know if France still had a government, much less if they still had a job.

In less than nine months, the Second World War had apparently come to an end. It had started the year before, when Germany crushed Poland, it had seemed finished when Nazi troops smashed the French army, occupied Paris and half of France, and forced the French government to surrender—leaving Hitler the master of continental Europe.

The French Consulate in Philadelphia was on the second floor of the Ledger Building. Although not luxurious, it was a spacious area overlooking

1

Independence Square. It had been divided into two parts: contiguous to the entrance, a waiting room for the public and, behind the counter, an office for the employees furnished with filing cabinets, a table, and two desks. Further back, close to the window, a separation formed a small office for the vice consul; opposite that was a large office for the consul fully enclosed with panels of frosted glass.

"Hey, what's going on?" said Moreau, the younger of the two employees who had just entered the office, when he noticed movement behind the closed door of the consul's office.

"I don't know," said Jacques, "except that we're expecting an important visitor."

Neither employee asked any further questions. They sat gloomily at their desks in their shirtsleeves, for the office was like an oven after the week-long heat wave. There was no air conditioning in the Ledger Building.

Suddenly the entrance door to the consulate opened. Solemn faced, a tall, clean shaven man in a neat grey suit came into the waiting room, walked briskly through the employees' office, entered the consul's office, and closed the door.

"Who's that?" asked Duprès, an elderly employee nearing retirement after years of service in the consulate.

"I have no idea," answered Jacques. "I've never seen him before."

No one spoke. Before long the consul opened the door and summoned Jacques and the two employees into his office. He introduced the visitor. "Monsieur de Lafarge has been sent here by our embassy in Washington to deliver a confidential message from the newly constituted French government, which has made its headquarters in the town of Vichy. Paris is now occupied by the Germans."

Mr. de Lafarge opened his briefcase and pulled out a large yellow envelope protected by five seals. *"Messieurs,"* he said, "I am delegated to read to you the instructions contained in this envelope, after which this document must be incinerated in your presence."

Downcast, in monotonous tones, he read the instructions of the French government in Vichy ordering all consular and diplomatic personnel to report on any American activity—military, industrial, or political—which would appear to assist England or be hostile to Germany.

After reading the two typed pages, he pulled a cigarette lighter from his pocket and lit the paper over the consul's desk.

Jacques said, "You are asking us to spy on the United States for the benefit of Hitler. I refuse to comply with these instructions."

The consul and the embassy's emissary looked at him in disbelief.

"Do you know what that means?" asked the consul. "It means throwing away what promises to be a brilliant career in the diplomatic service. You passed the competitive exam with very high marks, and you came here with an excellent rating after your courageous service in Jerusalem."

"I'm sorry, sir," Jacques said. 'Under no condition will I spy on the United States to help Hitler. I'll tender my resignation."

"Don't make that decision in such haste," said the consul. "Take forty-eight hours to think it over. Take a little time to consider your own future and your own interest."

Jacques could understand the servile attitude of the old man who had spent his entire life in the consular service, but he despised him for it. Jacques stood up. *"Au revoir, Messieurs,"* he said and walked out of the office.

In his apartment that night, he felt sick to his stomach—sick at the thought of his parents, his relatives, and his friends captive under the Nazi yoke. Sick at the thought that the new French government had told him, officially, to serve what he considered the worst tyranny of he modern world. He'd had firsthand experience with that tyranny the year before, in Austria, where he'd gone to improve his fluency in German.

In March 1939 he was in Innsbruck, Austria, staying with distant relatives. He had spent the day cross-country skiing in the mountains south of the city in the company or he two boys and their sister. When they returned the snow had melted in the outskirts of the city, so they put their skis on their shoulders and walked. Dusk was falling. Street lights had come on. At the Bozner Platz, within one block of home, a man wearing an arm band with the swastika confronted them. He shook a coin box, saying, *"Fur das Winterhilfs Werk,"* for the winter relief. The three Austrians, Franz, Klaus, and Anne Marie, hastily dug into their pockets and put a coin in the box. Jacques refused to do so. Upon a second summons, he refused again; before he knew it, two evil-looking characters sprang out of the shadows. Each seized one of his arms and marched him to the police station a couple of blocks away.

There, a Nazi official "greeted" him with the familiar *"Heil. Hitler"* and outstretched arm. The man's eyes blazed when Jacques answered, *"Gruszgott,"* the salutation used by anti-Nazi Austrians.

"You refused," said the official, "to give to the Winter Relief."

"Yes," said Jacques.

"Why?" asked the official.

"Because," Jacques answered, "I know that what I put in that box will come back on my own head in the form of bombs, shells, and bullets."

The Nazi official quickly realized he was dealing with a foreigner. He released Jacques immediately. He apologized. Hitler did not want the war which was being thrust on Germany by the "British-Judeo plutocracy."

When Jacques got home, his Austrian hosts were waiting anxiously behind the door. When he told them what had happened, they shook their heads. "You can do that because you are a foreigner. If any one of us had done it, we would have had a warning; a second offense, of any kind, would have meant being sent to a rehabilitation camp, or worse, a concentration camp—Dachau or Auschwitz, for men, Lindau or Ravensbruck, for women—without judgment or hearing. Terror prevails here!"

"Yesterday," Franz said to Jacques, "I'm sure you noticed the Mercedes with four flat tires on the Maria Theresien Strasse. The license plate showed that it belonged to a *Norddeutscher*—a north German—surely a Nazi. We walked by as though we had seen nothing. You may have wondered, when we got home, what we were whispering about and why suddenly here was such a loud burst of laughter. We were laughing about the four flat tires. We whispered because the walls are thin here, and *die Mausie*, who is a fanatical Nazi, lives in the next apartment. If she knew why we were laughing so loudly, we could all have been arrested. You foreigners don't understand this. You can't understand it."

The sight that left the deepest impression in Jacques' mind was thrust upon him as he traveled out of Germany in June 1939. He had boarded the train in Köln to leave the Nazi Reich. One other passenger sat in the first-class compartment: a woman in her twenties, athletic, neatly dressed, and blond with penetrating light blue eyes. What the Nazis would describe as a perfect specimen of Nordic beauty—beautiful without makeup—no lipstick. That kind of stuff belonged to the women of the effete democracies.

The train passed through the city of Lachen. Just after crossing the Ems River, it came to an unscheduled stop before arriving at the Dutch border. It was a beautiful day; there was not a cloud in the sky. But outside in the fields, behind barbed wire, a man, bareback burned by the sun, was straining, obviously exhausted, pulling a harrow. Behind him was a man with whip!

The blonde woman, seeing Jacques' look of dismay, said, "Sir, this man is one of the more fortunate among those who oppose the leadership of the Führer. He is being reeducated. This is the camp of Oberlangen, for political detainees."

A year later in Philadelphia, Jacques remembered all that as he tossed around in bed in the torrid heat. *At least*, he thought, *they are not going to reeducate me*, but he shuddered at the thought of what would happen to his country, his family, his relatives, and his friends in conquered France. How could he help them? What could he do? Would Britain hold out? Would she, too, be overrun like France?

His own world had collapsed around him. His dream of the future was shattered. He had no money, no job, no country. He was stranded in a foreign land, but he was still free. He fell asleep on that happy thought.

Early the next day, he drove to New York to sell his car. When he had come to the United States the previous year, he had brought an exotic car, a Bugatti, practically unknown in America. The firm had one representative in the United States, in a one-man shop in Manhattan. The owner agreed to buy

4

the car for a small sum. He gave Jacques some cash and promised to deliver the rest in small monthly payments.

Jacques returned to Philadelphia by train. When he got to his two-room apartment in suburban Villanova, the phone was ringing. By the time he'd unlocked the door, it had stopped. A short time later, it rang again. A gentle female voice said, "Mr. de Thoranne, I have been trying to contact you all day. The ambassador wants to see you."

"What for, *Mademoiselle?*"

"He wants to talk to you about your resignation."

"*Mademoiselle*," said Jacques, "that is perfectly useless. My decision has been made, and is irrevocable."

"Wait a minute, sir," she said. "Here is the ambassador; he wants to speak to you himself."

"Jacques," said the ambassador, "I did not get an answer to my cable requesting you to come to the Embassy this morning. I must see you to discuss the implications of your decision to resign from the service."

"Sir," Jacques answered, "I do not see what good that will do. I mailed my letter of resignation to you this morning, and my decision is final."

"Jacques," said the ambassador, "you do not realize what consequences your resignation will have. I cannot discuss such confidential material over the phone. I simply must see you."

"Mr. Ambassador," said Jacques, "I simply will not, under any conditions, take orders from Hitler, and I don't think you should."

"Jacques, I want to explain this to you. I must see you personally to do so."

"Mr. Ambassador, I'll come, but don't expect me to change my decision."

"Very well," said the ambassador. "I will receive you in my office, privately, tomorrow at eleven o'clock."

Jacques arose early the next morning and prepared a breakfast of bacon and eggs with toast and coffee. He was hungry. He'd been too upset the day before to eat supper.

He caught the suburban train from Villanova to Thirtieth Street Station; there, he got on the 8:00 A.M. train due in Washington at 10:30.

When he entered the French Embassy on Massachusetts Avenue, the first man he encountered was Benech, the French naval attaché, who greeted him with the words, "Ah, here is the deserter."

"Deserter yourself," Jacques answered. "What kind of future do you think France will have under the boot of the Gestapo?"

"Sir," said Benech, "it is beneath my dignity even to talk to you, much less discuss the matter with you. We have a legally constituted government in France, and I am following their instructions."

"Mr. de Thoranne, the ambassador is waiting for you," said the first secretary of the Embassy.

The ambassador, Doynel de St. Quentin, was alone in his office when Jacques entered. His ruddy complexion had turned into a washed-out grey. He had deep pouches under his eyes. His features were drawn, and he moved slowly as he held out a trembling hand. Jacques thought he had aged ten years since their last interview a couple of months earlier, when he had proposed to transfer the vice consul to Los Angeles.

He spoke slowly and hesitantly, as though it was an effort to express his thoughts. "Jacques," he said, "I cannot understand your decision to resign. This is the time, if ever, when all Frenchmen, everywhere, must stand united in opposition to the Germans. Marshal Pétain, our great leader, who is now head of the Vichy government, has asked for unity."

"That's not what your secret memo said, Mr. Ambassador," Jacques commented. "That just instructed us to spy on the United States for the benefit of the Vichy government—that is to say, for Hitler. Mr. Ambassador, I just won't do that."

"Jacques, you will be an émigré," the ambassador retorted. "My ancestors were émigrés during the French Revolution, and it did them no good."

"Mr. Ambassador," Jacques answered, "my mind is made up. Only a British victory can rescue France from a fearful tyranny. As a student, and later as a member of the service, I spent time in Austria after it had been occupied by the Nazis. I saw that reign of terror firsthand. That's not living. That's being a slave to the so-called master race. That's not for me. I don't know what I'm going to do for a living, but I'd sooner work as a stevedore on the docks in Philadelphia than take orders from Hitler or his emissaries."

"Jacques, we have always been good colleagues. I have appreciated your enthusiasm, your willingness to work and to defend our vital interests. I'm conducting very delicate negotiations with the State Department. They would be hampered if we failed to show a united front. Please delay your resignation for a week. May I ask that of you?"

"Certainly," said Jacques, "I can wait that long."

"Very well," said the ambassador. "Return to the consulate tomorrow. I will send your letter of resignation back to you."

The next morning Jacques found that, once again, the consul was first in the office. A deadly pallor tinged his drawn face. The deep lines around his mouth seemed even deeper. Even his white hair seemed a shade whiter.

"Good morning, sir," said Jacques.

"Good morning, Jacques," said the consul. "Give me the office keys. You have a week off...

"Thank you, sir," said Jacques. "Goodbye."

A week went by. The letter of resignation the ambassador had promised to send back did not arrive. So Jacques issued a press release which read:

I shall not venture to cast judgment on the Pétain regime or on its actions. I leave that to history. As far as I am concerned, it is my unshakable conviction that only one thing can redeem France in the near future: a British victory.

Propaganda in France may well attack Britain; it will not change the basic fact. If freedom of religion and thought, without which a world is not worth living in, are to be restored in my unhappy country, it will be through Britain.

It will do the French government no good to try to turn the French people against their former ally, now their only hope. It will not even get them any consideration from the conqueror. I personally prefer to resign than to serve such a regime.

However black things look at present, I am confident the world will not go under. I have faith in Great Britain, I have faith in the United States of America. I have faith in the future.

Almost every paper in the United States carried that press release; it was quoted *in extenso* in the *New York Times*. It was followed by a deluge of phone calls, visits by reporters, photographers, curious neighbors, and, of course, friends.

But that did not solve Jacques' problem. He was an exile, an alien, a man without a nationality, without a country, and without a job—and he needed one, soon. Job hunting was an immediate priority.

A week later Jacques went to Washington to answer a want ad. When he got off the train at Union Station, he ran into Janson, the vice consul at the French Embassy in Washington. They were good friends. Janson greeted him warmly.

"Jacques," said Janson, "the papers were full of your resignation. I'm so glad you made it public when you did. After your interview with the ambassador last week, before you'd had time to get back to Philadelphia, he sent an urgent 'priority' cable to the French government in Vichy, requesting authorization to dismiss you from the diplomatic service. I ciphered the cable. It was marked 'most confidential' and 'urgent.' I could not warn you. I'm closely watched here. There's been no answer yet, and the press release announcing your resignation caught them completely by surprise. I'm so glad you did it."

"I smelled a rat," said Jacques, "when I got back to Philadelphia and the consul demanded the immediate return of the keys to the office and to the safe and gave me a week's vacation."

"Your stand made them furious," said Janson, smiling. "You are public enemy number one around here. They hate you. They say you don't know what's happened in France, where 95 percent of the people support the new government. You'd better watch out. They will get back at you any way they can."

"All that may be true," said Jacques, "but I will never take any orders from Hitler—such as the orders contained in that secret memo sent by the Embassy."

"Yes, they are afraid you might make that public," said Janson. "They were livid when they read the papers that morning. Your resignation statement made front-page headlines in the *Washington Post*. I had the pleasure of delivering it to the ambassador in person. You should have seen his face. He hit the ceiling when he realized you had beaten him to it."

"The ambassador could have been a little more honest with me," said Jacques.

"I'm so glad his dirty trick failed," said Janson, "and I can tell you that there's more than one in the embassy who secretly agrees with you—the ambassador's secretary, for one, I'm sure. Congratulations, dear Jacques. I have to run for my train." He shook Jacques' hand warmly. "You'll understand that I prefer not to be seen with you. Good luck."

That luck did not take long to catch up with the man without a country, home, job, or money. He soon found that he was not an orphan but the adopted son of a great land.

He'd been invited to speak before the Optimist Club of Upper Darby, a suburb of Philadelphia. The members wanted to hear why he'd resigned and what might be the outcome of the war between England and Hitler.

Jacques had left the meeting quietly and was walking to the subway when he heard someone running behind him. It was the president of the club. "Here, you," he said, "don't be bashful. That was a wonderful talk. Here's ten bucks. We can't give you more, but we like guys like you. We'll get you plenty of more talks. Paid ones, too."

They did. That first talk developed into a thriving lecturing business with one message: "If you want to help France, support Britain."

Soon, a prestigious Philadelphia law firm offered him an office and a part-time secretary, Andrèe Scanlan. She was a great help.

As the lectures piled up and Jacques' reputation as a speaker grew, demands on his time by service clubs, luncheon clubs, women's clubs, and radio stations imposed upon him a strenuous program perfectly managed by his new secretary. Soon she spent all her time working with him, typing his lectures, each tailored to the audience he was to meet. His name became a household word on the Eastern seaboard; to many Americans he represented the true spirit of France, the spirit of "no compromise" with Hitler.

That's why he was invited to sponsor the premiere of a play conceived in the South, *The Sailors of Toulon*. It featured a rebellion, almost a mutiny, of a group of sailors of the French fleet at anchor in the Mediterranean port of Toulon who were determined to continue the fight against the Nazis while the officers accepted the surrender and abided by the orders of the Vichy government of Marshal Pétain.

The play, given in a theater in Nashville, was attended with great fanfare by many business and political leaders of the State of Tennessee, including the governor. Before the play the governor, in an impassioned speech, reminded his audience that the fledgling American colony owed its independence to the French and that it was thanks to the French troops and sailors of Lafayette and Rochambeau that Cornwallis was compelled to surrender in Yorktown. He went one step further and reminded the assembly of the help the British had given the Confederacy during the war against the North. The tumultuous applause, which repeatedly interrupted the speech, made it clear that south of the Mason-Dixon line, and in Nashville in particular, no one was about to forget the help which had come from both Britain and France.

It was a perfect setting for Jacques' message. If you want to help France, he told the people, support Britain. That too, was greeted by sustained applause. He was asked to repeat the message later on WSM, Nashville's main radio station.

When he got back to his office in Philadelphia, his secretary handed him a terse message: "Mr. John F. Wilkins, Director of the FBI in Philadelphia, wants to see you as soon as you return to the office."

Jacques wasted no time getting to FBI Headquarters, only a short walk from the Morris Building where he had his office. He handed his card to the receptionist. Mr. Wilkins received him almost immediately and greeted him cordially.

"Mr. Jacques de Thoranne, I need not tell you that we have followed your activities carefully since you resigned from the French Diplomatic Service, however, we are not the only ones interested in what you are doing."

"I'm not surprised," said Jacques. "I'm sure my former colleagues are most interested in what I am doing."

"Yes," the chief continued, 'you have become a thorn in the side of the Vichy government and of that section of the Gestapo watching known enemies of the Nazis beyond the borders of lands occupied by the Third Reich.

"No sir, I'm not surprised," said Jacques.

"These people," the FBI chief continued, "have gone one step further. We are told enemies have hired a hit man to eliminate you."

"Which enemies?" asked Jacques.

"I can't be more precise than that," Wilkins said, "but we know for sure that you are a target. That's the bad news. In this country, however, we do not tolerate such interference by a foreign power. We will give you twenty-four hour protection, but you must help us...."

"How?" asked Jacques.

The FBI chief sat back in his chair. "You are living with friends in Villanova," the official said, "but we can't give you the protection you need in this semi-rural area. You'll make our job much easier by moving into center city."

"Sir, I have not received threats of any kind," said Jacques.

"I don't think you will," the FBI man continued. "Your enemies know threats won't deter you, that you will make any threats public."

"Sir," Jacques said, "I'll move to Philadelphia as soon as possible."

"Good," Wilkins said. "Waste no time moving into the city. If you are out late at night, don't walk home. Take a taxi when you get off the train. Above all, be alert at all times. Your life depends on it. In the meantime, the U.S. government will bring its full power to bear on those we believe are behind this."

"Thank you for warning me," said Jacques. "I see that the long arm of terror that grips Europe extends to the United States."

"Do you have a gun?"

"Yes, sir, I do."

"What kind is it?" asked the official.

"It is a French *quatre-vingt-douze*, which is quite cumbersome; it's not something I can put in my pocket."

"Keep it within reach at night," said Wilkins. "Carefully lock your doors and latch the windows; keep in touch with us at all times. Here's a special phone number which will be answered immediately. Meanwhile here is a small revolver and a permit to carry it. Should anybody stop a car near you and try to force you into it, don't hesitate to shoot it. Call at any time you see or hear anything unusual."

"Thank you, sir," said Jacques.

"What on earth did the FBI chief want to see you about?" Andrèe asked Jacques when he returned to the office. "You seem disturbed."

"I've just been warned that one of my enemies has engaged a hit man to do away with me."

"My God, that's horrible!" said Andrée. "What is the FBI going to do about it?"

"The FBI will provide personal protection, but I must move to Philadelphia to make their job easier; I'll do that in a couple of days. He also said that representations 'at the highest level' would be made by the U.S. government against those suspected—by that, I'm sure he means the Vichy French and the Nazi embassies in Washington. Andrée, it's really reassuring to live in a country which provides that kind of protection to citizens."

"Will you continue to lecture?"

"Of course I will," said Jacques. "You should know me better than to ask such a question. The worst thing I could do would be to yield to intimidation."

"Don't forget you have a speaking engagement tonight in Pennsauken. Here's the script."

"A good thing you reminded me. Where's Pennsauken?"

"The other side of the Delaware River over the Ben Franklin Bridge. You don't have to worry about getting there. The president of the club said he'd pick you up at your apartment in Villanova at six this evening."

"Who's the president of the club?"

"His name is James Westcott."

"I remember him from the Reciprocity Club in Center City. He asked me then to address his group. I'd better get going."

Villanova, a suburb of Philadelphia, was about twenty-five minutes away from Suburban Street Station at Sixteenth Street. It was still daylight when Jacques got off the train there, but there were no taxis at the station, so he decided to walk the seven hundred odd yards to his apartment on Hillcrest Road. He hurried along, keeping a watchful eye around him.

He stepped off the sidewalk to avoid a batch of freshly poured cement before the entrance of a house. Without warning car zoomed up behind him. Jacques had a split second to jump for the protection of the pillar at the gate entrance as a blue Plymouth flashed by knocking down board and lights, tearing off the ropes, and churning up the cement. Its back fender hit the gate pillar with a loud crunch, and the car sped off in a cloud of dust—so fast it disappeared around the bend before Jacques had time to get a fleeting glimpse of anything more than the two letters FG of the dirty license plate.

The sound of the car hitting the pillar, followed by the scream of the tires, brought the owner out of the house.

"Did you hear that?" he asked Jacques.

"I sure did," answered Jacques. "I barely had time to get out of the way."

"Oh!" said the owner. "Another one of those drunks!"

Jacques knew better. As soon as he got to his apartment, he called the FBI. The chief was still there. "I'm very glad you called," said Wilkins. "This information comes just when it is most needed and will be very useful."

When he heard of the failed attempt against Jacques' life, the president of the club in New Jersey insisted on having Jacques spend the night at his home and drove him into Philadelphia himself the next morning.

"Did you see the paper this morning?" asked Andrée when Jacques entered the office.

"No," said Jacques, "why?"

"Look at this," said the secretary, handing Jacques the *Philadelphia Record*, with a dramatic front-page headline in bold letters, "HIT MAN SET ON THO-RANNE," followed by the subheading, "State Department Warns Vichy French Ambassador."

"With that kind of publicity," said Andrée smiling, "you'll get more speaking engagements than you can possibly handle. I've just signed you up for the

Town Meeting of the Air, in New York; it's not too well paid, but you'll reach an immense audience. Next week you already have three engagements in Massachusetts and one in Cleveland, Ohio.'

Threat or no threat, Jacques continued his appeal to America to help stave off the onslaught of tyranny engulfing the world. His message, delivered in terms suited to each individual audience, was always the same: "If you want to help France, support Britain." Each lecture was followed by comments in local newspapers and on radio stations. Eventually Jacques became an unofficial spokesman for those silenced by the Gestapo. As 1940 came to a close, a cloud of gloom fell over the civilized world. Hitler controlled land stretching from the Soviet Union to the Atlantic Ocean. Himmler's Gestapo ruled the conquered peoples with a ferocious reign of terror.

England alone stood free after the worst military defeat in her history. The British Expeditionary Force in France—virtually the entire British army—had narrowly escaped annihilation by fleeing in disarray across the English Channel, leaving behind every piece of war equipment. The Royal Navy had lost all of its G-class destroyers during the Dunkerque evacuation. The RAF was crippled by its devastating losses of planes and pilots in France. It had so few planes and such a dearth of fighter pilots that a Nazi invasion seemed a practical reality. These were the days when the survival of Britain depended above all on help from America—and Jacques appeared day after day, before every kind of audience, to request that help.

Christmas and New Years came and went and brought Jacques a few days of rest—but not many; the first two months of the year were studded with engagements. When he returned from a week-long lecturing tour in Chicago at the end of January 1941, his secretary said that the British ambassador wanted to see him. She had scheduled an appointment for the following week.

"Will you drive to Washington," she asked him, "or do you prefer to take the train?"

"I'll take the train; I can relax there. Besides, at this time of the year, no one knows what the weather will be like."

It was a bitterly cold day in early February when Jacques quietly entered the British Embassy on Massachusetts Avenue in Washington, DC.

"Good afternoon, Mr. de Thoranne," said the receptionist.

Jacques looked at her in surprise. "How on earth, miss," he asked her, "do you know my name before I have even handed you my card?"

"Sir," said the lively, trim receptionist, "I've seen your picture often enough in the papers and magazines to recognize you immediately. Besides, I know you have an appointment with the ambassador today. You won't have to wait very long."

The ambassador sat in a high-backed arm chair on one side of the fireplace. A roaring fire cast its cheery message throughout the vast, high-ceilinged, wood-paneled room. The ambassador rose slowly to greet his visitor, shaking his hand warmly.

"Please, sir," said Jacques, "don't get up. Your administrative assistant tells me that you are suffering from lumbago."

"Mr. de Thoranne," the ambassador said to Jacques, "I have wanted to have a few moments with you for a long time; I particularly want to thank you, personally and in the name of His Majesty's government, for the immense service you are rendering Great Britain at a time we need it most."

"Mr. Ambassador, if there is a service, it is not just for Great Britain. My own country will be the greatest beneficiary of a British victory. I want to make the American people understand that there can be no compromise with Hitler and what it would mean to the civilized world if Britain were to fall."

"Exactly," said the ambassador, "but our people would be called self-serving if we tried to convey this message. You can do it and are doing it very well. No one can accuse you of being a British propagandist. Is there any way we can help you?"

"No, thank you, Mr. Ambassador. I have developed a busy lecturing business. I am well paid, and my livelihood is assured so far...yet, on second thought, Mr. Ambassador, perhaps there is a way in which you could help."

"I will consider any request favorably."

"As a lecturer I must consider that the novelty of my resignation and of the collapse of France have worn thin. If I could see the war first hand, I could bring true life and death stories to the many organizations before which I speak."

"Mr. de Thoranne," the ambassador said, "our consul in Philadelphia told me of your desire to serve as war correspondent with the nationals of occupied countries who have escaped to Britain to continue the fight. I favor this project and have discussed it with a gentleman in London who enjoys the full power of government. He approves this and believes you are the person he is looking for to help us in an area where we are quite weak—I have in mind parts of Africa—where you could render a great service. When would you like to leave?"

"I have engagements scheduled until mid-March. Could I leave at the end of March or in early April?"

"I think so. That would give me time to make arrangements. How would you like to travel?"

"Could I travel on warship, escorting a convoy?"

"I think that can be arranged, too," said the ambassador.

"Then I will no longer need the guardian angels of the FBI," said Jacques, smiling.

"I am well aware, Mr. de Thoranne," said the ambassador, "that you have lived a dangerous and most unpleasant life during the last few months, but I can also tell you, relying on your discretion, that the American government has gone to great lengths to assure your personal safety. It made representations, in the strongest terms, to the foreign power powers responsible for this threat. It has also warned them of the serious consequences it would have for them were you to be murdered. I feel sure that those who had planned this attack realize now that it would not serve their interests, but that does not mean that you should drop your guard."

"I won't, Mr. Ambassador, but I feel much reassured by what you have told me, and I appreciate the time you have taken to talk to me."

"You will hear from me shortly through our consul in Philadelphia." The ambassador shook Jacques' hand.

"Mr. de Thoranne," said the receptionist, "a taxi will be here for you in a few minutes; you should be able to catch the four o'clock train. It has started to snow, and I'm sure you will want to get home as soon as possible."

"Thank you, Miss."

Jacques caught the four o'clock train with a few minutes to spare. It was snowing hard when the train pulled out of the station. It covered the ground when Jacques got off the train at Thirtieth Street in Philadelphia. He was fortunate to catch a local to Fifteenth Street. There were still many people in the street as he came out of the station, but there were no taxis. Despite the warnings he had received, he decided to walk to his apartment on Spruce Street. He walked fast, constantly on the alert. Nothing happened.

"While you were in Washington," Andrèe told him the next morning, "I got a call from Mr. Kelby, president of the Philadelphia Hundred Club; he wants to have you as guest speaker for his group."

"What is the Hundred Club?" asked Jacques. "I've never heard of it."

"That club is limited to one hundred members, all of whom are presidents of other clubs. It is a very select group. Can you imagine how many engagements that is going to bring?"

"What date did he propose?" asked Jacques.

"Thursday, March 20," said Andrée.

"That's all right," said Jacques. "I won't be able to take any later speaking dates. I'll leave for the war zone in late March or early April. The ambassador approved the project you and I have discussed many times."

The insistent ring of the phone interrupted the conversation. The secretary picked up the receiver. "Yes, Mr. Kelby, March 20 will be all right… yes… he is here."

Jacques picked up the receiver. "Mr. Kelby, I'm glad to make your acquaintance over the phone. It will be a pleasure to speak to your group. This will be the last engagement I can accept. I'm leaving a few days later for the war zone. I'm scheduled to serve as war correspondent with those who have escaped from the conquered countries of Europe and are fighting the Nazis with England. I shall look forward to your meeting."

"Andrée," said Jacques to his secretary, "Mr. Kelby said, that in view of the circumstances, he'll make this a bang-up affair, for men only, a send-off that I will never forget."

The "bang-up" send-off party was well attended. Nearly all of the members of the Hundred Club were there. It took place in Philadelphia, at Schrafft's on Chestnut Street; a large private room had been reserved for the club, whose president had great power in City Hall.

At the end of the meal, the president rapped his gavel. "Members, all our announcements are cut short this evening. This meeting is to hear from a well-known citizen, a member of the French Diplomatic Service, who now stands condemned to death in his own country for refusing to obey Hitler, a man whose message you won't soon forget, Mr. Jack de Thoranne...."

As Jacques sat down after an address repeatedly punctuated by applause, the president of the club stood up and gaveled for silence. "Members, now comes the second part of our special evening. I want everyone here to understand that this is art, pure art; if anyone here feels he should leave, he should do so now, during the ten minute scheduled break." No one left.

"Gentlemen," the president went on after the break, "let us resume the meeting."

When all members had returned to their seats at the tables arranged in the form of an inverted U, the door of the room opened and a young lady, elegantly dressed, entered, followed by a middle-aged man carrying a case containing a violin. "Members," said the president, "the second part of our special program is now underway."

To the lively tunes of the violin, the girl opened the short umbrella she carried under her arm, held it above her head (as an umbrella should be held), while with the other hand she slowly shed, rhythmically to the tune of the music, every vestige of clothing to reveal a body which would have been the envy of any woman in the audience. (There were none!). She walked around for a few moments, to the tune of the music, with the umbrella as her sole cover. Then she closed that colorful protection, folded it, and put it in her bag. Then she made the rounds and walked up to selected members of the club and, straddling each one, pressed his face in the depression between her shapely breasts. She came to the speaker's table and went directly to the guest of the evening (who was also the youngest man in the room).

The violin struck up a lively tune as she quietly sat astride him. With her right arm, she tenderly pulled Jacques' face against her lips while her other hand explored and gently caressed an area of the male body quite sensitive to a feminine hand—with the remark, overheard only by those close by, "What a feeling!"

Everyone stood up when the violinist intoned the French National Anthem, and a formidable round of applause greeted the player when he put down his violin.

The president of the club rose once again. "Gentlemen, I'm sure you'll all agree that we've had a wonderful evening. I can think of no better way of closing it than to ask our guest speaker from France to thank the artist for her outstanding performance." (She was still at the speaker's table, without the umbrella.)

The applause which followed gave Jacques a few seconds to recover from his surprise and time to think of what to say. Applause and expectations rose as he stood up to face the audience. What would he say? He waited for calm to return.

"Our two artists," said Jacques, "have provided a performance which will long be remembered, and I cannot think of a better compliment to the beautiful young lady, who played such a prominent part in this delightful evening, than to tell her that no one in Paris could have done better."

Chapter II

When Jacques prepared to sail for England in March 1941, he had a better perspective of the war—not a very encouraging one. He wondered what he was getting into. Was he on his way to disaster? No one knew who would win the war. Most people believed that Britain had lost it. She stood alone with a fledgling army and a small, terribly overextended air force.

Across a narrow strip of water, the English Channel, Hitler's Germany had built the most powerful war machine the world had ever seen. It seemed invincible. It had crushed all the barriers and armies of Europe with lightning speed. It held practically the entire continent under its yoke. It ruled with absolute power.

To the east Nazi and Soviet armies faced each other in an uneasy truce. To the west Nazis occupied all French harbors on the Channel and the Atlantic. The French government had signed an armistice dividing the country in two. The north was directly under Nazi rule, enforced by the Gestapo; the south was nominally free, administered by a legally elected government under the presidency of a man with great prestige, Marshal Philippe Pétain. Because Paris was occupied by the Nazis, he chose the town of Vichy, in unoccupied France, for his capital. His administration became known as the Vichy government.

Stunned by the suddenness and magnitude of the defeat, the French people and their leaders, almost to a man, had no doubt that Germany had won the war. Their hopes for the future rested entirely on the aging Marshal, convinced that only he might mitigate the exorbitant demands of the conqueror.

The British Expeditionary Force (BEF)—virtually the entire British army—was encircled and had retreated in disarray to the French coast. It was saved from annihilation by the sons and daughters of a seafaring nation, mobilized by a man previously retired by the Royal Navy for being too efficient. War had brought him back to service as the admiral in charge of the entire Dover area. Acutely aware of the catastrophe facing Britain, Sir Bertram Ramsey organized in a few days the rescue of the entrapped army from the

French port of Dunkerque and the beaches nearby. While others talked, he acted. In ten unforgettable days, from May 24 to June 4, he assembled everything that could float. He slashed red tape, bypassed chains of command, overruled admiralty and war cabinet objections, and rescued the defeated army of two hundred twenty-five thousand men who'd lost everything except their will to stay free. Thanks to Admiral Sir Bertram Ramsey, in early 1941 Britain was still a sovereign nation.

Thanks to the Fighter Command and to the English Channel, Nazi troops had not overrun Britannia. Hitler's armies were land armies, not prepared for a hazardous venture across the sea—even across such a narrow strip of water as the English Channel, called by the French *la Manche*, the sleeve. By the end of 1940, the British army had been reorganized and rearmed. It was standing guard over the green fields of southern England, ready to repel any invader.

So the land war in Europe became an air and sea war directed against Great Britain: an air war to destroy its industrial power and the morale of its people and a sea war to cut its lifelines and starve the British people into submission. Britain's survival depended mainly on materials brought over the sea lanes from Canada and the United States.

When the war had started in September 1939, the combined navies of Britain and France had a good command of the seas. Merchant ships, bringing vital supplies to both countries, sailed independently. Some were lost, but most got through.

After the collapse of France in 1940, the French navy was confined in ports and was no longer a major factor in the war. Britain had to protect the sea lanes alone, with an overextended navy which had been diminished by the loss of all her G-class destroyers. Stukas and the S-boats had sunk them during the evacuation from Dunkerque.

In January and February of 1941 alone, some 320 ships—700,000 tons—were sunk—some by surface raiders such as *Atlantis*, a disguised merchantman; some by warships; some by planes; but most by submarines. These losses were greater than the combined ship production of Britain, Canada, and the United States. The figures did not include ships damaged by enemy action, or with mechanical problems, or otherwise crippled waiting at anchor in ports for parts which took weeks, sometimes months, to arrive.

Because merchant ships traveling independently had no protection against submarines, the British Admiralty organized the system of convoys. Twenty or thirty or more ships sailed together, under the protection of small warships—corvettes, frigates, destroyers—equipped to detect, attack, and sink enemy U-boats. Britain's most vital lifeline started in the United States. Although neutral in the conflict, America sensed that world freedom was at stake.

Canada, then a part of the British Commonwealth of Nations, had already thrown its strength into the fray. Its eastern port of Halifax, nestled in a long protected bay, became gathering point for convoys bound for England. Warships, freighters, and tankers, loaded supplies and war materials from the United States and Canada, assembled there for the dangerous run to England.

On a morning in late March 1941, one of the largest freighters in the world, the twenty-two thousand ton *Tyndareus* of the Blue Funnel line, dropped anchor at Halifax. Painted dull grey, it sat low in the water, heavily laden with weapons of war—fighter planes, guns, ammunition, explosives, and depth charges—put aboard in the port of New York.

Jacques de Thoranne was aboard it.

He went on deck before breakfast. A cold wind blew from the west, spewing a fine drizzle which could almost have been snow. Throughout the bay he could see the dark hulks of the ships, blacked out and silent. A launch came toward *Tyndareus*. It stopped at the foot of the wooden ladder hanging over the side. A man in the uniform of the Royal Navy climbed up the ladder. The captain of *Tyndareus* greeted the newcomer, Commodore Williams, who asked to see passenger Jacques de Thoranne. The captain sent for him.

Jacques arrived a few minutes later.

'Sir," said the commodore, "the Ministry of Transport has instructed us to put you on a warship for your journey to England. Preferably a warship manned by sailors of a conquered nation who have sided with Britain."

"What kind of warship, sir?" Jacques asked.

"We have two escorts, manned almost exclusively by Free French crews. Both are corvettes. One, *Christmas Rose*, commanded by Captain Brunaud, and the other, *Marigold*, commanded by Lieutenant Commander Darcy. Do you have any preference?"

"Yes, sir, I do," said Jacques. "*Marigold.*"

"That was a quick decision," said the commodore.

"Yes, sir," said Jacques. "If Darcy is the former professor of submarine warfare at the Ecole Navale in Brest, I used to dance with his daughter Thérèse."

"That may be the case," said the commodore. "Both Brunaud and Darcy are former submarine commanders. They escaped from France when the French surrendered. They've been fighting with Britain ever since. They are among the best antisubmarine fighters in the British Navy."

"Have they been assigned to this route for any length of time?" asked Jacques.

"They are assigned to protect merchant ships whenever we have very important convoys. They have performed so well that the Admiralty has given them the newest, fastest corvettes."

"What makes these corvettes different?"

"They are equipped with the latest quick-firing weapons, a four-inch gun and Bofors 40mm pom-poms, also the latest technical advances, 10cm radars and the most sensitive asdics. Both ships fly the white ensign of the Royal Navy, although the crews are French except for a few Canadians learning anti-submarine warfare."

"Sir, what are asdics?" asked Jacques.

"They are instruments to pinpoint the exact location and distance of submarines under water. We feel pretty sure that submarines have been alerted for this convoy, which carries large amounts of war material. You can expect some action."

"When may I transfer, sir?"

"Immediately," said the commodore. "The launch that brought me here will take you there. Meantime we'll tell Darcy you're coming."

Jacques had never met any of the crew of *Marigold*, but he was greeted like an old friend when he boarded. Here he was among his own—a sharp contrast with the colleagues in the embassy in Washington, where he was the outcast.

From Halifax, Canada, to Liverpool, England, convoy distance varied between three thousand and four thousand miles depending to the route followed. Convoys did not travel in a straight line; they zigzagged to avoid two obstacles: enemy and weather. At convoy speed—six to eight knots for slow convoys—ships covered up to two hundred miles in twenty-four hours. Atlantic crossings took seventeen to twenty-two days, depending on weather, condition of the ocean, and enemy action. Across this vast expanse of water—sometimes sunny, sometimes gloomy, sometimes fearsome, always impressive—lay a zone of fear called the Gap, where there was no air cover and, lurking below the waves, Nazi submarines could operate almost at will.

Convoy HX 103 included forty-one ships: freighters, mostly fueled with coal and loaded with materials, and tankers loaded with oil and fueled with oil. The convoy was protected by warships fueled with oil: four corvettes, two Canadian, two Free French; three frigates, one English and two Canadian; and one British destroyer, *Warminster*, flagship of Commodore Williams, in charge of the convoy.

The convoy left Halifax at night, making it more difficult for Nazi spies to know its exact composition. Blacked out, with radios silent, the ships emerged from the bay.

As the officers of the *Marigold* and Jacques sat down for dinner, Commander Darcy said, "Now, we are getting underway, and I can tell you a few secrets which could not be mentioned until now."

"What kind of secrets?" asked Jacques.

"First," said Darcy, "this is the most valuable convoy we have ever escorted. We have thirteen tankers which must get through. England is running dangerously short of oil. Second, the freighters are full of critical war material, planes in particular. The ship you came on from New York, Jacques, is worth its weight in gold. Besides planes, it's carrying depth charges, guns, and all kinds of ammunition. It's a real powder keg; we cannot afford to lose it."

"How many planes?" asked Bousquet, the second in command on *Marigold.*

"I have no idea," said Darcy. "I don't know myself. The British are terribly tight-lipped about this."

"What's the next secret?" asked Mouchet, the ship's doctor and surgeon.

Why, Jean," said Darcy, "you've got a few secrets, too. Tell us how you got to England. You've had a long-standing reputation of being the most anti-British man in the French Navy. and here you are fighting with us and with them. How come?"

Mouchet, a navy doctor in his early thirties, carefully groomed and clean shaven, a quiet determined man, finally answered the question he'd been asked many times.

"I was on the French destroyer *Sirocco,* evacuating men from Dunkerque. Around 2:00 A.M. we were hit by one, perhaps two, torpedoes fired by a German S-boat. The ship was cut in half and went down in a few seconds. I had my life jacket on and floated around for about an hour before being picked up."

"Was the water cold?" asked Jacques.

"Not very," said Mouchet, "but I was beginning to feel the chill when I was rescued by an overloaded pleasure boat. It put us ashore in Dover and went to refuel to return to France to rescue more people."

"Did the English give you the choice of returning to France?" asked Jacques.

"They did," said Mouchet, "but the people in Dover received us so well, gave us dry clothes, hot food, and hot drinks, and seemed so grateful for what we were doing that...."

"That what?" asked Darcy.

"That my anti-British feelings started to mellow, and my anti-German feelings got the upper hand, especially when I realized that the English weren't going to yield to the Nazis. Besides, the sinking of *Sirocco* and the loss of so many of my friends simply infuriated me. So I stayed in England to continue the war—and I'm glad I did! My big problem is that I don't speak English!"

Darcy laughed. "No one on this ship does," he said. "The Canadians on board are from the Maritimes and are not good at it. Of course if we have any transmission problems, Jacques will help us. Besides Commodore Williams is very considerate and will see that his men don't transmit messages too fast."

"The cook has really surpassed himself," said Mouchet, savoring a leek and potato soup worthy of a chef at the Ritz.

"Better eat it before reaching the high sea," said the orderly, bringing a large bowl for a second service. "The wind is blowing pretty hard out there."

Beyond the lee of land, soup was no fare to serve, even on a corvette!

Corvettes of the flower class (all bore the name of a flower) were squat, stubby, 950-ton ships, superbly seaworthy, at home on the heavy seas of the

North Atlantic. They were not fast ships: sixteen knots flat out. They could not overtake the faster subs navigating on the surface under diesel power—that was a job for frigates or destroyers—but for sub hunting on convoy duty, they had proved their worth.

German submarines would wait in the ocean along a convoy's presumed route. When ships were sighted—the smoke of the coal-burning freighters could be seen from afar—submarines would let the convoy pass and trail it; at dark they surfaced and speeded up on the surface in position to fire torpedoes.

The two Free French corvettes, *Christmas Rose* and *Marigold,* were last out of Halifax harbor. Their job was to zigzag behind the convoy with radar and asdic, sniffing air and sea.

For days there was no action—an uneasy calm. Occasionally a Catalina would over fly the convoy, circle it, and disappear toward its Canadian base.

"While there's been no action so far," said Darcy, "we shall soon get into the danger zone, and we must be fully alert at all times. Remember, too, that submarines nearly always strike at night."

Jacques stood on the bridge next to the skipper, watching the ocean in the gloom of dusk. The north wind showered the deck with a thin drizzle of snow. How nice it would be to have a hot shower before turning in, an unthinkable luxury! No one could chance being in the shower if a torpedo hit. Since leaving Halifax, no one had had a proper wash. At best one got a quick change of clothes.

Darcy told Jacques, "When we enter the danger zone, I will not leave the bridge of this ship until we're through the Gap."

"How long will that take?" asked Jacques.

"Between five to seven days," said Darcy.

"Won't you get any sleep at all?" asked Jacques.

"I'll cat nap now and then for a short time when my second officer is on watch."

"Here he is," said Bousquet, who had just appeared.

"I'll rest a few moments now," said Darcy. "Bousquet, stay on the bridge; if there's anything unusual, send Jacques to wake me."

"This is my first tour of duty on a convoy," Bousquet said as they stood on the bridge watching the thickening snow. "I was about to graduate from submarine school in the Naval Academy at Brest when France collapsed. I escaped to England with several other students on the same ship as our commander. He is a fantastically competent man, so earnest and dedicated."

"From what I've seen," said Jacques, "he could send his crew through fire and they'd go!"

"Yes," said Bousquet, "we all have great faith in him."

Jacques and Bousquet belonged to the same generation. They had the same conservative, patriotic background and the same confidence in hard work. They talked about the past in France and what had led to the collapse. They remembered the friends who had lost their lives, mused on the events they'd just lived, and wondered when the war might end—and something more immediate, too. "This snow's getting awfully dense," said Jacques. "I can't even see the bow of the ship!"

"I can't either," said Bousquet. "Now we must rely almost entirely on radar for surface visibility."

"Say, Bousquet," said Jacques, "do you smell something?"

"I can smell fuel oil," said Bousquet, "but that's a constant smell on these ships."

"I know," said Jacques, "but there's more than that. I can smell burning phosphorous. That's an odor I remember well from the lab when I was studying chemistry."

"You mean," said Bousquet, "that sort of sickly smell with a rotten garlic-like flavor? It's very faint, but I do smell it."

"Do we have any phosphorous on board?" asked Jacques.

"Not to my knowledge," said Bousquet.

"That's not a normal smell at sea. I don't like that," said Jacques. "I think I'll wake the chief."

"For heaven's sake," said Bousquet, "let the poor man get some sleep! He doesn't get much of it anyway!"

"I know," said Jacques, "but he said to wake him in case of something unusual."

"I wouldn't do it," said Bousquet, "but you're sort of unofficial here, and you can probably get away with it."

Jacques rapped at the skipper's door.

"Yes. Come in."

"Sorry to wake you, Commandant, but there's a strange smell outside!"

"What kind of a smell?" asked Darcy anxiously.

"Something like burning phosphorous," said Jacques.

"What!" said Darcy, rising from his bunk in a split second. He went outside. "I don't smell anything," he said. He stood in silence on the bridge. "Yes, I do smell it," he said. "That's the smell of a phoscar."

"What's that?" asked Jacques.

"That's a float carrying a beacon containing a phosphorous compound. When it hits the water, the phosphorous ignites with a brilliant flame which illuminates a vast area around it. That smell, combined with the smell of fuel oil, disturbs me greatly."

"Why, Commander?" asked Jacques.

"I hope nothing has happened to *Christmas Rose*. That smell is coming from the direction where she should be. We'll scour the area to see what we can find."

The men on watch in the darkness of night had smelled the phoscar, noted the change of course, and were probing the area with radar and asdic. The crew were alert and tense as the skipper directed *Marigold* in the sector covered by *Christmas Rose*. Speed: 16 knots!

It's not easy for a submarine to torpedo a small ship at that speed at night, specially a ship equipped to detect and fight submarines.

The smell of the phoscar had long disappeared when *Marigold* reached the sector where *Christmas Rose* should have been. There was no blip on radar, indicating her presence.

Darcy did not return to rest; he stayed on the bridge, gloomly and full of foreboding.

"We can't even inform the commodore of our suspicions. We can't use the radio, and we can't leave the rear of the convoy unprotected."

"That means," Bousquet said to Jacques, "we'll have to wait for daylight."

Every morning at daybreak, Commodore Williams made the rounds of the convoy on his fast destroyer. Was any ship missing? Were there any stragglers?

As soon as *Warminster* was in sight, *Marigold* signaled the commodore over the blinker: "Fear something happened to *Christmas Rose* around 2:30 A.M. Stop. Smelled fuel, phoscar. Stop. Scoured area, found nothing. Stop.

The British destroyer acknowledged the message and sped astern of the convoy at high speed.

It was daylight now. The snow had stopped, and visibility was good. Scanning the horizon with trained eyes and binoculars, even with radar, nothing could be seen except the emptiness of the ocean.

On *Marigold* officers had finished lunch when *Warminster* returned to the convoy with four survivors of the French corvette. The men on watch on *Warminster* had found them adrift in a carley float, exhausted, half frozen, and black with bunker oil. With them were two crewmen dead from exposure. All were still wearing the lifejackets which had kept them afloat in the frigid water when the corvette was torpedoed in the black of night. They had climbed onto the carley float by the light of the phoscar, choking on its fumes. *Christmas Rose* had been hit with two torpedoes and had gone down in less than a minute, taking the rest of the crew with it.

Commodore Williams had radioed for more escorts. In the meantime *Marigold* was left to cover the rear of the convoy by itself. Darcy asked the commodore for authorization to take on bunker oil from the only tanker in the convoy equipped to refuel other ships at sea.

"The wind is picking up," Darcy commented. "We must refuel before the weather gets too bad. We've got to cover the rear of the convoy by ourselves. That means go faster, travel farther, and use more fuel...."

"How far can you go on one load of fuel?" Jacques asked.

"At twelve knots, we can go about thirty-five hundred nautical miles,' said Darcy. "By refueling now, we'll have enough to reach England, even with the higher consumption due to our added job."

The loss of *Christmas Rose* had cast a pall of gloom over *Marigold.* The crew was silent, but the disaster had not dampened their spirits. If anything It had inflamed their anger against underwater foe.

The weather worsened all afternoon. Convoy speed had been reduced to four knots. Jacques had been to sea before, but he'd never seen anything like this. "It can't be too bad," he said to Bousquet when he saw Darcy on the way to his cabin for a rest.

"Keep your eyes open, boys," said the skipper.

"Can the sea get much worse than this?" Jacques asked.

"It can," said Darcy. "The wind's about force ten. It can go to twelve. But in a sea like this, an attack is unlikely. When submarines are on the surface in this kind of weather, men in the conning tower must tie themselves down or be swept away!"

"The chief doesn't seem too concerned about this weather," Jacques said to Bousquet.

"He probably thinks we must grow our sea legs," Bousquet said, "but I'll admit, Jacques, I don't remember being at sea in a storm like this. When the wind whips up a fog from the waves, as it's doing now, we sailors say the sea is smoking."

"Bousquet, I wouldn't say this to the chief, but I don't mind telling you…this is really a bit scary…."

"Fortunately these corvettes are really seaworthy!" Bousquet said. "Jacques, hold on there while I go get something."

Jacques felt uneasy alone on the bridge until Bousquet returned a short time later.

"There's some good news, Jacques," he said. He had brought his binoculars. "The barometer's rising. By noon the worst should be over."

They remained there on watch until morning. In the grey of dawn, Bousquet scanned the horizon with his binoculars.

"There's trouble out there," he said to Jacques. "Take my binoculars and look at that ship astern!"

"It's listing," said Jacques, "and can't seem to come out of the list."

"It won't," said Bousquet. "The cargo has shifted, and it will founder."

"Shall I call the chief?" said Jacques.

"You can," said Bousquet, "but there's nothing we can do."

Darcy confirmed Bousquet's words. They drew closer to the stricken vessel. It was the *Ville de Tamatave.* It was no longer rising to the wave. Suddenly it keeled over. In horror Jacques watched it go to its watery grave. He'd never seen a ship sink before.

That was nothing new to the men on the *Marigold*, But it was the first ship they'd seen destroyed by the forces of nature. They pulled three terrified, trembling men from the sea.

The storm abated during the day, and the convoy increased speed with *Marigold* patrolling the rear. Visibility was good, but as dusk shrouded the ocean, an alert sounded by the radar operator sent tremors through the ship. A submarine on the surface was trailing the convoy a few miles astern. Radar showed the characteristic blip of a submarine's conning tower.

"Now let us see what we can do about him," said Darcy to Bousquet and Jacques, standing next to him on the bridge. He brought the corvette around and headed it slowly toward the enemy craft.

'We are among the first to test a new device," said the skipper. "It's called the snowflake. When we close in, we'll see how it works."

The gunners on the quick-firing four-inch gun were at the ready with the gun loaded.

"Fire snowflake!" ordered the skipper.

Moments later a full square mile of the ocean was bathed in daylight. Less than half a mile away, on the surface, was the sub!

Marigold's guns roared and roared again. The third shot struck the Nazi craft at the base of the conning tower as it submerged.

Guided by the asdic, the corvette bore down on the point where the U-boat had submerged. Sinking a U-boat was no easy job. Depth charges had to be fired at the right depth and at the right time. Two patterns set to explode at different depths were released. There was no asdic echo and no visibility, just the smell of fuel oil. Had the enemy vanished, fled, or gone to the bottom? No one knew. Only time would tell, and *Marigold* could not wait. It had to resume its job of protecting the rear of the convoy.

The ship veered eastward to catch up with the convoy, zigzagging on the way, its asdic and radar probing sea and air.

"From what I can see," Jacques said to Darcy, "your main problem is lack of escorts. You can't protect a convoy and then leave it to chase an enemy miles away."

"That's true," said Darcy. "That's the Admiralty's main concern now, but we are desperately short of ships and men to man them.

"The British are enlisting all the foreign seamen who have escaped from the conquered countries. They are training and equipping them. That takes time. Then there's the language barrier. In the meantime we are losing ships faster than shipyards can build them."

"Not counting all the war material that's lost, too," said Jacques. "Commandant, it looks as though you won't get much sleep tonight; can I be of any help?"

"You are an extra pair of eyes," said Darcy, "and we never have too many. Of course they are not much use in zero visibility. Why don't you get some sleep now, it's already two-thirty."

Jacques returned to his cabin. The sea was not rough, so he could sleep in his bed. The motion of the ship and the steady throb of the reciprocating engine lulled him to sleep.

When Jacques went up to the bridge the next morning, the skipper was having a quick breakfast.

"I should think that by now," Jacques said, "we should be almost halfway through the Gap, sir."

"Better than that," said Darcy. "We are about two-thirds through, but we are expecting the worst. The Admiralty has warned the commodore to expect attacks from packs of U-boats at any time."

So far convoy HX 103 had lost only two ship, *Christmas Rose*, to enemy action, and *Ville de Tamatave* to the forces of nature. Not one merchantman had been sunk by the enemy. The weather had improved. The sea was choppy, and visibility was good.

The convoy maintained a steady seven-knot pace. Watchmen on *Marigold* scanned the horizon with eyes and binoculars while radar and asdic sniffed air and water.

"I've had no news from anyone in my family since I left France in June last year," Darcy told Jacques, who stood next to him on the bridge. "No mail can get through, and it's the same for my crew."

"It's the same for me, too," said Jacques. "I've had no news from any of my relatives since the fall of France. I don't know if they are dead or alive."

"I know how you feel," said Darcy. "I feel relatively fortunate. My wife and children were in Brest, where there was no fighting. But all the men on this ship are very lonely. Few of us know anyone in England. Do you?"

"Yes," said Jacques, "I have some relatives there."

"Close relatives?" asked Darcy.

"Yes," said Jacques, "an aunt, her husband, and her son and daughter. I was always very close to my cousin Sheila. She came every year to spend the summer vacation at our home in France to perfect her knowledge of French. The boys in our family took turns going to her people in England to improve their fluency of English. For years I've loved that girl. I can -wait to see her."

"Where does she live?" asked Darcy.

"I know where she used to live—not where she lives now. She was bombed out of her home in London in the December 29 air raid of last year. All I know is that she works at the Ministry of Transport."

"You are lucky," said Darcy. "That's what most of us lack. Jacques, I'm going to get a little rest now. When Bousquet comes up, I'd like you to stay on watch with him."

"I certainly will, sir. You can count on me."

Jacques and Bousquet had much in common, and both were eager to destroy a U-boat. Together they watched over the convoy as *Marigold* zig-zagged astern until they got some help. Help came in the form of a Canadian frigate with mission to cover the port side of the convoy. These were English Canadians. It was not the same as having the crew of *Christmas Rose* as co-escort, but it did absorb much of the burden *Marigold* had been carrying alone.

Another day went by....

Darkness enveloped the convoy.

Suddenly a violent explosion rent the silence of the night. A huge flame shot into the sky, casting a red glow on a great column of black smoke and lighting up clouds and sea.

Unseen and undetected, a U-boat had slipped into the middle of the convoy and torpedoed the tanker equipped to refuel escorts. Oil in the tanker burned fiercely for a while, much of it pouring out onto the surface of the sea where it cooled and stopped blazing. Some crewmen were bobbing up and down in the oily muck. The light of the flames outlined the U-boat; quickly, before anyone could fire, the submariners disconnected the diesel and plunged beneath the sea on electric power.

Marigold was closest to the stricken vessel. The corvette followed the U-boat's course under water on the asdic and fired two patterns of depth charges. The U-boat changed course, seeking refuge under the last ships of the convoy, where the warships did not dare fire depth charges lest they disable a merchant ship.

The watch on *Marigold* reported to the bridge. "Sir, after that last pattern, there's a long slick of oil coming to the surface."

"Do you think we got the U-boat?" Jacques asked Darcy.

"We may have damaged it," said the skipper, "but only time will tell. We won't know what has happened until the U-boat surfaces. Oh! Oh! What's this? We're getting help!"

"What's that ship?" asked Jacques.

"That's *Warminster*, with the commodore in charge of the convoy. He looks as though he's coming in for the kill!"

The radar of *Warminster* had seen the U-boat trying to escape on the surface between the merchant ships. Maneuvering carefully, at full speed on its third pass, the British destroyer rammed the U-boat aft of the conning tower. There was a crunch of wrenched steel plates and clatter of splintered metal as *Warminster's* momentum carried it over the U-boat, lifting the stern of the destroyer out of the water and cracking the drive shaft of the starboard propeller.

In the semidarkness an urgent message came over the blinker: "*Marigold* stand by. Have rammed U-boat."

"Things are beginning to heat up," said Darcy to the men around him on the bridge. "For Williams to call for help, his ship must be badly damaged."

When *Marigold* arrived the destroyer had disengaged itself from its perch but was no longer a fighting ship. One propeller was out of commission and speed was reduced to ten knots.

The U-234 rammed by *Warminster* was too damaged to submerge and tried to flee on the surface. The corvette was hot on its trail. Holding the U-boat with its searchlight, the machine gun on the foredeck blazing, the corvette pursued the U-boat, slowly gaining on its prey. The pursuit must have taken an hour when *Marigold* closed in and rammed the U-boat just ahead of the conning tower. That was the *coup de grace*. As the U-boat sank, a few crewmen jumped from the conning tower into the frigid water, life jackets around their necks.

"*Hilfe, hilfe!*"

Four survivors were picked up.

The chase had led *Marigold* far astern of the convoy and miles from the damaged *Warminster*. At least, thought the men on board, we've got something to show for it: living proof that we've sunk a sub!

While *Marigold* was battling the U-234, other U-boats attacked the convoy. *Warminster*, now a straggler and far behind the convoy, had rescued the survivors of the *Trelawney*, a beautiful motor ship which had been torpedoed an hour earlier.

At 4:00 A.M. the convoy was attacked again. *San Amado*, a six thousand three hundred-ton tanker, burst into flames which colored in red the low-hanging clouds and a huge column of black smoke rising into the sky. Next to go was an ammunition ship; it disintegrated with a cataclysmic roar, blowing steel plates and the superstructure of the ship to pieces, showering the sea and a nearby ship with flying debris. Regardless of his own fate, Commodore Williams ordered *Marigold* into the fray. There were too many U-boats and too few escorts to fight them. No one in that convoy had any sleep that night, and it seemed that dawn would never come!

"Help is on the way," said Darcy to Bousquet and Jacques, who had joined him on the bridge. "Three more escorts, one of them a destroyer, will join us before the day is out."

"Sir," said the radio operator, "a message from *Warminster*."

"Am completely disabled. Join me at 50.13 N 27-36W."

Abandoning the convoy, *Marigold* zigzagged at full speed toward *Warminster*, some thirty-five miles astern. The sun was up when they sighted the crippled destroyer, now at a complete stop. When it was in full view of the corvette and less than a mile away, there was a muffled underwater explosion, and a column of black smoke erupted from the stern of the crippled vessel. "Torpedoed," was Williams's last message. "Get the sub."

The crippled destroyer, already listing, sank fast. It carried patterns of depth charges on deck, ready to be fired. The charges were preset to explode, triggered by water pressure, at various depths—twenty, thirty, fifty, seventy feet, etc., in the hope that some would explode close enough to cripple the U-boat under attack.

From a few hundred yards away, the sailors on *Marigold* watched in horror as the survivors, scrambling to inflatable rafts, were hurled into the air by great geysers of water churned up by *Warminster's* own depth charges.

Suddenly *Marigold* changed course, away from this scene of disaster.

"Aren't we going to rescue any survivors?" Jacques asked the skipper.

"We are," said Darcy, "but we have another priority."

The answer was terse and emotional. Darcy was very pale. Jacques did not know then that the asdic operator had an echo from a submarine fleeing under water—almost surely the U-boat which had torpedoed *Warminster.* Pursuit into nowhere seemed interminable. Suddenly *Marigold* fired a pattern of depth charges, made an abrupt one hundred eighty turn, and fired another pattern. Excitement ran through the ship. All eyes on board were glued to the sea. The gun crew stood at the ready.

"I'll bet all of my next pay," said the asdic operator, "that we've made a hit. Any takers?"

No one spoke. All respected his extraordinary expertise and knew his standard answer when a bet was proposed: "In every bet, there's a crook and a fool; as I'm not a fool and don't want to be a crook, I never bet."

When the asdic man did bet, the crew was sure the sub would surface. Tense, they watched and waited. They did not wait very long! Like some huge dark slimy sea monster, the U-boat surfaced violently from the sea. A number of men jumped out on deck.

Marigold opened fire. The second salvo was a direct hit at the base of the 88mm gun and made mincemeat of the gun crew.

"Cease fire!" ordered Darcy, "I want to bring this U-boat to England."

Marigold lowered a whale boat with a boarding party. The U-boat's deck was red with blood. Jagged pieces of metal mixed with human flesh. Three bodies lay there, motionless.

One glance at the U-368 told Darcy that his ambition, his dream since he'd hunted subs, was not for now. The U-368 could not be salvaged. Slowly it keeled over. The conning tower struck the sea, absorbing tons of water. Then it listed to forty-five degrees, and suddenly the enemy craft went to its final grave, stern first, bow pointing toward the sky.

Nineteen crewmen, life jackets around their necks, bobbed up and down in the frigid waters. Holding hands they formed a circle in a final desperate bid to survive. *Marigold's* whale boat rescued them, shivering and shaken but alive, prisoners of war now, all strangely subdued—all the more that they could not understand the language of their captors! These submariners spoke English, and *Marigold's* white ensign told them that this was an English warship. Yet they could not understand a word of their captors. They cringed when they learned they were prisoners of the French.

Jacques spoke to them in their own tongue. He learned that the second officer had been killed when *Marigold's* shell had exploded on deck and that the U-368's commander had gone down with his ship.

After rescuing the Germans, Darcy sped to the site where *Warminster* had gone down. Like all on board, he had a sense of achievement—but he now had another priority: to rescue fighting men adrift on the sea and anxiously awaiting his return. Eyes, unaided or helped with binoculars, strained to pierce the haze descending on the ocean.

Rain and mist were closing in as *Marigold* reached the scattered debris of what remained of *Warminster:* two rafts, one carley float, and one lifeboat sustained numbed and exhausted survivors. They had the strength to cheer when the corvette arrived. A few climbed aboard unaided; most were pulled on deck and cared for by men whose language they did not understand. Survivors afloat had managed to stay together, but the corvette searched in vain for the man everyone on board had hoped to save. As dusk set in, Darcy ordered his crew to abandon the search, convinced that Commodore Williams, the man all liked and admired, had gone down with his ship.

Alone on the vast expanse of the sea, *Marigold* sped to catch up with the convoy. Night and fog had set in, and visibility was nil.

There were other problems, too. There's not much room on a corvette, and the survivors had been given the run of the ship—except the German prisoners, confined to the lobby of the magazine, empty by now; all told, *Marigold* had only seven depth charges left! Food was also running out.

"Fog has a great advantage," said Darcy to his companions on the bridge. "Submarines can't see us, and it is very difficult, if not impossible, to take aim. That does not mean that we can relax."

"Is the asdic operator still at his post?" said Jacques.

"Of course he is," said Bousquet, "but so far he has not made contact. The radar man is guiding us now and will make sure we don't collide with anyone in the convoy if and when we catch up."

"Aren't we through the Gap yet?" asked Jacques.

"In a few hours we should be," answered Darcy. "Despite its advantages, this fog bothers me."

They were out of the Gap, and the fog had cleared when *Marigold* came within sight of the convoy.

"What ship?" signaled *Woodpecker*, the Canadian frigate astern of the convoy.

Marigold gave her name and code number and proceeded at full speed between the merchant ships. When she came in sight of the new commodore ship, *Engadine*, which had just arrived from Iceland, *Marigold* signaled over the blinker: "Request authorization to transfer *Warminster* survivors to rescue ship. Will keep German captives here."

The reply came forthwith: "Authorization granted. How many prisoners?"

"Nineteen from U-368; four from U-234," *Marigold* answered.

"Three cheers," came the reply. "Splice the mainbrace!"

Darcy scratched his head when he read the message. He handed the transcript to Jacques. "I can understand three cheers, but what on earth does splice the mainbrace mean?"

Jacques burst out laughing. "That's typical British sailor jargon," he said. "It means get out the champagne."

Everyone laughed. Tired, exhausted, unshaven, and dirty as they were, they still were able to laugh. "I must say," said Bousquet, "that Commodore has a distinct sense of humor."

"Where's the rescue ship?" asked Jacques.

"It is never identified," said Darcy, "but it has a different place in each convoy. Submarines have orders to sink these ships whenever they can."

Transfers between ships on the open sea and in hostile waters are no picnic—impractical when the sea is rough and treacherous in the dark—but the weather was favorable when *Marigold* discharged its excess passengers onto *Astoria* and received needed supplies in exchange.

In the meantime the convoy welcomed some new combatants: a Polish destroyer, Norwegian corvette, and a Greek frigate arrived to shepherd the convoy through the last leg or the journey.

Seven ships from the convoy had been lost and many seamen with them, but Admiral Doenitz's grey wolves had paid a heavy price: two U-boats destroyed and several damaged. The new escorts, manned by men driven by hate of the enemy who'd enslaved their kin, welcomed this chance to strike back and bring the remaining thirty-four ships to port.

Marigold was no longer a fighting ship. It had seven depth charges left, not enough for one good pattern. Yet with its prisoners from two U-boats, its battle-scarred side plates pocked with 20mm holes from the U-boats' machine guns, the long tell-tale streaks of rust trailing down from those holes, and its crumpled bow, it was the envy of every escort, even of the Commodore ship itself! It was ordered to join *Engadine* ahead of the convoy to probe air and sea for any signs of the enemy.

There was no U-boat attack that night.

The next morning the weather was clear. The sea was choppy. Shortly after dawn a Sunderland, a big four-engined flying boat equipped with radar and loaded with bombs, flew over the convoy, circled it, went and came again; it brought a deep sense of relief to the tired men on the freighters and the warships. All knew they were closing in on land.

They knew that with the "eagle eyes" on the great planes, the chances of being "fished" at night were much reduced. They sensed, too, that *Marigold's* asdic man would detect at night any U-boat that the Sunderland had missed.

"You've been our contact man with the German prisoners," said Darcy to Jacques. "Have you learned anything?"

"Yes," said Jacques. "They are split into two groups. The younger men appear to be Hitler fanatics. They are bitter, sullen, and above all infuriated because they've been captured by sailors from a decadent, conquered nation!"

"Anything else?" asked Darcy.

"They complained about being confined to such cramped quarters," said Jacques.

"What did you say?" asked Darcy.

"Pointing to the sea, I told them there was plenty of room outside," said Jacques.

"I would have given the same answer," said Darcy.

"Some of the older men," said Jacques, "had a different attitude. I got the impression they were pleased that, for them, the war was over."

The news of *Marigold's* kill had preceded the ship. When convoy HX 103 sailed up the Mersey River, preceded by *Engadine* and *Marigold*, the Frenchmen on board got a glimpse of an England they had never seen before, an England that was sentimental, that was admiring, that was grateful to the lonely foreigners far from their homes who'd been out there in the hell of war protecting British lives at the risk of their own.

A great crowd roared its welcome to *Marigold* as the battered ship came alongside—men; women; civilians; Wrens in their neat uniforms; Navy officers; sailors; and the Admiral, Western Approaches, himself were there to greet them.

First landed were the German prisoners, before a crowd suddenly silent and hostile: the survivors of both U-boats were hurried to waiting vans, which rapidly disappeared.

Next down the gangplank came the killer crew, dirty and unshaved, with tangled hair and drawn features, first the seamen, last the officers. A small band of musicians struck up a brief, lively, emotional *Marseillaise*, followed by a roar of applause from the crowd—all of whom stopped suddenly at attention. Tears welled in the eyes of the exhausted men. They'd never expected any welcome like this. With Jacques as interpreter, the Admiral, Western Approaches, said a few words. "Men of France, I know what you've been through! I followed your convoy from the start! I lived your anguish by the day, almost by the hour. I shared your triumph! Your record is unequalled: two U-boats sunk and one severely damaged and probably destroyed. I know what you need now: a bath and a bed.

"I came to bring the thanks of the British people, of the king, and of the Admiralty. With men like you, France will live again," adding in French, *'un grand merci!'*"

They, too, gave the Admiral *un grand merci*—thankful for his presence and thankful his comments had been so brief.

Chapter III

Jacques awakened and looked at his watch. He could hardly believe what it told him. He'd slept for nineteen hours.

He washed, shaved, put on his khaki war correspondent's uniform, went to the mess hall, and ordered breakfast. The waitress asked about his uniform and if he had come in on a cargo ship.

"No," said Jacques, "on a small warship—a corvette, a Free French corvette."

"Not the *Marigold?*" she asked.

"Yes," said Jacques. "Why?"

"Sir, we're all proud of you. I've been here since the war started. *Marigold* is the first ship ever to sink two submarines on one crossing."

She brought him bacon and eggs, with toast and butter, and sugar and tea. Jacques said to her, "In America, we've been told that things like butter and sugar are sharply rationed. It doesn't look like that to me."

"They are, sir, but not for you men. That's a terrible job you have, and when you're on land, we do all we can to make you feel at home."

"You certainly do that well," said Jacques.

"Are you shipping out again?" she asked.

"No. I'm going down to London this afternoon."

"I wish you a good journey," said the waitress. "When you get through the customs, be careful not to trip over the water mains."

"The water mains?" Jacques asked.

"They occupy a large part of the sidewalk. We're bombed so often it's not practical to dig up the road each time, so the pipes are on the surface, out of the way of traffic. Pedestrians must step over them."

"I suppose I'll get used to the bombings when I'm in London," said Jacques. "Before I leave Liverpool, I'd like to reserve a room at the hotel in London. Where can I find a phone?"

"I'm sorry, sir, the phones are restricted, but you'll have plenty of time when you get to London. The 2:00 P.M. train is very good and seldom late. You'll be in London at 6:00 P.M."

It was still daylight when the train pulled into Euston Station. Collecting his luggage, minus a stock of 16 mm color movie film which the customs official in Liverpool said had to be cleared in London, Jacques took the first available taxi to the Savoy Hotel.

"Do you have a reservation?" asked the clerk at the desk.

"No, I arrived yesterday from the United States. I wanted to call from Liverpool, but they said the phones were restricted."

"That's all right," said the clerk. "We always have room for our American guests." He gave Jacques a key and asked him to register. "I see from your badge you're a war correspondent. The Ministry of Information holds the daily press conference here at noon every day."

With most adults mobilized, the hotel used children for many menial jobs. The energetic bellboy, who could not have been more than twelve, made two trips to bring up the balance of Jacques' luggage. He was thrilled with a tip of two silver quarters.

Jacques sat down in an armchair. He had still not cast off the perpetual motion he had acquired on the ship that had been his home for three weeks. He was still pitching and rolling, rolling mainly, as he dozed off in the comfortable bed.

His first mission the next morning was to find his cousin, Sheila Hatherley. Her apartment in London had been destroyed by fire, so he didn't know where she lived, but he did know she worked at the Ministry of Transport.

At first the minister operator made trouble about connecting him, but when he said who he was, she put him through to Sheila.

"This is Miss Hatherley."

"How are you today, lovely?" said Jacques.

"Who's this?"

"Sheila, don't you recognize my voice?" said Jacques.

"Oh! Of course I do. Jacques, how wonderful. Are you in London?"

"Yes. I'm at the Savoy. Can you meet me there this evening?"

"Oh, Jacques, of course I can," she said. "I'll come as soon as I leave work. I'll certainly be there by six."

"Good," Jacques said. "When you get here, come right up to my room, number 319."

After breakfast Jacques went to the Ministry of Information, the MOI for short. He was directed to a lean, slender, neatly dressed woman in charge of

providing journalists with permits, requisitions, and transportation to join soldiers, sailors, and even airmen in action. Her name was displayed in large letters on her desk.

"Mrs. Stacpoole," said Jacques, "my name is Jacques de Thoranne, and—"

"Oh yes, sir," said Mrs. Stacpoole, "I knew you were coming. Will you
wait a minute while I get your file?"

She returned with a folder. "Several people in the Ministry of Information
want to meet you, sir, among them Mr. James Ferguson. You must also call on
your employer, International News Service. You must see Mr. Pleven at Free
French Headquarters...."

She took a sheet of paper from his file. "Here you have names, addresses,
and phone numbers of all the people you should contact. I'm also going to send
you to have some photos made for passes and other documents you may need."

"How many photos do you need?" said Jacques, pulling out his wallet. "I
had these made before leaving the States."

"Oh, how fine. That will save time," said Mrs. Stacpoole. "Now, where
would you like to go to obtain material for your articles?"

"I'd like to go where the action is," Jacques said.

She looked at him curiously. "Are you sure you want to see things for
yourself?" she asked.

"Certainly," he said, "why do you ask?"

"Because most of you people who come out here are cowards. They don't
want to go in the front lines to get shot."

"I've already been shot and torpedoed at on the way coming over. I didn't
come over here to sit behind a desk," said Jacques. "I'd like to go to Dover; I
know the Germans are shelling it from France every day. I'd like to go on one
of the launches that rescues pilots down over the water. I'd like to see
Coventry, Scapa Flow, the submarine base at Dundee.'

"There will be no problem doing that," said Mrs. Stacpoole.

"Maybe," said Jacques, "you can suggest still more interesting visits. I'd
like to know where to get a good story for the American public. As far as the
people in our Midwest are concerned, this war might as well be on the plan-
et Mars."

"I'll give you more suggestions another time," she said. "It is now close to
twelve o'clock. You may want to get back to the Savoy for the noon conference
of the MOI."

Fifty to sixty journalists, representing mainly American news services or
major newspapers, attended the daily news briefing. It lasted about forty minutes. Few questions were asked. The reporters took notes and went to their
typewriters or to the bar. Later in the afternoon, they were all in the bar.

If that's the usual routine, Jacques thought to himself, *I can see what Mrs.
Stacpoole meant.*

After lunch Jacques went to Carlton Gardens, headquarters of the Free French in England. The first person he met was an old classmate, d'Huart, who had been evacuated from Dunkerque at the collapse of France and had decided to stay in England rather than return to France.

"When you have time," d'Huart told Jacques, "I'll tell you what's going on here. This clique is a real mess."

Jacques returned to the Savoy by the underground and hurried to his room, hoping to get there before Sheila arrived. He was lucky. He'd had time to take off his coat before she knocked.

He opened the door.

"Jacques. How wonderful!"

"Sheila!"

She came into his arms. He kissed her, feeling the whole warm length of her body.

"Now," he said, "we've got a lot to talk about. Let's have dinner and come back up here. I'll reserve a table. Do you want to wash up?"

"Jacques," she said and looked at him anxiously, "could I take a bath? I've not had a real bath since we were bombed out last year."

"Of course, take your time—all the time you want—and enjoy it."

When she came out of the bathroom, she took a very short piece of lipstick from her bag and began to apply it sparingly.

The sight of her rationing her lipstick got to him.

She saw the way he watched her. "Don't make fun of me, Jacques," she said. "Lipstick is hard to get."

"I thought that might be," he said. "That package on the table is for you."

It was a small package in blue paper, from Macys. She opened it. "Oh, Jacques, a dozen lipsticks."

"Do you think" he asked, "that will last until the end of the war, even if you don't ration it? Now, open the grey package. It has stockings." He saw the pathetic run in one of those she wore.

She went into the bathroom and put on a new pair, they went down for dinner.

Over cocktails, he said, "It's been a long time since we've been in touch. What are you doing?"

"I'm working at the Ministry of Transport. A lot of the work is confidential. It's a relief to have what America is sending us now. We were about to go under.

"But you are the one that's news. We heard about your resignation. We heard you'd been condemned to death by the French Vichy government. We read about it here, in the newspapers; we heard it on the radio. Mother was so proud. But you, how did you manage?"

He sipped his drink. "Well, all of a sudden I was out of money, didn't have a job, and didn't have a country—but Americans adopted me. They gave me an apartment, no charge. They helped me develop a profitable lecturing business. After the Vichy government condemned me to death, I had more engagements than I could handle. My message to these clubs was: 'If you want to help France, support Britain."

"What are you going to do now?"

"I'm not sure," he said. "Tomorrow morning I'm going to meet a man named Sir James Ferguson. He's with the Ministry of Information. I've never heard of him. Do you know who he might be?"

"Oh, yes. He's very important. Few outsiders ever see him. He never gives interviews to the press and is never in the headlines."

"What does he do?" Jacques asked.

"He gathers significant facts. He compares British Intelligence data with what he collects from independent sources. He has a genius for judging what he learns. Everyone of importance studies his reports before any major undertaking, and they usually follow his recommendations. If Sir James wants to see you, it must be something important."

They relaxed in the comfortable dining room, enjoying a good meal.

"I've been trying to remember," Jacques said. "The last time I saw you was four years ago, in 1937, at the farm in France. It was your twentieth birthday."

"Yes," she said, "I've not been there since."

"The last I heard," said Jacques, "the farm was still there. My father and mother and sister are still living there, as best they can. My brother, Henry, is a prisoner of war. Poor Henry! At least he's still alive."

"I remember that holiday, Jacques," she said.

Then she couldn't look at him. She looked down at the tablecloth, which was brilliant white and reflected light upward on her face. She reached across the table and put her hand on his.

"How wonderful to have you here, Jacques; do you remember all the intimate things we used to discuss?"

"Yes," he said.

"Jacques," she said, "you may think I'm silly, but at twenty-four, I'm still a virgin."

He said, "I'm not surprised, and I don't think it's silly."

"Jacques," she said, "I'm so pleased to hear you say that. When I see all that's going on around me, I wonder. But now I have an incentive: I'm saving my virginity for the man I love."

"Sheila, you never told me you had a lover."

"I'm not sure that I do," she answered, "but I love him very much…although he is a second choice," she whispered, looking at Jacques wistfully.

He took her hand. He drew her to him and embraced her lovingly.

"Mother knew we loved each other," Sheila said. "She told me more than once that our blood relationship excluded marriage. She was always uneasy when I stayed at your home."

"I'm not surprised, my mother was a little anxious about it, too."

"Did she ever bring up the subject?"

"Only once," Jacques said, "and I told her that those laws were arbitrary, without scientific foundation, and that royalty bypasses them when it sees fit and commoners should have the same right."

"What did she say?"

"Nothing. Sheila, tell me more about your lover."

"He's a fighter pilot in brother John's squadron. He comes to John's home quite often. He's so quiet, so modest, so brave, and...so handsome. But he has never said a word to me about love."

"Have you said anything to him?" Jacques asked.

"No, I really never get a chance," she said. "Someone is always in the way. We are so cramped in wartime London. Our home was gutted in the December twenty-ninth raid last year. I lost all my belongings. Now I'm living in John's small flat with his wife, Kay, and their two children. There are only two bedrooms. There's no privacy."

"I'd miss that terribly," said Jacques.

"Oh, Jacques, that's bad enough, but what makes it worse is that I have no one I can confide in, no one to talk to about my inner feelings, my hopes, my despairs. Can you see what it means to me to have you here?"

"Sheila," Jacques said, "we're all lonely in this war. I know I am. If you weren't here, I'd feel alone in a wilderness."

She seized one of his legs between hers under the table. He felt the warmth of that embrace.

"Sheila," he said softly.

"Holloa, what's this?" she asked as the waiter wheeled up a cart, made in happier days, equipped to prepare *crêpes flambées* on the spot. "I didn't order this."

"I did," said Jacques. "That used to be your favorite desert. I assume it still is, so I changed your order and mine. Let's enjoy that little pleasure while we're still alive."

"You shouldn't be so extravagant," she said. "I would never have ordered that."

"I know. That's why I did. What do you want to drink, coffee or tea?"

"I'll have coffee for a change," she said. "I'll have to go after that. Last night I didn't get home. I couldn't even call Kaye. The phones were out of order. I'd love to stay longer, but there are so few trains after nine o'clock."

"All right," said Jacques, "after coffee, we'll collect your things. If we can't find a taxi, I'll walk you to the station. Oh! Here's the coffee."

"Here's something we don't want," Sheila said, as the sirens suddenly burst into their shrill, insistent scream.

"Sheila," said Jacques, "should we go to the shelter? You're the expert on London wartime life."

"It sounds as though it's coming pretty close," Sheila said. "Hear that? Let's go down."

The other diners rose from their seats. Without haste they quietly walked down to the shelter.

The shelter surprised Jacques. It was only a basement with a reinforced ceiling, supported by a forest of vertical steel pipes, two to three inches in diameter. Metal braces joined them in the form of an X. This ceiling might have supported the hotel if a bomb demolished the upper floors, but in no way could it withstand a direct hit.

"Mere improvisation," Jacques thought. "This country has been at war for more than a year and a half, and a shelter in a leading London hotel is no more than a makeshift structure that probably could not be evacuated in case of fire. Same mentality as in France—no one believed war could happen until it did happen, and when it did the nation was completely unprepared."

There was nothing much to do in a shelter, except to wait for the all clear and hope it didn't get hit. There were no seats. Packed like sardines in a tin, all the guests were standing. Most were silent. Time went slowly. It seemed that the raid would last forever. It seemed, also, that the dull powerful thuds of the bombs, clearly distinguishable from the rapid fire of the ack-ack, were closing in on the neighborhood.

Suddenly a nearby hit shook everything in the shelter. The lights went out. Dust fell from the ceiling. Jacques lit his flashlight. The air was like a thick fog. People were coughing. There were more heavy thuds, further away. The ack-ack continued. Then as suddenly as it started, it stopped. The all clear sounded.

As they walked up to the lobby, the hall porter commented, "A pretty bad one this time, sir. There's been a direct hit on the underground station, and there are quite a few casualties. There are arms and legs and bodies scattered all over the place. Lucky we weren't hit. All lights are out in the neighborhood."

"Sheila," said Jacques, "how do you manage without a flashlight?"

She shrugged, "Mine was lost when the apartment was burnt out. Just try to get one now."

"You can't go home in a mess like this. Smell the smoke? You may have to stay here. Let's go up to the room. I'll get my coat and take a look at things outside."

He lit the candle the hotel provided for power failures.

"Jacques," she said, "please don't be too long. Be careful. Put on your helmet and stay away from walls weakened by fire. They collapse without warning.

I'd go with you, but I have no change of clothes. You'll see what you look like when you get back."

Jacques got back in half an hour. "Sheila, it's awesome. It's one thing to see scenes like this in the movies, it's another one to be in the real thing with the heat, the smoke, the noise of the collapsing buildings, the showers of sparks, the bits of bodies, the ambulances, the fire. On Surrey Street there was the arm of a woman, white, cut off at the shoulder, rings still on the fingers! Ugh! It's absolutely horrible."

"We're getting used to this," Sheila said. "You won't see how dirty you are until you get some proper light."

"Well, dear," said Jacques, "before going outside, I didn't think you could go home tonight. Now I know you can't. You'll stay here. The hotel is full. You take the bed. I'll sleep in the chair."

"No, you won't," said Sheila. "We'll share the bed."

She undressed and went to the bathroom.

"There's no water," she said. "A water main must have been hit. Lucky I took a bath before dinner. Come and join me in bed."

Jacques was writing a few notes on his first experience of being bombed. "First let me clean some of this soot off my face," he said, wetting a towel with some of the mineral water he'd ordered before dinner.

"Jacques," Sheila insisted, "I've made a nice warm place for you in bed. Come and make yourself comfortable."

She watched him undress and reach for his pajamas.

"You don't need those. I want to feel you, especially tonight. I've dreamed of that—often. Now we can do it." He took her in his arms. He, too, had often dreamed of that. Now—it was real. His nerves were still tingling from what he'd seen. He was excited and relaxed as he felt the passion of her embrace.

"Jacques," she said, "you'll never know what this means to me. I feel so comfortable, so protected, so relaxed, and yet so excited. Let me tell you: I would not mind if a bomb hit and killed us both in each other's arms."

"Sheila!"

"I mean that," she said. "I really mean it. How long will this awful war last? I'm so lonely. What makes my life so unbearable is that I have no one to whom I can cry, no one I can talk to like this, no one to whom I can confide my feelings, my despairs, my hopes. You understand me, dear Jacques—you always did. I can tell you all this, dear Jacques, and…."

She burst into passionate sobbing. He let her sob as he squeezed her in his arms; wiped her tears; he stroked her blonde hair; he caressed her forehead and kissed her affectionately.

"Jacques, dear, you've made me forget for a moment this awful life, you've made me want you."

"Sheila, I want you, too, but I know you want to save your virginity for the man you love."

"Jacques, I've never slept with a man. I love this. We've always been so intimate…Why couldn't we get married? You don't know what it means to have you here. You're a breath from the outside world, which I love so much, and which I may never see again."

She sobbed softly as Jacques caressed her neck, her ears, her shoulders. Gradually, calm returned to her trembling body.

"Darling, lovely, beautiful," Jacques said to her, "I need you, just as much as you need me. I've been shaken like never before by that awful scene I witnessed tonight. I need you, your presence, your love."

His lips found hers. He could feel her slender, vibrant body, her tender breasts, her warmth, her passionate love; he could feel, too, her worries, her sadness, her doubts about life and about herself, and behind it all, he sensed her quiet resolve to help her country win the war—however demanding, however impersonal, however trying that job might be.

Exhausted, they fell to sleep in each other's arms.

In early morning she woke him up.

"Jacques, dear, we'll have to do this again. I loved it! I feel so much better. So refreshed. I've got new courage to face the future. But we must be careful. I've been thinking. Many hotels are so stuffy, and this is one of them. It might be better if we don't have breakfast together."

"Sheila!" Jacques said. "It can't be that bad. We are in the twentieth century."

"I know," she said, "but this is a first class hotel. It has a worldwide name, and they are very sensitive about having pros here."

"Pros?" said Jacques.

"Yes—prostitutes."

"Sheila," said Jacques, "you certainly don't look like one. Besides you *had* to stay here. You could not be chased out into the street with nowhere to go and no taxis, no trains."

"I know," she said, "but that's not the kind of logic that prevails around here."

"Sheila," said Jacques, "I won't have my behavior controlled by some hotel manager. This hotel may be first class, but I'll move if I must. Let's go down to breakfast together. After breakfast, we'll take a taxi, and I'll drop you off at the Ministry of Transport and go on to the Ministry of Information."

They sat down to a breakfast of bacon and eggs. Yes—you could still get bacon and eggs in a first class hotel in wartime London following a heavy air attack. You couldn't get much sugar, only a very little butter, and cream was out of the question.

After breakfast, they went up to "their" room, picked up their coats and belongings, came downstairs, and hailed a taxi.

"Jacques," said Sheila, "I can't tell you how I've enjoyed our reunion. It was so exciting and so peaceful. Let's do it again, soon."

"We must," said Jacques. "After I've seen Sir James, I'll know better what to expect. I'll let you know what he wants. Oh, here we are at the Ministry of Transport. Good-bye, my love, my beautiful dear cousin. I'll call you tomorrow. If the phones are out, I'll leave a note at the Ministry of Transport."

"Sir," said the cab driver, "I'll get you to the MOI as soon as I can. That air raid last night did a lot of damage. Some streets are impassable, but they did get the trains running this morning."

The cab threaded slowly through the blackened streets. Many traffic lights were dead; but drivers gave the right of way to those emerging from the most cluttered areas.

Jacques opened the window to get a better view of things. There were pedestrians going around or over the rubble. They seemed unperturbed, dodging obstacles as a matter of course. Some carried umbrellas, although it wasn't raining. It might be as well to carry gas masks, Jacques thought, for the sour, acrid smell of smoldering debris of what had been homes the day before rasped nose and throat. There was no wind; the air was heavy, damp, foggy, and laden with vapor that oozed from the scorched belongings of Londoners who'd lost all they owned—now homeless Londoners in search of a place to sleep and eat. Despite the delays, traffic jams, detours, and slowdowns, the taxi put Jacques at the MOI a few minutes before the scheduled time.

Chapter IV

Although he arrived early, Jacques de Thoranne was ushered immediately into Sir James's spartan office. The minister greeted him with the old-fashioned courtesy traditional among Englishmen in high places.

"I have followed your movements since you embarked on a new career," he said, smiling. "You stand out as the only official in the French Diplomatic Corps to have resigned and sided with Britain when all seemed lost."

"Sir James," said Jacques, "I could see no other choice."

"That's why you convince people. You have delivered a most effective message to our friends across the Atlantic—through the news media, on the radio, in conferences, and in lectures. I was particularly impressed by your silent message to the Great Masonic Lodge in Philadelphia."

"A silent message, sir? I don't quite—"

Sir James smiled. "Yes. A member of our consular staff in Philadelphia attended the meeting where a United States senator, in an impassioned speech, urged Americans to stay out of a European conflict which was nothing more, in his words, than the continuing shifting of borders that has been going on for centuries."

"Yes, sir," said Jacques. "There were many in attendance; the hall was full."

"When the audience gave the speaker a rising cheer of thanks," said Sir James, "you sat stony-faced with your hands in your pockets, in the first row, in front of the important officials at the head table. The consular official, who was here recently, could not repress a smile when he told me about it. He said, 'There's a man not afraid to express his opinion.'

"Yes," said Jacques, "I remember that meeting. The speaker was Senator Nye of North Dakota. I expressed my conviction that because England's war is the civilized world's war, it is also America's war. England cannot win without American intervention—industrial and military. England has neither the industrial power nor the manpower to remove Hitler from Europe."

"That's true," said Sir James, "but however well you understand the main issues, you cannot know how our back is to the wall at this very moment. I wanted to see you because I think you can be of great help. Our consul in Philadelphia told me you plan to report on the activities of the Free French in England, on the seas, and in the French African colonies which rallied to our side."

"That was my intention when I left the United States."

Sir James sat back in his chair. "It would be very useful for us to know how much we could count on the Free French if Hitler were to implement a plan proposed to him by Grand Admiral Raeder."

"What plan is that, sir?"

"The code name," said Sir James, "is Attila and Felix. It is outlined in this confidential memo. Please read it while I look into something."

He handed Jacques a folder marked, "Attila and Felix — Most Confidential."

> Intelligence sources have obtained details of Grand Admiral Raeder's proposed plan to seize North Africa, including West Africa, now controlled by the Vichy French government, in order to gain full control of the Mediterranean and eventually occupy Egypt. The plan has been prepared with typical German thoroughness; it would be carried out in several steps. First German troops would cross the line between occupied and unoccupied France, thus seizing control of the entire country.
>
> German armies would then enter Spain, passing at the Western end of the Pyrenees Mountains; they would assemble a major force in southern Spain. From there, they plan a combined attack against Gibraltar by land, air (paratroopers), and sea.
>
> The second part of the plan is to invade Greece and thus neutralize Malta and the Suez Canal. Cut off from sources of supply, Egypt would inevitably fall.
>
> The third part of the plan is to obtain the full cooperation of the Vichy French Government, which still controls the French fleet and the territories of Morocco and Senegal. Both Laval and Darlan, who control the French Navy, have promised their help. With Dakar, the best deep-water port in West Africa, in German hands as an air and sea base, an all-out war against our sea-lanes would almost surely be successful; this would cut off supplies from the Far East and Australia. Were this plan to succeed, Britain would be in grave danger of losing the war.

Jacques sat there for a while, pondering the consequences of what he had just read. He'd started to read the brief report again when Sir James returned.

"Sir James," said Jacques, "I'm very disturbed by what I've read. This is a frightening perspective. I have never heard of this project. Is it technically feasible?"

Sir James's features contracted for a brief moment. "Yes," he said, 'we believe it is technically possible. It would be costly, but the Nazis are not concerned about that. Their army and their air force are full of self-confidence after the crushing defeat of France and the disastrous evacuation of Dunkerque."

"I should think that they would need naval support also."

"They would," said Sir James. "The navy is their weak spot. They have two very modern battleships, *Bismarck* and *Tirpitz*, which are almost ready. From what we know, these ships have no match in the British Navy. They have several pocket cruisers roaming the Atlantic. They have two heavy modern battle cruisers, already operational, *Scharnhorst* and *Gneisenau*. They are short of destroyers. They lost their best ones during the invasion of Norway, but they are rapidly building new ones, and they are building twenty to thirty submarines a month."

"Frightening," said Jacques. "I had no idea how tenuous our hold on Africa is. Have you any idea how soon this plan may be carried out?"

"I think that it would have been carried out already if it had not been for one stumbling block."

"What was that?" asked Jacques.

"General Franco."

"General Franco? I thought he was Hitler's ally. He's not very popular in the United States."

"I know," said Sir James, "but the American people don't understand General Franco. Their minds have been poisoned by writers like Hemingway who never knew what was at stake in the Spanish Civil War. We'd have a communist Spain today were it not for Franco."

"How could Franco be a roadblock in Hitler's plans?"

"Franco won't allow Hitler to use Spain as a base to seize Gibraltar. He told Hitler so in no uncertain terms. Franco has a well-equipped, well-organized army. Its officers and men are experienced veterans of the civil war. To a large extent, Franco holds the key to Attila and Felix, and his mind is set: No German troops through Spain, period."

"I can hardly believe this, Sir James," said Jacques.

"Franco doesn't like the Nazis any more than the Soviets. He used Nazi help to win the war because French and British help was denied him, but he won't let the German army use his territory to attack the key to the Mediterranean."

"I had no idea that Franco had any such view as this."

"The liberation of Europe," Sir James continued, "depends on the intervention of the United States. Meanwhile you can help us. Our intelligence service in the part of Africa you intend to visit is not particularly good. Africa is far away. Many of our observers there are looking at the war from a distance. Too many feel secure and are lackadaisical. You plan to report on African territories in allied hands—Chad, French Equatorial Africa, and perhaps the Belgian Congo.

"As you do this, it would help us to know how much Britain can count on the free territories should the Nazis attempt to carry out Attila and Felix."

"Yes, I can see the need for such information."

Sir James studied Jacques intently. "I must warn you," he said. "This is a very dangerous job. These areas are infiltrated by elements dedicated to the Nazis. They won't hesitate to get you out of the way—permanently out of the way—if they suspect you of being a British agent."

"Sir James, I've already been through that in the U.S., except there I had the protection of the FBI."

"You won't have any protection in Africa," said Sir James. "Your safety will depend entirely on your discretion, your alertness, and your wits. We will give you any help we can, which is not much. Being British by birth entitles you to the British passport, which you now have. That's perfectly justified now that the Vichy government has deprived you of your French nationality. You won't be suspect among the French truly dedicated to an allied victory. From them I believe you can get confidential information no Englishman could ever hope to obtain."

"I am sure you are right, Sir James. I've already had some indications to that effect," said Jacques.

"Mr. de Thoranne, I want to make one thing clear. You do not have to take this risky job. You may proceed exactly as you had planned before this conversation. You'll find the same cooperation from our official and unofficial representatives in these territories, and you don't have to decide now. Take all the time you wish to think it over."

"I appreciate this, Sir James."

"In the meantime, you have *carte blanche* to go anywhere you wish in Britain," said Sir James. "There will be no restrictions for you. You may visit our top-secret night fighter radar installations and learn how pilots are trained to attack German bombers at night. You may take a trip on a submarine, on a warship, or on a bomber if room can be found. Just ask for any trip you want, and the MOI will arrange it."

"Sir James," said Jacques, "this mission appeals to me. From what you have told me, I gather that I would not be a member of British Intelligence."

"That is correct," said Sir James. "We gather information in two ways. First through British Intelligence, a network of trained professionals, and also from what we call the irregulars, operating independently. None of our irregulars are British nationals. They operate independently."

"So, I'd be one of those," said Jacques. "An irregular. How do you know that I fit that category?"

"I don't," said Sir James. "You'll have to decide that for yourself. In almost all areas where you plan to go there are British consulates, which will give you all the help they can."

"It's certainly a challenging proposal. I'll think it over and give you my answer shortly. In the meantime, I'll take advantage of your offer and get a firsthand look at some of the devastation Hitler's air force has showered on England."

"Mr. de Thoranne, do you have any plans for lunch?" asked the minister.

"No, sir, I don't."

"I'm sure Miss McNeill will be pleased to accompany you and give you any other information you need. You may talk with her as confidentially as you do with me. She is my right hand. Here she is."

"Mr. de Thoranne, you have delivered a message of 'Help England' that no Englishman could have given. I have a small token of appreciation for you," she said, "but we must first have your photograph taken."

"That isn't necessary," said Jacques. "I had a stock made before leaving the United States. How many do you need?"

"Two are enough," she said.

"What are they for?" asked Jacques.

"I'll give you a special pass," she said, "that will allow you to go almost anywhere you like. Only a handful of these passes have been issued. You may not use it outside of England, and you must return it to me before you leave. Let's go out for lunch now. We have a cozy little club nearby where only members of our group are admitted."

Miss McNeill was in her thirties; she was of medium height, with blue eyes and neatly groomed blonde hair. Although not beautiful, she had a certain charm, a magnetic personality, and a way of stepping into her guest's frame of mind, blending it into her own.

"I needn't tell you that England's situation is still very precarious," she said as they sat down to a table for two, which was covered with a red and white checkered tablecloth and laden with *hors d'oeuvres*. "Most of the outside world thinks Germany has won the war and that England will face a stalemate and eventually be compelled to end hostilities."

"Miss McNeill, there can be absolutely no compromise with Hitler."

"Of course not," she said, "but before the war, even until the disaster at Dunkerque, many in England favored an accommodation with Hitler. There were powerful pacifist forces at work in the House of Commons, in the House of Lords, among the ruling classes, and in the news media, not to mention in the public. Those who disagreed were called warmongers. Who knows what would have happened if the British Expeditionary Force had been destroyed in France? Churchill might have been forced to resign and, conceivably, peace could have been signed with Hitler."

"That, of course," Jacques said, "would have been followed by Nazi occupation of England, which would have suffered the fate of Czechoslovakia and become a satellite of the Nazi Reich. I shudder to think of it."

"It was at this point," said Miss McNeill, "that Sir James gained great influence with the prime minister. He had warned the government about the pro-Nazi forces at work in Belgium and France, about the incompetence of the French general staff, about the mentality of the unions, and I think, about the pacifist forces at work here in England."

"I've heard some things that I find hard to believe," said Jacques. "One of the crewmen of the corvette that brought me over here said that the Belgian Railroad Union had gone on strike when it was imperative to transport troops to the front to block the advancing German Army. Is that true?"

"It is. You can be sure there will be no more strikes now that the Germans are in control."

"Do you know what's going on in France now, under the occupation?"

"Yes," she said. "By and large the ruling classes are settling down, convinced that the Nazi occupation will last forever. Entertainment is proceeding as usual. Mistinguett and Cecile Sorel are still at it. Edith Piaf is very popular. She makes 20,000 *francs* for an evening performance. She gives most of it to the poor. Maurice Chevalier still lives in the Paris suburbs but comes to the city for singing performances and broadcasts over Radio Paris."

"Entertainers' lives have not changed that much," said Jacques.

"No," she said. "Neither have those of writers like Cocteau and Colette who contribute to the collaborationist press; Sacha Guitry is back, writing new plays."

"I begin to understand what kind of an outcast I am—and why Sir James needs the kind of information he wants me to gather."

Miss McNeill signed a check for the lunch. "Remember," she said as they walked back to her office, "for anything you need, come here. Call me the day before if possible. If not, just come. I'll manage to fit you in. Where are you going now?"

"To Canton Gardens, to the Free French headquarters. I'll need some sort of document or visa to visit the territories, and I might as well start the formalities as soon as possible. There's probably a bureaucratic thicket there, too."

She smiled, "Good luck."

At Carlton Gardens Jacques looked up Pierre d'Huart, who was in his late twenties, well-built and athletic, full of spirits and energy, and clean shaven with grey eyes and chestnut hair. He and Jacques were old friends.

"I'm so pleased to see you," he told Jacques. "After hearing about your resignation, I felt sure you'd be coming through sooner or later."

"As for me," said Jacques, "I never expected to see you here. How did you get here?"

"I was ADC for General Blanchard. I was also an interpreter. The general didn't know a word of English. He sent me with an urgent dispatch to Lord Gort after the Nazis broke through our lines. I managed to get to Lord Gort but was unable to return to General Blanchard."

"Then you were caught in the Dunkerque pocket?"

"I was," said d'Huart. "I escaped to England with a few other soldiers on a large white yacht. The skipper of that boat was a blonde girl, about twenty. As soon as the boat was loaded, she gunned the engine, and we were off."

"I understand that the weather cooperated.

"To some extent it did," said d'Huart. "The sea was like a mill pond—not a ripple. But as soon as we got out of the smoke of the burning city, German planes attacked us. Some strafed us; others tried to bomb us. Suddenly a Stuka dive-bomber came at us, but just as suddenly the clatter of machine guns broke out on board our ship. We could see the tracer bullets engaging the dive-bomber. When it was quite low, there was an explosion and the plane crashed into the sea about a hundred yards away. The yacht had a Bofors pom-pom, fired by a man who must have been in his fifties and was perhaps the girl's father. Neither she nor the man said a word. The yacht pressed on, full speed ahead, zigzagging now and then, until it landed us in Ramsgate and refueled for a return trip. That was the last we saw of it."

"In the U.S. we heard that this fleet of small boats saved a great part of the BEF," said Jacques.

"That's correct," said d'Huart, "and now that I'm back here alive, I can say I wouldn't have missed that experience for anything. The trip left a deep impression on us all. They gave us food, hot drinks, dry clothes. Later on they gave us a choice to stay in England or return to France. Under no condition would I go back to live under Nazi rule, although things are not that good here—I mean, of course, among the Free French. You'll find the same ridiculous feuding as there was in France before and during the collapse."

"Some people will never learn," said Jacques.

"There's a major conflict between de Gaulle, who represents what we might call the army, and Admiral Muselier, who controls what is left of the French Navy. There are quite a few French warships in British harbors, but there are no men to man them. Jacques, you are lucky, representing the American press. You are a free agent."

"I was born in England and am therefore British by birth and a British national. I intend to remain a free agent."

"I don't blame you," said d'Huart. "De Gaulle is not here. I doubt he would receive you anyway. Muselier is out, searching for new headquarters. He will be glad to welcome you. Come back later."

"I'll be glad to," said Jacques. "I'll keep in touch with you."

"And I'll tip you off about any scoop," said d'Huart. "As a matter of fact, I have one right now, but it's super hush-hush. Some French soldiers captured by the Germans last year escaped from a German prisoner of war camp in East Prussia and went to the Soviet Union. The Soviets are sending them to England. They should arrive tomorrow at Euston Station around ten. You might want to interview some of them, but you'll need luck. Only two of us know about it, and it's positively no journalists—of course, your source remains secret."

After leaving d'Huart, Jacques hurried back to the Savoy. He had two broadcasts to write: a fifteen-minute broadcast for the BBC's *Empire Program* and a five minute broadcast in French. It was past midnight when he got to bed.

The next morning, when he opened the door of his hotel room, he noticed an elderly man, balding, with thin grey hair on the sides of his head and a ruddy complexion, who appeared interested in his movements. He paid no further attention and turned the corner of the corridor to go downstairs.

Suddenly he remembered that he had left his wallet under his pillow and returned to his room. The door stood ajar. He breezed in and stood face to face with the man he had just seen in the storage compartment across the hall.

"What are you doing in my room?"

"Oh! I'm sorry, sir...I...uh...just went in to make sure all the taps were turned off. Water is...so difficult to get...we can't waste it...."

"A likely story! Get out of here." said Jacques.

"I'm sorry, sir...."

That man was looking for the girl. *After all that confusion following the bombing*, he wondered *how could they know that Sheila had stayed here all night? The room must be bugged.*

After breakfast he returned to his room and called the Cumberland, an American-style hotel at Marble Arch.

"Yes, sir, you may have a room with bath. It will be ready for you after lunch."

Then Jacques called his cousin. "Sheila, I'm moving. I'll be at the Cumberland, room 305. A good thing you weren't with me last night," he said and explained what had happened.

"You won't have that trouble at the Cumberland," she said, laughing. "There's another hotel in the neighborhood that's even less fussy, the Mount

Royal, but I don't recommend it. It has the reputation of being...what should I call it, the headquarters of the fair ladies who roam the streets at night in search of customers."

It was only a short distance from the Savoy to Euston station. The underground station Strand wasn't far from the hotel, and trains followed a direct route to Euston station. Soon, however, Jacques regretted he had not taken a taxi. The train suddenly stopped between Leicester Square and Tottenham Court Road stations and remained stopped, doors closed, silent. It was almost eleven o'clock when he reached the platform where the train from Liverpool was due to arrive. Obviously the secret had been well kept. The area was cordoned off, and the travelers in the front part of the train had passed the gate. Jacques walked quietly toward the cars remaining to be discharged. A wary official stopped him, "Sir, this is off limits. No one is allowed here."

"The remaining passengers are French. They don't speak English. I am here to help them," Jacques said.

"I am sorry, sir. I cannot let you through. I am under very strict orders."

Jacques drew the special pass from his wallet.

"I'm sorry, sir, you should have shown me this in the first place. Go ahead."

The ex-prisoners were allowed to alight. Some could walk, but many had to be carried to the waiting ambulances. Those who could walk looked haggard and wan, but all had that semi-satisfied expression of human beings escaping from a nightmare and hardly able to believe that it was over.

"We've been told not to say a word to anyone," said one of the men Jacques addressed. So Jacques, talking to him in Frenchmen's French, asked him where he was from, if he had a family, wife and children. That broke the ice. "After all," the ex-prisoner said, "between Frenchmen, there's nothing to hide. Our story started after the German tanks broke through the French lines at Sedan."

"When was that?" asked Jacques.

"That was on May 15. We were captured by the Sixth Panzer Division, at Rozoy-sur-Serre, and sent to a prisoner of war camp in East Prussia. Things were so bad there that we escaped and went to the Soviet Union. They imprisoned us, too. There the filth, the cold, the starvation diet, if you could call it a diet, made us regret what we'd done. So we planned another escape to return to the German prison."

"You must have been pretty desperate to do that," said Jacques.

"We were," said the ex-prisoner, "but a few days before we were ready, the Russians moved us back far into the Soviet Union, in cattle cars with no sanitation, no light, and no food. They said they feared a German invasion and wanted us out of the way. We ended up in another prison camp, worse than the first."

"How did you ever get out?"

"Somehow our leader, Captain Billotte, convinced the Soviets to let us go. We boarded an English hospital ship in Murmansk. For the first time since

May of last year, we had a proper meal—but that was nothing compared with the return to liberty."

"Does everyone in your group hate the Soviets more than the Germans?" asked Jacques.

"I would say they do," said the man. "The Germans, at least, didn't seem to think that we were some kind of inferior human beings. They let us keep our watches, our rings, our wallets, and the photographs of our wives and children. The Russians treated us like animals. They took everything we had. Look at this, *monsieur,*" he said, opening his mouth. "Before leaving Murmansk they put us in a dentist's chair—I should say a butcher's chair—and he pulled bit of fillings from our mouths. They took all the gold out of my mouth. One inlay would not come out, so the dentist just broke off the tooth to remove it. No anesthetic, nothing! They could not get the gold ring off one fellow's swollen finger, so they just cut the finger off. The Germans may be brutes, but the Russians are barbarians If they do get into a war with Hitler, I hope the Germans wipe them out. I can tell you, *monsieur,* there's not a communist left in our group, now they've seen the real thing."

That afternoon Jacques paid his bill, removed his belongings from the Savoy, and checked in to room 305 at the Cumberland.

He was finishing a broadcast when the phone rang.

"Jacques, are you very busy just now?"

"Never too busy to listen to you, my dear cousin. What's up?"

"My assistant has returned," she said, "and I could probably come over for an hour or two."

"Wonderful. Come whenever it suits you. I'm writing a couple of broadcasts. I'll just stop when you come. How about dinner?"

"I'd love it," she said, "but I don't want to get home too late."

"Think there'll be another bombing tonight?" he asked.

"Jacques, stop it!" she said.

It was not an easy assignment to speak to the conquered people in his homeland. He felt sure his parents, his sister, and many relatives and friends would tune in to hear him. What could he tell them, especially after what he had learned from Sir James? The war was going to be a long one. There was no quick solution to the rescue of Europe.

When Sheila arrived, she came into his arms; he embraced her tenderly. He felt her trembling body.

"You don't know what this means to me, to have someone of the family so close to me, someone I know so well, and who knows and understands me, especially at a time like this…."

"Sheila," he said, "you do have brother John."

"I know, but I've never been able to talk to him as I talk with you, and he has an awfully small flat for a couple with two children and one extra adult."

"Why don't you stay at your mother's place—in Hampstead, isn't it?" asked Jacques.

"It was," she said, "but no longer. When the Blitz started, we took Mother to the summer cottage near Tiverton, in Devon, where she would be safe from the bombs. John had the weekend off, and we helped pack her clothes and the few belongings which were very dear to her. I returned there the following weekend and took about half my clothes for safekeeping, just in case."

"Did you drive?" Jacques asked.

"Yes, I did," she said. "When I came back, I could not even get close to what had been home. The whole area had been burnt out. I lost everything I had, my photographs of our vacations together, my typewriter, my camera—all things that can't be replaced. That's why I'm staying with Kaye. I could put up with the loss of all I owned, but the greatest loss of all is the loss of my privacy. Jacques, it's gone, all gone, and it's just plain horrible."

"Look darling, I can get you a little privacy this week. Tomorrow, early, I'm leaving for Coventry. After that I'm going to the super secret night fighter training center, then to Scapa Flow, and to some of the bases for the long-range planes that hunt submarines. I should be back Friday. I'll keep the room here and give you the key. You'll have privacy for a few days. So let's go down to dinner. Just let me finish the last lines of this broadcast to France,"

"What? Are you writing all this in longhand?" Sheila asked.

"I learned to type rather late in life," said Jacques. "I can't think and type at the same time. So I first put it down in longhand, correct it, and then type."

"Where's your typewriter? I'll type what you've already written while you finish the broadcast. That will help me brush up on my French."

"Before we go to dinner," Jacques said, "don't let me forget this. I would have given it to you the other day, except that the bombing prevented you…."

From the closet, Jacques drew the basket of fruit still wrapped in the newspaper he used to hide it from view in Liverpool. "Some friends gave me this basket of oranges when I left New York. I thought you'd like it, but wait a minute. I have to make a selection."

"What are you doing?" she asked.

'These moldy oranges are going into the wastepaper basket," he said.

"Don't you dare do that!" she screamed.

"Sheila, these oranges are moldy."

"It's easy to see that you haven't been deprived of oranges for two years," she said. "We'll eat them first."

"No, you won't!"

"Jacques," she screamed, "you and I have never had a quarrel, but I'm ready for one now."

"Sheila, don't be silly. Let's go down for dinner."

He had never seen his cousin like this. He felt something had snapped. She didn't say a word as they walked down the stairs. He sensed that the pressures of war were taking their toll. He realized that anything he would say could make matters worse and that he'd better let the storm blow over and discuss the problems connected with his upcoming trip another day.

They sat down for dinner. "Sheila," he said, 'what will you have for dinner?"

"I'm not hungry," she said.

"Well," Jacques said, "this looks like a pretty good menu. How about some lamb chops? You used to like them when you came to the farm, with fried potatoes and salad. Won't you try some?"

As she glanced half-heartedly at the menu, the elderly waiter came up to the table.

"Waiter," she said, "I'll have the lamb chops, somewhat underdone, the fried potatoes, and the salad, please."

"Make it two," Jacques added, "and also a half bottle of rosé wine."

The dinner went by, broken now and then by a desultory conversation. Jacques did not press the point and did not ask questions. Sheila was not herself. They went up to the room in silence.

"Sheila," he said, as he camouflaged the basket of oranges with a newspaper, "before eating any of these oranges, please remove the moldy parts."

"I will," she answered softly.

He called for a taxi.

"What are you doing now?" she asked sharply.

"I want you to go home by taxi," he answered. "I don't want you to take that basket in the underground and in the train."

As they went through the lobby, Jacques stopped for a word with the hall porter. "Sam, this is my cousin, Sheila Hatherley. She has been bombed out and is living under difficult conditions. I'll be away this week, but I've kept my room, which has been paid for. I have told her to come and stay here. When she comes, please give her the key."

"I certainly will, sir. Your taxi is waiting."

"Thank you."

"Sheila, get in. Take this, it should be enough for the fare."

"Oh! Jacques," she kissed him softly.

He noticed her hand was trembling, and he saw tears in her eyes.

She got into the taxi and waved good-bye.

Sheila's attitude left Jacques depressed and anxious. He had much on his mind as he walked up to his room. Would he take the job proposed by Sir James? What had he come here for, if not to do his share to free his homeland? He'd wait to see

Seymour Barker, who was in charge of the London office of International News Service, and hear what he proposed and what guidance he offered. Should he go off to Africa or stay in England? What kept him in London? One woman: Sheila! He'd always loved her and had always dreamed of marrying her. But was the blood relationship too close? Maybe. And now she loved someone else...or did she?

On his broadcast he would tell the people in France what true Frenchmen were doing to free *la patrie*, tell them about the Free French corvette, how it had sunk two U-boats and had rescued members of the crews. He would use no names, no dates, but would give vivid details of what had happened. That should kindle some hope in their hearts.

After that he'd tell them something to make them laugh: the question he'd got in a service club in West Orange, New Jersey. During the question and answer period, a man in the audience asked if it were true that Napoleon wore a red vest so that, if he were wounded, blood would not show, thus avoiding panic among his soldiers. Jacques said he didn't know that detail. "Well," the man said, "perhaps you can tell me if Mussolini wears brown pants for the same reason." Jacques knew that that kind of a story would be all over France in a few days. The only problem would be to get it through the censors in England.

It was almost midnight when he finished writing his final script. He fell asleep the moment he got into bed, hoping the sirens would not wake him up. They didn't, but the telephone did—at two-thirty!

A soft voice, almost in a whisper, greeted him apologetically.

"Jacques, I'm so sorry I was so rude and nasty to you this evening. I feel terrible about it, and you were so patient and understanding. I tried to put on a good face when I got to the hotel, but I'd had some horrible news just as I left the office."

"What upset you so?" Jacques asked.

"I'll tell you about it when you come back...but we were so thrilled to get the oranges."

"I hope...," said Jacques.

"Yes, I did."

"Sheila," said Jacques, "I have not been here very long, but I'm beginning to see what kind of lives you Londoners are living. I hope you'll use my hotel room while I'm away."

"I wanted to thank you again for that," she said. "That will be wonderful. Privacy for a few days. I'm sorry I woke you up, but I couldn't sleep until I'd spoken to you...."

"Good night, Sheila dear. See you on Friday. I'll try to get back to London early. Let's spend Saturday together. I want to talk to you. I'll let you decide where to go and what to do."

"Jacques," she said, "I'll be able to sleep now."

Chapter V

Jacques arrived early the next morning for his eight o'clock appointment with Seymour Barker, the bureau chief of International News Service.

Barker greeted Jacques amicably, "I see you're five minutes early."

"Yes, sir," said Jacques. "I try to be five minutes early for any appointment to make sure I'm not late."

"We need people like you in this agency," said Barker, who opened the door himself. "You'll fit in. I know what you've done in the past, and I have great expectations for you in the future. Jacques, just call me Seymour."

Seymour Barker was a man of medium height, with aquiline features, clean shaven, with neatly groomed hair with a shade of grey in the black. He had light green eyes and a piercing gaze. His office was small and functional: a desk, a telephone, a typewriter, and a couple of chairs.

"You're going to Africa?" he said to Jacques.

"Am I?" said Jacques. "I suppose I am. I've been asked to go to the Free French and Free Belgian colonies."

"We have practically no coverage in those areas. The agency doesn't think the cost is justified. In Brazzaville, the capital of French Equatorial Africa, we have Karl Bigley, who writes and delivers broadcasts beamed to the United States. There's not much worthwhile news out of there, and Bigley never gets out of the city. Contact him when you get there."

"I will," said Jacques.

"His contract with the Free French is almost up. He'll give you the low-down before he leaves. I have a couple of important assignments for you."

"Which are?" asked Jacques.

"First get acquainted with the area. Then take a few excursions into neighboring Angola and Mozambique."

"Portuguese territories?" said Jacques.

"Yes. They're riddled with Nazi agents. The Gestapo, the Abwehr, and the

Sicherheitdienst all have emissaries throughout these territories. Find out what you can about them. I'm particularly interested in the rivalry that exists between these groups and the agents and sympathizers they have planted in the Portuguese administration."

"That's a tall order," said Jacques.

"I know," said Barker. "It's a dangerous one, too. Keep a low profile. Observe what you can. When you get back to London, the two of us will decide what to publish."

"What's the other assignment?"

"What do you know about cobalt?" asked Barker.

"Cobalt? You mean the substance used by the Chinese to color the famous blue porcelain made during the Ming dynasty? I know that it's a metal that looks something like nickel when it's pure. That's about all that I can tell you."

"I didn't know any more than you until very recently," Barker said, "when I found out that the outcome of the war may hinge on cobalt supplies."

"What? Seymour, where did you hear that?" Jacques asked incredulously.

"Cobalt is a vital strategic metal," Barker said. "Industrial production depends largely on tools which cut steel. That operation produces much heat. Cutting tools made of ordinary steel burn up fast, but tools made of steel/cobalt alloy remain effective even when red hot."

"Then Germany's production of war materials would decrease considerably if the Nazis couldn't get cobalt."

"Exactly. From what I've heard, it would fall by 30 to 50 percent"

"Where do the Nazis get the cobalt?"

"Some comes from Vichy-controlled territories in North Africa, but I have it on good authority that most of it comes from the Belgian Congo."

"The Belgian Congo? But the Congo is our ally, isn't it?

"It is, but remember Belgium is occupied by the Nazis. They can exert much pressure."

"How does the cobalt get to Germany?" Jacques asked.

"According to my informant, it's mined in the east of the Congo, in the Haut Katanga. From there it's sent overland on the Portuguese railroad to the port of Lobito in Angola. It's loaded on Spanish, Portuguese, or other neutral ships and sent to Spain or occupied France."

"How do those ships get past Nazi submarines?"

"They are clearly identified. Huge Spanish and Portuguese flags have been painted on their sides. At night they are illuminated with floodlights, and they have all other lights on, too. Submarines leave them alone."

"How do they get through the British blockade?"

"The British don't want to upset Portugal or Spain. They need the Portuguese islands of the Azores, and it is vital for them to keep Franco neutral. So the ships get through."

"I'm learning a lot about the war!"

"Jacques, anyone can understand why the Germans need gold. The German mark is worthless outside of Europe. The Nazis need a hard currency—gold—to pay spies, embassy personnel, rents, etc. Very few people realize the crucial importance of cobalt and black diamonds for the prosecution of the war. Cobalt to produce super-hard tools, black diamonds to sharpen them."

"Well, what do you want me to do?" asked Jacques.

"I'd like you to find out all you can about the operation. What quantities are involved? In what form is the cobalt shipped? Refined, semi-refined, or in the form of ore? How is it paid for? In what currency? Who makes the payments? To whom do payments go?"

"That's another tall order," said Jacques.

"And another dangerous one," said Barker, "but I don't want you to take any chances. Use your own judgment and be careful."

"I will," said Jacques.

"Where are you going now?' asked Barker.

"To the BBC," said Jacques, "for a broadcast to the people of France."

"I'll drop you off there," said Barker. "I have an appointment near Portland Place."

Jacques was longer than he had expected at the BBC. He reached the Cumberland a few minutes late for his 10:00 A.M. appointment with the driver who was to take him to Coventry. He was in his room, gathering his luggage, when the phone rang.

It was the hail porter. Jacques' transportation was waiting.

A small, khaki-colored car waited at the door of the hotel. It was driven by a trim female chauffeur of the Auxiliary Transport Service (ATS) who apologized for not being exactly on time. "I was supposed to pick up another American war correspondent at the Savoy," she said. "I waited fifteen minutes, and he didn't show up. They do that to us all the time."

"Maybe he had a little too much yesterday," said Jacques.

"I wouldn't be surprised," she said. "There'll be just the two of us to go to Coventry. Later this afternoon I'm to take you to a place without a name. It's a top-secret night fighter-training center. You'll spend the night there, and tomorrow you'll leave for Glasgow. I'll be your guide in Coventry."

"You must know the area pretty well," said Jacques.

"Yes, sir, I do," she said. "I've been told to show you anything you want to see. Coventry is about one hundred miles from here. It will take two and a half to three hours to get there, depending on road conditions and the possibility of air raids."

De Thoranne sensed right from the start that his chauffeur was slightly ill at ease with just one male passenger in the small car. She drove in silence, her full attention devoted to the road.

"Oh! I'm sorry, sir," said the chauffeur as she swerved suddenly and braked hard, coming to a full stop on the sidewalk. "Quick, sir, get out and lie down—quickly."

"What's that?" de Thoranne asked as a screeching vehicle passed them at breakneck speed along Aldersgate Street, which in seconds was deserted by everything that moved, leaving an open road for the speeding truck.

"That's the BDS." she said. "The bomb disposal squad. They take unexploded bombs with delayed-action fuses, timed to explode hours or days after impact. I hope that's the live bomb that was at St. Paul's."

When they had resumed driving, Jacques said, "May I ask you what your name is?"

"Yes, sir, I am ATS Gladys Pritchard."

"In the United States, we are somewhat less formal than you people in England. May I call you by your first name?" said Jacques.

"Certainly, sir," she said.

"My first name, as you've seen on your order, is Jacques. Please call me that."

"Oh no, sir, I would feel uncomfortable doing that, but I like it when you call me Gladys. Do you see, sir, that field on the right with a sentry at the fence?" she asked.

"Yes," said Jacques.

"That's where they detonate the unexploded bombs. Look! See that smoke? That's one going off. Hear? We're getting so used to those bangs that we pay no attention anymore."

De Thoranne felt completely relaxed; his driver was exactly what he would have chosen as a private chauffeur: precise, smooth, attentive, and lively. He felt detached yet a part of her driving, perfectly comfortable delegating all responsibility to her. She drove in silence, a perfect picture of self-control, not even muttering a word of reproach as she swerved and braked hard to avoid a young cyclist bursting out of an alleyway who scraped the front fender and fell flat on his face to the left of the car. She stopped and got out quietly, but he had already picked himself up.

"Are you hurt?" she asked him.

"No, ma'am, just grazed my hands," he said, picking up his bike, which seemed little the worse for the fall.

"I'm sorry, sir, for making you hit the front seat," she said.

"Don't be sorry. You are an excellent driver. Where are we now?' Jacques asked.

"About five miles from the center of Coventry. I will show you whatever you want to see," she said.

"We might as well have lunch before seeing the town," said Jacques. "Is there a good restaurant in Coventry?"

"Yes, sir, The Black Swan. I'll drop you there and pick you up after you have eaten."

"No, you won't," said Jacques. "You are my guest. We will both go to The Black Swan."

"Sir, we are not supposed to do that. I go to the canteen for lunch."

"Maybe you do," Jacques told her, "but today is an exception. If anyone complains, just tell them you're following orders."

There were no signs of war at The Black Swan on that sunny spring morning. The crocuses were in bloom, birds sang, and people walked around leisurely, as though the world were at peace.

ATS Pritchard parked the car. An elderly waitress seated them at a table for two, brought the menu, and disappeared.

What impressed Jacques most about his driver was the subtle spirituality of her delicate features—her intense blue eyes, her sensitive mouth, her blonde hair, and her pink complexion. Under the coarse military uniform, he imagined a body as beautiful as the head.

"The Black Swan has a remarkable menu," he said to the waitress who had just returned. "*Quenelle* is on the menu. That is a dish which is most appreciated in the east of France."

"We have a French chef," the waitress said. "He escaped from Dunkerque and volunteered to join the Free French in London. They told him that at forty-seven he was too old, so he came here. He's really made a reputation for the restaurant."

"Would you like to try some *quenelles?*" Jacques asked his companion.

"What're they?" she asked.

"Fish dumplings made with pike and served warm with a tasty sauce."

"I'm sure I'll like that," she said, "and I'd like chicken after that."

"This doesn't look like a war-time menu," said Jacques. "Let's enjoy it while we can."

"It feels like civilian life again," said Gladys, smiling. "I won't need any dinner tonight. Depending when we get there, I'll almost surely spend the night at the air base and return to the office tomorrow and then home."

"Where is home?" Jacques asked.

"In Carshalton, just south of London," she said. "We've been lucky so far and have had no bombings of which to speak. I live there with Mother. The rest of the family is at war. Father was recalled to active duty to command a destroyer. She was sunk during the Dunkerque evacuation. His ship, the destroyer *Furious*, was attacked by five Stukas. They shot two of them down, but one bomb went down the stack and exploded in the engine room. The ship sank in no time. Father was in the water for about an hour. A lot of small ships picked up the survivors. He was one of the last to get on board a passing yacht. He was put in charge of another destroyer. That one survived until the end of the evacuation. He's on convoy duty now."

Jacques sensed that, with the help of the warm meal, the Portuguese wine, the cheery fire, and the relaxed atmosphere, Miss Pritchard's shyness and reserve were melting away.

They discussed the events that led up to this war and Britain's lack of preparedness when it started.

"Even today, almost two years into the war, your ack-ack can't reach Germany's high-flying bombers. Even the older Heinkels, the HE 111Ps, fly practically out of range of your anti-aircraft defenses. You'll not be able to protect London at night, or any other city, until you have a big radar-equipped force of night fighters."

"Yes, we are building one. That's what you are going to see tonight."

They had finished lunch. Jacques said, "Suppose we take a look at what Mr. Hitler has done to Coventry in the absence of any proper air defenses."

They toured the blackened skeletons of the industrial inner city, which had once been factories and homes, and toured the new factories, where resolute men and women were building parts of Spitfires.

When he left Coventry that afternoon, Jacques had once again seen the plight of people who had refused to believe a disaster could happen—until it did happen. He relaxed in back of the car and enjoyed the ride. He wondered why Gladys was so silent.

"Gladys," he said, "don't think I'm bored with riding. I love it. When do we get to the secret base?"

"We'll be there in about a half hour. They wanted me to get there before sunset. We don't use the headlights any more than we have to."

"You'll have to use them to return to London."

"No, I must spend the night at the base, and I don't like that."

"You seem awfully quiet, now."

"Mr. de Thoranne, you've given me a lot to think about. Don't think I haven't enjoyed the day. It's the nicest outing I've had since I joined the ATS. But you've made an awfully unpleasant prediction...."

"Which was?"

"You said it would take American intervention to win the war. You are right. You talk just like Father, and we wouldn't listen to him. I realize we've brought this on ourselves. You've made me face it. This is no life for a girl—or for anyone."

"Gladys, you shouldn't complain. You're meeting all kinds of people, and you're not regimented. Many others are worse off than you are."

"I know," she said.

"Here's my card. If we both survive and you come to America after the war, look me up.

He spent the night at the secret air base, watching the night fighters take off and land in the darkness and return to their underground bunkers; he saw the new radar equipment and how it worked. He was entrusted with many secret technical details.

Next he went to Greenock. There he saw an old friend. *Marigold* was being repaired, cleaned, and repainted in camouflage black, white, green, and brown. The scars were gone she was getting a new bow. He asked about the crew. They had a new and faster corvette and were back escorting North Atlantic convoys.

In Glasgow Jacques visited an old classmate, Gilles Dubarle. Dubarle was a quiet, athletic, unassuming man with inquisitive green eyes, a clean-shaven face, and light brown hair; he wore a neat dark blue French naval officer's uniform. He was an ensign on a modern French destroyer, the *Maillé Brézé.*

"I'm not supposed to," he told Jacques, "but I'll show you what carelessness does. You're in uniform, so there should be no difficulty getting into the arsenal."

"I have a pass which opens almost any door—if I need it."

"We were ready to take off to escort a convoy," said Dubarle, "and I was doing some last minute shopping in town. When I got back, I saw this frightful mess."

Jacques examined a gaping hole in the center of the ship, torn plates, and jagged metal. "How did it happen?"

"How it happened is absolutely unforgivable," said Dubarle. "A sailor was doing some last minute cleaning around the torpedo tubes. He pushed the wrong button and fired a live torpedo into the ship's stack. The explosion killed forty men and wounded about fifty—not to mention the four or five months we'll need for repairs at a time when destroyers are desperately needed—just as we were ready to go to sea."

"In addition to the waste of time," said Jacques, "you'll probably have a hard time replacing the trained men who've been killed or wounded."

"Of course, we will," said Dubarle, "not many French Navy men have volunteered to help England. I'm about the only officer left here with a thorough knowledge of this ship."

"I'm sure Admiral Muselier will do all he can to find the men you need," said Jacques.

"Of course he will, but he can't provide what's not there," said Dubarle. "It will be easier to replace enlisted men than officers. Muselier said as much when he was here."

"I bet he was angry when he saw this devastation," said Jacques.

"You bet he was," said Dubarle. "This whole thing has to be blamed on carelessness and lack of supervision."

"I guess this sort of thing happens in any of the armed forces, but it's certainly no way to win a war," said Jacques.

"Of course not," said Dubarle, "but there was too much of that in pre-war France. This was the carryover of the lack of discipline and sloppiness and the expression of a general social attitude in France and much of Europe before the war. Remember when we were students, how we used to curse all those strikes—all that antimilitarist propaganda?"

"Yes," said Jacques, "and all that pacifist talk and the eventual breakdown of French war production when the leftists elected the Blum government."

"The whole country's paying for it now," said Dubarle.

"And paying through the nose," added Jacques. "Can you guess how much money the Germans are exacting from France now?"

"I have no idea," said Dubarle. "Do you?"

"Yes, I do. They're taxing France four hundred million francs a day."

"What?" said Dubarle. "Four hundred million francs a day? That's impossible! Are you sure?"

"I got it from the State Department just before I left the U.S. Hitler had ordered France to pay six hundred million francs a day, but the Vichy Government managed to reduce that to four hundred million and hopes to bring that down to three hundred million, but I'm not sure they'll succeed."

"How can the French people afford it'?"

"I've no idea," said Jacques. "I'd love to discuss this further, but I must get back to London this afternoon."

"You have a train in about forty-five minutes," said Dubarle. "I'll run you down to the station."

"In a way," said Jacques, "I'm in the company of a man back from the dead. You were really fortunate."

"I know," said Dubarle. "I'm one of the few officers to survive. I was delayed because I could not find the type of film I wanted for the trip and searched for it all over town, with no luck."

"I'd say with much luck," said Jacques.

"Yes," said Dubarle. "In war life hangs by a thread. Look what's happened to our lives. You studied for five years to pass that horrible competitive exam for the Diplomatic Service, and you've had to leave the career for which you worked. I was looking forward to my career in the navy, and here I am far from my family wondering if I'll ever see them again. I have no idea what has happened to my wife and two children. I have no news from my parents or from my in-laws and for how long? Here's your train."

"Let's plan to get together after the war," said Jacques. "*Adieu!*"

Chapter VI

It was dark when Jacques reached London. He wondered if Sheila had used the hotel room. He did not stop at the desk for the keys. He went right up. He knocked at the door.

"Who is there?" came a soft female voice.

"Sheila, it's me—Jacques. I just got back."

The door sprang open. She jumped into his arms and clasped him so tightly it slowed his breath. She remained there, her blonde hair on his shoulder, and her lips against his. He felt her emotion, her electricity, her warmth, and her anxiety.

"Jacques," she said, "I'm so glad you got back this evening. I've missed you so much at a time when I needed you most."

He didn't ask her why she needed him so much.

"Sheila, I guessed that Chris had been shot down. How did it happen?"

"One of my friends works at the Fleet Air Arm," said Sheila. "I got some details from her. They asked for volunteers for the dangerous job of bombing the two German battle cruisers under repair at Brest. Chris volunteered. Five Swordfish attacked on April 5. Two were lost, and Chris was flying one of them."

"What did brother John say?" Jacques asked.

"I haven't seen him since," said Sheila. "Oh Jacques, I've lived in constant fear of this, and now it's happened."

She sobbed and came into his arms. He held her there in silence. He could feel her loneliness and her anguish. He gave her what she needed most: companionship in her grief. He could feel her sobbing, softly, as though she were unwilling to express her pain. He wiped the tears from her eyes. She opened them, looking at him lovingly.

"Jacques," she said softly, "I'm going to be awfully late arriving at Kaye's. I should have left already."

"You're right," said Jacques. "You will be very late. You'll be so late that you're not going. You are going to stay here, both today and tomorrow. You should have all you need: clothes, toiletries, lipstick, I presume," he said, smiling.

"Jacques," she said shamefully, "I've got all the lipstick you gave me here in my bag."

"This room isn't too warm,' Jacques said, pulling a pair of warm pajamas from his bag. "Aren't you cold?"

"We're used to it," she said. "For days last winter we had no heat at all. Which side of the bed do you prefer? Don't give me that story that you'll sleep on the couch. There are no sheets on it, no blankets, and you have no sleeping bag. As a matter of fact, there aren't many blankets on the bed. But you don't need those pajamas." She snuggled into his arms.

Outside a cold wind drove a thin, drizzly rain in swirls through the dark streets, in moaning or screaming and beating against the windows. Here the windows had glass, and Jacques didn't care about the outside. He had Sheila in his arms.

He felt her warmth as he drifted off to sleep; he sensed, too, that she was soothed and consoled. She had decided that fate had changed her life, that she had to accept it and continue life as best she could. At least fate had been kind to her in one way: It happened when the cousin she preferred among her relatives, the cousin she trusted and loved, was there with her. She could talk to him and he'd understand.

He didn't know how long he slept. He didn't know if he was dreaming, but he felt a soft feminine hand slowly bringing him out of the land of dreams.

"Jacques," she said softly, "forgive me for waking you up. You've helped me through this awful time. This has done something to me. Remember that night when I stayed at the Savoy?"

"I certainly do," he said.

"You remember when I wouldn't let you sleep alone on the couch, and we slept together in bed?"

"Of course I do," he said.

"You said I shouldn't worry about getting raped."

"That still holds true, my darling," he said.

"I know," she said, but...."

"But what?" he asked.

"As I was falling asleep in your arms...."

"Yes, what?" he asked.

"I was half dreaming that I might like to be raped," she whispered.

"Sheila!"

"I know I shouldn't, and I know we shouldn't. I know it's not reasonable. I know I told you I was saving my virginity for the man I loved."

She wasn't sobbing, but her tears ran down his neck.

"Sheila, dear, you'll get over this...and you do have your childhood lover to talk to."

"I'd be terribly lonely without you here now," she said, "but you're going to leave England soon, aren't you?"

"I'm not quite sure about my future plans yet."

"Why not?" she asked.

"I haven't yet been authorized by the Free French to visit their territories, but that's not the main hitch," he said. "Something else is holding me in England."

"What is it?" she asked, looking sharply into his eyes.

"You," he said.

She squeezed him tightly. She was breathing hard.

After a long silence, she said, almost in a whisper, "Jacques, I can really feel you, and it's doing something to me."

"I know," he said, "and it's doing something to me, too. Your eyes have been wetting my shoulder, but that's not the only wetness I feel...."

"Jacques, I feel so comfortable with you here."

"Sheila, I've always loved you. When we were children, I loved you. I love you still more today. I've always wanted to marry you, but it's that blood relationship. I'm sure the law would call that incest."

"We don't have to worry about that here."

"Darling, let's marry now."

"I've been waiting for you to say that," she whispered, and she gave him her love, her soul, and her body in one long passionate embrace.

They lived the dream they'd dreamt so long, alone, in a London at war.

After breakfast, where sugar was rationed and butter a little more so, she said to him, "I've put on my best dress and a pair of the stockings you brought to go out with you. I want to show you what's left of the flat where we used to live. We can take a bus first, then walk for about a mile, and you'll see what's left of the family home."

She wanted him to experience the life she'd lived for the past few months, severed from her happy past, from her family, from her belongings, and now deprived of her hopes for the home she'd dreamed of "when this miserable war is over."

He thought what a wonderful wife his cousin would make for a man who would really appreciate her—pretty, almost beautiful, athletic, intelligent, affectionate, and reliable.

On that Saturday morning, the big red bus was almost empty. There was just one couple at the opposite end of the upper deck, so they could talk freely.

"Sheila, Sir James wants me to evaluate the true situation in the so-called Free French territories in Africa. If the Germans and Italians were to gain control of the north of that continent, could he count on the Free French to stand by England, or would they fold up and side with the Nazis?"

"It would be a catastrophe if the Germans occupied Dakar," Sheila said. "It would be almost impossible to supply Egypt and to hang on to the Gold Coast and Nigeria."

"Sir James outlined the German plan, called Attila and Felix, in much detail," Jacques said. "He said how weak British Intelligence was, and is, in that part of the world. He was particularly interested in Chad, French Equatorial Africa, and the Belgian Congo. He would also like an appraisal, an objective one made by an outsider, on the Sudan and Egypt."

"I gather," said Sheila, "that things are pretty confused in those territories."

"I got the same impression from Sir James," said Jacques. "He warned me that this would be a very dangerous job. He said I didn't have to take it."

"I know," said Sheila, "those territories are riddled with Nazi sympathizers. What did you tell Sir James?"

"That I'd think it over," said Jacques. "He said he had full power to approve this mission and that no one besides himself, Miss McNeill, and I would know about it."

"And now," said Sheila, "four know about it, since I have been added to the conspiracy. I don't like it, although it may be very useful. But Jacques, it's your safety that concerns me."

"Sheila, we're at war. You're living in danger here every day," Jacques said.

"I know," she said, "but I didn't choose it. It's been thrust on me, like it or not. You don't have to choose this."

"I know," he said, "but the British do need the information. From what I've seen, there's an awful lot of dissension here among the Free French."

"Yes," said Sheila. "There's already a split between the army and the navy. De Gaulle hates the British because they won't recognize him and his small following as a government in exile."

"Thank God," said Jacques, "that Admiral Muselier, who controls what's left of the French Navy, is really working with the British. Britain's greatest need today is for ships."

"There're plenty of French ships—freighters and warships—in British ports," said Sheila, "but there are no crews for them. A few sailors, escaping from France, show up now and then."

"I've been trying to encourage that fighting spirit in my broadcasts," said Jacques. "I avoid all mention of politics. I just tell them what some Frenchmen are doing to free their country. I told them about the two Nazi submarines our corvette sank. I gave them graphic details but no names of ships or U-boat numbers."

"Did you tell them about the Free French submarine *Rubis?*" asked Sheila.

"Yes," said Jacques. "I told them that the sub had mined Narvik Pass where the Nazis lost two destroyers—that *Rubis* had been crippled by depth charges but had been nursed back to England by two British destroyers."

"That story didn't get into the papers here," said Sheila.

"Maybe it didn't," said Jacques, "but all the French sailors I've met seem to know about it. That boosted morale. The sub is under repairs now, and I'm going out on its shakedown cruise next week."

"Jacques, we get off at the next stop. We'll save time on foot. The bus hasn't followed its usual route because of the bombing the night before last. You just avoided it. Look at this mess."

A mess it was. No vehicle could pass through the narrow winding street. Sidewalks and roadway were choked with debris of all kinds. Some of the rubble was still smoking.

"You mean to say we're supposed to go through this street? Rather, I should say, climb through this street?" said Jacques.

"If you want to see what life in London is like these days, yes," Sheila said. "I'll take my stockings off first. They're too precious. More than once I've gone to work in debris like this. That's why I brought these old tennis shoes. The soles are still in good shape."

"I'm wondering if my colleagues at the Savoy go in for this kind of exercise."

"They don't. They go as far as they can in a taxi, take a look, return to the Savoy, and write articles about it."

Jacques watched her climb over the debris that barred the way. "I can see you are used to it," he said. "You're just as agile and nimble as you always were. Traveling over this stuff is some exercise. Hold it a minute, Sheila. I want to take your picture atop that unforgettable mountain."

"Jacques, do you see that house on the left, which still has its roof on?" Sheila asked as she slid down the pile of debris.

"Yes, I do," said Jacques, "what about it?"

"When we get to the house that used to be next to it, take a good look." she said.

"I can see it from here," Jacques said. "There's one wall still standing, and there's a piece of floor jutting out from it with...it looks like a bathtub on it."

"Exactly," she said. "When the house was blown apart, a man was taking his bath. He survived in it unhurt, but Civil Defense had a terrible job rescuing him from that third floor. That story made the newspapers."

They progressed slowly through the chaos. It took them roughly a half hour to reach the family home. What had been a house was now four walls, still standing, blackened inside and out, with no windows and no doors. A misshapen pile of rubble was piled outside the walls. It wasn't smoking, but the sour smell was still there. It was waiting for someone to remove it.

"See that third window from the left-hand corner on the second floor?" said Sheila.

"Yes."

"That was my bedroom. See what's left? Don't you think we were right to send Mother out to the country? Against her will, too."

"As I know her," said Jacques, "she would have refused to go down to a shelter."

"Jacques, where would you like to go now?'

"Provided we can get transportation, I'd like to visit the seashore where we played when we were children—Felpham, near Bognor."

"That's a good idea," she said. "It fits in with what I want to do today and tomorrow: forget the present and relive the happy past. We can use the family car."

"Where is it?" asked Jacques.

"It's in a private garage near Surbiton. We can get there by train."

"Isn't gas—I mean petrol—rationed?"

"It is, but I save my coupons," Sheila said. "I haven't used the car for several months. Put on your war correspondent's uniform and take your special pass."

"Can't I go like this?" Jacques asked.

"No," she answered, "all the southern coast of England is under special regulations. They're still afraid of a German invasion."

The Sunbeam was a small, blue-grey, two-door sedan. It appeared in mint condition under its thin coat of dust. Sheila made the rounds: tires in good shape, half a tank of petrol, and engine oil up to full mark.

"Do you remember, Jacques, how you taught me to take care of the car? I'm the only one that uses it now, and I don't use it much. Before I take it out, I check all those details, including the level of water in the radiator. We're ready to go."

The engine started almost immediately. Sheila stopped at the Shell station to fill the tank. A grey-haired woman came to the pump.

"Any news of your husband, Mrs. Stewart?" Sheila asked.

"Yes, miss. After the Germans sank his ship, he was adrift in a lifeboat on the North Sea for five days with five other men. A British destroyer picked them up, and they're all back home. He had frostbite and lost three toes, so there's no chance he'll go back to sea now. He'll have some desk job on the home front."

"I'm so pleased he's in good shape otherwise. Mrs. Stewart, I'd like you to meet my cousin who arrived from the United States a short time ago. He's a war correspondent for American newspapers."

"Glad to meet you, sir. Thank God America supplied us with all those destroyers. We were in great difficulty after losing so many ships during the evacuation at Dunkerque."

"How do you know about all that, Mrs. Stewart?" Jacques asked.

"I should, sir," she said, "with a husband in the merchant navy. Every time he got home, he asked when we were going to get more destroyers. Tell me, sir, how long do you think this war will last?"

"Mrs. Stewart," Jacques said, "I've had that question every day since I've been in England. I can't answer it. I know one thing: It won't be over tomorrow, and it won't be over until America gets into it, and God knows when that will be."

"Sheila," said Jacques, as his cousin drove over the narrow, winding roads in Sussex, "I believe that's the question foremost on everyone's mind—here, in occupied Europe, and probably in Germany, too."

Some distance from the sea, a soldier stopped them at a roadblock.

"Miss, where are you going? You cannot go any further than here; this is army territory."

"Mr. de Thoranne, here, is a war correspondent who has just arrived from the United States," she said. "He would like to see the shore defenses and visit the beach at Felpham."

"I'm sorry, miss. Our orders are very strict. No one is allowed past here."

Jacques got out of the car and addressed the sentry. "I understand very well that you are following orders, exactly as you should. Here's my pass to visit restricted areas."

The soldier examined it carefully.

"Sir, with that special pass, you may enter. Go to the office about three hundred yards from here and register. They will give you a guide, because the whole beach front is mined."

"Will you allow Sheila, my cousin, to accompany me?" Jacques asked the soldier. "She works at the Ministry of Transport and is cleared for confidential work."

"That will be all right, sir. These rules are made for your own protection and safety. I'll call the office."

There an officer in a neat uniform greeted them cordially.

"I see, lieutenant, that you have already had more than your share of the war," said Jacques, looking at what remained of the officer's right arm.

"I have, sir. I was wounded as we were boarding ships off Bray Dunes in France. Is there anything we can do for you?"

"Yes, lieutenant," said Jacques. "As a child I used to go to Felpham for vacations in summer. I have a weekend to myself, and my cousin Miss Hatherley volunteered to bring me here for the afternoon. I would like to see your defenses and, if possible, have a look at the beach."

"By all means, sir. Sergeant Cosgrove, here, will be delighted to guide you, but do not stray from the path. The whole area up to the beach is thick with mines."

The narrow, winding path to the sea led them through fields of clover, broken by hedges of hawthorne, elderberry trees, and overgrown brambles, mainly blackberry. They walked in silence and in single file, the sergeant leading the way. Presently they came to a clearance that offered a full view of the beach.

The tide was low. Big black boulders, covered with brown kelp and green seaweed, dotted the expanse between the sea and the high water line. It was just as it had been when, as a child, he had climbed over their slippery sides. Just as it used to be except that it was deserted—there was not another human being in sight: the seagulls had taken over. Just as it used to be except for the rolls of barbed wire, the muzzles of machine guns, the tank traps, and the other obstacles erected by man— puny barriers that were no match for German armies. Were it not for the sea....

"We can go no further," Sergeant Cosgrove said, "we'd be taking our lives in our hands."

They stood there for a brief moment and turned back. A fine, penetrating rain began to fall as they left the fortified coast. Somehow that visit, made to rekindle the happy times of the past, had worked in reverse: it had thrust back in their minds the realities of war and the contrast between the "then" and the "now."

For miles they drove in silence. Jacques felt awkward, unreal, sitting next to his beautiful cousin with nothing to say. Finally he could stand it no longer and broke the silence. "Sheila, I don't know about you, but this visit which meant so much to me has left me with mixed feelings. To see such changes in the place I loved has left me with a sense of frustration and gloom."

"Jacques," she answered, "I was going to say the same thing. See how we think together? We always did anyway. Now we're returning to the blackout, to groping in the dark."

"Do you think we'll get to Surbiton before dark?" he asked.

"Yes," she said, "we will. Then we'll catch the next train and return to the hotel...."

"....where we will have a pleasant evening together after a good meal," said Jacques. "You can't return to your sister-in-law's place that late."

"I'm looking forward to our spending another night together."

The rain was still falling as they arrived at the hotel, drenched. They didn't have far to walk, but progress was slow in the wet darkness of the blackout, even with the help of the blackout flashlight which cast a feeble blue light through the gloom.

"There's one good thing about this rain," said Sheila, as she changed into dry clothes. "We won't have to go to the shelter tonight."

They didn't have to go to the shelter; after a good dinner, they went to bed early, where she melted into his arms.

"Jacques," she whispered, "there's something I've wanted to tell you since you've been here. It's something I've not told anyone, and yet it weighs on my mind. It has for a long time."

"What is it, dear?"

"It's been with me almost from the start of the war. You may think I'm silly, but I have a terrible sense of foreboding. I feel absolutely sure that I won't get through this war alive. You will, but I won't. I wouldn't tell anyone else, but I want you to know."

"Sheila, dear," he said, "you aren't fanciful. Knowing you as I do, this disturbs me terribly."

"I knew it would, Jacques. That's why I hesitated to tell you, but now that I have, it's a weight off my mind. I feel better now that I've told you this secret. I can't explain it, it's not rational, it's just there…."

He squeezed her in his arms; her lips found his. They lay there in silence, feeling each other's body, sharing each other's doubts.

"Jacques," she said, "I'm so happy you're here, but I don't know for how long. That's why I need your thoughts now."

"About what, darling?" he asked.

"Everywhere about me I see my friends enjoying life while they are still here, and some of my colleagues at work are just plain promiscuous. You and I were brought up to cultivate personal responsibility. I don't seem to fit in with those around me."

"That's right, lovely," he said. "We're both squares, as they say in America."

"Yet," said Sheila, "if we all demand and obtain satisfaction of our desires and wants, how will we return to the sensible, peaceful, and civilized world in which we used to live? Right now it's an incredible scramble to satisfy minimal needs: enough sugar for tea, some decent butter, some nice stockings, a place to sleep comfortably in privacy, a man to sleep with…."

"You've got one now, darling," said Jacques, "right here."

"I want you so much," said Sheila. "Let's make love again.'

"Sheila," said Jacques, "I want you just as much. But I didn't want to take your virginity unless you were to be my wife. I don't see why you can't be—now…especially after what we did last night and tonight, and…."

"And what?" she asked.

"Now that things have changed for you. Ever since your first vacation in France, when you were about fourteen, I used to dream of sleeping with you, of squeezing you in my arms, and…but my religion held me back."

"Jacques, I didn't want to mention that. Do you still believe in God, as you did when we went to church together?"

"I certainly do, my love, more so than ever. Since that fanatic across the Rhine unleashed this war, I've been closer to death more often than ever. At each crisis I have felt closer to the Creator. I was going to ask you to come to church with me tomorrow."

"Of course, I will," she said softly. "Why are you going? I need you here. All the more now that we've lived our childhood dreams."

"I know, darling," Jacques whispered. "I'm not sure why I am going. Let's go to church tomorrow and ask God to help us overcome our doubts. In the work that may lie before me, I'll need God's help and his protection. I don't know if I'll survive, but I trust in the word of the great African explorer—was it Stanley or Livingstone, I don't remember which? 'Man is immortal until his work is done.'"

"I love that," said Sheila.

"Darling," said Jacques, "I hope your foreboding is not correct, and that we'll both survive the war. If you don't my soul will be torn apart. Through my bleeding heart, I'd have to say. 'She was too good and sweet to live in this sordid world.' Sheila, I don't want to think of it."

The next morning they went to a small church on Farm Street, and both prayed. The sermon seemed spoken for them. It stressed the frailty of life and dealt with the will of God and His Providence—His protection for all his human beings until it was best for them to enter life eternal. It was a beautiful sermon by a Jesuit, and Sheila's eyes were wet.

"Jacques," she said, "I'll go to that church every Sunday now. I feel refreshed. I'm going to think over my life. You've got me out of the rut of thinking how to get to work next morning and wondering where to get some tea without standing in line for hours."

"Sheila," said Jacques, "aren't we all in that rut to some extent?"

"I suppose we are," she said. "Jacques, what is your next move before you make the final decision? I'll miss you terribly if you leave."

"Sheila, I'll miss you just as much. I'm leaving tomorrow for two days in Dover. This seems to be the time when the Nazis lob shells into the city from guns on the coast of France. I'll try to get back to London on Tuesday in time for you. Maybe we can have dinner."

"I'd love that," she said.

"On Wednesday I'm going to Dundee for a shakedown cruise on *Rubis*, the Free French submarine damaged by German depth charges near Narvik, now repaired. When I come back from that, I'll decide either to stay here or to carry out Sir James' proposal."

"Jacques, I want you to stay here," she said, as Jacques put her into the taxi. Her tear fell on to his cheek as he kissed her. His own eyes were wet.

Chapter VII

Free France in England, in 1941, was not a government, although it liked to consider itself as such. It had no legal standing, no popular mandate, and no administrative power. It was a disparate group of Frenchmen (and a few Frenchwomen, including a famous woman tennis champion) who had fled to England when France collapsed and stayed there.

These exiles, numbering a few thousand, were dominated by an army colonel, Charles de Gaulle, who had been appointed general on an interim basis *(general de brigade à titre temporaire)* a few days before France signed the armistice with Germany. De Gaulle insisted on full political, administrative, military, and naval control of all the Free French in England. That split the group. De Gaulle's leadership was not accepted by the highest ranking French Navy officer in England, Vice Admiral Muselier, who went his separate way. He had been an admiral long before de Gaulle became an interim general. De Gaulle had no experience and little understanding of naval warfare, and neither Muselier nor his men were willing to operate under his orders.

Both de Gaulle and Muselier were condemned by the Vichy French government, presided over by Marshal Philippe Pétain.

Under these circumstances the Free French in London conducted their affairs as best they could. While de Gaulle decided the course of all political affairs, routine administrative matters were reviewed by a small committee at weekly meetings every Monday.

These meetings were chaired by René Pleven, Free France's foreign secretary. He was a quiet, mild man of medium height, pale faced, with a stubby greying mustache. He was always carefully dressed in a neat dark blue business suit.

Also attending every meeting was Solange Morel, assistant to de Gaulle and recording secretary—a tall, lanky woman in her early forties, with a handsome, clear-cut face, dark hair, neatly trimmed just below the ears, and strong dark eyebrows shading soft brown eyes. She wore a long dress down to her ankles.

Usually in attendance was de Varvin, de Gaulle's ADC, in a lieutenant's uniform, with the light blue *képi* of the *armée coloniale*. Most of the time he spoke for de Gaulle, who seldom, if ever, attended.

Sometimes present was Alfred Cassin, a discredited politician who had fled France at the time of the collapse, perhaps hoping to restore some glitter to his tarnished image.

D'Huart had briefed Jacques on the constitution of the committee. He had informed him that it would consider Jacques' request to visit Free French territories in Africa during its last meeting of September 1941. He added that he'd do his best to obtain a copy of the minutes of that meeting.

Jacques went to Dover on that Monday but didn't see much of the war there. The Germans hadn't fired on the city from across the Channel. There Jacques went out to sea patrol boats which rescued fliers that were shot down in aerial combat, but there were no dogfights, and all he did was bounce around in rough water.

When Jacques returned to London on that Tuesday evening, he was again reminded of the formidable power of the Nazi Luftwaffe. Hitler, infuriated by a British raid on Berlin, had ordered his bomber force "to obliterate London."

There were no taxis at Victoria Station. Jacques caught a crowded underground train for a connection at Charing Cross. There women and children were lying on the cold concrete platform with sheets of newspaper as their only mattress. He had to step over their bodies to enter the carriage.

At Oxford Circus the station was on emergency lights. Trains were still running at the lower level, but the wait seemed interminable. He was about to take his chances on foot when a packed train pulled in to that station.

When he reached his destination, Marble Arch, he was thankful he had his flashlight. He emerged from the underground into a world full of smoke, under a cold and misty rain that seemed to sharpen the rancid smell of smoldering debris. The whole atmosphere seemed hostile and left him with a feeling of dread and impending doom.

At the Cumberland everything was dark. There were no lights in the hotel; there was no heat; there were no elevators; the phones were dead.

He went up to his room. He lit a candle and got into a damp bed, shivering from cold and dismay. He had not been able to reach Sheila, and that disturbed him very much.

He arose early the next morning, aware that the trip to the station might be a long one. As he was loading his belongings in the taxi, the hall porter handed him a small, hand-addressed envelope.

"Sir, this came while you were preparing your luggage."

"Thanks, Sam," said Jacques, thrusting the envelope into one of his pockets as he got into the taxi.

"To Liverpool Street station, please, cabbie."

"Yes, sir. Looks like you're going on a long journey. Liverpool?"

"No, cabbie, I'm on my way to Scotland and then off to sea."

"I don't envy you, sir. You think it's bad here, but we're on dry land. Out there they're sinking them all the time."

The cab stopped close to the station. "Sir," said the cab driver, "I can't go any farther. See, they haven't cleared all the rubble from Monday night's raid, but you're lucky. Here's a porter."

"What train, sir?" asked the porter.

"The ten-fifteen, but first I must get a ticket."

"That's over there," said the porter, "the sort of box with the tin roof. The ticket office received a direct hit in one of the last raids."

Finally Jacques sat down alone in the comfortable compartment.

He had a few minor details to attend to: a reservation for the dining car— yes, there was a dining car on this train, even in war—and some order was needed among the papers and change he had thrust pell mell into his pockets. Out of one pocket, with the railroad ticket, came the hand-addressed envelope the hall porter handed to him when he left the hotel. He had completely forgotten about it. It was addressed to him in a handwriting he had never seen. He opened the envelope.

The terse note inside stunned him. It was written by Sheila's brother, John. It read:

> Jacques.
> Sheila was killed in Monday night's raid. The trolley she was
> in received a direct hit. Enough of her remains were found
> for positive identification. John.

Those few words wrenched Jacques' soul. The note struck him like a close-by explosion. It left him limp and exhausted. His head swirled. His legs felt weak and wobbly. His stomach seemed gripped in a clenched fist.

He sat there, dejected, in the corner of the compartment, watching the rain make long streaks on the window. In every part of his body he felt sick, horribly sick. His dearest cousin, the one being he loved most on Earth, the woman whose warm body he had held in his arms all night, who had told him she would not outlive the war—his beloved was gone forever.

He did not go to the dining car. He felt too sick to eat. He sat there, listening to the heartless tac-tac-tac of the train, watching the countryside unravel in the rain. Again and again that vision of his first air raid in London sprang back into his mind—vivid, dancing before his eyes: the flames, the heat, the smoke, and in the red glow of the fires, that woman's arm, neatly severed at the shoulder, with rings still on the fingers. The grief that hand left behind—a grief that had become all too real now that he was sharing it—a grief that he felt as he had never felt grief before, a grief that made up his mind for him. He knew that now he would not stay in London.

The train was delayed somewhere along the way, and it was dark when Jacques arrived in Dundee. The rain had stopped. He went to the naval base and presented his requisition.

A Wren in a neat navy uniform accompanied him to a small room, sparsely furnished with a camp bed. "We'll wake you up at four-thirty tomorrow morning, sir. Your ship will leave at 7:00 A.M."

Exactly on time the next morning, there was a rap at the door. Another Wren entered briskly, set down a tray with hot tea, two scones, and butter, and vanished as fast as she had arrived. Although Jacques was half-asleep, he saw that she looked very much like Sheila—elegant, slender, and lively—a reminder of the beloved who'd gone forever.

Commander Cabanier, captain of the submarine *Rubis*, greeted the visitor at the gangplank.

"Welcome aboard, Mr. de Thoranne," he said, shaking Jacques' hand warmly. "We all heard your broadcast about the *Rubis*."

"I hope I didn't make too many mistakes, Commander," said Jacques. "It was all hearsay; I had no firsthand knowledge."

"No," said Cabanier, "but it was the broadcast about *Marigold* sinking two U-boats that was outstanding and terribly dramatic. It was so graphic. You could almost hear the crunch of the plates as *Marigold* rammed the U-boat. You could almost feel the bow of the corvette lifted out of the water and plunging back into the sea as the U-boat went under. What type of submarine was it?"

"I don't know," said Jacques, "but I can tell you what the number was. It was U-234."

"Let me check," said Cabanier. "That could be a pretty big sub, probably a type WII-C. Those U-boats have crews of forty to forty-five men."

"We rescued nineteen German sailors," said Jacques. "The survivors said that many crewmen had gone down with the ship. I should have asked them what their full complement was."

"You'd better be prepared to answer all kinds of questions," said Cabanier, smiling. "This is the first time anyone here can question an eyewitness to the ramming of a submarine. Even at the Naval Academy no one ever had that opportunity."

The shakedown cruise was short lived.

Rubis glided out of port on the surface on its electric motors; when it reached the high sea, the diesel engines were connected to the propellers; when the engines revved up, trouble started. The starboard drive train began vibrating, and the chief engineer and the commander decided to return the ship to port for further work before another shakedown cruise.

Jacques had no idea when that might be so after thanking his hosts, he took the next train to London.

On arrival he went to the Cumberland and called Sir James's office. Miss McNeill set up an appointment for the next day.

Sir James received him with his usual courtesy.

"I understand that the Attila and Felix plans may be hampered by the damage done to the German warships at Brest. *Gneisenau* apparently has been hit and will be out of commission for months."

"Where did you learn that?" asked Sir James.

"That's the rumor floating around among the officers of the Free French Navy," said Jacques.

"It could be true," said Sir James. "When would you like to leave?"

"At the first opportunity," said Jacques.

"A Free French warship, commissioned by the Royal Navy, will leave Liverpool a week from today. It will escort a convoy to Egypt and will take you to Port Said. You can begin your trip there. Whenever you come across anything I should know, contact our nearest consulate."

"Yes, sir, I will," said Jacques.

Sir James summoned his assistant. "Miss McNeill, please prepare Mr. de Thoranne's passport as we discussed."

"Yes, sir," she said. "Mr. de Thoranne, it will be ready tomorrow morning; you may pick it up any time then."

When Jacques left, Sir James dictated briefly the agreement made with Jacques.

"I am sure," he said to his trusted colleague, "that de Thoranne is the right man for the job. I'm far more positive now than I was after our first interview."

"Why is that, sir?" she asked.

"He has a knack for finding things out—ultra secret things. He has found out something known to less than a dozen people in this country. He knows that, following his run-in with the prime minister, de Gaulle negotiated with the Soviets to have them underwrite the cost of the Free French in England."

"I did not know that," said Miss McNeill.

"You do now," said Sir James, smiling. "De Thoranne was furious about it. It has shaken his faith in de Gaulle. Of course he knows that this must remain secret."

"How could he find out something so secret as that?" she asked.

"I have no idea," said Sir James. "He also knew all the details about de Gaulle's feud with Admiral Muselier. And that's not all. He mentioned that the Germans were working on a bomb which could release the energy stored in matter; if that were successful, he said, one bomb could destroy an entire city. I can't imagine how he found that out, but if he follows that path in Africa, he'll provide all the information we need."

"Sir," said Miss McNeill, "the French in London—and I'm not speaking of those in Canton Gardens—know he's genuine. They hear his broadcasts. They know he's been condemned by the Vichy government. They know he could have remained comfortably in the U.S. with a salary and nothing to worry about, as the other diplomats have done. They know he's no opportunist, because he resigned when it appeared Britain would go under. They trust him."

"I'm sure you are right," said Sir James.

"That's not just my opinion," she said. "I've heard this from a French naval officer I go out with from time to time; I'm just repeating his words as I remember them."

"Miss McNeill, I agree. He is the right man for the job. I only hope he doesn't get murdered on the way. If the Abwehr knew of his potential, they'd dispose of him in a hurry. When he comes tomorrow for his passport, I want to see him."

The visit was brief.

"Your passport," said Sir James, "is marked to provide you with any help you may need at any of our consulates or with any of our agents the consul may indicate. We are not providing you with a list of any of these agents, for your own safety."

"I understand, sir, and fully agree. The more I think about it, the more important this mission is. I am nothing more than a war correspondent working for an American news agency."

Sir James rose and grasped Jacques' hand. "Good luck and take care."

Chapter VIII

Jacques spent his last weekend in London preparing for the African venture. He was sitting at the table in his hotel room when there was a rap at the door. It was his old friend d'Huart.

"Jacques, I've arranged an appointment with Captain Moreau, a Free French navy pilot who's enrolled in the RAF. He's very interesting, and what he has to say should provide good material for a report. I've made reservations for the three of us at *L'Ecu de France*, the best French restaurant in London. But before we go there, read this—the minutes of the meeting where the Committee reviewed your request for an *ordre de mission* to visit Free French territories in Africa."

> Pleven: Jacques de Thoranne has requested an *ordre de mission* to travel to Free French territories in Africa.
>
> de Varvin: What for?
>
> Pleven: International News Service is sending him to report on the war effort of the Free French in territories which have rallied behind de Gaulle.
>
> Cartier: How can he travel? When he resigned from the Diplomatic Service, he lost his passport.
>
> de Varvin: And we can't issue one.
>
> Morel: He has a British passport. He was born in England. I'm sure the British were pleased to give him a British passport after all the help he gave them following the collapse of France.
>
> Cartier: What help?
>
> Morel: He lectured extensively throughout America, urging those who wanted to help France to support Britain.
>
> Cartier: I can see why he gets so many favors from the British.

Pleven: Favors?

Cartier: Not one of us could get a permit to meet the prisoners released from the Soviet Union, but de Thoranne was there. Also he can broadcast whatever he wants to France over the BBC, and we have no control over what he says.

De Varvin: There's nothing wrong with his broadcasts. I listen to all of them. Did you hear the one about the two Nazi U-boats sunk by the Free French corvette and the fury of the German survivors when they learned they had been rescued by men of a conquered nation?

Morel: I heard that one. I'm sure they loved that broadcast in France.

Cartier: That's not the point. The point is that he can say anything he wants, and it gets through the censors. Our broadcast on the U-boats was held up for days. There's no point in airing it now. De Thoranne has too much influence with the British. Before long he'll have too much influence in France. The sooner we get him out of here, the better.

Pleven: He has asked to tour the Free French territories in Africa, and he can be very useful there. General Sicé, the commander there, needs someone with excellent knowledge of English for the daily broadcast to the U.S. Bigley, the American who's doing it now, says he won't stay on when his contract expires.

Morel: I think we should tell de Thoranne that General Sicé may need his services there.

Pleven: No, absolutely not, or he might not go at all, and he is badly needed. When will he pick up his *ordre de mission?*

Morel: When he returns from Dundee. He's going on a shakedown cruise on *Rubis.*

Cartier: The main thing is to get him out of here as soon as possible.

After reading the minutes, Jacques turned to d'Huart. "I'm very grateful to you for warning me. Is this how they conduct business at Free French headquarters in Canton Gardens?"

"Generally speaking, it is," said d'Huart. "Do you still intend to go?"

"I'll think it over," Jacques said. "If I didn't have a British passport, I'd certainly call the whole thing off."

D'Huart stood up and started for the door. "Let's go to lunch. We can walk. The weather's fine. Jermyn Street is only a mile or so from here."

They arrived at *l'Ecu de France* shortly after Captain Moreau, who was already seated at a corner table covered with a red and white checkered tablecloth. The table provided as much privacy as could be expected in a crowded restaurant. It was usually occupied by preferred guests, such as d'Huart. He and the *maitre d'* had escaped from Dunkerque on the same boat.

Moreau was a slender, determined looking man with sharp features and a clean-cut face. His dark hair contrasted with his pink cheeks and blue eyes. He'd arrived in England when only Fighter Command stood between the German Army and the invasion of Britain.

Shot down on his third mission, he'd parachuted into the sea, where a British patrol boat rescued him. He returned to the fight the next day and already had three German planes to his credit. He said it should have been four, but he'd been obliged to crash land his Spitfire, which was damaged in a dog fight with a Nazi fighter last seen losing altitude and trailing smoke on its way to France—but no one saw the Nazi plane crash, and so it wasn't counted as shot down.

"The problem," Moreau said to Jacques, "is to gain experience in direct combat. Going through school and training missions is one thing, but the real know-how comes from actual combat. The Germans have been at it much longer than we have and have many very good pilots. I'm feeling more confident now—but not overconfident.

"Now we are more than a match for the Luftwaffe in the air over England and over the Channel. Today, in an operation similar to the evacuation of Dunkerque, we'd shoot down practically all their dive bombers."

"Yes," said d'Huart, "I've been told the Germans lost almost 12 percent of their bombers in the last raid on London a few days ago."

I don't see how they can sustain such losses for very long," Jacques said. "If 12 percent, or even 10 percent, of their bombers were shot down over England, how many more were damaged, crash landed in France, or are otherwise inoperable?"

"You are right," said Moreau. "No air force can sustain those kinds of losses. I think we've seen the last of the massive raids for a while.

"And you," he said to Jacques, "where you going?"

"I'll be on my way to Africa in a couple of days to report on the activities of the Free French for an American news agency."

"Do you plan to return to England after your trip?" asked d'Huart.

I don't know," said Jacques. "I have to get to my destination. I'll travel on a small Free French warship, escorting a convoy carrying war materials for the Eighth Army, to Port Said in Egypt. We'll go round the Cape of Good Hope, then north along the East Coast of Africa."

"How far is that?" asked Moreau.

"I can't give you the exact distance," said Jacques, "but off the cuff, I'd say it's fifteen to sixteen thousand miles. If all goes well, it will take between three and four months. Most of the ships in the convoy are coal burners. They must stop to refuel several times on the way. Certainly in Freetown, probably in Capetown or Lourenço Marques, and perhaps in Mombasa."

"My God," said Moreau, "how awful! On the sea all that time amid the U-boats. I think I've got a lousy job, but I spend most of my life in comfort on dry land. I wouldn't take your job for anything. I don't envy you."

"I think I've got the best job of all," said d'Huart, laughing, "especially if the massive raids over London are coming to an end."

When Jacques arrived in Liverpool to board his transportation to Africa, the ship's doctor was waiting for him at the station and greeted him cordially. Bernard Moleux and Jacques were old acquaintances and had attended the same public school, the Lycee Janson de Sailly, in Paris. More than once they had been in the same class and had passed their baccalaureate in science on the same day. They'd lost sight of each other when Moleux went to medical school.

Moleux was used to acting decisively, with brisk but courtly manners. He was of medium height, clean shaven, with grey penetrating eyes and slender, well-groomed hands perfectly suited to the delicate job of surgery. He shook hands with Jacques warmly.

"What a pleasure it is to get together again," he said to Jacques. "You have no idea what a sense of kinship exists between all of us rebels. There are so few of us. It's so nice to add one more to the company."

"I know I'll feel at home on board that ship," said Jacques.

"In addition," said Moleux as they boarded a taxi, "you'll probably have a beautiful cabin all to yourself. The BNLO is in the hospital."

"The BNLO?"

Moleux laughed. "That stands for British Naval Liaison Officer. Our man is sick in the hospital, and no replacement has been found. Practically no one on board speaks any decent English. All Scott transmissions are in English, so there could be problems. I know they're counting on you to serve as translator when needed. Here we are at the customs. They're going to examine all your belongings."

"I took care of that in London before I left," said Jacques. "Here's my pass."

The customs officer examined the document. "Go ahead, sir, everything is in order. With that pass, nothing need be opened."

When they arrived alongside *Commandant Dominé*, Jacques was surprised to see how small the warship was. Compared with the huge hulks of the freighters nearby, it looked like a child's toy, six hundred tons next to twenty thousand tons—a fly next to elephants.

Tea with the officers of the ship was waiting when they came aboard. There were two Englishwomen, one the wife of a French naval officer. They greeted Jacques warmly.

Moleux took Jacques on a tour of the ship. On the foredeck he admired a neatly polished four-inch gun, supplied by the British to replace the original three inch; amidships, a couple of Bofors pom-poms; astern, a collection of depth charges and the devices to fire them.

They disembarked for a closer look at what was left of the port of Liverpool: charred remains of warehouses, bomb craters in wharves, sunken ships, scattered ack-ack batteries, and grey freighters disgorging war materials from the United States. Beyond the wind-whipped waters of the harbor, the outline of the city of Liverpool, shrouded in a grey mist, was gradually vanishing into the darkness of night and the blackout gloom.

When they returned they found the *Commandant Dominé* as dark as its surroundings; not a light was visible from the outside. To move on deck the crew carried flashlights with blue lenses.

What a mess, Jacques thought to himself, as he sat down to dinner with the officers of the ship.

The cook, a clean-shaven fellow in his early thirties, brought a large soup tureen.

"I'm serving this watercress soup," he told the party, "because by the time we get back—if we ever do—you'll have forgotten what soup tastes like. This ship rolls so damned much that you'll be eating sandwiches and canned food."

No one laughed. Though the mood was somber, the conversation was lively. It turned around stories of how they'd escaped from France during the collapse and why they'd decided to fight on with England.

Arthru, the chief engineer, told how his ship, the destroyer *Sirocco*, was torpedoed by an E-boat as it evacuated British and French soldiers from Dunkerque.

"I'll never forget the night of June one, nineteen-forty,' he said. "Our ship sank awfully fast. Although I had my life jacket on, I was sucked under with *Sirocco*. When I surfaced I heard a few men yelling for help, but I couldn't see them. It was very dark. Thank God the water wasn't too cold."

"How long were you in it?" asked Moleux.

"I must have floated around for about an hour," said Arthru, "before I was picked up by a private motor boat. It was overloaded and low in the water. They had to help me on board, I was so numb with cold and fatigue. When I landed in Dover, I had only one thought in mind: to get back on a ship from where I could send some kind of Nazi craft to the bottom."

"Do all you men on board this ship feel the same way?" Jacques asked.

"Most, if not all of us, do," said Moleux. "You'll have to hear the story of Emile, our diesel mechanic, to know how bad it is in France. He should be here any time."

"Yes," said Arthru, "Emile had returned to France after escaping to England from Dunkerque. He wanted to get back to his fiancée, who lives in Cherbourg."

"You have to hear stories like his to know what it's like to live in France since the Nazi invasion."

All citizens were under constant watch. Every home, every apartment, was compelled to display a poster inside the front door at all times. That poster had to carry the list of all persons living there: name, sex, and occupation.

Owners and tenants had to be listed separately. Each individual had to indicate where he or she could be found and show the time of exit from home, destination, and time of return.

Any Nazi, SS, or member of the Feidgendarmerie or of the Gestapo, could open the door at any time and check who lived there and where they were. God help those who were not where they'd said they'd be.

The occupying power suspected everyone of aiding the British bombers aiming at port facilities and submarine pens. Any citizen on the street could be picked up at the whim of an SS, questioned, and tortured on a mere suspicion or because someone did not like his looks. When help was needed to load a truck, unload a train, or clear up the rubble after bombings, the occupier could commandeer anyone in the street or in his home.

"You can understand," said Emile, who had just joined the others at table, "that such a life was intolerable."

"Why did you return to France?" asked Jacques.

"I returned because my fiancée lived in Cherbourg," said Emile. "I had no idea how bad things really were. It didn't take long for me to know how terrible it is to completely lose one's liberty."

"Weren't you afraid of being drafted for work in Germany?" asked Moleux.

"I was," said Emile, "but when the German Navy advertised for diesel mechanics, I applied and was hired immediately. One day when there was no diesel work, I fixed a periscope."

"That must have put you on the right side of the Germans in the arsenal," said Arthru.

"It was a great help," said Emile. "I got *ausweise*, permits, when I wanted to go to Barfleur on weekends. That's a small fishermen's village where Denise's aunt has a home. There were no bombings there, there were fewer soldiers, and the atmosphere was less oppressive.

"Why didn't Denise and her mother move there?" asked Moleux.

"They'd been talking about it for a long time," said Emile, "but pulling up roots is something else, and then an ugly incident jarred them into action."

"An ugly incident?" said Arthru.

"Yes," said Emile. "In Cherbourg, overlooking the sea, there's a statue of Napoleon on horseback. His right arm is raised, pointed toward England. One morning a few onlookers were laughing at the advice someone had placed at the foot of the statue. It read:

> *Mon p'tit Hitler*
> *C'est en voulant attaquer l'Angleterre*
> *que je m'suis cassé le nez*
> *N'fais pas comme moi!*

> My little Hitler
> It is by wanting to attack England
> that I came a cropper
> Don't do like me.

Everyone laughed at the free advice Hitler was getting, but Emile was not laughing. "Can you imagine," he went on, "what happened? The Nazis were so enraged at this lack of respect for their great leader that they picked up four men off the Street and shot them—to teach the French a lesson. What the French learned was to hate the occupier a little more."

"I find that hard to believe," said Jacques. "Is that true?"

"I think it is,' said Emile. "They were shooting people all the time. I wondered who might be next. I decided to go back to England—a risky undertaking at best—from Barfleur, something like sixty miles of open sea...no picnic, even in peacetime, but in war, with patrols everywhere...."

Denise's younger brother, François, loved the sea. He had put all his savings in a two-seater Hart-Sioux kayak. It was carefully folded and hidden in his aunt's house in Barfleu. He had not dared use it since the occupation, lest some German confiscate it. It was equipped a waterproof compass and a small Sachs two-cycle outboard engine (made in Germany!) for propelling kayaks.

At seventeen he could see no future other than being conscripted by the Germans into a labor crew or joining the underground resistance movement. He did not trust that. There were too many amateurs in those groups, and too many of them talked too much.

The best solution, he thought, was to get to England. But how? He dared not undertake the trip alone. He had discussed the project with Emile many times, but for months, it remained what it had always been—a dream.

It was the murder of the men in Cherbourg that plunged them back into the world where your life could be snuffed out for laughing at an amateurish handwritten poster taunting Hitler.

The getaway required darkness—the darker, the better. Best of all would be a long, foggy night. The wind? No more than a gentle breeze, if possible, blowing west to east and no moon before 4:00 or 5:00 A.M. Tide flowing east; sea, fairly calm, at least not rough.

All that was a tall order from nature. For the men, the capacity to paddle for hours on end if the engine failed, which meant getting the muscles of arms and abdomen in top shape. The engine needed gas and oil, beyond the reach of most civilians. There was plenty of gas at the arsenal, but getting it out was something else. Although the guards at the entrance were French, no one could be trusted. Every day Emile went to work at the arsenal on his bike. On the handlebar he had installed two metal containers which he filled with water and sometimes wine when he went to Barfleur. Guards at the gate never bothered to check their contents. From time to time, before going to Barfleur on weekends, Emile would fill one container with gas.

That's when he got the scare of his life. It was on a fine day, a Sunday, and he was pedaling leisurely with one hand on the handlebar. As he was about to enter the little village of Théville, a car of the Feldgendarmerie, coming from behind, pulled up alongside, and the driver yelled in excellent French, "*Monsieur*, that's no way to ride a bicycle. Hold your handlebar correctly, with both hands."

"Fancy that," said Emile, as he related the incident, "telling me in my own country how to ride a bicycle. The insolent bastard. He just wanted to show who was the boss. I could have killed him, but I said nothing; I just put my other hand on the handlebar and went on my way pretty shaken and thanking my lucky stars he hadn't checked anything. That kind of stuff was going on all the time."

By August enough gas and oil had been obtained for the trip. All that was needed was the right weather on some weekend when Emile happened to be in Barfleur. It seemed that every weekend there was something wrong: too much wind, moonlit nights, patrols very active in the area. The delays were maddening. Finally fate seemed to smile at the adventurers on a Sunday evening late in October. A light, drizzly rain was falling gently through a shroud of fog. There was very little wind, and at 8:00 P.M. the tide was right.

"I'll never forget those last moments," said Emile. "I kissed Denise and her mother good-bye. There were tears in their eyes, but they did not cry. Their last words are engraved in my mind, "We are proud of you.""

Dressed in warm, dark clothes, Emile and François carried the kayak the one hundred yards or so which separated the house from the beach. Before crossing the walkway, they laid the slender craft alongside a wooden shack and listened intently. The monotonous, heavy footsteps of the night patrol came along the walkway. The guard passed within a few feet of the two adventurers, quite unaware of their presence.

Then they carried the kayak over the stone embankment, walked over the sand, and put it into the water. They pushed it far enough to make it float and paddled off.

"I'll never forget that last moment when we left the soil of our dear land," said Emile. "Would we make it to England? Were we going to our death? I had butterflies in my stomach. So did François. The thought of leaving Denise behind almost paralyzed me. Would I ever see her again? But her last words still ring in my ears, "We are proud of you.""

"I can understand how you felt," said Moleux. "All of us here have more or less gone through some of that.

"Well," Emile continued after swallowing hard, "we paddled off. We could see absolutely nothing, but our compass was guiding us, and we could tell from the hissing of the sea where the reef was. We passed a few feet east of it and vanished into the night. There was no moon. We had two compasses: the one in front of François was luminous and was our only guide. I was in the back seat."

Soon a heavier swell told the travelers that they were out of the lee of land, but there were no breakers. Emile rigged up the engine, put the propeller over the side, and pulled the rope. The engine started at the first tug of the rope. Its regular throb was exhilarating. It sang, "Away from slavery, away, away!"

The engine propelled the kayak at something like four to six miles per hour. The tide, which at that time should be drifting east, was of some help. With any luck, if the engine held up, the escapees could expect to reach the Isle of Wight by morning. Midnight came and went, and they felt relaxed enough to eat a sandwich and have some hot coffee from the thermos. That kept them warm for a while, but by 3:00 A.M. they began to feel the cold, so they started to paddle to warm up; besides, the engine had begun to sputter.

The sea was still calm, just a big swell but no breakers. They went up and down on me slow, rhythmic motion of the sea, like a feather in a gentle breeze. They could only guess how far they'd gone: at least thirty miles they figured, perhaps forty at most.

After paddling for about an hour, Emile tried again to start the engine, but it would not even cough. Apparently the spark plug was fouled, and they had no spare. It was too dark to clean it, so they paddled until dawn.

While François paddled, Emile removed the spark plug. The insulation was cracked; there would be no more engine power.

They paddled on in the morning haze. Their arms ached, their hands were blistered, and some blisters oozed blood.

Suddenly when they reached the top of a big swell, a faint line appeared on the horizon in the mist. The English Coast? It to be! That faint line, so far away, galvanized their waning strength. On and on they went, aiming for that faint line. It firmed as the sun rose slowly in the east. England all right. It had to be! It was still far, far away, but at least it was in sight.

"You people who have never lived in slavery," said Emile, "will never know how we felt. Just the idea of setting foot on a free land filled us with hope and pride."

The sun rose further in the east, the mist cleared, and a grey patrol boat bore down on the slender craft. A man on deck examined it through binoculars. He'd surely seen the little French flag on the kayak's prow. François pointed to it. The grey ship circled the kayak for a few moments, and then...it hoisted the Union Jack. It came close by and stopped the ship for the escapees to board it.

"I was so tired and stiff," Emile said, "that they had to lift me out of the kayak. François was in better shape and got out with little help. They took the kayak out of the water and put it on deck. You know what," Emile went on, "I never was so angry at myself for goofing off in school as when I boarded that ship. I couldn't speak a word of English."

"Welcome to the company here," said Moleux. "None of us speaks decent English."

"The crew of that patrol boat was just wonderful," Emile continued. "They bandaged our bleeding hands, gave us hot drinks and food, and took us to the Naval Club at Southampton. There we were received by the French Naval Attaché."

"Who was it?" asked Kermadec, the first officer, who had just joined them.

"I don't remember his name," said Emile, "but he wanted to know all about our escape, where in France we had come from, and what we were doing there. When I told him I'd been working on the diesel engines and the periscopes of Nazi submarines, the English brought in some technical people, and I thought their questions would never end."

"What in particular did they want to know?" asked Arthru.

The answer was cut short by the appearance of the commandant. "I've just had word from Admiralty that our departure is scheduled for tomorrow. If any of you have any last minute shopping to do, you must do it in the morning. All hands must be on board by noon. We are going to escort a convoy to Sierra

Leone, and don't expect good weather. The forecast is for very stormy seas. Good night."

"Well, I'm going to turn in," Moleux told Jacques. "If you need any more tropical gear, come with me tomorrow. There's a shop that has not been bombed out where you can get anything you will need for the tropics."

The two spent the next morning shopping. Jacques bought an extra pair of khaki shorts and increased his stock of quinine as a precaution against malaria.

It was pitch dark when *Dominé* finally left the war-scarred city of Liverpool for the open sea. It was a moonless night. A howling wind whistled and screamed through the stays of the small ship, driving before it a cold, penetrating rain.

There was little cause for exultation among the Frenchmen who manned the ship, exiles far from families and homes until the end of the war. In October 1941, who could tell when that might be? Who would win? Would they ever see loved ones and homes again?

The convoy which preceded *Dominé* chugged slowly out of the widened Mersey River into Liverpool Bay.

The bay was choppy enough, but when *Dominé* passed the points between the cities or Wallasey and Bootle, both invisible in the blackness of night, the violence of the ship's rolling and pitching told them they were nearing the open sea.

The men on watch could only guess where the huge hulks of the freighters might be and, in the meantime, hang on to anything they could grab when *Dominé* emerged into the Irish Sea.

Jacques turned in early, only to find that on a six hundred ton warship in a heavy sea, you can't sleep in a bed. He was tossed out of his comfortable bunk by a particularly violent lurch of the ship. There was no way to install a hammock in the BNLO's cabin. He went aft to try to sleep in a hammock rigged up in the chief engineer's confined quarters. He lay there, swaying violently all night.

At midnight Arthru came in after being relieved from his watch. "Terrific," he commented, seeing that Jacques wasn't asleep, "I've never seen it this bad. The wind hit force eight as soon as we got out of Liverpool Bay into the Irish Sea, and it's still increasing. The Old Man won't leave the bridge. It's the first time I've seen him so worried. I waited ten minutes for a chance to come astern along the lifeline, and see how I'm drenched. My boots are full. The waves are washing overboard, like a river over a dam—listen to that now."

The sickening sound of the diesel engines racing as the propellers cleared the water was becoming ever more frequent, and the motions of the ship ever more violent.

Jacques got up to take a look at things outside. The sea was a rearing mass of churning foam. The sky was a dark greyish buff, so similar to the dirty foam that one could hardly tell where it melted into the sea. For Jacques at that time, there was nothing much to do except hang on. He went to the galley. Fernand the cook was baking a roast.

"That's about the only cooking I can do now," he told Jacques and the two crewmen enjoying the warm dry air in the galley, "but at least I'm not working for those damned Nazis any more."

"What were you doing?" asked Jacques.

"The Germans conscripted me to build submarine pens in Brest," said Fernand. "That was backbreaking work, but we were better off working in France than the Frenchmen sent to work in Germany. I had to leave suddenly this year after the incident of April twenty-eighth."

That incident had stirred up the entire city of Brest and the surrounding sub-urbs, where it had traveled by word of mouth despite the efforts of the Nazis to keep the matter secret. The censor's control of the press and of the news media, including the radio, did not extend to the private conversations of citizens. The Germans, the Abwehr particularly, had long been concerned by the open hostility of the population. In dismay they watched that population cheer when British bombers attacked the arsenal, even when the bombs missed their target and fell on the city of Brest.

"I saw a group of women in tears when a British bomber was shot down," Fernand told his listeners. "They hate the Germans more than the men do. They won't speak to them; they won't have anything to do with them."

There was unrestrained rejoicing in town when a bomb, aimed at the arse-nal, hit the Hotel Continental, headquarters of the German naval staff, while the officers were having dinner. Most of them were killed immediately or died in the rubble of the hotel which burned to the ground in the fire that followed. When the fire alarm sounded for that fire, every hose company encountered unforeseen problems: a flat tire, a shortage of hose, engine failing to start, traf-fic jams, etc.

None of this was lost on the Germans. They saw in these repeated inci-dents a spirit of defiance, a conspiracy to aid the British, a spontaneous and quasi-universal movement to remain aloof from the occupying power, a clear message that they were more than unwelcome. Yet the Abwehr had no hard evidence to confirm its suspicions, nothing concrete anyway, until April 28, 1941.

On that evening three French workmen, employed at the arsenal, got into a fight with four German soldiers at the Café du Port on the Rue de Siam in Brest. Two Germans were killed, and one of the French workmen, badly wounded, was carried away by sympathetic onlookers. A thorough investigation followed, and there were numerous arrests.

"I knew one of the men they arrested," Fernand said. "He had asked me to help organize a few patriots to inform London about German activity in Brest. My name was probably on his list which had been seized by the Germans. Not knowing what he might say under torture, I took off the moment I heard of his arrest. I hid with a relative for several weeks until the worst of the commotion had blown over. Then I got over to England."

"How did you do that?" Jacques asked.

'That,' said Fernand, "is a secret I'll take with me to the grave. I informed only one person, my girlfriend, Sophie. All she said was, "I love you. I hate to see you go. Better to die in an escape attempt than in a German death camp. I'm sure you'll make it anyway. *Adieu.'* She was right. See, I'm here."

He swore as a particularly heavy lurch of the ship sent the magnificent roast of beef scurrying to the other end of the galley while his listeners grasped anything within their reach to avoid doing the same.

"I can't possibly do any good cooking in a mess like this. To think of it. We've been less than twenty-four hours in the open sea, and it's almost as bad as Cape Horn. Doesn't look as though it's improving either."

After rescuing the joint, he eyed the horizon thoughtfully through the galley door.

"Doesn't look so good," he added knowingly. "We're in for a hell of a dustup, or I'm no sailor."

The cook wasn't mistaken. The Irish Sea was bad enough, but when the ship emerged from St. George's Channel, the narrow stretch of water between England and Ireland, it was struck by the full force of the gale. Until then the wind, which sailors evaluate according to a scale of one to twelve, had hovered constantly between seven and eight. Now even an inexperienced eye could tell it was getting worse as the ships headed almost directly into the wind. All Jacques could do was to hang on. The crew was hanging on too: one hand for the ship and one hand for themselves. No one got any sleep that night either. The ship's motion was too violent and too erratic.

Despite the rolling and pitching, she maintained her course, battling wave after wave like a boxer parrying ceaseless attacks; suddenly she would be caught off guard in the trough of a wave before she could rise to the next one. A mountain of water would pound her with the ponderous weight of the sea and bury her forecastle under churning foam. There would be a sickening thud. She would shudder from stem to stern, hesitate as though the blow had been too great, then slowly, gathering her strength, she would emerge.

"Sir, the fo'c'sle headrails have been sheared off!"

"Aye, aye."

"Sir! That last one we took over the port side smashed the port lifeboat and bent the davit."

All day long, reports came in telling how the ship was being hammered to bits. But when the boson announced that a couple of depth charges had been washed off the stern, the Old Man, despite his fearlessness, decided to go down and see the chief.

"Is she standing up to it?" he asked the chief engineer.

"I don't know how many more of those she can take," the chief replied gloomily. "One of her sister ships was broken in two in less than this. Can we ease her down a bit?"

"Could, but I'm afraid the convoy will bump into us if we do. Can't see anything in pitch."

Speed was reduced by a few knots. Immediately the blows of sea against ship slackened. The storm had not abated, but the ship took time to rise to the waves and was no longer being torn apart.

The men on watch had long since lost sight of the convoy. Visibility was very bad. In the pale, washy light, the obscurity of day faded, almost imperceptibly, into a howling, shrieking night. During the day you had some idea of what you were up against; at night you were tossed hither and thither like a child's toy in a bathtub.

After another sleepless night, the morning found everyone worn out by the violent ceaseless motion, almost as indifferent to themselves as was the sea.

A sudden swerve the ship made around 7:00 A.M. was hardly noticed, but when Kermadec, the first officer, came down to breakfast and announced he had narrowly avoided a collision with a freighter of the convoy, no one seemed impressed. Everyone took it listlessly, as a matter of course.

In the morning, through the spray, corvette *Wallflower* signaled over the blinker: "Are you all right?"

Dominé's "Yes" came erratically from the crest of the waves.

Yes meant, "We're holding fast...so far," and "We know you'll stand by, *Wallflower*, if we go...although we know, too, that you could never rescue anyone from a sea like this." There's some sense in the old French saying concerning the captain: *Maitre, après Dieu* (Master, after God).

The gale slackened toward daybreak of the third day. Sometime after dawn a pale watery sun tossed a few windy rays through a sky of lead. The sea was still enormous, heaving and swelling, but the vicious, foaming horses had fled. The little ship was dirty and battered but she had weathered the storm.

"You were right, cook, about that dustup," said Jacques. "If only the weatherman were as good at forecasting as you are, we'd have a superb weather service. Hey!" he said suddenly. "We seem to have left the convoy. Where is it?"

"We're not leaving the convoy," said Kermadec. "We're looking for it. The storm scattered everything. That ship over there is *Hollyhock*. We don't dare communicate by radio lest we disclose our position. Only the blinker can be used."

The day-long search yielded nothing. Not a ship, not a smoke in sight. Only an empty sea. As *Hollyhock* put it over the blinker, "Tomorrow is another day. Good night."

The next day *Dominé*, much faster than any corvette, scoured a wide area and by midday came across what remained of the convoy—fifteen ships. The commodore, captain of *Egret*, ordered *Dominé* to take its place in the convoy, already short of escorts.

As the big red sun sank over the western horizon, *Dominé*'s weary crew welcomed its first restful night in twelve days. The sea was as smooth as a lake—none too soon for all on board. Now they could look forward to setting foot on dry land. Freetown was a few days away. Almost everyone's mood changed. There remained only three malcontents on board: two British sailors and one South African, all with the same ambition to reach Freetown to get off "this damn ship."

The next morning *Egret* dispatched *Dominé* to round up *Hollyhock* and the freighter she was escorting. They were nowhere to be found, and *Dominé* returned to Egret for instructions:

"Please go back and watch over *Cornish City*, which has broken down about fifty miles astern. When repaired, should be able to do about seven knots."

It was already past 7:00 P.M. but it was a bright, moonlit, cloudless night. At seventeen knots it didn't take long for *Dominé* to find the disabled ship. She was sighted by the man on watch, to starboard, drifting, big and helpless. *Dominé* circled and called her with a small lamp used for Scotting. No answer.

Dominé continued to circle. She repeated the question: "How long will repairs take?" Still no answer. *Dominé*'s men on watch could sense the nervousness of the freighter's crew. What was this low, slender craft powered by diesel engines? Friend or foe?

Finally, a terse answer: "Expect to be ready 10:00 A.M."

When *Cornish City* got underway, it could not exceed three knots, so *Dominé* escorted it to the Azores for more permanent repairs. There the Old Man was told to proceed to Freetown as fast as possible; that meant at twelve knots if *Dominé* were to reach Freetown with some fuel to spare.

Now the crew could relax. It was safe to have a shower and a change of clothes. The cook could prepare decent meals again. Jacques could return to the comfortable bed in the BNLO's cabin.

Dominé's route took her between the Cape Verde Islands and the West Cost of Africa. Dakar, controlled by the Vichy government (and somewhat, perhaps, by the Germans), was about four hundred miles to the east.

The Dakar latitude was passed at noon, and no enemy action was expected. In the evening a special dinner was served for the purser's birthday, and dusk set in as officers and crew returned to their stations. Arthru, Moleux, and Jacques remained in the mess room sipping strong French coffee. "Hey," said Moleux to Arthru, on hearing the sudden acceleration of the diesel engines, "what's going on?"

"Don't know," said Arthru, rising from his chair. "I'll go and see!"

"There's someone yelling in the gangway," said Jacques. "What's he saying?"

When the cry was repeated, everyone got the message: "Enemy convoy in view!"

The blasts of the hooter sent shivers through the crew as the men hastened to action stations. *Dominé* sailed at nineteen knots, rapidly overtaking the nine ship convoy consisting of slow coal-fired freighters.

"Doesn't that convoy have any escort?" Jacques said to Arthru.

"Yes, it does. It's a ship just like ours. This series of ships has three-inch guns, but the British have replaced our gun with a four-inch."

"Will there be a fight?" Jacques said.

'That's anyone's guess," said Arthru. "It depends on the commodore of the convoy. Jacques, put on your life jacket."

When Jacques returned on deck, *Dominé* and sister ship, *La Boudeuse*, were traveling side by side, and the two commanding officers were talking over the megaphone.

"There won't be a fight," said Kermadec. "The commodore in charge of that convoy is Capitaine de Frégate Meunier, who was formerly the Old Man's immediate superior. They were good friends then and surely still are now, even though Meunier sided with Vichy."

"I don't doubt that secretly Meunier hopes the British will win," said Arthru.

"And neither he nor our Captain will engage in a gun duel which would benefit only the Germans," Kermadec said as *Dominé* headed for its destination in Freetown and the two commanding officers exchanged parting salutes.

Freetown was several days away now. There was still nothing to see but the sky, the clouds, and the blue waters of the sea, sometimes enlivened by flocks of flying fish. As the ship went further south, heat became a problem in the innards of the ship where motors and generators yielded constant warmth. There was no air-conditioning in a ship built for coastal patrol in the waters around France.

One morning as the day crew took up its stations, there was something new: the smell of land. There was no land in sight, but the smell was there.

After many days at sea, land can be smelled long before it can be seen—and this time *Dominé* could not be rerouted: its reserve of fuel was less than 10 percent. At last, in the distance through the haze, a low, bluish-grey line separated sea from sky. Land!

Chapter IX

Land, but what land! A dismal, forbidding coast. A town sprawled on the north bank of the Sierra Leone Rive, Freetown was the port and main city of the British colony and protectorate (depending on where you were) of Sierra Leone, West Africa, about five hundred miles north of the Equator.

A hot, humid, oppressive climate! In the wet season, rain penetrated everything everywhere. Humans lived in a bath of vapor and a cocoon of sweat, under constant attack by mosquitoes bred by the millions in the neighboring swamps, fungi proliferating on dripping bodies! Soon this hostile environment dulled the senses, fogged the brain, and slowed activity to a crawl. Those bred in this morass cared about little more than primitive shelter, food, and sleep.

In the Sierra Leone River, a mile off shore, *Dominé* was ordered to drop anchor in the sweltering heat; for how long, no one knew. Not a breath of air. Stifling humidity. Everyone dripped with sweat.

After what seemed an eternity, a small white launch manned by a black native pulled up alongside and made fast. A man in the white uniform of the French Navy stepped aboard and introduced himself to *Dominé's* commanding officer as Commandant Lebreton in charge of the Free French Naval Commission in Sierra Leone. He informed the Old Man that a larger launch would arrive later to take a small number of *Dominé's* crew ashore, but that in the meantime, he wanted the purser, Le Boucher, and the war correspondent to accompany him to the port

Freetown, 1941! The hub for northbound and southbound sea lanes...the port of call...the haven...the supply point for convoys, merchantmen, supply ships, tankers, warships, submarines, coal-burning freighters, and oil hungry motor ships. Jacques had never seen a harbor quite like this: a mass of lighters, barges, tugs, launches, rowboats, rafts, and every imaginable craft that could float or

100

ever did float at anchor off-shore or tied up to wharves, makeshift piers, docks, platforms and embankments. On shore, near the water's edge, coal piles, oil tanks of all shapes and sizes, some filling, some emptying—all this was thrown together around a natural harbor on the north bank of the Sierra Leone River, a river that opened its mouth into the ocean and formed huge swells when its heavy current bucked the great tides.

The launch landed its passengers at the foot of a muddy embankment, at the top of which Lebreton had parked his car.

"As you can see, this place is pretty primitive," Lebreton said to Jacques as they drove through a messy weave of low, wooden, unpainted shacks, tenements, and houses with corrugated tin roofs. The car threaded its way along roads bordered by V-shaped gullies two to three feet deep to channel the tons of water periodically disgorged from the skies on this town of fifty-five thousand souls.

As they passed a large, unpainted wooden building, with a dirty-looking front porch, Lebreton said, "That's the Savoy, the so-called best hotel in Freetown. No screens, no protection from mosquitoes or any other flying pests. No rooms are available, anyway, but in a pinch, if you're really desperate, they may offer you some space on the porch."

"Is there no protection at all against mosquitoes?" Jacques said.

"None whatever," Lebreton said. "Screens are unknown here. The American Naval Attaché's office and house are an oddity and an attraction. They're the only places in Freetown with screens."

"Doesn't everyone have malaria?" Jacques said.

"The place is full of it, and to make matters worse, quinine is almost impossible to get. If you want protection here, bring your own."

"How about food?" Jacques said, as they passed the local market, which seemed well supplied with oranges, bananas, avocados, coconuts, and chickens.

"As you can see, there's all you want of the local stuff. There are plenty of imports, too. Butter, tea, grapefruit. Manufactured items are abundant: razor blades, tissues, shirts, shorts, even bathing suits. They're mostly from Hong Kong."

Women? Plentiful, none of them white, supplying anything you could want—and don't want!

"There seems to be an extraordinary mixture of races here," said Jacques.

"There is. It's a mingling of incredible variety, four to five thousand aboriginals, colonists, settlers—Syrians, mostly Moslems and some Greek Orthodox, all of whom retain their individual identities."

"I suppose English is the main language here," said Jacques.

"Don't be fooled," Lebreton said. "This is a real Tower of Babel. Many of the settlers have married local women, haven't returned to Europe in twenty years, and speak broken English. Then there's the Yoruba language of Nigeria, but the two principal languages are Henda and Temne. Just try to make yourself understood."

Administration? A mini British Government with an information officer and a police officer (or commissioner) was all that was needed to run the colony.

There was a Free French Commission on Charlotte Street headed by a military man, Commander Allegret, but there was not much use for a military man in Freetown. The bulk of the work went to Navy Commander Lebreton.

Jacques gave Lebreton the letter from Sir James Ferguson. He read it attentively and said to Jacques, "I suggest we go this afternoon to Lumley Beach, where I have a cabin. There's no telephone there, and we can talk privately and confidentially. There will be no interruptions and no unwelcome visits. As I mentioned, there's no room available in any hotel in Freetown. For tonight you can stay in the Free French Commission's office, but we can't give you a bed."

"Don't worry about that," said Jacques. "I have a folding bed, an inflatable mattress, and a mosquito net."

"Perfect," said Lebreton. "You're self-sufficient. I wish we had more people like you. Let's go to the British Officer's Club for lunch, and then we'll drive to Lumley Beach."

"As you have seen," said Lebreton as they sat down before the rolling surf on the deserted beach, "Freetown is a makeshift harbor. It's all been hastily slapped together because we, the Free French, had counted on occupying Dakar with its modern port facilities."

After the capitulation of France, all civilians and most of the military in the colonies wanted to continue the war. The general consensus was *la guerre à outrance, a* war to the finish.

The French government in Vichy opposed such action. When it signed the armistice with Hitler, it agreed unilaterally not to undertake any action hostile to the Nazi Reich and to prevent any French citizen from doing so. Marshal Pétain was convinced the Germans had won the war. He believed the Nazis would respect the terms of the armistice and that the French should do the same. He sent Marshal Weygand, Supreme Commander of the Army, to rally governors in the French colonies of Africa to that view. Weygand went to Algeria, Morocco, Sénégal, even to Syria.

Dakar, capital of Sénégal, was of particular importance, as it had the only modern water port on the West Coast of Africa. Some powerful units of the French navy were there. It was the headquarters of Governor Pierre Boisson, whose authority extended over most French territories in black Africa—Mauritania, Niger, Dahomey, Togo, etc. Boisson was a loyal supporter of the legal French government, and he agreed to comply with the terms of the armistice it had signed.

A committee of citizens in Dakar had been formed to continue the war against Germany and receive the Free French who were doing so, but the committee had been infiltrated by agents of the Italian secret service. They warned the governor that a small task force of Free French warships had left England for Dakar. Boisson immediately replaced all army men sympathetic to Free France with pro-Vichy, anti-British navy men.

"The Free French ships," said Lebreton indignantly, "were received with shells and bullets. *Dominé* was one of them. The negotiator, Capitaine de Frégate, Thierry d'Argenlieu, standing in a launch with a white flag, was seriously wounded; his white uniform was red with blood!"

The Free French withdrew under cover of a smokescreen provided by their escorting British warships, who also returned the fire—exactly what the Nazis wanted.

The next day German-controlled Radio Paris broadcast the report that the English, trying to capture Dakar, had fired on the city and had been repulsed, the only casualties being women and children killed in a native hospital.

"So you see," Lebreton continued, "after that fiasco we are left with this miserable, vital, port of Freetown. The Germans have the power and the strategic points they need to seize French colonies in Africa. Fortunately they don't have enough surface warships to carry out a combined operation against Dakar. To get to that port, they would need the full cooperation of the French authorities."

"Britain," said Jacques, "is obviously in a very precarious position. I can see why the British government is so scared that the French navy could fall into German hands."

"It could still happen," said Lebrcton, "especially after Dakar."

"Can't the men in the French navy understand who the real enemy is?" said Jacques.

"You would think so," said Lebreton, "but they can't seem to get over the rivalry that has always existed between the two navies."

The rivalry had exploded into fury when the British, afraid the French fleet would fall into German hands, destroyed or disabled the greater part of a French naval squadron anchored at Mers el Kebir, Algeria, killing over twelve hundred men. That was followed by Dakar, where the Free French were repulsed with a violence hitherto unseen during the war.

"You must remember as you go into Free French territory that this Dakar incident has left very bitter memories among all the supporters of the Free French—many of whom are in prison where they are horribly mistreated. There's a fierce hatred on both sides, exacerbated by German propaganda. The German armies, with their experience, equipment, and organization, are the most formidable fighting force the world has ever seen."

"So far," said Jacques, "it would appear that the Nazis have won the war, although Britain has not yet lost it. It will take the might of the United States to tip the scales—and that's not yet ready to happen. How did you manage to get out of territory controlled by Vichy?"

"I was on assignment at the time in Dahomey," said Lebreton. "I heard about the surrender of France over the radio on June eighteenth, the day it happened. I didn't wait for de Gaulle's call to help rally the colonies to continue the war, I immediately contacted key people to find out who was for surrender and who wanted to carry on the fight with England. I contacted de Gaulle's headquarters through the English in Lagos. I heard about the Free French plan to occupy Dakar and organized a team of volunteers to seize all the centers of power Togo, Niger, and Dahomey: power plants, airfields, telephone exchanges, army depots, etc."

On September 23 these patriots got a surprise. Instead of hearing from de Gaulle, they were treated to a broadcast from Boisson, ordering governors in each colony to arrest all individuals dangerous to the security of the colonies. One of Lebreton's friends in the police hurried to tell him that an arrest warrant had been issued against him as one of the most dangerous men in the colonies. He departed immediately in a front-wheel-drive Citroen for Nigeria but was stopped at a roadblock on the Kandi-kotonou highway by a police commissioner and six black guards. He was handcuffed and driven to Kotonou. There Commissioner Minette of the Sureté punched him in the face, saying, "Here's what we do to traitors." He was thrown into the yellow fever quarantine station, which had been hastily transformed into a concentration camp.

There Lebreton was locked in a cell with a guard at each door. The heat was unbearable under the tin roof. His wife was not allowed to bring him any food. Instead he was provided with meals delivered in a case for gasoline cans from a local restaurant, which usually spoiled before they got to him. After he had been there for some days, a friend passed him a scribbled note informing him he was to be transferred to Dakar for trial. That hastened his resolve to escape.

"During the change of the guard at 9:00," A.M. Lebreton continued, "the cell remained unguarded for a few minutes. I had gradually loosened one of the hinges of the shutters and was able to push one shutter open and was off. Bullets whizzed around me, but I had the protection of a big tree, which kept me out of the line of sight. I scrambled through the barbed wire, which tore my clothing and skin, and was off into the bush.

"Instead of following me through the wire, the guards ran the length of the camp back to the gate. By the time they got out and started after me, I was half a mile away into the dense bush.

"I walked all night through the bush, guiding myself by the stars. The next morning I was exhausted and lay down sometime after daybreak, after making sure there was no village in the vicinity. I ate wild bananas, drank water out of the swamps, and everywhere avoided tracks and villages. That evening there was a terrible storm. I welcomed it, knowing that the guards would remain sheltered. I guided myself as well as I could, walking as though in a dream. I fell down several times. My feet ached and were so swollen that I didn't dare remove my boots for fear I couldn't put them on again.

"Before daybreak I heard the sound of European voices and natives answering—one white man and six natives passed about thirty feet away. It was obviously a border patrol, and there, about one hundred yards away, was the French customs. I could see the sentry under the lantern; he was completely unaware of my presence. I passed behind him on tiptoe and quietly went from one coconut tree to another to reach the British customs, which was another hundred yards away.

"There I hid until daybreak, lest the native guard push me back to the French border. I impressed him by using the name of the British district commissioner and requested the use of the phone. There I was welcomed. They gave me a cup of tea and some food and sent me to the district commissioner's office, which was about six miles on foot and eight miles in a native canoe.

"At the district commissioner's I got a much-needed bath and the loan of a pair of pajamas and a camp bed. I fell asleep in the late afternoon and woke up the next morning as stiff as a board but a free man.

"From there they took me to Lagos by launch, where I arrived on October thirtieth. days after my escape from Kotonou. Some friends put me up at their house, where I rested until November seventeenth."

You've certainly had your share of troubles," said Jacques. "But at least you were able to escape."

"I haven't told this to anyone in Freetown," said Lebreton. "Although I have given a few details to the head of the Free French commission here, Commander Allegret. In any case, keep this under your hat. I've told you about it because you are one of our own. We've been hearing your broadcasts from London; we also heard that the Vichy government had honored you with the death penalty *in absentia.*"

At the outbreak of war, France had a vast colonial empire in Africa. From Morocco, Algeria, and Tunisia in the north, to the vast expanses of Mali, Niger, Chad, Ivory Coast, Dahomey, and Togo further south, hundreds of thousands of square miles of the continent were under French administration.

Most governors in these territories followed the Vichy government's orders and arrested all army officers and private citizens unwilling to accept defeat, but the governors of Chad and French Equatorial Africa (AEF) defied Vichy's orders and sided with the British. They were a handful of Frenchmen beyond the reach of their legal government and of the Nazis.

But these rebels, these Free French, were so few! Why? That haunted Lebreton as it haunted de Thoranne.

"Most of those who were free to express themselves," said Lebreton, "have remained silent. Last year they were convinced that Germany had won the war. They still believe it today, but with less conviction. I'm sorry you are leaving tomorrow. We have so much more to discuss. We would be delighted to have you among us longer, but I know you want to get on your way. You may want to board *Dominé* this evening, in case she leaves early tomorrow. We'll have dinner at the Free French Commission, and I'll get a launch to take you to the ship."

After they reached the Free French Commission's office, Lebreton said, "Whether you like it or not, you're our guest here! *Dominé* was ordered out this afternoon on an emergency. What it is, I don't know. But she was refueled and won't return here. I'm very happy to have you here."

This did not suit Jacques. He had planned to begin his African survey from Egypt, travelling there on *Dominé*, after stops in Capetown, Lourenço Marques, then north in the Indian Ocean, through the Red Sea and the Suez Canal to Port Said. Then from Port Said, he had intended to go through Egypt, the Sudan, Ethiopia, Uganda, the Belgian Congo, AEF, Chad, and Nigeria.

Jacques discussed this contretemps with Lebreton. "I think that, all things considered, I may just as well reverse my itinerary. I'll start with Nigeria, Chad, AEF and then go through the Congo and the Sudan to Egypt."

"I agree," said Lebreton. "This change in itinerary has decided advantages. It will take at least two or three weeks to provide you with transportation to Nigeria, so we'll have you in Freetown for a while. You can be very useful here, and, in the meantime, you'll learn a lot. All along your new route are friends of mine who were imprisoned by the Vichy government or who escaped to avoid arrest. A number of them are in key positions in the territories you plan to visit and are people you can count on in case of need. I'll give you a personal note for each of them."

What he learned in Freetown opened Jacques' eyes to the true significance of Attila and Felix. First Lebreton introduced him to the staff of the Free French Commission. The organization, set up by a former major in the French Colonial Army, occupied the building owned before the war by the Woerman Steamship Lines, a German company that had served as the Nazi intelligence center in Sierra Leone.

When the French occupied the building, there were no office supplies or equipment, not even any paper. Their first written communications were typed on the letterhead left behind by the Woerman Lines—until they received a caustic note addressed to the Woerman Lines, telling them to use a better disguise than the Free French if they wanted to continue their spying activities!

Correspondence thereafter was typed (on a rickety old Remington typewriter) on shorter paper, with the Woerman name and logo cut off. Getting blank typewriter paper in Freetown in 1941 was almost impossible, and as for typewriter ribbon, forget it!

The Free French office in Freetown was kept busy mainly with naval affairs. It screened the French sailors brought into port on ships captured by the Royal Navy and the ships anchored in the mouth of the Sierra Leone River. The French sailors were given the choice of returning to France or continuing to fight the Germans with the British Navy or joining the Free French who were training men in the colonies or in England.

For these men, this was no easy choice.

They were housed in Mabang, a camp set up to accommodate sailors from captured ships, escapees from lands controlled by the Vichy government, and volunteers arriving from neutral territories. To call it uncomfortable would be an understatement, but it provided shelter from the rain and shade from the blazing midday sun. It was very hot and the food was miserable, but this was war and the men had one consolation: they were free.

Morale was low among these captured sailors. They were far from their country, their homes, and their families. They were confused and bewildered. Many had been brainwashed with tracts proclaiming that, "England is the enemy, her treacherous government sank our ships and killed your brothers at Mers el Kebir in an unprovoked attack." They were told that satisfactory peace conditions had been negotiated with Germany (which was not true, of course), counting on the Germans' sense of honor. These peace conditions were never defined.

The escapees from Vichy's clutches or from occupied lands were a different breed. They knew what they wanted: a chance to fight the oppressors and expel them from the fatherland, however remote that idea might seem.

Jacques put his forced stay in Freetown to good use. He prepared pamphlets giving facts and figures on the German occupation in France: 300 million francs taken from the French people each day by the Germans; examples of arrests made on mere suspicion; conscription of men to build the Atlantic wall; hostages shot when a German soldier was killed.

In one pamphlet he gave the reasons for his own resignation: secret orders from the Vichy government to spy on the United States. There was no question of England here. Spying on a country most French admired and liked was a cardinal sin. They couldn't accept that. This deceit demonstrated that the Vichy government was little more than a puppet of the conquerors.

The contents of these pamphlets were aired in five-minute broadcasts, in English for Sierra Leone and Gambia and in French for Dakar and other French territories under the control of the Vichy government.

Jacques interviewed every escapee from Vichy territory and assembled and analyzed significant facts. He was particularly interested in any information remotely connected with Attila and Felix, such as the construction of airfields in strategic areas, work performed with native labor and supervised by French engineers. Through these interviews Jacques got some insight of a nation bitterly divided in defeat. Many who supported Marshal Pétain's Vichy government hated their Free French compatriots more than they hated the Germans. "To give you an idea of their feelings," said Lebreton to Jacques, "read this letter I have just received. Look at what they did to my friend Gilbert Picour. His own words will tell more than anything I can say."

Dear Lebreton:

I have heard that you are in Freetown. So, before leaving for Capetown, I thought you would be interested to know that I am again a free man, enjoying life without that feeling of being watched and followed everywhere, which was my fate in Dahomey.

The American Consul at Dakar arranged to exchange me for a Vichy Frenchman from Douala. After three weeks in the quarantine station and after another five months in solitary confinement in Kotonou, I arrived, blindfolded, at Porto Novo. There an English police officer and four Nigerian policemen took charge of me; I was put aboard a beautiful government launch and taken to Eboué House. This, you will agree, was a more comfortable way of arriving in Lagos than the dramatic way in which you reached that city, which was related to me by your wife.

I had been arrested on November 20 by Morere and Minette. I asked for an explanation, but received none. The instructions to arrest me had come from Dakar after your escape. Minette said I was responsible and no doubt told Dakar. The customs clerk was also held responsible and was sent in chains to Dakar.

The governor of Dahomey, the police, and Peuvergne were sharply criticized for your escape, and they took no chances with me. I was constantly guarded by one sergeant, one corporal, and two natives. They slept a few yards away, and during the night, four men kept a close watch on me. Even when I went to the latrine, two native guards with drawn bayonets accompanied me. There was absolutely no chance to escape.

Now that is all over and seems like a bad dream. I heard from your wife and was pleased to know that she had reached Algiers safely. We all admired her great courage and the steadfastness she had shown. She is a courageous and determined woman, and I hope you will soon be reunited with her and with your daughters.

The doctor has ordered me to South Africa for a rest, and I shall leave by the next boat. I wanted to do some touring there, but my motorcycle has not yet been returned to me. The Vichy government in Dahomey requisitioned my refrigerator and my Triumph.

Some day I hope to hear from you verbally and discuss with you all that has happened since that unforgettable day when you made good your escape. Until then, good bye and good luck.

"I can see," said Jacques, "why some citizens are bitter. I don't detect any hatred from the writer. The viciousness seems all on the other side."

"You're right," said Lebreton. "The French so-called government, which is little more than a rubber stamp for the Germans, cannot stand the living reproach that Free Frenchmen represent for them. Our very existence shames them; our refusal to accept their surrender is heresy.

"Since you are truly one of our own, I'll give you a clear idea of the disparity of forces off the shores of the Atlantic. We'll start here, in Freetown. Get into my car, and we'll make the rounds."

First Lebreton drove Jacques to the huge piles of coal strewn along the water front, coal from England and even from Poca Huntas in the U.S., to feed the hungry furnaces of the coal-burning freighters.

"See," said Lebreton, "there's just not enough deep-water space to allow many ships alongside at the same time, either to load or unload."

"Considering that something like 80 or 90 percent of the freighters are coal fired, this must be a terrible bottleneck."

"Of course it is," said Lebreton. "The Germans and the Vichy French control the only good harbor between Liverpool in England and Capetown in South Africa; and very few, if any, freighters can make the trip without refueling on the way. See what a mess we're in!"

Jacques said nothing. His mind turned to Attila and Felix. What could happen to Freetown? How could the eighth Army in Egypt be supplied if Dakar were fully under German control? He shuddered at the thought.

Next Lebreton took him to the tanks storing bunker oil for the steam-propelled tankers and to the diesel reserves for the motor ships. Here again, everything was makeshift, poorly organized, and insufficient.

"See what we have to do," said Lebreton. "That tanker out there is refueling the ship next to it."

"Mere improvisation," said Jacques, "due to lack of foresight and to the collapse of France."

Next they toured the supplies of food and drinking water needed by the freighters. Here again, improvisation was obvious.

"Pretty depressing," said Jacques.

"Yes," said Lebreton. "We'll need a little more than muddling through if we are ever to win this war."

Neither man spoke as Lebreton drove his small car back to the office. Both were tense and depressed by the reminders they had just seen of the frailty of England's fight for liberty and of the immense task required to free the continent of Europe.

Back in the office, Lebreton pored over a few messages.

"I've got some good news for you. In the not-too-distant future, you'll have transportation to Nigeria on a warship. That's bad news for us."

"Why?"

"Because you're making inroads at the Mabang camp against Vichy's propaganda. Your pamphlets have been read all over the camp. The facts you've given them about the German occupation of France have made many of the men think twice. Even Dakar has acknowledged the effectiveness of your messages."

"Dakar? How?" asked Jacques.

"They are jamming your broadcasts," said Lebreton laughing. "While that may be effective in and around Dakar, their jammer doesn't have the power to reach most of the other colonies in Africa. You'll soon be public enemy number one in Dakar, as you are among your former colleagues of the Diplomatic Service!"

Chapter X

During World War II, travel in areas affected by the conflict was a major problem: there was no transportation. Air travel was out. The military and top government officials themselves constantly engaged in a battle for priorities. Sea travel? Except for a few neutrals such as Portugal, no one had passenger ships. With some know-how and much perseverance, berths could be obtained on freighters—some traveling in convoys, others sailing independently.

It was not comfortable travel; it was not safe travel; often it was dangerous travel. Many ships in convoys went to the bottom. Passengers of ships sailing independently did not always reach their scheduled destination: 300 men, women, and children on the Egyptian ship *Zam-Zam* ended up on the *Dresden*, a Nazi supply ship, when the *Zam-Zam* was sent to the bottom of the sea by *Atlantis*, a German surface raider.

Jacques' travel priority was to get to Nigeria. He couldn't get there overland. There was too much enemy territory in the way. By sea the capital of Lagos was about one thousand miles from Freetown, but from Lagos transportation overland was possible to the area Jacques wanted to visit.

Lagos has been provided on corvette *Burdock*, assigned to escort two freighters. Departure scheduled in two days." *Burdock* had just arrived from England, escorting a large convoy. The ship had refueled in Freetown and taken on fresh supplies of food when Hanson, the skipper, received orders to escort two merchant ships loaded with much-needed supplies—one for Takoradi, Gold Coast, and the other for Lagos, Nigeria. There was another, unusual assignment: to transport a passenger from Freetown to Lagos.

"Glad to have you on board," Hanson said to Jacques who arrived shortly before departure on a launch provided by the Royal Navy. "This is the first time we've had a passenger on this ship. It's nice to have someone from the outside. Living all the time with the same crew, you begin to feel cooped up after a while. You'll get many questions, because all the news we get is censored."

"I hear that complaint everywhere I go."

"You won't be too comfortable here," said Hanson. "There's no bunk available, but you can sleep in the officers' mess room."

"I have a folding bed and a sleeping bag," said Jacques. "Could I sleep on deck?"

"You could," said Hanson. "The sea rarely gets rough here, but you'll get up in the morning drenched from the dew unless we put you under the gun shield. We'll move you if there's a call for action stations, which is quite possible. Two submarines have been signaled in the area."

"What would you do if you were attacked by two submarines at the same time?" said Jacques.

"We'd have a problem, and it would be up to me to solve it. I'll be my own boss on this assignment," said Hanson, smiling.

The two submarines never appeared, and the escorting seemed like a piece-time cruise. There was no wind; there was not a ripple on the water; there were no long swells. At night the air was clear, and the two blacked-out merchant ships were plainly visible against the sea. While the corvette's crew had to keep a watchful eye on everything around them, this escorting provided a welcome rest from the ceaseless motion of the North Atlantic run and from the of Freetown.

All on board wanted to hear everything about America. None had ever been there, and their knowledge was confined to what they'd seen in the movies or heard on the radio.

Although Jacques was impatient to reach his destination, the week on board went by very fast.

"It seems to me that I smell land," said Jacques late one morning.

"You do," said Hanson. "We're about twenty-five miles from Lagos. We'll be there before sunset."

Corvette *Burdock* docked before dark on the western side of the lagoon. Lagos was on the east side, and the last bus for the city had already left, which meant spending the night on board, in the stifling heat, amid swarms of mosquitoes, and with no way to install a net. This was not for Jacques, but there was no means of transportation to shore where the ship had docked.

When three natives in a long, unstable pirogue came alongside offering transportation across the lagoon, Jacques bid good-bye to his hosts and took off amid the horrified looks of the corvette's crew.

"I'd never put my foot in that kind of thing," the bosun commented. "Hope you get there. Good luck!"

The three boatmen handled their long hollowed-out tree trunk with great ability. In less than an hour, just before dark, they landed their traveler on a sloping beach on the eastern side of the lagoon within Lagos' city limits.

A tall native official came out of nowhere to meet him. "Visa, sir."

"No need for a visa. I'm off the warship and missed the last bus. Here's my war correspondent identification," said Jacques, brandishing the official-looking card. "I'm going to the Grand Hotel. Call a taxi."

"Yes, sir," said the sentry.

Jacques had no idea how much the guard had understood, but he quickly rounded up three natives to carry the luggage and guide the traveler to a taxi, a two-wheeled cart, drawn by an energetic cyclist.

"Grand Hotel," Jacques ordered.

"Yes, sir."

As he sat in the taxi, Jacques sized up the new environment, with its oppressive heat, humidity, unpainted wooden hovels, unfamiliar smells, the quiet, the calm, and the remoteness of war. Freetown had given him the first taste of colonial Africa, but Lagos seemed to take him a step further.

The Grand Hotel might not have been grand, but it was acceptable and always open. Any official guest wearing an officer's khaki uniform could find a room with bath. No reservation was needed despite the dire shortage of hotel facilities.

Jacques was thrilled with his special passport. Its magic touch opened almost any bureaucratic door.

Everywhere he was received as a friend and was prevailed upon to bring fresh, first-hand news from the motherland. He was a guest at various clubs— even at a scout's troop. Colonials who had not returned to the metropolis in years wanted to know if such and such a street in London or Plymouth was still a part of the landscape.

Everywhere he was asked about America. What did Americans in New York think of the war? Were they afraid of being dragged into it? He spoke on the radio every other day and was repeatedly interviewed by the local press. He was the guest at private homes where people wanted to know the real stuff. "All we get here is censored news which tells very little."

For all the good will in Lagos, he encountered the same problem as in Freetown: transportation. Sea travel was a one-way street to Freetown, and air transportation was out of the question. Land transportation was the only way to get to Chad.

Colonel Adam, a fat and pompous administrator with a bulging abdomen, was an extraordinary source of information. His knowledge of West Africa and Lagos was unsurpassed, and he dispensed it freely.

Jacques was anxious to protect himself from yellow fever, endemic in West Africa. Its deadliness had impressed him during his student days. He had never forgotten the quip of his professor of biology, "Yellow fever epidemics leave 20 percent of the victims with a long convalescence and immunity and the remaining 80 percent in the cemetery." In Freetown the vaccine was unobtainable; Colonel Adam sent Jacques to Yaba, in the outskirts of Lagos, to the office of a Dr. Smith, a specialist in the disease who prepared his own vaccine.

Then the obliging official requisitioned a first-class compartment on the Nigerian railroad to Jos, the closest station to Chad. He also gave Jacques a letter of recommendation for the British Resident at Jos and a letter for the Syrian-Arab whose trucking service offered daily transportation from Jos to Fort Lamy in Chad.

One formality remained: an exit visa to be obtained from the chief of police in Lagos. The official examined the passport curiously.

"How is it, Mr. de Thoranne," he said finally, "that there is no entrance visa on your passport?"

"I arrived on the warship *Burdock*," said Jacques.

"You saved yourself a lot of trouble," said the chief. "Entrance visas are very difficult to get."

With his exit visa in order, Jacques returned to the Grand Hotel. The porter secure a taxi, a black Ford station wagon. Into it he loaded what remained of Jacques' luggage. Jacques had entrusted most of it to Hanson, to be returned to the U.S. from Freetown. Extra luggage was out of the question anywhere in wartime, especially in Africa.

Lagos' Iddo station was an extraordinary place, teeming with natives of all ages and reeking of poverty and good humor. Every member of this human flood wanted to help unload and carry luggage. Thank God for the porter of the Grand Hotel. He put some order in the swarm of would-be helpers, entered the station wagon next to the driver, and accompanied Jacques and his belongings to the reserved compartment.

Alone in his compartment, Jacques looked forward to some rest and quiet, sorely needed after his social whirlwind in Lagos and his 102° body temperature which had followed the yellow fever vaccination. Jacques had little more to do than watch the scenery and collect his thoughts. He basked in this world at peace contrasting so sharply with the world at war he had left. A snappy little locomotive with traction wheels fore and aft of a big boiler and tanks drew the train on a narrow-gauge track. The reserve of water was not enough for the thirsty locomotive. That meant a stop every fifty miles or so to quench its thirst. The pulling power of the traction wheels was dictated by the steep inclines and the sharp curves the train had to negotiate.

The first-class compartment was clean and comfortable, although the seats were hard. One could be pulled out to make a bed. The windows of smoked glass reduced the glare of the sun, but there was no protection from the heat, as no one in Nigeria in 1941 had ever heard of air-conditioned trains.

The train pulled out of Iddo station slowly a few minutes after noon. It stopped once on the outskirts of Lagos and then started toward its destination. A few minutes later, the steward informed the first-class passengers that lunch was ready and that a proper meal would be served in the evening. Lunch was not so bad. It consisted of canned meat, a salad of sliced tomatoes and cucumbers with sliced boiled eggs, Heinz sauce, a dessert of fruit salad, and finally, coffee.

After leaving Lagos the train passed through dense bush country, above which towered innumerable palm trees. Often vegetation was so close to the tracks that the foliage brushed the carriages.

After lunch Jacques returned to his compartment to collect his thoughts. What had he done so far that could give Sir James an unbiased, precise picture of Britain's shaky hold on Africa? He had learned much during his stay in Freetown. Above all, he had understood the vital role this West African outskirt played in the war, and he'd been horrified by its vulnerability.

Nothing in Freetown had been prepared for war. Everything was makeshift. There were no defenses and no adequate repair facilities for ships. An old aircraft carrier, *Vindictive*, a very fast ship in its day, had been partly dismantled to perform minor repairs. One boiler, one stack, and two propellers had been removed, but even thus amputated, it could do twenty-four knots.

She had four four-inch guns and four Bofors pom-poms. Other than that Freetown had no defense, but those pom-poms came in handy when Boisson, Governor of Senegal, sent navy plane to photograph the harbor's facilities. A burst of fire from the pom-poms disabled the plane and forced it to crash land into the water, where the crew of two were rescued. Both men were prisoners on the *Vindictive*, where Jacques interviewed them. Brard, the Lieutenant de Vaisseau, vented his anger against the British; he was still smarting from Mers el Kebir and Dakar. Didn't he realize, Jacques asked him, that Germany was the true enemy? Why were French merchant ships carrying raw materials for the Germans? To help them keep the French people enslaved?

"Because," Brard answered tartly, "we must carry five hundred tons of materials for the Germans in order to get one hundred tons for ourselves."

There was no adequate fire-fighting equipment in Freetown and only sloppy manpower to handle the little there was. Jacques remembered the big bang the night a lighter caught fire, destroying precious tons of badly needed fuel, and how the port was unable to extinguish the blaze. The fire was allowed to burn itself out for want of proper fire-fighting equipment. *Maybe that, too, should be brought to the attention of Sir James. Although,* Jacques thought, *he must surely know this."*

As the train rattled along, the bush faded from thick to sparse. When the train stopped at Azo, crowds of smiling natives stormed it. Most of them were very young.

Jacques bought six oranges from a native girl. She asked for two pennies. He gave her three, and she went away smiling. Jacques had seen poverty in France when, as a student, he had helped some deserving poor in shantytowns, but this was destitution. Many had no home and slept outside. Their sole possessions were the few rags that served as clothes.

The day was fading when the train pulled into the station at Ibadan, a city of half a million, then said to be the largest all-black city in the world. The stop lasted for half an hour. Jacques walked around the station neighborhood, amid homes made of mud and palm leaves. It was the density of the population which impressed him most. A lone white man, an object of discreet curiosity in the black throng, he had to thread his way through swarms of natives. He returned to the train well before its scheduled departure, anxious about what might happen if it should leave without him.

After dinner, in the privacy of his compartment, Jacques set up his mosquito net over the bed the steward had prepared. The bed had only one sheet, but a consideration for the kindly native brought a big smile and a second sheet, obviously dried in the blazing sun.

Jacques locked the door, turned off the light, and continued to assess the reports he'd collected from escapees from Vichy-controlled territories of Mali, Guinea, and Senegal. The story was always the same. The government of Marshall Pétain was pressing its supporters in these colonies to build airfields, runways, and service facilities where none, or only limited facilities, had before existed. For what purpose—Attila and Felix?

By the end of the next day, the train passed the five hundred-mile mark. In Jacques' compartment the temperature was 98°. The train continued its stop and go progress, up and down inclines, around innumerable bends put there mainly, it was said, to increase the profits of the Italian contractors who built the track.

At 7:45 P.M. the steward called for dinner. The day had faded into dusk, and the travelers could watch the hills, delineated by winding snakes of fire, as the natives burned the brush in their yearly custom. Meals, including the dinner, soup, fish, meat, string beans, potatoes, and carrots, banana jelly, and coffee, cost ten shillings a day. Someone said that the railroad's profit was eight shillings and that meals cost the company less than two shillings. The cost of eggs in Nigeria in 1941 was four for a penny.

There were no symptoms of war in Nigeria, no damaged railroad stations, no repaired tracks. This was another world. The main enemies were insects, mosquitoes particularly. Jacques was the envy of fellow travelers. He had the only mosquito net on the train.

The train was broken up at Kaduna. One portion was routed to the walled city of Kano, where snake charmers held sway; the other part was for Jos, Jacques' destination. During the day the heat was torrid, but temperatures dropped sharply during the night. Shortly before dawn a blanket was comfortable.

The dining car vanished during the breakup, so no breakfast was served the next morning. Jacques ate the oranges he had bought at Azo.

When Jacques alighted in Jos, the district officer waited to greet him. *Thank God for his presence*, Jacques thought. He alone knew how to control the scramble of natives wanting jobs as "boys for master."

"Mr. de Thoranne, my name is Pembleton, and I am the resident here," said the official. "I hope you will accept our hospitality during your stay in Jos. I understand you are from Philadelphia. My wife was born in Germantown. We've lived here for years, and she will be delighted to have some fresh news from home."

Mrs. Pembleton showed Jacques to his bedroom. "I'm sure that you'd like a bath after more than two days in the 100° heat on the train with no facilities to wash. You have all you need in this bathroom. I can't wait to hear all you have to tell us about England and Philadelphia. I know the dining car was disconnected, so while you take your bath, I'll prepare breakfast for all of us. Give me any clothes you need to have washed.

Before they sat down for breakfast, the Pembletons introduced Jacques to the Willoughbys. Willoughby was an administrator in Nigeria; his wife had returned to England shortly before the outbreak of the war and was only recently able to rejoin her husband.

"After the collapse of France," she said, "it was almost impossible to get a passage out of England for Nigeria. It required all kinds of priorities and several months' waiting time. Finally I was booked *Abasso*, but we were dive-bombed at sea a short time after leaving England. It was a terrifying experience; one bomb missed us by no more than fifty yards. I'll never go through that again, even if I must stay here until the end of the war. And you, Mr. de Thoranne, how did you get out here?"

"On the six hundred-ton sloop *Commandant Dorniné*, the first Free French warship commissioned in England after the fall of France. A warship is the only practical way to get out of England these days."

"I know," said Pembleton. "My vacation is long overdue. Both my wife and I could obtain transportation to England, but returning here is another matter. She wouldn't have a priority, so we've decided to vacation in South Africa. Even that will mean traveling on a freighter in a convoy, not a very pleasant prospect."

"Exactly. The submarines are after the freighters."

"At least here," said Pembleton, "we are better off than in England. There's no shortage of food. Now and then we receive some manufactured articles from Hong Kong, mostly cheap stuff, but at least it's something. Outside of food, everything not produced locally is difficult to obtain. There's no aspirin in any pharmacy. When you get a headache, you just let it blow over.

As for quinine? Forget it! Milk of Magnesia, even Eno's Fruit Salt, widely used here before the war...well, people must do without them."

"There's a shortage of so many things we've always taken for granted," said Mrs. Willoughby. "I can't even get a new ribbon for my typewriter. How were things in the States when you left, Mr. de Thoranne?"

"That was a few months ago," said Jacques. "There were no shortages, and everything was in abundant supply. There was a pick-up in business, particularly in that part of industry which made war material. There was also a vague feeling of uneasiness among many citizens who wondered if the U.S. could forever stay on the sidelines during this war."

"You're our latest arrival from England," said Mrs. Pembleton. "How did you find things there?"

"Plenty of shortages," said Jacques. "Almost everything was rationed, from petrol to sugar. Many items which were not rationed, such as lipstick, were almost unobtainable, and the little there was did not seem satisfactory—at least according to the women to whom I talked. They were also unhappy about the quality of the stockings they were able to obtain after waiting long lines at the shops."

"How did you find the morale?" asked Mr. Pembleton.

"It was good," said Jacques. "I believe that by bombing England, Hitler has strengthened Britain's resolve to win the war. There is also a cautious hope that Hitler will be stopped somewhere in Russia, despite his initial victories and an unspoken, foggy dream that some day America will be drawn in. In the meantime Britain will do her best to muddle through."

After breakfast Mr. Willoughby said, "We can't let you go through here without showing you the pagan tribes, something you will not see anywhere else in the world."

They went to Bukuru by car and then walked through the cacti. In those few miles on foot, they went back some three thousand years in time. They regressed from the age of mechanized man who killed his own kind with shells, bombs, and torpedoes, to this peaceful primitive village, where natives who owned nothing but a minuscule mud hut with a thatched roof lived in peace with their neighbors. Their wardrobe consisted of a loincloth for men and for the women a kind of flat hat, which was attached to the backside. This hat was about the size of a frying pan, made of leaves and held together by their long stems with the handle jogging up and down at every step.

There was no war in Nigeria. War was on the news. The BBC blared this news every day to those who would listen. Few did, but even those who didn't listen were jarred out of their complacency when on Monday, December 8, 1941, the BBC stunned the world by announcing that Japan had attacked Pearl Harbor with catastrophic loss of life and had declared war on Britain.

The automobile was the only practical way to travel from Jos to Fort Lamy. An enterprising Syrian had set up a trucking service between the two cities. His business depended largely on the good will of the colonial powers: England in Nigeria and the Free French Chad. The favors he distributed to influential administrators on both sides of the border ensured a trouble-free transportation system.

When Jacques presented a requisition drawn up by the district officer in Jos, a green Chevrolet semi pick-up was immediately put at his disposal. The boss himself, Shaheen, would drive.

On December 10, 1941, at 5:00 A.M. the two men left in the black of night; by 6:00 A.M. the darkness had faded into a glorious red dawn. They had traveled about thirty miles.

"If you want, mister," said Shaheen, "I can take you to Fort Lamy tonight."

"No thanks," said Jacques. "I've made arrangements to stop at the residence of the district officer in Maiduguri."

"That's fine. Maiduguri's a little more than half way. It's just under six hundred miles by road from Jos to Fort Lamy, and about three hundred fifty miles to Maiduguri."

The road wound through dense bush which thinned from time to time. What did not thin, though, was the density of the local population. Vast numbers of natives were scattered along the road, almost without interruption. Where the concentration of mud huts increased markedly, the area became a town.

Leaving Bauchi to the east, Shaheen followed the track to Dasaso. Progress was slow. Of course Shaheen stopped every time he encountered one of his many trucks, heralded distance by the cloud of reddish-brown dust churned up along their path.

In late morning Shaheen stopped at Potiskum, a village of mud huts, for something to eat. While he went to transact some trucking business, an employee took Jacques to a rest house serving Syrian food—eggs cooked in a horrible-looking sauce. The mere sight and smell of it made Jacques feel sick. The employee seemed hurt when Jacques declined to eat. He said that he had a headache and would be content with two oranges. He wondered how people could survive on such awful stuff.

By 5:00 P.M. the twelve-hour ride ended in Maiduguri, where Shaheen delivered his traveler to the district officer's home. Mr. Neven greeted him cordially. "We shall be delighted to put you up for the night and to have you as our guest for dinner."

Jacques thanked Mr. Neven for his hospitality, adding, "I've heard no news all day. Is anything new?"

119

"I'm afraid there is," said the district officer, "and it's not good. Two of our most powerful battleships, *Prince of Wales* and *Repulse*, have been sunk in the Far East by the Japanese. There's a heavy loss of life."

"How did it happen?" asked Jacques.

"I don't know," said Neven. "There were no details."

"We seem to be going from one setback to another," said Jacques. 'We've been living with our heads in the sand for years, and now we're paying the price."

"A high price, too," said Neven. "In the meantime life here continues as in the past. Would you like to attend a meeting of natives tonight? You can get an idea of how we apply colonial rule. Before the meeting ends, we'd welcome a few comments about America, if make them."

"Of course I will," said Jacques.

This meeting of the average citizens was conducted in the local *hauser* language, in a public square known as the big yard. It was followed by another meeting at the school, where the more educated native clerks could listen to the news and Jacques' comments in English. Most of them had a good sense of humor. All wanted to know what life was like in America and what was going on since she had come into the war. Jacques told them how Americans lived and gave a few details about their industrial power, which he said would eventually decide the outcome of the war, to the loud applause of the natives present.

Jacques left Maiduguri early the next morning for the last lap of his journey to Fort Lamy. The car bumped and bounced over the rough dirt track which varied in width from fifteen to one hundred fifty feet. It was an endless unraveling of holes and ruts, of sand piles and stones, winding through the timeless bush, punctured here and there with wide open spaces.

In one of those clearings, Jacques got his first glimpse of the local amazons, completely nude, riding bareback on black bulls; they were armed with poison darts, which they fired through blow tubes. They guided their steeds off the track at the sight of the oncoming car.

"Keep the windows of the car closed as we pass these women," warned the driver.

By noon the travelers reached the border of the French colony and entered Fort Foureau, on the west bank of the Chari River. The river was several hundred yards wide at this point, and there was no bridge across it, but there was a ferry consisting of two barges, assembled catamaran-style with thick boards fastened to each barge to form a platform large enough to carry one vehicle. The whole contraption was towed by a third barge, propelled by a gasoline motor without radiator or circulation pump. The engine was cooled by water drawn from the river in a can suspended by a chain. A native, as black as coal, filled the can in the river and poured the water into a reservoir made from an old gasoline tank. The water was then piped into the motor from where it was discharged hot into the river.

It took some twenty-five minutes for this primitive contraption to reach the opposite bank. Primitive it was. No anchor, no life jackets, no means of escape if the thing were to sink. All around, crocodiles were on watch.

Lieutenant Catan, a friend of Lebreton and the head of the Free French Commission in Freetown, was in charge of the border on the east bank of the Chari River. Living in this wilderness, he was thrilled to receive visitors from the outside world and invited them both to lunch.

It was a welcome invitation; they were very hungry. Jacques handed Catan the letter prepared by Lebreton and introduced himself.

"You need no introduction," said Catan. "We've heard your broadcasts over the *Empire Program.*"

"I came to report on the activities of the Free French in Chad," said Jacques. "You may not have much to report," said Catan.

As they sat down to lunch, Catan briefed his guests on the situation in Fort Lamy. All was not well on the east side of the Chari River.

"The Free French in London have put Lapie in charge here," said Catan. "He's not a leader."

"Isn't he a former deputy of the French Parliament?" asked Jacques. "That's correct," said Catan.

"That's correct," said Catan. "He's a politician. He settles disputes by talking to each party separately and telling each one he's right. He satisfies no one. Recently he infuriated the American military attaché, Cunningham, so much that Cunningham walked out of the residency where he was staying, at ten o'clock at night, and went to stay with the military residence of Colonel Leclerc."

"What was the argument about?" asked Jacques.

"Lapie was mum about it," said Catan. "Remember, don't ask him for anything. He'll say yes and do nothing. Both civilians and military are vying for control. The result is no one knows where responsibility lies or who controls what."

The Syrian, Catan, and Jacques lunched quietly in the torrid heat under the shade of a tall tree in front of Catan's Spartan dwelling. The men were enjoying coffee when a cloud dust on the track a couple of hundred yards away announced the arrival of two trucks, one apparently in tow.

"Excuse me for a moment," said Shaheen anxiously. "There seems to be a problem with a part of my fleet."

"I'm glad that we can speak confidentially for a few minutes," said Catan. "Lebreton tells me I can trust you. I'm telling you this so you can pass it on to the British. The most modern part of the French fleet, about eighty to ninety ships, which they call the *Flotte de Haute Mer*, is at anchor in Toulon, France's naval port on the Mediterranean. It's under the control of Admiral de Laborde."

"I had no idea there were so many warships there," said Jacques.

"Admiral de Laborde is violently anti-British. He has proposed a plan to the Vichy government and to the Germans to recapture Free French territory in Africa, Chad particularly."

"How on earth do you know this?" asked Jacques.

"I used to be communications officer in Toulon. I managed to get transferred to Dakar. From there I was able to get to British-controlled territory. Don't ask me how."

"I understand," said Jacques.

"My girlfriend is secretary to Admiral de Laborde," said Catan. "She types all his correspondence. One day when she was filing, she came across a handwritten letter the Admiral had addressed to Admiral Darlan, who controls the French navy and is a power in the Vichy government. It described Laborde's plan to recapture Chad. It estimated the amount of equipment the Germans would have to supply—tanks particularly; it proposed the creation of an African legion of volunteers, French officers, NCOs, and native soldiers, for a total of fifteen to twenty thousand men, and finally, that the whole project be under the supreme command of Field Marshal Rommel. My girlfriend hates the Germans. She was absolutely shocked."

"Catan," said Jacques, "that's an enormous undertaking. It will take months to prepare. When did you hear about this?"

"Just before I got to Dakar in March. I haven't mentioned this to anyone in Chad. Most of them are opportunists and will side with whoever wins the war. Besides, they don't know how to keep their mouths closed."

"I'll pass it on to the right person when it can be done safely without revealing any sources."

"Fine," said Catan. "Have you any information that ties in with what I've told you?"

"Yes, I do," said Jacques. "The Pétain government is building airfields in various parts of Vichy-controlled territory in Africa."

"I've heard the same thing," said Catan. "In any case I've made arrangements to take off to Nigeria if Vichy invades Chad.'

The return of Shaheen put an end to the conversation.

"Mr. de Thoranne," he said, "I do not want to deliver you too late to Fort Lamy. Are you ready to leave now?"

They thanked their host for his hospitality and got on their way.

Lapie, the politician, received de Thoranne cordially and insisted he stay at the residency. "I'm not popular because I'm an iconoclast. I'm trying to break tradition here. It's not easy. These military people think they're the bosses and refuse to recognize civilian rule. I've communicated repeatedly with London but can't get a clear answer. I doubt that Colonel Leclerc, who is in charge of the military here, will receive you because you stopped here first."

Lapie's assumption was correct. Leclerc saw no need for a war correspondent. He didn't care what America thought of the Free French. He wanted soldiers. Who needed journalists?

Jacques decided to leave Fort Lamy without delay. It was an awful place anyway and consisted mainly of an agglomeration of mud huts, surrounding something called a European town: a palace for the governor, a shack called a post office, and a hotel, at least by name.

Jacques was lucky enough to dispense with its services. Lapie was about to leave for Fort Archambault, and he invited Jacques to stay at the residency as long as he wished.

Before he left Jacques wanted to see the parts of Fort Lamy he hadn't had a chance to visit. To do that he had to enter his cameras. That required preparing innumerable forms in duplicate, which took the better part of the afternoon. Final Picut, the mayor (he bore the title of *administrateur maire* gave him the permit to carry the cameras. "But don't use them except for civilian objectives, at least when the military are around," Picut warned.

"I'll leave them in my bag," said Jacques.

"You'll be safe that way," said Picut. "A few weeks ago I gave an American a permit, and while he was photographing the barracks, the military confiscated his camera. It made quite a fuss. Finally I settled it with Colonel Leclerc, who told me unequivocally that I'd better remember that the military are in control here. When I asked Jean de Lanne, his ADC, if the Colonel would receive you, he said, 'Tell that man that Leclerc has no time to see him, and the sooner he gets out of here, the better."

"Lapie told me as much," said Jacques, "and I'm leaving in a couple of days. I've already made a reservation on the auto service for Fort Archambault."

"I might as well show you all there is to see. Let's tour the town. It won't take long.

"May I tour the barracks?" asked Jacques, "Without taking any pictures, of course."

"I wouldn't recommend it," said Picut. "With Leclerc, no one can tell what might happen."

Picut and his guest drove through the native village. Mud huts had a single circular room with a thatched roof in the form of a cone, with a hole at the top to vent the smoke the wood fire which was lit in the evening on the dirt floor. Beds were a wood frame supporting a web of meshed stalks—small protection against the cool at night.

Much of Fort Lamy's food supply came from vegetable gardens managed by the city. Carrots, beans, tomatoes, yams, what have you, grew in neat patches without a weed in sight. "We must rely on ourselves here," said Picut. "All our vegetables are grown in gardens like these. There are plenty of bananas and tropical fruits, and there's always a good supply of fish from the river. Of course manufactured articles are something else."

"How about clothes?" asked Jacques.

"They're hard to get," said Picut, "but as you've seen, the natives live practically nude. For Europeans it's another matter.'

"How about soap?" asked Jacques.

"We make our own," said Picut. "Now I'm going to take you to see something interesting. Get in the car."

Picut drove the car cautiously along what seemed like a dirt road laced with gullies. He swerved continuously to avoid boulders and holes deep enough to entomb the vehicle while the occupants of the car hit the roof of the Citroen when an oversize bump couldn't be avoided. Finally Picut brought the car to a stop a short distance from the east bank of the Chari River.

"See those two boats in the middle of the river?" said Picut. "What do you think of them?"

"They look in pretty good shape," said Jacques, "but they have too much draft for this shallow river."

"You're right: They won't be able to move until the rainy season. Then they can bring in supplies from Fort Archambault."

"What supplies in particular?" asked Jacques.

"All the heavy stuff," said Picut, "particularly fuel, parts for cars and trucks when available, ammunition, and other supplies for the military."

"Anything for the civilian population?" asked Jacques.

"That's a good question," said Picut. "That issue sparked a furious conflict last year between Leclerc and Lapie. Lapie wanted to bring in food, Leclerc ammunition. Leclerc prevailed. The boats brought in very little food. Leclerc isn't popular. Even his men call him the Führer."

"Picut," said Jacques, "I share Leclerc's concern and approve his decision. Don't forget that Chad shares a long border with Niger, which is Vichy-controlled territory. Who knows what those people might do?"

"Holloa! Holloa!" exclaimed Picut suddenly. "What's this? What's going on here?" A group of about a dozen planes was rapidly approaching.

"Nothing good," said Jacques. "Those planes have no business here. I'll bet they're...."

"What?"

"...going to bomb us," said Jacques. "Here they come. See the bombs falling? Quick Picut, get down in this gully. Quick! Lie down."

There was a muffled roar. Both men were showered with a rain of debris and stones and smothered in a fog of dust.

'That was a close call," said Jacques after the dust cleared. "Do your ears hurt?'

"I thought they were being punctured," said Picut feebly. "I feel shaky and weak, especially in the legs. My knees feel woolly and ready to collapse." After a while, he said to Jacques, "I seem to have lost all energy...but you...you don't seem affected,..."

"You wouldn't have said that if you had seen me after my first really close call. It was in London, at two in the morning, as I was coming out of the BBC. I was just as shaken then as you are now. After that first experience, I more or less got used to it."

"Are the planes gone?"

"I think so," said Jacques.

"What's all that noise, then?" asked Picut.

"They must have hit the ammunition dump," said Jacques, "and it's continuing to explode."

"What were those planes?" asked Picut. "They didn't seem to have any markings?"

"No, they just had camouflage, but they were made in Germany. They were Heinkels 111 Ps."

Jacques helped the official out of the gully. His pith helmet had protected his hair, but his clothes were covered with dust. His face was pale. He staggered awkwardly up the steep side of the gully. When he reached level ground, he walked slowly and hesitantly.

"That bomb fell about one hundred feet from where we were," said Jacques. If the bomb had been released a fraction of a second later, we wouldn't be standing here talking. Obviously the attack was aimed at the Fort Lamy military installations."

"Probably," said Picut, "but the bombs that fell here were far off the target."

"You're assuming that the only target was the military complex," said Jacques. "I believe the pilot was aiming at the ships, and he came awfully close to hitting them. The bombs straddled the target, one bomb on the other side of the river, two on this side. This one just missed your car, too. It's covered with dust and debris, but doesn't appear to be damaged. Want me to drive?"

"No," said Picut. "I'm still groggy and weak, but I'm a little better now. It's my knees. They feel...I feel as though they're going to collapse."

"It'll probably take you a day or two to get over it," said Jacques. "A good night's rest will restore the energy that's been drained from your body."

As they approached the base, they could see the fuel dump burning fiercely and pouring a huge column of black smoke into the blue sky. The hangar housing Fort Lamy's two planes was still smoking, and the ammunition was still spluttering.

Fort Lamy was knocked out as an effective base. Jacques was unable to access the full extent of the damage as Colonel Leclerc had ordered the whole area cordoned off.

"Where would you like me to drop you off?" asked Picut.

"I'm staying at the residency," said Jacques. "I'll wash up and go to the hotel for dinner; I'm not that hungry anyway."

"Why don't you come to my place for dinner?" asked Picut. "My wife will be at her bridge party, and there'll be just the two of us. It will be a very plain dinner—nothing fancy."

Jacques accepted his invitation with pleasure. After washing up, changing clothes, and removing as much as possible most traces of the dust shower he'd received in the bombing, he walked over to the official's home. "I'm glad you're here," said Picut. "It's nice to have some companionship after a thing like that. From where do you think those planes came?"

"Without doubt from Vichy-controlled territory," said Jacques. "We can take a good guess if you have a map of the area and a compass."

Picut brought both and unfolded the map on the table.

"Put one leg of the compass at Fort Lamy," said Jacques, "and draw a circle to scale four hundred miles from here."

"Why four hundred miles?" asked Picut.

"Because Heinkels with a bomb load have a range of about eight hundred miles," said Jacques.

Picut anchored the compass at Fort Lamy and drew a circle around it.

"Those planes," said Jacques, "could have come from any area in Niger encompassed by that semicircle. Your guess is as good as mine—Zinder, Nguigmi, Agadem?"

"There are rumors that airfields are being built in several areas within that circle. I'll pay a lot more attention to those rumors in the future."

"The immediate problem," said Jacques, "is to replace the supplies of fuel, ammunition, etc., which were destroyed in today's attack. If the roads between here and Fort Archambault are anything like what I've seen between Jos and Fort Lamy, you have a problem."

"They are," said Picut.

"That means that all the heavy stuff must be brought in by boat. Lucky the boats weren't hit. When will the river be navigable again?"

"During the next rainy season," said Picut.

"When's that?" asked Jacques.

"From August to November," said Picut.

"What? We're in December now. Do you mean to say those boats can't move until next August—eight months?"

"That's correct," said Picut. "When you get to Fort Archambault, you'll know why the river is the only practical way to haul large supplies."

"Does navigability of all rivers in these areas of Africa depend on the period of rainy seasons?" asked Jacques.

"Generally speaking, I would say yes," said Picut. "With the exception of the Congo River, only two of the tributaries, the Sangha and to some extent the Ubangi, are still navigable at their low."

Chapter XI

There was one hotel—of sorts—in Fort Lamy—Amadani's. Jacques went there for breakfast: a loaf of French bread, crusty, rock hard, a superior tooth breaker, eatable only after a long soak in tepid tea. No butter, some jam, enough of which to starve. Jacques paid the bill and left with an empty stomach—nothing new for him in these parts, where the appearance or taste of the food made it prudent to abstain.

Jacques was discovering that abstention wasn't necessary at the homes of French colonial officials. Their food was always good. At Fort Lamy in 1941, the pleasures of life were terribly restricted and were, for many, limited to what the French called the pleasures of the table. Raw ingredients were produced locally, and all that was needed was expert preparation. The French were good at that.

Jacques was invited to lunch at the home of Delmas, the acting governor. Madame Delmas greeted her guest cordially. He was someone from the outside world, with different views from the colonials who'd been confined to Fort Lamy for as long as four years.

Madame Delmas was a distinguished, elegant woman, apparently in her late forties. She had dark hair, cut just above shoulder level; big brown eyes shaded by heavy eyebrows; refined features; and a pale skin obviously never exposed to the fierce tropical sun. She wore a loosely fitting, thin, blue and white knee-length dress and no stockings. She had supervised the preparation of a meal of fresh river fish, served with a tangy sauce, followed by chicken and vegetables and a dessert of exquisite tropical fruits spiked with a potent alcoholic liquor brewed locally. At lunch the main subject of conversation was a discussion of the confrontation between Governor Lapie's civilians and Colonel Leclerc's military.

"Lapie is a part-time governor," said Delmas. "He's away most of the time. When he's gone, I'm in charge, and the conflict erupts. The military have the power of the gun, so they usually win. Now, though, that power has been curtailed. The bombing destroyed most of their gasoline and practically all their ammunition. There's no way to bring in more supplies except by truck, so the priority goes to tank trucks. With the water in the river so low, boats can't navigate for the next eight months."

"There must be a better way to supply Fort Lamy than through Brazzaville," said Jacques.

"There is," said Delmas. "Supplies could come routed through Accra in Gold Coast, but it requires trucks and bridges, and the materials are not there at the present time. Everything must be improvised. No one believed war would break out. When it did, only Germany was ready."

"There's a new equation in the war since Pearl Harbor," said Jacques.

"We won't feel that for a while. Meanwhile we have to hold out. Fort Lamy can't defend itself since the raid. There's nothing left, no ammunition, no gasoline, not even a reconnaissance plane," said Delmas.

"I'd like to continue this conversation, but I've got to get you on your way to Brazzaville. As you travel you will see that in French Equatorial Africa, everything depends on communications."

Delmas drove Jacques to the point of departure of the overland auto service. There were four cars, all Chevrolets. Each carried a driver and five passengers. The caravan traveled single file over a dirt track. Progress was slow, and the travelers reached Loumia, the first stop, after dark. They couldn't see much of the village of mud huts; the only light at the rest site came from the mantles of kerosene lanterns, which cast a greenish glow over the dinner table where the travelers found some rest and food.

Sleeping quarters were primitive. Beds were rough wooden frames with mattresses of woven reeds installed under a pitched thatched roof with a dirt floor.

The night was chilly; mosquitoes were everywhere. Thanks to his mosquito netting and his sleeping bag, Jacques was not too uncomfortable, but he couldn't sleep. The natives in the village a few yards away coughed from dusk to dawn. Wood fires burning in the center of the native huts spewed much smoke and little heat.

Jacques got up early and watched the preparation of the morning coffee. The cook drew water from a barrel fed by a rainspout. The water was filthy, thick with mosquito larvae. It was warmed—not even boiled—over a charcoal fire and poured, tepid, over the ground coffee. *Ugh*, thought Jacques, of coffee made from a few beans and thousands of mosquito larvae.

Jacques took a small Primus camp stove and an aluminum saucepan from his rucksack, filtered the dirty water through a clean handkerchief, and boiled it for fifteen minutes, much to the amusement of his fellow travelers. With that water he made some tea, hoping it wouldn't be too poisonous.

The caravan got under way at 6:00 A.M. By leaving early it reached its destination around 2:00 P.M. avoiding the worst of the day's heat. In the morning it was uncomfortable. In the afternoon it was unbearable. The cars traveled with windows open, smothering passengers, even in the first car, with the red sand, churned up from the dirt track. Visibility was nil; drivers just guessed where to go.

The fine reddish dust of the dirt track penetrated everything: eyes, ears, nose, throat, and lungs. The travelers coughed, sneezed, and tried to wet their parched lips with dry tongues. Everyone's eyes were red and watery. Wiping them with dust-covered handkerchiefs only added to the misery. Blinking was like rubbing eyeballs with sandpaper. One woman with dark hair became a redhead as the trip proceeded. All were caked with a dust paste wherever sweat was abundant: behind ears, under arms, in the groin. Clothes, shoes, and belongings were caked with dust. The holes, bumps, and ruts in the track seemed never to end.

There was some relief from the dust and motion when the cars came to a river and waited for the ferry—the usual catamaran style, many of them drawn to the opposite bank by hand. Few ferries could handle trucks, so trucks had to make great detours to cross the rivers over bridges. After crossing the Bahr Illi on a ferry consisting of three hand-drawn barges, the caravan arrived at Bousso.

At 2:00 P.M. the thermometer stood at 99°! All the travelers, except Jacques, slept; he boiled water which he stored in his only container, a thermos flask. That meant drinking hot water in the searing heat. That boiled water was still hot enough to make tea the next morning.

The caravan left Bousso at 6:00 A.M. and pulled into Fort Archambault at noon. Here, the rest house consisted of tents with a double roof nestled under tall trees about two hundred yards from the Chari River. Even here the heat was oppressive.

Fort Archambault was a showpiece for AEF and French colonization. The land had been planted with banana, orange, and lime trees, but the produce fields were the real achievement: potatoes, tomatoes, carrots, beans, peas, eggplant, and cucumbers.

Governor Lapie, Chief of Cabinet Mérot, and Chief of Administration Cassamatta organized a party at the Governor's residence. Minguet, head of the STOL (general store), produced from his prewar stock a couple of adequately chilled bottles of *bière de la Meuse*, which was served only on special occasions.

"We're pretty safe here," Lapie told Jacques. "To invade us from Vichy-held territory would entail extraordinary communication problems. The territory of Niger, of course, is controlled by Vicky, but they have only a skeleton force with practically no troops, no equipment, and few trucks. There is not much danger of invasion here."

"I agree," said Jacques. "The main danger is from paratroopers. From what I've seen, there's not an antiaircraft gun anywhere in Africa."

"That's correct," said Lapie. "There are none."

"That was why Fort Lamy was bombed with impunity this week," said Jacques.

"What? Fort Lamy was bombed?"

"Yes. Didn't Colonel Leclerc tell you?" Jacques asked.

"Mr. de Thoranne," said Lapie, "there is no communication between Colonel Leclerc and me. What was the damage?"

"The ammunition dump was destroyed and some fuel tanks were set afire. Both of their planes were gutted. The only defenses were the rifles of the army. They fired at the planes, but if there were hits, they were not obvious. It was believed the planes came from somewhere in Niger."

"When I escaped from Vichy territory," said Minguet, "the French in charge had orders to set up a number of airfields. The exact locations were to be disclosed later."

For the travelers Fort Archambault was a milestone in the journey from Fort Lamy to Bangui. The better part of the harrowing drive on dirt tracks was behind them, and there remained only the two-day trip from Fort Archambault to Bangui, where they were to board the riverboat for a leisurely cruise down the Ubangi River.

The four cars that came from Fort Lamy were joined by three more at Fort Archambault to accommodate the increased number of passengers, including several women. The party had the same cook and food handler, both of whom traveled in a truck carrying the supplies and food—meat or fish, vegetables, and fruits. The truck would leave the village, where the travelers had spent the night, two hours ahead of the convoy of cars. Usually it arrived where lunch was to be served in time to do the cooking, set table, and serve the meal when the travelers arrived.

The day the caravan left Loumia, the truck broke down, and the cook and the food arrived at the next stop only a few minutes before the travelers. Jacques toured the kitchen, camera in hand. The stove was made from two rusty five-gallon gasoline cans from which both ends had been removed—no need for gas or electric ranges in these parts. Notwithstanding, meals were always good and tasty. What intrigued Jacques particularly was the preparation of the excellent mayonnaise, which was served each day at noon with hearts of palm. It was light and fluffy with a very peculiar taste.

While the assistant lit the charcoal fires in the stoves, the cook went to work on the mayonnaise. He was a heavy man with a chubby head, thick lips, and a wide mouth, baring now and then the single tooth left in the upper jaw.

His ears were thick and wide at the lower end and slanted into a point which disappeared into a crop of bushy black hair. He sat on the ground, tailorwise, his legs folded under him, holding the wooden mortar in which he vigorously beat the mayonnaise with a homemade wooden pestle in each hand.

Jacques readied his camera for a shot but couldn't see the source of the oil until the cook put both pestles in his left hand, continued to beat the mix, seized the bottle of oil in his right hand, put it to his lips, and filled his mouth. Then he placed the bottle on the ground, mixed oil and saliva with energetic movement of cheeks and tongue, and gradually dribbled the emulsion into the mortar. Jacques pressed the camera's release, but the camera's shutter, apparently horrified by the scene before it, refused to record for posterity the African manufacturing technique of producing fluffy, tasty mayonnaise.

At lunch, which was excellent as usual, Jacques passed the hearts of palm and mayonnaise to his neighbor without helping himself, to the astonishment the table. "What happened?" they asked.

"Ah!" said Jacques, "I must watch myself. My liver is kicking up," he added, patting the lower part of his thoracic cage with his right hand.

The explanation produced no surprise. In Africa, when a colonist was sick, local physicians usually diagnosed the trouble as "hepatic dysfunction."

One of the women who joined the travelers at Fort Archambault sat next to Jacques and immediately showed interest in him. Here was an American who spoke French—and good French at that, almost like a native. "How useful it is to communicate," she said. How she regretted her failure to learn English in school. How nice it would be to speak that language fluently.

She was of medium height, slender, and of average build. Her features were regular, her skin pale, her brown hair cut just below shoulder level. She wore a short-sleeved, thin, whitish dress, with nothing under it.

She was divorced. Her husband had been too interested in native girls. Since her divorce, she had slept with men of many nations, but never with an American, especially one who spoke French. The woman was refined and articulate, almost distinguished. She had a pleasant personality and was enticing and seductive, but Jacques was too wary to accept the not-too-subtle proposal.

When he studied biochemistry, bacteriology had been his hobby. He'd taken extra courses in the subject. While others sat in cafés playing bridge, he spent hours examining bacteria under the microscope. He was considered an expert by students and professors.

What kind of vaginal flora proliferated in this woman who had slept with so many different nations, but who had, so far, been deprived of Americans—particularly of any speaking French? Jacques knew exactly what he wasn't going to do, but he didn't want to hurt the woman. He felt sorry for her, she exuded an underlying sadness and was drifting, with nothing to hang on to. He didn't want her to hang to him, but he wanted to put her off in a nice way.

"There's not much privacy in these rest houses along the way," Jacques said to her. "I don't know about you, but I can't feel relaxed in such an environment. Making love is so intimate...."

"I understand that well," she said. "This is the kind of man a woman can really love and enjoy."

"All right," said Jacques, "then let's wait until we get on the boat."

The rest house at Boucca was a copy of the previous ones; however the forty-odd travelers were squeezed into a much smaller space. The bunks were only a couple of feet apart, under the sputtering light of a kerosene lantern with a broken mantle. The travelers chose bunks as best they could.

Jacques' nearest neighbors were the woman who had slept with men of many nations and a thin man with a stubby mustache and a loud snore. It was not so much the lack of privacy that marked this stop of the journey (travelers were used to that); it was the noise. Inside was cacophony of snores, burps, groans; at one end of the rest house, gurgles of someone vomiting; somewhere in the middle, moans of a woman in the throes of lovemaking; not to mention all the other discordant sounds humans can make. Against this background a chorus of mattresses crunched under the weight of restless bodies. Outside the relentless coughs in the native villages, and further away, the dismal wails of hyenas. There were no showers and nothing deserving the name of toilet.

Jacques slept in his clothes and kept his shoes on, unwilling to put his bare feet on dirt floor, which he surmised was probably infested with chiggers and other parasites of the jungle. Clothes were welcome when the chill of the night and the clammy air of the river crept into the rest house.

When departure time finally came, Jacques got up and assembled his belongings, verifying that none had grown wings during the night. His female neighbor changed from warm nightclothes to her day gear, baring an elegant, slender body. She displayed it leisurely, unconcerned by the lack of privacy.

The caravan started just before dawn. The woman took a seat next to Jacques in the lead Chevrolet. She was a pleasant, intelligent companion. She said she had lived for years in AEF and acquired much knowledge of the land, its natives, and its politics. She loved to show her knowledge and appreciated a good listener.

"Even in Fort Archambault," she told Jacques, "there were many in the colonial administration who remained loyal to Pétain and the Vichy government. These people are bureaucrats; they consider their jobs first."

She told Jacques about a man she had met a month earlier. He had managed to get out of France, go to Algeria, and make his way to Dakar. There he went through the bush to British territory and eventually ended up among the Free French.

"You should have heard what he had to tell about the shooting of hostages when German soldiers are attacked or killed. The Nazis make the French authorities choose the hostages to be shot. Can you imagine what will happen if the British win the war?"

"Somewhat vaguely, I can," said Jacques.

"Now that America is in the war," she continued, "some sitting on the fence or working with the Germans are beginning to have doubts. They are not so sure they are right."

"You meet many different people here," said Jacques.

"I do," she said. She told Jacques that she had served as guide for a South African commander visiting the area. He spoke enough French to make himself understood and had told her about the vast quantity of diamonds at the mouth of the Orange River. He had found one himself and sold it for seventy-three hundred dollars. He told her how De Beers controlled the diamond market and roped off the entire area to prevent the collapse of the market and AEF and particularly the Belgian Congo are rich in low-grade black diamonds, which are essential for many industrial operations.

Jacques wondered who this woman was who was so well informed and at what she was driving. He was ever more suspicious, yet ever more interested in what she had to say—true or false, it was worth recording. So far all he knew about her was that her name was Gisèle.

At dinner that evening there was the usual laugh when the travelers saw Jacques boiling water. One man told him sarcastically that he had lived long in the region and never had any serious complications—just a few bouts of diarrhea from time to time.

"From the point of view of the bacteriologist," Jacques said, "I find it hard to understand how you people can avoid infections after drinking coffee prepared with such contaminated water."

"If you were to live here long enough," they told Jacques, "you'd get used to it, too."

The next morning the caravan seemed tired and departed sluggishly. The road was shrouded in a thick, woolly mist, which hung over the silent land, a mist so thick that native huts a few yards away were barely discernible—huts where the natives shivered and coughed.

Beyond Fort Archambault the landscape changed to tall rubber trees, palm trees, and a thick undercover bush. The track through it was narrow; it was not quite as rough as before, but just as dusty. The caravan and its occupants, covered from head to foot with fine red sand, arrived in the afternoon at Bangui, on the Ubangi River.

When they entered the Hotel Pain, the manager had an urgent message for Mr. de Thoranne from Governor Lapie, who was delighted to provide him with a place to stay.

Mr. Latrille, Lapie's chief of cabinet, a huge towering man, received Jacques cordially and conducted him to a cozy apartment, which he had all to himself. It had a clean bathroom and a shower. For the first time since leaving Nigeria, Jacques washed and changed to clean clothes. He enjoyed a welcome rest from the brutal hammering of the dirt track, the unsanitary conditions and meals, the restless nights in makeshift beds, and the intolerable, invisible, and uncatchable sand fleas.

The governor gave a dinner at his residence the night the caravan arrived. Guests included several local notables, a South African major on his way to Stanleyville, an administrator from Fort Archambault and his wife, and an Englishwoman and her husband who managed the general store in Bangui. As usual conversation dealt mainly with the war, the problems it caused the expatriates, the lack of communications with relatives in the motherland, and the shortages of items usually taken for granted, such as mantles for kerosene pressure lamps—a main source of concern as there was no electricity in Bangui.

There was, however, no shortage of food. The colonists had taught the natives how to grow vegetables. Almost any vegetable grown in Europe was available. There was also no shortage of that fuel so necessary to so many: alcohol—whiskey, beer, liqueur, and even wine.

After dinner the chauffeur drove Jacques back to his apartment. There was no light there, not even a candle. He really appreciated his flashlight, but didn't let it shine too long: batteries were unobtainable! He undressed fast and snuggled into the clean sheets where there were no sand fleas.

Jacques didn't visit the other travelers' rooms at Hotel Pain, but he assumed his apartment was luxury compared with them. He didn't, however, spend much time in the apartment. His *ordre de mission* from London, his recent stay in England, and his background from the United States made him a much-wanted guest by many local colonists who had not been out of Bangui since the start of the war. For them someone from the outside world was uncensored news.

Jacques lunched the next day with the South African major and dined that evening with the governor. Before dinner he was introduced to Duplessis, in charge of Brazzaville's Ministry of Information for the Free French. Duplessis was on his way to Fort Lamy to see firsthand what damage the bombing had done to the military base.

"I'm very glad to meet you, Mr. de Thoranne," he said to Jacques. "For weeks now we have asked London to send us a man articulate in the English language. There's a job waiting for you in Brazzaville. Until now our English broadcasts beamed toward the United States have been delivered by an American journalist, a correspondent for the United Press. He has been transferred and is leaving early next month. You are arriving just in time."

Officially Jacques had never heard of this assignment. It had not been mentioned to him in London. Thanks to d'Huart, he'd been forewarned. Jacques had no intention of remaining in Brazzaville until the end of the war in a position where he was no longer his own master. By now, however, he expected the unexpected and knew he had to deal with it.

"Who should I see when I get to Brazzaville?" he asked, as though this unwanted assignment was no news to him.

"You will have to be approved by General Sicé, who is in charge of the entire Free French operation in French Equatorial Africa, but that is just a formality," said Duplessis. We know of your proficiency in English. We listened regularly to your weekly broadcasts from London, over the *Empire Program.*"

To hell with them! Jacques thought to himself. *To think of the nerve they have to assign me to a position without consulting me.*

Brazzaville would be a trap. Getting out against the will of the local authorities would not be easy. That was on his mind all evening. He joined the conversation now and then. Most of the time he half listened to what was said, and his thoughts were elsewhere. At least he'd have time to think things over. The boat for Brazzaville would not leave for a couple of days. What could he do? Turning back now wasn't possible. Besides, if he did, his main assignment would be a failure. Sir James had warned him to be wary and to use his wits in this dangerous job.

When he went to bed that night, he turned things over in his mind, what his options were and how he could beat the system which had entrapped him. His first priority would be to get out of Brazzaville, where the officials could claim him as a French national. That meant living in Leopoldville on the south bank of the Congo River, in Belgian territory, where he was a British subject.

On his last evening in Bangui, an English couple, the Youngs, invited him to dinner. He admired her knowledge and control of French. She spoke it fluently and faultlessly, almost like a native—a rare thing among the English. He sought their advice about where to stay in Brazzaville at least temporarily.

"Oh, don't stay there," said Young. "That's an awful dump. Go across the river to Leopoldville. There's a pretty nice hotel there, the ABC. We have a good friend in Leopoldville who runs the SEDEC, the general store. I'll give you a note for him, and I would ask you to deliver a small package. It is quite confidential, concerns business, and I don't want to send it by the mail; that's too unreliable. His name is James Goodridge. He will be a great help to you in finding a decent place to stay."

Since arriving in Bangui, Jacques had not eaten a meal at the Hotel Pain, except breakfast the first morning. He hadn't seen any of his fellow travelers. He expected to find them assembled at the hotel for breakfast before boarding the riverboat at 7:00 A.M. None were there. *This is strange,* Jacques thought to himself, just as one man of the party appeared, disheveled, unshaven, and very pale.

"Where are our other companions?" Jacques asked the man.

"All in the hospital with dysentery," the man answered. "I thought I was immune, but the same problem hit me during the night, and I'm sure I have a high temperature. You're the only one of us who can travel on the boat. It's your turn to laugh now."

"I don't think it's funny."

"You don't, but we all laughed at you when you boiled your water and took Stovarsol. Let me tell you," said the man, very slowly, "I'd sooner go to the hospital for a week than be bothered with all the precautions you take."

"Have you found out what the problem is? Was the dysentery amoebic or bacterial?"

"It's all the same to me," said the man. "I don't think they're equipped to find that out at this hospital. Besides, they're short of medicine. I said short! Short's not the word. There's no medicine here whatever against dysentery! I went there yesterday to see if I could get some when I felt this coming. I got nothing!"

"Take care of yourself," said Jacques. "Good luck!"

On his way to the river boat, Jacques thought to himself, *That eliminates one problem; I won't have to ward off Gisèle. I feel sorry for her, but no one can constantly defy the laws of physiology without suffering the consequences.*

The primitive city of Bangui lay on the west bank of the Ubangi River, which was a tributary of the much larger Congo. Although the Ubangi was navigable all year round, it could not accommodate the large river boats which plied the Congo. Smaller steamers linked Bangui to Zonga, where travelers to Brazzaville or Leopoldville were transferred to one of the much larger river steamers.

Jacques was the only traveler from Fort Lamy to board *Kobb* that morning for the journey down the river. He arrived shortly before the scheduled time of departure but was informed the ship would be delayed for at least a couple of hours, due to the dense fog. Visibility was reduced to a few feet, making navigation impossible. The fog was so dense, Jacques could barely see beyond the two barges moored on each side of the ship.

The barge on the port side carried an automobile on deck. A unit of native soldiers, known as *tiraileurs*, occupied the barge to starboard. The *tiraileurs* were recruited in the colonies and used in the French army as foot soldiers. They were cooking some foul-smelling meat over a wood fire in a small gasoline drum with both ends removed. The smoke streamed lazily over *Kobb*. The stink was nauseating, but no one dared complain.

Kobb was a relatively small river boat with a paddle wheel astern, driven by a reciprocating steam engine. The ship's flat bottom enabled it to pass through the shallow parts of the river.

When the fog cleared at about 9:00 A.M. the captain, a short, stubby, pot-bellied man with a ruddy face topped by a pith helmet, blew the hooter. The crew detached the moorings and got the ship underway.

The Ubangi River wound through the dense equatorial forest, almost strangled at times by sandbanks, some barely emerging from the water. Navigating this river required experience, skill, and constant attention. The captain himself was at the helm, zigzagging the craft around narrow bends, avoiding invisible sandbanks, and coming to a stop at night or whenever, for any reason, visibility failed.

At Zonga more passengers for Brazzaville boarded a larger craft, *Alphonse Fondère*. 360-ton ship with a six-foot draft and a 450 horsepower reciprocating steam engine with direct drive to the paddle wheel. With the current, speed was about seven miles per hour.

The trip down the Congo River from Zonga to Brazzaville took five to eight days when the weather was fine. It took longer when days were foggy, when nights were cloudy, or when there was no moon. It took unpredictably longer when the captain invited a female passenger to dinner.

When *Kobb* transferred its passengers to *Alphonse Fondère*, an attractive redhead with blue eyes and a shapely body showing conspicuously through a thin white dress with a floral design caught the captain's eye. All the passengers knew where she was invited after dinner when the ship remained moored at Zonga for the night instead of leaving at 4:00 A.M. as scheduled.

The ship had been in service since it was built in 1929. Accommodations were acceptable. There was a good cook on board, and the dining room could hold all the passengers at one time. Civilians and military were divided into groups, seated at separate tables. Jacques soon discovered that both groups were like Gaul, divided into three parts: the pro-Vichy British haters, the pro-Free French, and the neutrals—by far the majority. Mealtime offered an excellent opportunity to judge the feelings of the travelers. Every meal bred conversations and discussions on two main subjects: local conditions, their scandals and corruption, and international conditions, the war, the surrender of France, and the actions of the Vichy government, its policies, and the territories and ships it controlled.

Scandal comments usually started with arguments over who among the women passengers had slept the previous night in the captain's stateroom.

Political arguments usually arose when an aggressive British hater, Krechelle, a Vichy supporter, focused on some outrage perpetrated by the British, such as sinking helpless French navy ships at Mers el Kebir, or when he stated that Hitler was right to exterminate the Jews. "They are the cause of this war," or when France elected Leon Blum, "She signed her death warrant."

A woman from Cameroon added that the Free French government there was "in the hands of the Martiniquais, the Jews, and the Free Masons."

Her immediate neighbor was a young aviation mechanic who escaped from occupied France by crossing into the part still nominally free. There he obtained an assignment for Dakar, where mechanics were badly needed. He volunteered for a job to dismantle a Potez 25 which crashed near the Gambian border. Slipping away from the wreckage at night, he walked through the bush and found his way to Bathurst. From there the British sent him to Free France.

The mechanic remained silent during the heated arguments. Finally, turning to Krechelle, he asked quietly, "Sir, have you spent any time under Nazi occupation?"

"No, I have not," said Krechelle.

"Well then, tell me, sir, what would you think of a government ordered by the Nazis to choose fifty hostages to be shot in retaliation for the killing of three SS Germans by the *maquisards* operating in the countryside? What do you think of an occupier who grabs people off the street and sends them to work in the most exposed jobs in the German factories? I am surprised, sir, that you cannot distinguish facts. The enemy of France is the Nazi occupier, not the English aviators who are bombing Brest to disable the Nazi battle cruisers harbored there. The people in Brest cheered the British planes, and I was one of them. You won't find anyone in Brest agreeing with your attacks on the British."

That comment coming from a man who knew put a damper on the violent attacks on the British, and the discussion turned to more mundane topics.

That evening Bauer, a Free French lieutenant, asked Jacques to join him in his cabin. I heard you say at dinner that, after witnessing all this nonchalance and sloppiness, you could understand the collapse of France. I do not accept that you should speak so disrespectfully of my country. Do you know what respect is?"

"Do you want to start all over again with the same mistakes if the allies win the war?" Jacques asked him. "I find it strange that, as an officer in de Gaulle's forces, you justify Pétain as you have done. I spent several weeks on *Dominé*, a fighting Free French ship, and never heard a word in favor of Vichy."

"Then," answered Bauer, "we have nothing more to say."

They did not say any more, and a few minutes later Jacques joined in a rubber of bridge with three other passengers.

When the river boat reached Brazzaville, Jacques realized that pre-war divisions, which were partly responsible for France's defeat, were still there. He suspected, too, that the German victory over French society had not helped traditional values, at least in territory under colonial administration. Over and over again, he heard repeated, mainly by women, that there was not a single married woman in the colonies who had not had affairs with other men, any more than there was a single married man who had not had affairs with other women, and he was lucky when those affairs were not with native girls infected with gonorrhea or syphilis.

The nine-day river journey gave Jacques some idea what to expect when he stepped off *Alphonse Fondère* into an environment he'd never before seen.

Chapter XII

Alphonse Fondère docked at 10:00 A.M. at the wharf in Brazzaville on the north bank of the Congo. At this point the riverbanks were several miles apart, and the vast expanse of water between was called the Stanley Pool. The south bank was barely visible in the morning haze. Most of the passengers on the boat were colonials who had traveled the route before. They knew the ropes. Jacques did not. When he got off the boat, there was not a taxi to be found. No one was at the wharf to meet him. The air was hot and muggy, and he sensed that the social environment was about the same—certainly unfriendly, perhaps hostile. An hour after the ship docked a taxi appeared. He went to the Hotel Congo-Ocean, reserved a room for the night while the taxi waited, and then went to the British Consulate where George Farr, the consul, received him warmly.

"It's nice to enter into a friendly atmosphere," Jacques said to the consul. "I don't think I'm very popular around here among the Free French!"

"Of course you're not," said Farr. "You're genuine; that makes you suspect amid a group interested only in remaining here in comfort until the end of the war. They are posturing as Free French, but they are just as liable to side with Vichy should the Germans win the war. Before America was in the war, they were sure the Germans would win. Now they are not so sure. You were different. You took sides when a German victory seemed certain. They've heard your broadcasts from London. To many of them, you are suspect. Let me introduce you to Major Black, our military attaché; he will be delighted to meet you."

"I've heard much about you," said Major Black, "and, to this day, you are the only member of the French Diplomatic Service to have refused to stay in the service of the Vichy government. I'll be introducing you to Desjardins, the Free French information officer, and to Karl Bigley, the INS man in Brazzaville, who writes and delivers all the Brazzaville broadcasts beamed to

America. After that I'll take you to lunch. The Congo-Océan is really the only place here to get a decent meal. The hotel itself is horrible, but they have an outstanding cook; you know how fussy the French are about their meals. I'll ask Bigley to join us, and we can all three have lunch there. In the meantime I'll show you Brazzaville."

Brazzaville, four degrees south of the equator, consisted of one long road along the north bank of the Congo River, with decrepit houses and buildings on each side of the road. Behind the houses, away from the river, stood native huts of flimsy walls and thatched roofs, accessible on dirt roads. The climate was terribly hot and humid—so humid that, on most mornings, the south bank of the river was invisible, shrouded in the mist created by the cold night air.

Mosquitoes abounded; fungi attacked the unwary, or merely the unadjusted, and proliferated in the sweat behind the ears, under the arms, and in the groin.

"There you have it," said Black, as they entered the dining room of the Congo-Océan where Bigley was waiting. "Karl, I'd like you to meet Mr. de Thoranne, who arrived from this morning."

'Mr. de Thoranne, welcome to this hellhole!" said Bigley. "You are badly needed! The powers here have no one who can speak decent English. They put all kinds of pressure on me to stay on the job until you arrived."

"I heard nothing of this in London," said Jacques. "I wasn't consulted, nor even told about it. The first I heard was through a third party in Fort Archambault."

"Not surprising," Bigley said. 'That's how they do things around here. Where are you staying?"

"For tonight, right here at the Congo-Océan," said Jacques. "It's a horrible place! My room has four rough cement walls and an unfinished cement floor. It contains two beds with rotten, stinking mattresses. There's a French window that won't close, a mere trickle of water when the faucet is turned on at full blast, an opening at the back with a broken screen, and further, it's on the ground floor!"

Black and Bigley burst out laughing. Bigley said, "You can have my house when I leave. You can have my secretary, too. She's a very intelligent, well-educated English girl, who, I believe, had some problems back home and came out here to forget and be forgotten. She's an excellent typist and was thrilled when she heard you were coming, saying 'Here's a man who speaks English-English, not American-English."

"She must have heard some of my broadcasts," said Jacques.

"We monitored all of them," said Bigley. "They disturbed the brass here. You're too straight from the shoulder, and they won't let that kind of stuff go out. Today when I arrived at the studio, I found someone else had prepared a broadcast and was about to deliver it in terribly bad English. Roussy de Sales, who is the right-hand man of the governor, General Sicé, told me I wasn't needed. I chalked the following statement on the studio door: 'Free French unfair to American journalist. Office closed until further notice.' The governor was furious. He considers himself governor of civilians and general of the military. He called me into his office and I sat down in front of him. 'Stand up, sir!' he yelled at me. 'People who come into this office stand. We don't need you here anymore. So you might as well understand you are leaving with a bad reputation."

"I haven't been here long," said Jacques, "but I've already got some idea of the mentality of these people, their philosophy, and why they stay here."

"Jobs in Equatorial Africa keep them out of the war, and they look as though they are doing something," said Bigley.

"That doesn't offer much meat for broadcasts to the U.S. When are you leaving?" Jacques asked Bigley.

"My contract expires in two weeks I won't hang around after that."

The conversation drifted on to the international situation, the loss of *Prince of Wales* and *Repulse* to the kamikazes in the Far East, and the failure of Hitler to capture Stalingrad. All that seemed far away from Brazzaville.

Major Black rose from his chair. "I must catch the afternoon boat to Leopoldville. I have work left at the consulate."

"Major Black," said Jacques, "would you be kind enough to reserve a room for me at the ABC Hotel? I'll arrive tomorrow."

"I certainly will," said Black. "I'll reserve it under my name. Check with me when you get over there. If you don't find me at the consulate, they'll know where I am. I'll tell Mr. Parminster, our consul, that you have arrived."

"Now," said Bigley, "come over to the office with me and meet Miss Garth, and I'll show you the equipment. Remember to register tomorrow. If you don't, you'll be in real trouble."

"I registered this morning," said Jacques.

Miss Garth was a charming woman with grey-blue eyes and reddish-brown hair. She wore a loosely fitting dress, sandals, and no stockings.

"You need only a minimum of clothing," she said in answer to Jacques' looks, for he had spoken no words. "The work would be interesting if it weren't for all these quarrels. They've made life pretty unpleasant for Karl."

"I can't wait to get out," Karl added.

When Jacques went to bed that evening, he made up his mind to not take Bigley's job. He realized he was caught in a trap. There was no way to get out of Brazzaville against the will of the local authorities. He'd seen enough of the colonial Free French (a different breed from those on the ships) to guess how much Sir James could count on their cooperation. He knew that he would not write any articles praising their spirit, their initiative, and the help they were contributing to win the war. The only thing he liked to write, or would write, was the truth. He realized he would be of no use in Brazzaville; his only problem was how to get out.

He installed his mosquito netting, put a brace against the door which would not shut, jammed the window closed despite the torrid heat, put his revolver under the pillow, and went to sleep. He had entrusted his two canteens (small, rectangular metal trunks used by officers in the English army, in which he carried his belongings) to the English consulate, so he could sleep without fear of being robbed.

Governor Sicé was too busy on that Saturday morning to see him. His ADC, Desjardins, said he'd try to arrange an interview on Monday. At this point Jacques didn't care whether he saw the general or not. He collected his canteens from the consulate and went to the ferry which had the hourly service between Brazzaville and Leopoldville. Once he boarded the ferry, Jacques was struck by the contrast between the two colonies. On the French side of the river, there was integration of the races; on the Belgian side, there was segregation. The ferry belonged to the Belgians, and the forepart of the boat was reserved for the whites, the back the natives.

After the ferry docked on the Belgian side of the river in Leopoldville, there was a fierce fight on the wharf. *A tirailleur*, apparently drunk, had jolted a white man who was accompanying two other men to the ferry. The white man yelled at him, "Knock it off! You're in Belgium here! You're not going to behave here as you do on the other side of the river!" The man's face was pale with fury! At that moment two black guards arrived and knocked the *tirailleur* down with incredible brutality—this was colonialism.

As Jacques got off the ferry after gathering his belongings, a man waiting on the wharf confronted him.

"Jacques," he said, "I felt sure it was you!"

"Gérard!" said Jacques. "What a surprise! It's a pleasure to see you! What on earth are you doing here?"

"I came here to meet some people coming over from Brazzaville, but they've apparently missed the boat. Where are you staying?" Gérard asked.

"At the ABC," Jacques said. "I'm told that's not a bad hotel."

"It's the best here," said Gérard. "Let me help you with your luggage. Have you reserved a room?"

"Yes. At least, Major Black did so for me. Gérard, I haven't seen you since, well, 1937, at your trial at the *Assises* in Poitiers, when you were accused of killing your woman friend."

The trial of Gérard Hauterive attracted national attention and captivated public opinion from one end of France to the other. The scion of a wealthy family of bankers stood trial, accused of murdering his girlfriend. It was a double scandal. He'd been living with a woman of wedlock and then was accused of murdering her. The story made headlines in every newspaper and tabloid in France.

The murder happened during the days of social turmoil after the election of the Blum government and the *Front Populaire*, which was followed by sit-down strikes everywhere. The leftist press had long portrayed the Hauterive family as a member of the *deux cent familes*—the two hundred families said to control the destinies of the Republic through their wealth and influence. The *Hauterive Scandal* was a godsend for those with a political axe to grind. The communist paper *l'Humanité* and the socialist *LePopulaire* did not miss their opportunity to knock the hated *bourgeoisie* and to press their campaigns of detraction and misinformation.

The trial was held in the quiet university town of Poitiers, a city of some fifty thousand in western France, built by the Romans atop a promontory overlooking the Vienne and Clain Rivers. Space was at a premium at the peak of the steep hill, and many of the narrow winding streets, lined by drab stone houses with slate roofs, were barely wide enough to allow the small European cars to pass abreast. Built at a time when people moved on foot or on horseback, there was little place for modern traffic in Poitiers, not to mention parking spaces.

Court sessions were held in a high-ceilinged room, paneled on all sides, including ceiling, with heavy oak wood, burnished by the passage of time and generations of low-paid cleaners.

In France criminal trials are held before a specialized court, the only one to empanel a jury, the *cour d'assises*, consisting of a presiding judge, two assistant judges, and nine jurors. The *cour d'assises* is a sovereign court and its decisions are final. For all practical purposes, its verdicts cannot be appealed.

Prosecution of Gérard Hauterive was based on an accumulation of circumstantial evidence which appeared to leave little hope for the accused.

The defense presented two key witnesses. The author of the forensic report—a well-known expert—stated that the woman had died of strangulation between 11:00 A.M. and 2:00 P.M. on the day of the crime. He was positive about the time of death.

Gérald's lawyer then put Jacques on the stand. He told the court how he and Gérard had spent their time on the Sunday of the crime. How they had left Poitiers early in the morning with the folded kayak in a friend's car. When and where they had set up the kayak. Where they had put it in the river. He even gave the route they had followed and the time they returned to the city that night. When the presiding judge asked Jacques how he could remember so many details so precisely, Jacques handed his diary to the jurist.

A hush fell over the courtroom as the judge silently read the handwritten comments; then he examined the diary's preceding and succeeding pages.

Convinced that the testimony was genuine, he read the notes aloud for all to hear. The jury had proclaimed Gérard not guilty.

"Whatever happened to you after the trial?" Jacques asked his friend.

"I got out of Poitiers as fast as I could. I left without even thanking you."

"Gérard, you didn't have to. All I did was to state the facts as they had occurred."

"I know, but your testimony was the one bright spot in the nightmare. You were so calm and precise on the witness stand. The clear statements you made about where we were, at what place we started, where we stopped for lunch on the sandbank, what we ate, at what time we got home—all that was so exact that no one could doubt it. You got me acquitted. I owe you an eternal debt of gratitude."

"You don't owe me a thing! All that was in my diary. I drew from it as I spoke. You couldn't have murdered her. Dr. Malard's forensic report was unequivocal: the girl was killed while we were on the Vienne River."

"I know, I know," Gérard said, "and that's what made your testimony so dramatic! Everyone was against me, including my father who was in court. My mother refused to come. She knew that I was leading a wild, dissolute, irresponsible life, but she couldn't believe I was a murderer."

"Of course she couldn't; neither could I."

"I haven't seen my parents since that day. I'm the outcast, the black sheep of the family, which otherwise had an unblemished reputation. I'm sure my mother...."

"I know what you're going to say. Your mother wrote to me after the trial. You know me, Gérard, I'm not very emotional. But that letter brought tears to my eyes. It overflowed with grief. I saved her letter; it's with my papers in the States. The whole affair pierced her heart. I answered her letter. I told her that you and I had more than once discussed your love affair with that nymphomaniac girl and your spendthrift ways. I told her that you'd pull out of it and live up to the family standards. After that I went to Austria for my studies. I didn't know where you went, and we lost track of each other. You don't know how thrilled I am to find you here, where I know no one. What on earth brought you here, of all places?"

"My uncle, who is president of the Société Générale in Belgium, has no children," said Gérard. "After the trial, he accepted me in Belgium and told me he'd give me a last chance to do something with my life. My uncle is a hard man, yet he took pity on me. I got a miserable job at the bank in Brussels. I was one of the lowest paid employees, and it was up to me to prove myself.

"That fearful ordeal in court had made a man of me, and two years later my uncle called me into his office. He said to me, 'Gérard, you have lived up to my hopes. I am sending you to our main overseas branch in the Congo, to Leopoldville. There you will be safe. We shall be at war with Germany very soon, and we will be crushed.'

"That's why I'm here, Jacques, and I owe it to you. I'm going to pay off at least a part or the debt. Right now I'm warning you that you are not welcome here. I'll come and pick you up one evening and tell you why. *A bientôt*"

Jacques went to his room at the ABC Hotel but did not unpack his gear. Not much was needed: a shirt, a brief, and a pair of shorts. After a cold shower, he relaxed on the terrace of the hotel. In ten minutes, despite the light clothing and a cold lemonade, his shirt was wringing wet in front and back.

What a climate, he thought to himself. *I can understand why people who live any length of time in this oppressive atmosphere lose all energy and initiative. I can see, too, why Miss Garth wears no more than sandals and a thin dress.*

She was sitting at a table next to him. "I would love to have you as my new boss," she said, "but you don't seem too enthusiastic."

"Would you be?" said Jacques. "It has nothing to do with you. It has to do with the job. What is there to write about?"

"That's the question," said Miss Garth. "The answer is: nothing! Oh, here, Jacques, I'd like you to meet Dudley Holman. Dudley, this is Jacques de Thoranne."

"I'm glad to meet you," she said to Jacques. "I was in Washington at the time of your resignation from the Diplomatic Service. We were all rooting for you—except the people in the French embassy! You were not very popular there! By the way, Jacques, you look pretty well. I understand that some of the people on your boat were fairly sick!"

"Fairly sick is a slight understatement. They weren't on the boat and never even got to it. They went to the hospital in Bangui instead."

"What? Malaria?" asked Dudley.

"No," said Jacques. "Dysentery, probably from contaminated water. I alone was immune because I boiled my water all along the way on my portable cook stove. I was the laughing stock of the whole group!"

"Let's shake hands," said Dudley. "I'm doing the same thing, and they laugh at me, too. Someday I'll laugh at them."

"What are you doing here?" asked Jacques.

"I came to report on the Free French—and for the adventure, of course," Dudley said. "I used to work on the *Washington Post*. I came over at my own expense, but I'm afraid I wasted my money. There's nothing to report."

"We can shake hands again," said Jacques.

"It's true," said Miss Garth. "There is nothing to report, but they intend to keep Jacques in Brazzaville to replace Bigley."

"At least that's what *they* have planned," added Jacques.

"Dudley," said Miss Garth, "we're going to have dinner. Would you care to join us?"

"I'd love to," she said.

Dudley Holman was a perfect beauty, just above medium height, blond, with blue eyes and soft, regular features, exuding both charm and determination.

"You'll be a welcome addition to the Brazzaville crowd," Dudley said to Jacques. "When are you going to start?"

"That, Dudley, is a moot question, and you have all but answered it. What can I do here? You have just said there is nothing to report!"

"I know they want you very much. When Karl leaves, there will be no one to write and deliver their broadcasts. I'd like to do it, but they don't want a woman." Dudley added, "How about a dance?"

As they danced Jacques could feel the warmth and intensity of her lithe body. "I wanted to get away from the table," she whispered, "to tell you just one thing—something I know sure. They will go to any length to oblige you to stay here."

"I appreciate your warning," said Jacques. "I'll not take it lightly and will be constantly ready for anything. They have a problem, of course. I'm a British citizen on a British passport. I realize, too, that they don't care about that."

"I'll keep you informed of anything I hear," said Dudley. "Of course, I've not spoken to you about this. I'll see you again soon, but I don't want to miss the last boat. Garth and I both live in Brazzaville. When you do come over, if there's anything you need, don't hesitate to call on me. I'll be watching this with much interest."

"I may call you," said Jacques, "but I'll say nothing over the phone. It may be monitored. When will you come back here?"

"In a couple of days," she said.

"I'll leave a note for you at the desk of the ABC," said Jacques, "telling you where we can meet. Again, many thanks for the help."

That evening Jacques lay awake, turning the problem over in his mind. How should he handle it? He was promised an interview with Sicé the following week. Were they preparing a trap? If so, how would he get out of it? He remembered Sir James' warning: "Don't take this job if you feel it's too risky."

When Jacques went down to breakfast the next morning, the desk clerk handed him a note that said, "Meet me at the boat at 6:00 P.M. this evening. Gérard."

The morning was cool and foggy, and the north bank of the Congo was invisible from the ABC. Jacques went to the British consulate to introduce himself. The consul received him promptly.

"May I see your passport, Mr. de Thoranne?" said the consul. "What? Issued to you my old friend, Jim Walsh. How are things in Philadelphia?"

"They were fine when I left," said Jacques, "much better than things are on the other side of the river in Brazzaville."

"It hasn't taken you long to find that out," said the consul.

"I came to make your acquaintance and to keep you posted on my job with the Free French," said Jacques. "London sent me to report on the activities of the Free French, but Brazzaville sees it differently."

"That has been the problem all along," said the consul. "In defeat, the French have been unable to overcome the problems that divided the nation before the war."

"It's the same in London," said Jacques. "The army and the navy are at loggerheads, but there the antagonism is based largely on personalities and personal ambitions. I believe I have done all I can here. I'll stay a while in the Congo, however. In the meantime I must get an identity card and a permit to take photographs.

"I'll call Mr. Troprès, who handles identity cards and permits," said the Consul. "That will make things easy for you. If I don't call first, he may keep you waiting for an hour or so. It makes these officials feel important."

"Thank you, sir," said Jacques. "Before I go, however, I would like to give you a confidential message for Sir James Ferguson in London; can you transmit it in a very secret code?"

"Yes, I can," said the Consul.

"Here's the message," said Jacques.

> Admiral de Laborde, commanding French fleet in Toulon, submitted plan to Admiral Darlan to recapture Free French territories in Africa and reestablish control of Vichy government there. Proposal suggests use of French officers, native soldiers (*tirailleurs*) and German war material and would be carried out under control of Marshal Rommel.

"Please sign this with my code name," said Jacques. "You have it on my passport."

"This is potent stuff," said the consul. "Are you sure of it?"

"No one can be sure of anything these days," said Jacques, "but it does come from a reliable source."

When Jacques arrived in Troprès' office, he was received immediately. He provided the official with the required photos and walked out of the office with a *permis de séjour* and a promise of a photography permit within a few days.

From there he went to meet Miss Garth, who was due on the noon boat. When he greeted her, he could see she was upset. She was furious at her boss, calling him a rotter because he meant to go off without paying his debts. Already bills were pouring in, and the woman was convinced she would never recover the canteens she had lent him some time before. She said that she had been his girlfriend, but that she would not sleep with him any more. After expressing her resentment and pouring out her anger, and particularly after enjoying a good lunch, she announced that she felt "more like a human being again."

Miss Garth had various errands to complete and expected to return to Brazzaville by the 6:00 P.M. boat. Jacques said he'd see her off at the wharf. There he rejoined Gérard, who had accompanied two Belgian officials bound for Brazzaville.

"Get in my car," Gérard said to Jacques, "and we'll go to a place where we can talk."

Gérard stopped the car on the riverbank in a clearing used by citizens for family outings. The place was deserted.

"What I have to tell you is too explosive, and I don't want to discuss it in my car," said Gérard. 'I don't believe the car's been bugged, but you can never be sure."

As they got out, Jacques said, "You may be slipping a time bomb in my pocket—or should I say into my head—because if it's that hot, I'll never put it in writing."

"I need not tell you," said Gérard, "that the Société Générale is one of the greatest banking institutions in Europe. Here, it is *the* power—political, financial, administrative—in effect, it controls the Congo."

"Completely?" asked Jacques. "Police and all?"

"Absolutely," said Gérard. "I've seen enough to know. Ever since I came here, I've been disturbed by the philosophy of the bank's management. These people don't believe in democracy. They're convinced that the average voter elects only candidates who tell him what he wants to hear. Once elected these candidates ignore their campaign promises and seek only to retain power. To do that they create among their constituents the illusion that their wishes are being carried out. They say that's why the system doesn't work and never will work for any length of time. That leaves only one way to govern effectively: dictatorship!"

"Hitler must be their idol," said Jacques.

"Yes and no," said Gérard. "They believe in his methods, but they don't trust him. If political boundaries had remained what they were before the war, it would not be too bad. But after the Nazis conquered Europe, the bank management felt compelled to go a step further and entered into an agreement with the Nazis to help them rule Africa when Germany wins the war. Because of my thorough knowledge of German, I was thrust into the middle of this. It's been my job to compare the German and French texts of the agreement and to make sure there is no discrepancy or misunderstanding."

"That must have been very interesting," said Jacques.

"It was. The main terms of the agreement stipulate that, when they win the war, the Germans will give Angola to the Société Générale. The bank has always wanted an outlet for the copper, cobalt, and uranium mined in the Haut Katanga.

They can't put the heavy stuff on barges and send these materials down the Congo, because there are two breaks of bulk: portage is required around the Stanley Falls at Stanleyville and the Livingstone Falls just below Leopoldville. That compels the rulers of the Congo to use the Portuguese railroad, built by Italian engineers with native labor and English capital. The narrow gauge track links Elizabethville and the Haut Katanga to the port city of Lobito. The distance is close to a thousand miles, and as there's no competition, the Portuguese charge what they want! As you may imagine, that's expensive transportation! Do you follow me?"

"I do," said Jacques. "The Nazis care very little that they have no rights to Portuguese Angola. If they win the war, they will just take it."

"Exactly," said Gérard, "and the brass in the Société Générale in Leopoldville are convinced that they will win. The Nazis have already set up camp in Portuguese territory."

"What do the Nazis want in exchange for their generosity?" asked Jacques.

"To obtain the agreement they sought, the Germans sent two excellent negotiators, in absolute secrecy, to meet the top people of the bank. One of them, Kurt Heimrichsen, spoke fluent French like a native. The other, Walter Reichard, who appeared to be his superior, spoke excellent English, but very poor French. Negotiations were conducted in French. I was there to monitor the discussions when both switched to German. I do not think that either of them suspected that I was fluent in their language."

"What did these men want?" asked Jacques.

"First they wanted the authorities to close their eyes on the traffic of black diamonds, which are mined in the Congo and funneled into German hands by a circuitous route. The diamonds go through Leopoldville and along the river, generally on the Belgian side. Then they are taken in native canoes over to the north bank of the river into the small enclave of Cabinda, which is Portuguese and therefore neutral territory. From there they are carried to the coast and, to avoid suspicion, taken by natives in small fishing boats to German submarines lurking in the muddy water at the mouth of the Congo."

"I gather these diamonds are useful to Germany's war production."

"Useful is not the word. You should say vital. Black diamond may influence the outcome of the war."

"What makes it so important?"

"I found out about a month ago that the Congo produces about 95 percent of the world's supply. A Belgian engineer came here from South Africa to get black diamonds for his company. They needed black diamond urgently because it's the only material hard enough to sharpen cobalt steel cutting tools used in lathe operations. Cutting tools sharpened with black diamond increase production speed by at least 50 percent.

"You see, cobalt steel cuts when it's red hot. Ordinary steel loses its edge long before that. Besides its uses for sharpening, black diamond is incorporated into grinding wheels; it's used as powder, mixed with oil or water; it's essential for the rapid production of ball bearings for diesel engines, submarines, tanks, et cetera. There's no substitute for it."

"I can see why those negotiators insisted on obtaining black diamonds," Jacques said.

"They wanted gold, too. They also demanded a share of the gold mined in the Congo. The Nazis' paper money is worthless outside of their conquered territories. They need gold to pay the personnel of their embassies, their spies, and numerous other expenses in neutral countries. I'm sure you remember how, when we were students, we discussed the methods used by Hitler to finance Germany's preparedness for war. At the time the Nazi Reich professed to despise gold, calling it the symbol of capitalism and the financial mainspring of the corrupt, degenerate democracies."

"I remember that well," said Jacques.

"Well, what do you think!" said Gérard. "After the Germans conquered France, almost the first thing they did was to demand information concerning the location of the gold reserves of the Banque de France—although that was not required by the terms of the armistice. A good part of that gold had been sent to the United States and some to Africa. The Germans demanded the return of the gold sent to Dakar. They also demanded delivery of the Polish gold in France's safekeeping, but the French authorities denied that request. They did agree to deliver all the gold Belgium had entrusted to France for safekeeping."

"I'm sure that did not endear the Vichy government to anyone in Belgium or the Congo," said Jacques.

"It did not," said Gérard. "Even here I know the Société Générale viewed that part of the agreement as a worthless commitment to be disregarded systematically.

"In France the Nazis looted the gold of private citizens," continued Gérard. "An escapee told me they ordered banks to open all safe deposit boxes in the occupied part of the country. They grabbed all the gold they found, but they did indemnify some of the important politicians who'd cooperated with them by paying them in worthless paper francs!

"Here the Société Générale agreed reluctantly to the demand for gold, but they weren't too concerned about delivery of the black diamond."

"I can understand that," said Jacques. "Black diamond is hardly used as a reserve of cash!"

"The Nazis' next demand," said Gérard, "was that the administration assign German agents, often trusted Belgian collaborators, to some key posts in the Congo to gather information of all kinds: strategic information, profiles of pro-Belgians, pro-allied, and pro-German citizens of the colony. They have the help of the Gestapo when they want someone rubbed out, but they are very careful about that. To my knowledge they haven't bumped anyone off so far.

They have no obvious office here. The headquarters of the Gestapo, for everything south of the Congo River, are in Mozambique. There they have practically taken over the Polana Hotel, which stands on a bluff overlooking the estuary of the Espiritu Santo River."

"I had no idea that the Portuguese were cooperating with them."

'They don't do it willingly," said Gérard, "but everyone in Europe is afraid of the Nazis' formidable power. That's why they've been able to prevail on Portugal to ship needed minerals from Belgian territory to the port of Lobito, where they are loaded on neutral Spanish or Portuguese ships."

"Those minerals must include ore-containing cobalt," said Jacques.

"Yes, but the Portuguese have compelled the Germans to pay all freight charges in gold; they won't touch any of the phony paper money the Nazis print in Europe!"

"Sure," said Jacques, "the Portuguese are also cooperating with the allies. Our ships are refueling at the Azores."

"The Portuguese have no army to speak of," said Gérard, "and they have to be very careful. I might say that the same thing applies to me. Until recently I enjoyed the full trust of top management in the office, however, I was so disgusted with this cooperation with our enemies that, although I have said nothing, they suspect that I may no longer be one of the boys. I know that they don't trust you, because you showed your true colors when you resigned. They will be very nice to you, very friendly. They will invite you to their homes and will want to find out what you know."

"I appreciate the warning," said Jacques. "I can't know anything at all, or they'll really suspect me. I assume that criticism of the clique on the other side of the river won't be out of order."

"Certainly not," said Gérard, "as long as you stick to administration and 'morality.' I have good reason to believe that they, too, are in the black diamond racket. You have a good reason to wander into no-man's land: photography. I have spoken to Zigorski, the official photographer here, whom you have already met. In a few days he will show you that I am not spinning you a yarn. He will also show you something that exists nowhere else in the world."

"Gérard, your help is invaluable," said Jacques.

"From now on, you and I will be just casual acquaintances," said Gérard. "Remember, I'm counting on you to get this information into the right hands. Also, be very, very careful. I know these birds. If they as much as suspect you know too much, they will kill you!"

"A very encouraging prospect," said Jacques, half-smiling.

"In the meantime," said Gérard, "I have spoken to the owner of a small *pension de famille*, called La Rotonde. She will give you a room at a very reasonable cost. If she introduces you as an American who speaks French and you hang around the café in the evenings, you will probably learn a good deal about what kind of allies the British have in the Belgian Congo. I'll drop you off there now and introduce you. Then I'll disappear."

Two days later Jacques stopped at Zigorski's store for a roll of film he had left there earlier.

"I'm so glad you came," said Zigorski. "I was going to call on you this evening at La Rotonde. Can you meet me here tomorrow at 5:00 A.M.?"

"I can," said Jacques.

"I understand you have a sixteen millimeter movie camera. Do you by chance have a telephoto lens?" asked the photographer.

"I have a four-inch and a six-inch telephoto lens," said Jacques.

"Perfect," said Zigorski. "Set up your camera with the six inch telephoto and bring a hundred feet of film. I'll bring some food and drink. It's an all-day expedition."

When Jacques met Zigorski the next morning, he found the photographer in a state of depression.

"Two things that can spoil this expedition are man and nature. So far, nature has always been the worst. It's the same again this morning. The fog is so dense we'll be lucky if we there on time."

"Where are we going?" asked Jacques.

"Down a trail along the river," said Zigorski.

"In this soup?" asked Jacques.

"Yes," said Zigorski. "By the time we reach the kayak, which I have entrusted to a faithful servant, it will be daylight. But if this fog does not clear soon, our adventure will be spoiled."

They walked in silence for about an hour in the thick fog. In the solitude of the river and the tall trees, the morning fog chilled the body and numbed the mind.

It was daylight of sorts when they reached the kayak.

"This is a very precious tool for me," said Zigorski, as he showed Jacques the blue and silver kayak. "I received this Klepper Faitboot from Germany about a week before the outbreak of the war.

"I'll get in front, and we'll let the craft drift with the current, paddling from time to time. We must follow the bank closely, or I won't see my markers in this fog. Now we are out of earshot of any human being, let me tell you where we are going. When we reach a place I have identified with a marker, we'll hide the kayak and proceed on foot down a trail that parallels the river. Then I hope to reach a point from where I can take photos and you can film a ceremony that, to my knowledge, is unique in the world."

"What kind of ceremony is that?" asked Jacques.

"At the time of the first or second full moon of every year," said Zigorski, "there is a native tribe which performs a ritual of human sacrifice. To remain on good terms with the god of the river, the crocodile, they offer him a sacrifice of the most beautiful girl of the tribe. They take her out a few hundred feet from the riverbank and just dump her into the water."

"How horrible," said Jacques.

"The authorities have tried to stop it," said Zigorski, "but all they've done is to drive underground. I've been out there several times, but only once succeeded in getting a picture of this ritual, and a bad picture at that. I was able to help the juju man of the tribe with various problems he's had with the government. He reciprocates by informing me where to go for the ceremony. I am afraid this miserable fog will spoil this project once again, although the performers of the ritual do stay closer to the riverbank when fog is this thick. This isn't the only ritual that takes place here. If you know where to go, you can still buy human meat in the native market at Leopoldville—ritual, of course."

"Charming country," said Jacques.

"Yes, from our point of view," said Zigorski. "Think of what the natives say. The white man is throwing fire over white men's homes and killing others by sinking boats and giving human meat to the fish. What god are they trying to placate?"

"They've got a point," said Jacques. "We don't have much of an answer to that!"

"See that marker?" said Zigorski. "This means the end of the river journey. Now we must go on foot along the trail through the forest. We must not speak. Just follow me."

"How do you know the natives won't find us?" Jacques asked.

"I expect to get there before they do," said Zigorski. "That's why we left so early. We'll stop at a place where we'll have a good view of the river and where we'll be beyond their reach.

Zigorski had made sure no natives would prowl around the spot chosen by the photographers to set up their cameras. The juju man has declared the area bewitched. The vantagepoint offered a good view of the river. Visibility had improved, but haze still hung over the water. The men set up their cameras and prepared for a long wait. They were both hungry and ate their sandwiches in silence. Zigorski pulled a bottle of beer from the Brasserie de Leopoldville out of his pack, and Jacques poured some tea from his Thermos. It was late in morning, and even along the river, the muggy air was oppressive and depressing. Jacques was constantly amazed at how cold the nights and early mornings could be and how hot the days were.

Suddenly the muffled sound of tom-toms rumbled through the heavy silence of the jungle. Just as suddenly, it stopped. Several crews of canoeists, in their frail crafts made from hollowed tree trunks, paddled rapidly away from the riverbank toward the middle of the river, to be lost in the haze. Then the terrified shrieks of the victim...silence...the boatmen returned to the riverbank...the god of the river was appeased.

"Another failed attempt," said Zigorski in low, quiet tones when he thought it safe to speak. "The mist spoiled everything. Your color film will just record the haze. Besides from where we are, the main action was hidden by the natives standing in the canoes. How much film did you take?"

"About one roll, fifty feet," said Jacques.

"Now, the problem is to get it developed," said Zigorski. "I'm not equipped to do it."

"Major Black told me he'd send anything like that to South Africa by the diplomatic pouch; it's the only place where this film can be developed," said Jacques.

Tired and unhappy about the failure of their photographic project, they started back to the kayak silently.

At a bend in the path a group of natives, accompanied by whites, suddenly appeared going in the opposite direction. Zigorski saluted one of the Europeans, who returned the greeting; he turned to Jacques when the group was out of sight and earshot.

"I'm sorry we ran into that gang," he told Jacques. "I'll be asked who I was with and what we were doing there. They came so suddenly out of nowhere that trying to hide would have made matters worse. By the way, did you hear the tune they were humming? I've heard it before!"

"It's a German sailor's song," said Jacques.

"I suspected as much," said Zigorski. "I suppose that tells you something. Well, the day's been a complete failure, from start to finish. Let's get home and have a good night's rest. I'm dead tired."

Jacques did not think the day had been a *complete* failure. The German sailor's song seemed to him like a straw in the wind....

Chapter XIII

On the outskirts of Leopoldville, within walking distance from the center of town, the mix of tropical vegetation and moderate-sized houses gave way to a neatly maintained park, superbly landscaped with exotic trees and flower beds ablaze with color.

A high wall topped by a glass coping surrounded the park. Entrance to the property was through an iron gate, opened for each visitor by an armed guard. Beyond the entrance a second gate stopped all visitors while identities and credentials were checked. Only then could the visitor proceed toward a squat stone building with thick walls, heavy doors and windows protected by iron bars, deeply sealed in the masonry. Security was tight. Day and night guards with trained German shepherd dogs were on patrol.

This was the nerve center of the Société Générale in the Belgian Congo, the richest colony in Africa. After the Nazis conquered Europe and occupied the Bank's headquarters in Belgium, Leopoldville became the headquarters for all the Société Générale's branches beyond Hitler's reach.

The building itself was divided into two sections: offices and a modern conference and living quarters for the concierge and his wife and rooms for the guards on duty. Because of the thick walls, the building maintained fairly steady temperatures in the low eighties.

The walls and floor of the conference room were paneled with slabs of white and rust-colored marble. At one end a long rectangular table spanned the width of the room; deep leather armchairs lined the remaining walls, with a large Bukhara carpet in the center.

It was in this conference room that the Conseil d'Administration of the Société Générale held its regular meeting on the first Tuesday of every month to discuss policies and events or the previous thirty days.

The trusted secretary, thirty-five-year-old Madame Amblard, was not present at the March 1942 meeting. As with most other European women who lived in the tropics, her menstruation had been perturbed by the persistent heat, and, unwilling to return to a Nazi-occupied Belgium, she had gone to the mountains in Rhodesia to recuperate. In her absence Gérard was told to serve as recording secretary.

Only routine matters were discussed before the Board, and before adjourning, Robert Delacroix, Président Directeur Général, asked if any of the members had further comments or questions.

Alain Bouchard, the premier vice president in charge of security and confidential material, stood up, "Sir, I have been watching closely the performance of a former French diplomat. He is the one who resigned from the French Diplomatic Service in America and sided with Great Britain. De Gaulle's headquarters in London have provided him with an *ordre de mission* to report on the war activity of the Free French in Africa via articles written for the American press. While he is without doubt a genuine patriot, we are keeping an eye on him and will continue to do so, although at present we have no evidence of any suspicious activities."

"I am aware of this, but there is nothing to worry about," said Delacroix. "General has informed me that he intends to retain the man in Brazzaville to write and deliver in English the broadcasts beamed to the United States."

"What if the man won't accept the job?" asked Bouchard.

"That will be too bad for him," said the chairman. "General Sicé is no man to stand any kind of opposition. In the meantime I understand that you, Grévin, have already had him to your home and are planning to invite him again."

"That is correct, sir," said Grévin. "So far I haven't detected anything suspicious. The man is a gentleman and is very knowledgeable. He has traveled widely in the United States and has many fascinating stories to tell. My daughters didn't even give him time to eat for all the questions they asked."

"Your method is excellent," said Delacroix. "We will learn more about the man in this way than by official questioning."

A few days later, when Jacques was again invited to dinner at the Grévin home, questions were asked before anyone sat down at the table.

As she graciously showed Jacques to a seat in the luxuriously decorated living room, Madame Grévin began the low-keyed interrogation, "I understand that you went down the river with Zigorski on a photographic expedition. We know him well; every amateur photographer does. He is an institution here."

"Yes," said Jacques. "Zigorski is a fascinating man. It was an interesting trip. We tried to get pictures of native rituals on the river, but the fog ruined our project."

"Did you see anything else?" asked Grévin.

"Nothing of any significance," said Jacques. "We came home quite tired after a disappointing day."

"Where do you plan to go from here?" asked Grévin.

"I'm not quite sure," said Jacques. "I have cabled London and should receive an answer soon from Pleven, who's in charge of foreign affairs for the Free French."

At that moment the door burst open, and the two Grévin daughters rushed to greet Jacques. "We're so glad you're here," said the younger daughter Christine. "We've got a bag full of questions about the U.S. The KKK—does it really exist? Are there still chain gangs in the U.S.? Does Al Capone's Mafia still control Chicago? What is it like?"

"My children,' interrupted Madame Grévin, "you must let *monsieur* relax a moment."

"Yes, Mother, but when else do we get a chance to find out so much about the United States from someone who speaks French?"

Jacques was delighted with the questions. They interfered with any further pumping by his hosts, and *Madame* was obviously more interested in Jacques' answers to these questions than by any comments of interest to the authorities.

After dinner Jacques returned his room at La Rotonde and found a note saying General Sicé would have time to see him on the following Wednesday at 3:00 P.M. Jacques informed Major Black and the British Consul in Leopoldville of the invitation.

"Are you going there?" asked Black.

"Yes," said Jacques, "although I am prepared for almost anything. I am, of course, a British subject."

Five people were waiting to see Sicé. All had been convened at the same time, and Jacques was last.

General Sicé received him as an oriental potentate would treat a lowly servant. "I have cabled London about your mission. Headquarters agrees with me that it would be very difficult, if not impossible, to accomplish, due to the mentality of colonists and officials. You are too young for the job, and I've asked London to send us no more young men like you."

"Sir, after my resignation, I offered my services several times to de Gaulle but had no response," said Jacques. "So, when INS offered me the job, I took it."

"The Free French," Sicé went on, "have their own dignity and have no particular good will toward the United States."

"General, the British—not to mention the Free French—won't win the war without the U.S. I am awaiting an answer from London and will inform you of my decision when I hear from Pleven."

As Jacques went out, Roussy de Sales, Sicé's assistant, asked, "How did you make out? You know, there's only one answer for you, and that's to get mobilized, which means you won't get out of here until the end of the war."

157

After leaving Sicé's office, Jacques went to the wharf to catch the boat for Leopoldville. As he was about to board, two *tirailleurs* barred the way at the head of the gangplank.

"Where is your exit permit?" they asked.

"Exit permit? For what? There is no need for an exit permit," said Jacques.

"That rule has been in effect since this afternoon," said one of the men.

Jacques had more sense than to force his way to the boat by attempting to pass these soldiers. This was probably what Sicé was looking for anyway—for Jacques to create an incident in which all the cards would be stacked against him.

"Very well," he told the *tirailleurs*, "I will go to get a permit."

As he turned back, he ran into Dudley Holinan, who had accompanied a friend to the boat.

"What happened?" she asked.

"I need a *permis d'embarquer*," he told her loudly. "Could you give me a lift?"

"Of course I will. Where do you want to go?" she asked.

"Please drive toward the administration building where they issue permits. Once we get there, I'll show you the way to go.'

"Why didn't you take the ferry?" she asked.

"Because two *tirailleurs*, obviously on instructions from Sicé's staff, barred the way. Trying to get by them would have led to a fight, and I probably would have lost it and been arrested." Jacques directed Dudley past the administration building and onto a rutted dirt track that of the city and up the river.

"I told you, Jacques, these people are utterly ruthless. They are determined to keep you here, whether you like it or not,'

"They won't keep me here."

"But this is no way out. This road dead-ends in the jungle. You can't possibly escape from here. Oh, Jacques, I'm really worried about you."

"Please, Dudley, trust me and keep driving.

"Jacques, I've never been this far from town on this track. I tell you, it won't get you anywhere."

"We'll go up the river until the Stanley pool narrows. You'll see why."

Dudley drove on, steering the car as best she could around deep holes. They left any semblance of a suburb, and only native huts and thick brush lined the road. Jacques watched the side of the road carefully, obviously watching for familiar landmarks.

His voice thick with tension, Jacques barked, "Dudley, please turn right here."

"What is this?"

'It's a ferry the poor use," said Jacques. "They charge two francs for a crossing."

"How did you ever find out about this?" she asked.

"Dudley, when I'm in hostile territory, I keep my eyes open. I consider every option," he said.

"You're not going to cross the river in *that*!" she said in horror.

"I am. This is a fairly wide canoe, made from a hollowed-out tree trunk, and has four sturdy paddlers. You watch these fellows."

Addressing the canoe owner, he explained, "I have just missed the boat and do not want to miss an appointment. Can you get me across fast? One hundred francs if you get me to me to the other side of the river without delay."

The promise of one hundred francs—perhaps more than they earned in a week—galvanized the four crewmen. As they pushed off, Jacques called to Dudley, "Mum's the word. Please say absolutely nothing to anyone. I'll call you when I get to my hotel. See you tomorrow. Many thanks."

The day faded into dusk and dusk slipped into night as Dudley stood there, watching the canoe vanish into the evening gloom. Jacques waved to her. She waved back. He guessed what she was thinking, *He's crazy—crossing that crocodile-infested river in that canoe in the hands of those natives.*

She had been home for a while when the phone rang. "Dudley," said a familiar voice, "I'm here, thanks to you, but please don't mention a single word to anyone. Tomorrow I'll just happen to bump into you at the terrace of the ABC between twelve-fifteen and twelve forty-five. Again, thanks."

When Jacques arrived at the terrace of the ABC to join a few friends, he saw Dudley sitting with Roussy de Sales. He went to greet them.

"What are you two doing here in this oppressive heat? Rehydrating bodies dried out by the scorching sun?" he asked.

"Yes," said de Sales. "I was wondering where you were. I couldn't find you after you left Sicé's office yesterday. I wanted to give you some advice about how to proceed around here. How did you get across the river?"

"How did you?" Jacques asked.

"By boat," said Roussy.

"So did I," said Jacques. "Until a bridge is built, there seems to be no other choice."

"Well, I'd better be on my way. It was nice to see you," de Sales said as he departed.

"Won't you sit down?" asked Dudley.

"Not now, Dudley," said Jacques. "Come to La Rotonde, where we can have a quiet lunch out of the limelight, at one o'clock."

"I'll be there," she said.

She was smiling broadly when she met Jacques in the small dining room at La Rotonde.

The *patronne* was an excellent cook, and Jacques had got to the right side of her. There was, among other things, a platter of cold fish, served with mayonnaise, which Dudley eyed suspiciously.

"You needn't worry," Jacques assured her. "It's not made by the cook on the caravan from Fort Archambault. I personally supervised the manufacture. Our cook has added some crushed garlic cloves to produce what is called *ailloli* in the South of France. It's potent stuff. You don't want to eat too much or go dancing afterwards…."

"This is delicious," she said, savoring the potent mixture.

While they ate, Jacques thought of the job he'd agreed to perform for Sir James. He couldn't carry it through if he were stuck in Brazzaville. Still more important than the original task was the information he'd gathered about the Nazi plan to destroy Freetown and seize Africa. It was terribly urgent to get that to London before it was too late.

Dudley smiled and said, "You should have seen them this morning. They sent Roussy de Sales over to find out how you got here."

"I told him, didn't I?" said Jacques. "His questions weren't very subtle."

"They're completely mystified. They had each boat watched. They can't find out how you did it. Some think you got on the boat disguised. They'd never believe you crossed the river in a canoe. Your disappearance was the topic of official discussion this morning, and your answer to Roussy de Sales will merely add to the confusion. What's your next move?"

"The environment here is unhealthy," said Jacques. "Don't you think that the better part of wisdom is for me to get out of it?"

"Of course," she said. "But you can't. You're in a trap."

"Dudley, consider the facts. On the other side of the river they could argue that I am a French citizen over whom they have jurisdiction. That's not true here in Leopoldville. To the Belgians I'm a British citizen, with a British passport and the protection of the British government. I have my *permis de séjour,* a permit to use my cameras. I have complied with all legal regulations. The French have absolutely no power over me on this side of the river."

"I agree," she said. "You've made a lot of progress since yesterday. You're beyond their reach, but they're desperate to get you. They'll go to any lengths to keep you here, I can assure you."

"Why?"

"First, they've got no one for their broadcasts to the U.S. The Free French in London told them you had been sent to fill Bigley's job. With Sicé it's a matter of prestige to keep you here. I also think that they're scared if you return to England, you'll tell London what a mess it is here. What's your next move?" she asked.

"Thanks to you, I'm out of the Brazzaville trap. Now I must get out of this one," he said.

"How?"

"I've taken a first class ticket on the riverboat to Stanleyville."

"Why Stanleyville?" she asked.

"Because that's the only way out. I can't go through Free French territory. I could, of course, go down to Matadi and catch a Portuguese boat to Lobito or Capetown. Then what?"

"You're right," she said. "Every escape route is fraught with danger. Where will you go from Stanleyville?"

"There's an overland car service to the Sudan."

"I don't envy you," she replied.

"I'm telling you this because I trust you."

"Jacques, you can be sure it will go no further."

"Monsieur, monsieur," said the *patronne*, "you are wanted on the telephone."

"By whom?' Jacques asked.

"I do not know, *Monsieur*; but he speaks French," she said.

"Excuse me a moment, Dudley," said Jacques.

He had a wry smile on his face when he returned to the table a few minutes later.

"That was a call from Brazzaville," he told Dudley, "from Sicé's deputy administrator, Clapot. He said Sicé had a very interesting proposal to offer me and asked me to come over tomorrow afternoon at three o'clock. I asked Clapot if I would get the same treatment as I did yesterday, being made to wait until everyone else scheduled for three o'clock had passed and waiting until the last. I told him to ask Sicé. Well, he did, and Sicé is alleged to have said that I would be first. I then asked what was the interesting proposal. Clapot replied that it was confidential and could not be discussed over the telephone. I said to him, very well, put it in writing and I will consider it. You can either mail it or send it over by Roussy de Sales; however, if Sicé absolutely wants to see me today, I'll be pleased to receive him here."

"What did Clapot say to that?" Dudley asked.

"Nothing," said Jacques. "That ended the conversation. They must think I'm a complete idiot to offer such bait to get me back. In the meantime I must stay here another week until the boat leaves for Stanleyville. Until then I'll maintain a low profile."

"I'm sure of that," said Dudley. "I'll come over every so often and tell you what's going on."

"Don't mention anything on the telephone," said Jacques. "Today is Wednesday. How about if we meet here on Friday at twelve-thirty for lunch?"

"That's fine. I'll be here," she said.

That afternoon Alain Bouchard was called into the office of Robert Delacroix. Gérard was there as recording secretary.

"Bouchard, it's again the problem of that American war correspondent traveling on a British passport. General Sicé called me this afternoon and wants him back in Brazzaville. I told Sicé I had absolutely no jurisdiction over the man and that as far as I am concerned he is a British citizen. He has complied with all our rules and regulations, he has been given a *permis de sèjour*, and we have no reason to take any action whatever against him. He is a well-known citizen with much prestige in the U.S. and England.

"Sicé was very angry. He said the man had escaped from Brazzaville when ordered to stay there. So I told Sicé not to expect me to solve a problem his people have bungled. He was furious and slammed the telephone down. So much for Sicé, but I do think de Thoranne still bears watching. He seems to be a very shrewd observer, and we have no real way of determining just what he knows or how much he knows."

"Sir, we are still watching him," said Bouchard. "This morning he booked a ticket on the *Georges Philippar* river boat for Stanleyville."

"So much the better," said Delacroix. "He'll be out of here in a week.'

"Karl Bigley, the American who has been broadcasting to the U.S. from Brazzaville, is leaving on the same boat," said Bouchard. "He has taken a ticket to Stanleyville and made a reservation on the overland auto service for the Sudan. To my knowledge, de Thoranne has only a ticket for Stanleyville. If you agree, sir, I have been thinking of putting Simone Aré on the boat to see what she can get out of the man."

"That may not be a bad idea, Bouchard," said Delacroix, "but if I am to believe Sicé, the man you are watching is as wary as a beast of prey. It is that wariness and his great discretion which makes me suspicious. Grévin has been impressed by the man's circumspection, but beyond that, we have nothing concrete against him."

"That is correct, sir—absolutely nothing," said Bouchard.

Robert Delacroix leaned back in his chair pensively. "I do not know, Bouchard, if your plan to use Simone Aré will work." After a while, he said, "As a matter of fact, I'm afraid it won't."

"Simone has performed a number of jobs for us, with some success. She is very attractive, highly sexed, and persistent, but she does have one drawback: she is not too subtle. I'll caution her that any clumsiness will be very counterproductive in this case and may, in fact, ruin the whole project."

"I wish you luck!" said Delacroix, half smiling.

In conversation with Dudley, Jacques had no inkling of the preparations made by the Belgian authorities to coax him into sharing any, or all, of the observations he had made with the designing woman the powers-to-be planned to enlist for that purpose. He did sense the hostility of the crowd in Brazzaville, their anger when he eluded their trap, and their vindictiveness, which had become public knowledge on the north side of the river.

At Sicé's headquarters in Brazzaville, they did know one thing, confirmed by Roussy de Sales: Jacques was now on the south side of the river in Leopoldville, in Belgian territory and out of their reach. How he got there remained a mystery. Guards had been posted at the departure of every ferry with strict orders to prevent Jacques from boarding the ship. The *tirailleurs* who had intercepted him the day before had been repeatedly questioned; all they could say was that Jacques had turned back, telling them that he would get an exit permit. He had departed by car in the direction of that office. Which office that was, the *tirailleurs* did not know.

Sicé's henchmen were baffled. Some conjectured that Jacques had simply slipped by the guards. Others guessed that he'd gone to the boat disguised as a woman. Still others surmised that he'd added a mustache and a beard to get past the guards. They questioned Dudley, who had seen Jacques the day before at the ABC in Leopoldville. All she knew was what Jacques had told her: he had crossed the river by boat.

Dudley briefed Jacques on the latest news from Brazzaville when she joined him for lunch at La Rotonde on Friday.

"Excellent!" said Jacques. "Do you think they believed you?"

"I don't know, but I'm sure they don't doubt you crossed the river by boat."

"Dudley," said Jacques, "your warnings are not falling on deaf ears. Every night when I turn in, I barricade door and windows and sleep with my revolver under my pillow."

"I'm so glad you're taking precautions. I'll come on Wednesday and see you off," she said, looking at her watch. "Oh Jacques, I've just missed the boat."

"I'll accompany you to the next one," said Jacques. "In the meantime, let's go to my room and take a nap.'

"Everyone else does at this time," said Dudley.

"I'm glad to have you for another hour," said Jacques when they'd gone into his room. "It's so nice to have a true friend when you're surrounded by foes, someone I can talk to and who will keep anything I say to herself."

He drew her toward him and held her in his arms tenderly; he felt her warm body, quivering in her thin dress. He kissed her delicately, on her fore-head. She looked at him with her big blue eyes, and her lips found his. They kissed for what seemed hours. They withdrew their lips, and he looked into her eyes. She looked into his.

"Darling," Jacques said to her softly, "do we stop here?"

"I don't see how we can," she whispered.

She missed the next boat.

Dudley had secretly felt the desire for what they were doing, and so had Jacques. Only the opportunity had been missing, and now it had come and been seized.

As Jacques accompanied her to the boat, he said, "Dudley, now we're beyond the reach of microphones and enemy ears, I have something to tell you."

"What?" she asked.

"I know I can trust you. This is for you only, unless something happens to me. Then it will be up to you to inform the right people. This knowledge could cost you your life, as it could cost me mine, if anyone were to suspect that we know about it."

As they walked to the boat, Jacques outlined the traffic of gold, black diamond, and cobalt that was taking place in the Congo. He told her he would bring the information to the right people and that it would be up to her to do the same if he were murdered. In a flash she realized the portent of the secret they now shared.

"You can count on me," she said resolutely, "but, Jacques, now I am even more concerned about your safety. Oh! Jacques, please do be careful."

"I'll be more than careful," he said.

"Perhaps I'll come back to see you again before you leave on Wednesday," she said mischievously.

As Jacques considered every option and every danger, he decided to entrust his diaries to the British Consul in Leopoldville. He also informed him of the anger in Brazzaville over his escape and of Sicé's determination to catch up with him and forcibly mobilize him.

"We will watch your future moves with very great interest," said the consul smiling.

Dudley was on dockside as *Georges Philippar* was being loaded and the lighters were being secured on either side of the bow.

"I've had plenty of feedback since I last saw you," she told Jacques. "Sicé considered it a personal insult when you told him to come over here if he wanted to see you. He is very vindictive and wants your recapture. Be very careful."

"I will," said Jacques, "and I'll let you know as soon as I get into friendly territory. Good-bye, sweet lovely girl."

With a loud blast of the hooter, the river boat started sluggishly upstream for its twelve-day journey to Stanleyville.

From the first day of the journey, the other passengers on the boat noticed that Simone Aré was up to something, and it did not take long for Jacques to realize who was the target. Naturally suspicious and made still more wary by the hostility encountered in Brazzaville, he decided to play the game, be very nice to the fair lady, tell her nothing, and make her talk. She was a striking beauty, apparently in her early thirties, of medium build. She was elegantly attired in light clothes, or rather, in a thin dress without much else, a low-cut neckline barely enclosing her well-formed breasts. She had dark green eyes, sensuous lips, hazel-colored hair, and a pleasant, distinguished voice as smooth and enticing as a lullaby.

At the first meal, she seated herself at the long table just opposite Jacques, constantly engaging in conversation with him.

The travelers on *Georges Philippar* were a different breed from the groups Jacques had met on *Alphonse Fondère*, on which he had traveled to Brazzaville. *Georges Philippar* passengers were mainly Belgian administrative personnel, some with wives and children. These were well-educated citizens, treating the natives benevolently but firmly, apparently much as the distinguished Americans of the Jefferson era had treated their slaves. No disrespect and no drunkenness were tolerated on *Georges Philippar*. It made for a very congenial company. Bigley was on board, but he had enough sense and *savoir-faire* to deal moderately with the bottle.

All the passengers spoke French, and conversation avoided the divisive issues of war. It dealt with education, climate, and customs among the different native tribes. It dealt especially with America, everyone repeatedly questioning Jacques about all aspects of life in the United States. He did not ask any questions about Madame Aré but soon learnt that she was married, flighty, and designing. He was told, too, that her persistent attitude toward him had caused much irritation, to the point that one of the travelers suggested to Jacques that he tell her to "shut up."

Jacques' indifference became one of the main topics of gossip on board. When the boat stopped at Coquilhatville, one debarking traveler asked a friend remaining on board to let him know if Madame Aré's seduction efforts were successful before the boat reached Stanleyville.

Another topic was Jacques' photographic activities. At every stop of the ship, throngs of natives came alongside, and Jacques took many pictures. At Irebu, the crowd became nasty and threatening, screaming at the photographer. Jacques asked a Belgian administrator, who had watched the scene, what the problem was.

"They are angry," he said, "because you are not giving them their picture."

"Can you tell them that the film must be developed first?" Jacques asked.

"They won't understand that. Don't you have any old photos you can spare?"

"I'll see," said Jacques.

He went down to his room and rummaged through his canteen. He found an eight-by-ten print showing Muselier, the Free French admiral, on the deck of the submarine Rubis, bestowing a decoration on Commander Cabanier, who had mined the pass at Narvik.

"Do you think this will do?" he asked the Belgian.

"Perfect. Just throw it to them."

The anger of the crowd vanished. Suddenly the natives were all smiles. The last Jacques saw of them, they were looking at the photograph upside down.

Occupations and distractions on board riverboats plying African rivers were sharply limited. One could watch the monotonous scenery with its thick equatorial forest and the islands of floating grasses moving downstream with the current. There were no newspapers or radios on board. One had to wait for a stop to hear news from the outside world. The main distractions on board were meals, exchanging ideas, playing cards, and sometimes playing chess. All these activities took place in the dining room after waiters had cleared the deck.

By the time the riverboat left Coquilhatville, the day was well on its way. The boat had taken on a supply of wood for the furnace, fresh vegetables, fruit, and meat, mainly chicken. There was no chance of reaching the next stop that day. Bogbonga was a good one hundred miles upstream. From there, Stanleyville was still five to eight days away, depending on weather and geography (fog, moonless nights, and sandbanks).

The boat dropped anchor at dusk. Swarms of mosquitoes confined passengers to the dining room, which was protected by screened windows and the periodic passage of a crewmember armed with a spray gun, profusely showering any intruders with clouds of DDT. There was no protection from the stifling heat. While the boat moved, there appeared to be some flow of air, but at anchor it was a sweat bath. Passengers sat listlessly at their tables, some playing bridge, others *belote*, some half-asleep, drinking cold beverages from the ship's icebox. Everyone was subdued. Even the river water was more than tepid—it was actually warm.

In the midst of this torpid scene, Simone Aré appeared, not quite as subdued as everyone else. She sat down next to Jacques' table, where a rubber of bridge was underway.

"I don't know how you people have the energy to play a game of cards in this suffocating heat," she said. "I've lived quite a while in this area, and I can't recall a more sultry evening. Look, I've just put on this light dress, with nothing on underneath, and it's already wringing wet, front and back."

No one answered. Maybe it took that comment to remind them that they, too, were wringing wet, front and back. The dining room was like a sauna. The game went on.

"How do you people manage to sleep at night in these lower cabins," Madame Aré commented further. "I'm in an upstairs cabin, and even there the torrid heat is so oppressive that I have to sleep in the nude with not as much as a sheet to cover me."

No one answered. Discouraged, she rose, walked around a couple of other tables, and left the room.

"I wonder who she thinks is interested in the way she sleeps; I couldn't care less," said one of the bridge players, looking at Jacques, who merely shrugged his shoulders and remained absorbed in the game.

"I'm just puzzled," he commented, "about which card I should play."

Everyone smiled, and the game went on.

Madame Aré appeared the next evening as the travelers were in the midst of dinner. Carefully groomed, make-up plentiful and perfect, dress cut to the navel, she went straight to the table where Jacques was dining with the Belgian administrator van der Wuip, his wife Marielle, and two children.

"Jacques, would you do me a great favor? I am dining with the captain and running late. Would you mind taking care of this?" she asked, handing him a crocodile-skin leather satchel. "If you don't know what to do with it, here is a key—the key to my bedroom," she added in a loud voice for all to hear and disappeared, leaving the bag on the table.

"Do you often get proposals like that?" asked Marielle with a smile.

"No, I don't," said Jacques, wryly, "but I have a pretty good idea of how I'm going to deal with it."

Simone Aré occupied one of the two staterooms on the upper deck, which were usually reserved for important bureaucrats or political figures. After dinner Jacques quietly put a salt shaker in his pocket and took the bag and the key to her bedroom.

"I wonder what on earth he's going to do?" said Marielle.

When Jacques returned to the table some ten minutes later, he called upon the administrator's young son, "Gilbert, I wonder if you can perform a very confidential mission?"

"Oui, monsieur," said the child.

"Would you please take this key," said Jacques, "politely knock at the door of the captain's dining room, hand the key to Madame Aré, and tell her that I have placed her precious bag on the dresser next to her bed and that I have locked the cabin door."

"Very well, monsieur," said the youth and, taking the key, he disappeared.

"Monsieur, what have you done?" asked Marielle under her breath.

"I believe," said Jacques, "that Madame Aré will not make another brazen public invitation to me again. But only time will tell...."

At breakfast the next morning, when the river boat had been underway for almost two hours and the steward had started to remove the dinnerware, the missing person everyone awaited finally appeared, dressed in a long robe, disheveled hair, red-faced, with deep black pockets under her eyes. She strutted abruptly in silence to the one unoccupied table in the dining room and, in a crackling imperative voice, ordered breakfast. She finally looked toward Jacques, who had his back to her, her eyes blazing with fury.

"My God," said the administrator. "If her eyes had been pistols, you would be dead, Mr. de Thoranne. What on earth did you do to her last night?"

"I didn't see her last night at all," said Jacques.

"Well, tell us!" said the administrator's wife.

"Madame, when I left the table last night to return Madame Aré's bag to her bedroom, I concealed a salt shaker in my pocket and gently spread an imperceptible, very fine layer of salt on the bed sheet. I smoothed it into the material, so there was no chance she could suspect anything in the subdued light of the bedroom. She had told us that she slept in the nude and that, even then, she was bathed in sweat. The result, of course, would be a somewhat unpleasant, itchy night, but from all appearances it was worse than that. Both the body and the ego seem to have suffered."

There was a chorus of subdued laughter at the table.

"How did you know to do that?" said Marielle. "I've heard of a similar prank before, but I think pepper was used."

"Madame, I am a biochemist, and I suspected, for various reasons, that salt might solve the problem. Apparently it has."

"Did you know, Mr. de Thoranne, that on river boats, the water is turned off from midnight to 6:00 A.M.?"

"I didn't know that, Madame. She must really have had a bad night."

In a group of only twenty-five first-class passengers confined in a small space for twelve to fifteen days, everyone knows everyone else's doings. In a flash all knew the source of Simone Aré's fury.

"C'est bien fait," was the general comment. "She really deserved something like that. It will not sit well with her to lose face."

Madame Aré was not seen at any table in the dining room from then on, and when the boat arrived in Stanleyville, she was the first passenger off, brushing everyone else aside. The others, including the administrator, had to take their turn in the blazing afternoon heat.

Jacques waited in his cabin. He was in no hurry to get off the boat, since he had decided to spend the night on board, an option the river boat company offered passengers when the ship docked after 2:00 P.M. A few other passengers, who had reservations for the overland car service to Juba in the Anglo-Egyptian Sudan, did the same.

There was a rap at the door of Jacques' cabin. It was Bigley. "Say, Jacques, did you see the two guys at the gangplank when the passengers started to disembark? One of them was a short stubby fellow with a mustache and colonial pith helmet."

"Yes, I did," said Jacques. "Why?"

168

"He's the chief of police. He was here with three black aides and a warrant for your arrest," said Bigley.

"Karl, you have to be kidding."

"I'm dead serious," said Bigley.

"What was the charge?" Jacques asked.

"Well, that's the point. The charge was taking photographs of military objectives going up the Congo River."

"Ridiculous!" said Jacques.

"I know. That's what the passengers thought, too," said Bigley. "The Belgian administrator was indignant about such a trumped up charge, and he signed a statement declaring this was untrue. Before they got off the boat, all the passengers co-signed it. I did, too, but my signature doesn't count for much. You want my opinion, Jacques? I believe Sicé is behind all this. That whole good-for-nothing gang in Brazzaville was infuriated when you left. They're afraid you'll bring the true story to London."

"It wouldn't do any good if I did," said Jacques. "I'm awfully grateful that you've warned me, Karl. When are you leaving?"

'Tomorrow at ten," said Bigley. "The overland car service starts from the Place des Roches, just a stone's throw from here."

In the meantime all the other passengers had left the boat; so had the chief of police and the district commissioner who accompanied him.

Jacques hailed a taxi and went straight to the SEDEC, a general store, where he asked for the manager, John Weiland. He told Weiland about the trumped up charge, the arrest warrant, and the declaration the other passengers had signed.

"Farr, our consul in Brazzaville, told me you would stop in and see me," said Weiland smiling. "But things are worse than I expected. Just be at the airport between twelve-thirty and twelve forty-five tomorrow. At that time the city is deserted. Everyone is having lunch or is asleep in the midday heat."

"Do I need a ticket? Any documents?" Jacques asked.

"Give me your passport," said Weiland.

He examined it and took down the number and the data on the visa.

He handed the passport back to its owner. "Here's a requisition. Show it to the airport clerk. That's all you'll need to board the plane. Good luck!"

Chapter XIV

If there were one place which might be called the center of the Continent of Africa, Stanleyville would be it.

The Mediterranean Sea is about twenty-one hundred miles to the north; the South Atlantic is some twenty-one hundred miles to the south; the Indian Ocean is some eleven hundred miles to the east; and the Gulf of Guinea is about the same distance to the west. The city, almost smack on the equator, is built on the north bank of the Congo River, only a stone's throw from the rapids known as the Stanley Falls.

Stanleyville was surrounded on every side by the dense, impenetrable equatorial forest. There were only three ways to get out of the city: the river-boat to Leopoldville; the Interfina, an auto service overland to the Sudan; and a plane.

No white man could get out of there against the will of the local authorities. On a Monday evening in mid-1942, that's where Jacques found himself: wanted by the police, cornered by nature, and stifling in the 100° heat. After a frugal dinner, he went to bed in his cabin on *Georges Philippar*—*not* to sleep, but to think. The local authorities would be watching the departure of the Interfina to the Sudan on Tuesday morning. Finding that Jacques was not among the travelers, they'd relax, secure in their belief there was no other means to leave the city, as no plane was scheduled until later in the week.

Meanwhile he'd apply for a *permis de séjour* and a new identity card, just to remain on the safe side of the law. He would create the illusion that he was in no hurry to leave and would wait until he received instructions from the news agency which employed him.

The next morning he told the steward on *Georges Philippar* that the room he'd reserved at the main hotel in the city, the Hotel des Chutes, would not be available until 12:30 P.M. He asked the steward to care for his luggage until he came to pick it up and tipped him generously.

The Interfina auto service was due to depart for Juba at 10:00 A.M. Jacques assumed that the chief of police would be watching to make sure he was not among the passengers; so that time, he went to the commissariat de police to obtain his *permis de séjour.*

He was received by a woman in her fifties. "I am sorry, monsieur," she said, "but I am not authorized to issue these permits. Only my husband, who is chief of police, may sign these documents."

"Madame, when do you expect him back?" asked Jacques.

"He should be here any time," she said.

"May I wait here?" said Jacques.

"Of course you may," she said. "You are *Monsieur...?*"

"Jacques de Thoranne is my name," said Jacques.

"Oh yes, my husband was speaking about you," she said. "You are the American war correspondent?"

"Yes," he said.

"Where are you going now?" she asked.

"I am going to stay here for a while, until I receive an answer from my agency," said Jacques. "I do not know where they want me to go next. In the meantime I shall stay at the Hotel des Chutes. I would like to see the pygmy colonies in the Irumu forest. Do you think that can be arranged?"

"Of course," she said. "As a matter of fact, I can help you."

Mrs. van der Meer was an enthusiastic historian and student of primitive societies. That was her main interest in life. She was delighted to have an avid listener. Although Jacques enjoyed her conversation, he decided it was time to get some breakfast, so he thanked Mrs. van der Meer and assured her he would come back later when her husband returned. He walked to a nearby café and seated himself in the back of the dark room. He could see without being seen. He ordered fried eggs, French bread, and coffee.

The native waiter had just laid the breakfast before him when the chief of police returned to his office. He remained there a short time and departed again. A few minutes later, Jacques returned to the commissariat. "Oh, you have just missed him," said Mrs. van der Meer. "I told him of your visit, and he will, of course, give you the permit. Please leave your passport with me."

"Madame," said Jacques, "I will come back; however, I never leave my passport anywhere under any circumstances. I will go now to inspect the room I have reserved at the Hotel des Chutes. Why don't you ask Mr. van der Meer to meet me there in the lobby around 3:00 P.M."

When Jacques returned to the center of town, the police station was closed for the noon siesta, and the town had sunk into its usual mid-day slumber. He found a taxi, picked up his luggage at the boat and, when out of earshot of the taxi driver, casually mentioned to the steward that he would stay at the Hotel

171

des Chutes for the next few days. Then, out of earshot of the steward, he ordered the taxi driver to take him to the airport.

The driver eyed Jacques suspiciously upon reading a large sign at the entrance of the air terminal, *pas de départ aujourd'hui* (no departure today).

Just beyond the gate, a tank truck was about to pull away from a twin-engine plane it had just refueled. There was one airline employee at the desk; he examined Jacques' passport and the requisition, handed them back to their owner, and loaded the luggage on the plane. As Jacques paid his fare, he noticed the taxi driver's wistful glance toward the flit gun, which was perched atop the rucksack Jacques was about to carry onto the plane.

"Very useful tool, that," said the native. "Can get liquid, but can't get pump."

"Want it?" said Jacques.

"Ah, ah, want it! I take right back to woman. Thank you, sir. Thank you!"

"Please board the plane," said the clerk as the joyful taxi driver returned to his jalopy, hugging his loot.

The plane, a Lockheed Lodestar, was filled to capacity with British servicemen and technicians being rushed to Egypt to bolster British defenses against Rommel's advancing Afrika Korps. There was one vacant seat.

"You've got the only seat left in this plane," said the soldier next to Jacques as he sat down. "E's'ad a bout with malaria."

The pilot started the two radial Pratt and Whitney air-cooled engines, revved them up, and taxied along the not-so-smooth runway. After a short run, the plane lifted off the ground, borne aloft on the heavy, saturated air of the equatorial forest. It gained altitude rapidly, circled the town, and headed northeast.

It banked sharply as it veered toward its destination. From his window seat, Jacques watched the scene below—the Stanley Falls, the Hotel des Chutes.

Uneasily he watched the dim green of the equatorial forest, barely discernible in the bluish haze, gradually fade into the bush, where giraffes and flocks of scared antelopes scattered at the approach of the plane. He kept a close eye on the angle the plane made with the sun to make sure it had not changed course. Hitler's allies in the Congo would not hesitate to order the plane back. Too many secrets were escaping in it.

Two and a half hours into the flight, Jacques knew he had won the day. The plane would not have enough fuel for a return trip. He knew exactly what he would have done had the plane been recalled. He smiled when it landed and looked at his watch. He wondered what the chief of police and the district commissioner were doing. By now they'd surely discovered the journalist's absence. An uproar must be taking place. He'd probably never hear about it, but he could imagine what it was like.

When the Lockheed came to a stop on the airstrip in Juba, a bus took the passengers to the Juba Hotel. From there the servicemen were directed to barracks nearby. They were on their way to the war in Egypt's western desert, but for Jacques this was something else.

For him everything in Juba was exhilarating. The air was light, the humidity was gone, and the sun beat down upon the sand with its breath of fire. The nightmare he had lived for so long had come to an end. The tenseness of his mind, of his muscles, of his entire being, evaporated in the thin, hot air of the Sudan. Now he was beyond the reach of the men in the Congo. He was free!

He was pretty sure why they were desperate to catch him. They must know that he'd learned too much from the careless talk at La Rotonde and that he'd followed the rumors about how gold and black diamonds were smuggled to the Nazis from Belgian territory. Did they suspect that he'd learned anything more about the dealings of the Société Générale with the Germans? That he could not guess, but they must have had compelling reasons to arrest a British citizen, the national of an allied country, on trumped up charges.

Juba was a small city of native huts and European barracks, built on the west bank of the Bahr el Jebel, the White Nile. In 1942 its links to the outside world were limited to a dirt track to Stanleyville, which crossed over the Lindi, Aruwini, and Bomokandi Rivers on primitive barges; to a link with Kosti on the Nile on antiquated paddle steamers fueled with wood; and to a trickle of air transportation, with planes flying low and slowly to conserve fuel.

Not everything in Juba was primitive. The Juba Hotel was modern, well supplied, and comfortable despite the heat. Elegant fans graced the ceilings of guestrooms and dining room. A few British officers based in Juba lived there, as did transients awaiting the departure of the next riverboat to Kosti.

Boat schedules were unpredictable. They depended on how many sandbanks the swamp boats had hit or missed during their twelve-day journey.

There were some twenty guests in the dining room of the Juba Hotel on the evening Jacques arrived, among them the pilot, copilot, and navigator of the Lockheed on which he'd traveled. He went to their table. "I see you have a vacant spot here. May I join you for dinner?"

"It will be a pleasure to have you," said Gillard the pilot.

"Before I sit down, however, I feel it is my duty to warn you," said Jacques.

"Warn us, of what?" said Gillard.

"You men have transported a very dangerous passenger," said Jacques.

"Well," said the copilot Trenet, "there was only one journalist on board."

"You must also know that this journalist was wanted by the police with an arrest warrant," Jacques told them.

"This is interesting, very interesting," said Gillard. "If the police were after you, you must be a good man. I saw your passport, but you aren't a true Englishman."

"What do you mean by that?" Jacques asked.

"If you were a true Englishman," said Gillard, "you would not come here and sit down at a table with three representatives of a lousy little conquered nation like Belgium. The Germans think they are a superior race and proclaim it. The English think they are a superior race, but they don't say it—they just show it."

Jacques laughed. "You're right! I am only half an Englishman. I have a foot on either side of the Channel. French father, English mother. So, I, too, am a part of a lousy bigger nation, also conquered by the so-called Master Race. All those people are angry at me because I resigned from the Diplomatic Service."

"Oh! You're the one. My hat's off to you," Gillard said, grasping Jacques' hand. "We're proud to have you at our table. Now let's hear why the police are so interested in you."

Jacques drew his revolver from its holster and laid it on the table. "See this? I was ready to use it on the plane."

"This is becoming more interesting by the minute," said Trenet. "What's the story?"

"I was afraid that the plane would be called back to Stanleyville if they discovered you were carrying me. They feared I knew too much about the black diamond and gold traffic. I was ready to force you to continue your route to Juba."

"You wouldn't have had to threaten us with your gun," said Gillard, "if you had told us what you have said now. Thank God someone is getting out with that story. The whole thing stinks! All three of us have families in Belgium. If we say anything, they'll take it out on them. But you would not have known if we had turned back progressively over the equatorial forest."

"I would have," said Jacques. "All the way, I watched the angle the plane made with the sun.

"I can see why they were worried about you," said Gillard. "What's the scoop?"

"I came to Africa from the United States as a reporter for International News Service, with instructions to report on the activities of the Free French at sea, in the air, and in the colonies. I found that the sailors and airmen were doing a fantastic job, but in the colonies, with few exceptions, I found cliques of opportunists. Their main ambition was to sit out the war in Africa while the others did the fighting. I also found worse. I learned that a number of corrupt officials were supplying the Nazis with essential strategic materials, black diamond, particularly. I found the route these materials followed to Cabinda and Fernando Po. From there the diamonds are sent on neutral ships to Spain and Portugal and from there to Germany. In Leopoldville I stayed at a little inn, La

Rotonde, where gossip flowed freely like beer. I even managed to obtain a sample of the diamond, which is with my diaries."

"How did you dare carry that out?" asked Trenet.

"I didn't," said Jacques. "Diaries and diamond have been entrusted to a source who can get them out without trouble. Don't ask me who."

"Now I can see why they wanted to arrest you," said Gillard. "They must be frantic! I'll bet everything I own when we fly hack tomorrow, they'll be at the airport to find out what we know. Don't worry. We won't tell them anything. We'll just make fools of them."

He went on, "Since you are one of our own, we can tell you something. The plane you flew on was seized from the French as a reprisal for the seizure of a similar Belgian plane by the Germans in North Africa. The crew of the French plane was strongly for Pétain, while the crew of our plane wanted to continue the fight. Our pilots were imprisoned by the Vichy French. We retaliated by imprisoning theirs. Eventually a swap was arranged. We went to pick up our crewmen at an airport near Bamako, and what do you think? An airport was under construction near Koulikoro, just off the Niger River, and there were three Heinkels on the ground there.

"The government of the Congo would not allow us to fly our plane into Vichy territory. They were afraid it would be confiscated. We left it at Fort Lamy and flew over Niger, Haute Volta, and Mali to get to Bamako in a rickety old Dewoitine which required several stops for fuel. The thing was falling apart. I was never so scared in my life."

"What you tell me about the Heinkels is very interesting," said Jacques. "What do you think the Germans are up to?"

"They probably want to occupy all of North Africa," said Gillard.

"You may well be right,' said Jacques.

"Mr. de Thoranne, you must know many people," said Gillard. "Both Trenet and I really want to join the RAF. Could you help?"

"I'll certainly give your names to the right people," said Jacques. "That may take a little time, though. I'm taking the riverboat down the Nile to Kosti and then the train to Khartoum. From there I'll go to Cairo, and you can count on me to transmit your request in absolute confidence. Let me have an address where you can be reached without creating suspicion. I will ask anyone contacting you to use my name, but I think you should memorize it rather than writing it down. I'm sure you understand why."

They laughed. Gillard gave his address, saying he would contact the other members of the crew.

"One more thing," said Jacques, handing an envelope to Gillard. "Would you mail this letter for me from Stanleyville with a Congo stamp on it? Please put it in the mailbox unobtrusively."

'I'll be pleased to do that," said Gillard.

The envelope, addressed to Dudley, contained a cryptic message, "All is well. The weather in Juba is wonderful. The man they've missed."

"Gentlemen," said the head waiter, who was dressed in a long white robe, "ten o'clock, time to close the restaurant."

Jacques was anxious to get to bed anyway. For the first time in weeks he could sleep in peace with the gun left in his bag.

It was broad daylight when he awoke. There was not a cloud in the sky and the sun streaming through the east window.

There were only two British officers seated in the restaurant. Jacques sat at a table nearby.

One of the officers rose and approached him, "I see that you are a war correspondent. Would you care to join us for breakfast?"

"Yes, sir, with pleasure," said Jacques. "My name is de Thoranne."

"I'm Captain Wilson. My colleague is Lieutenant Harker. Where do you come from, Mr. de Thoranne?"

"From the U.S., said Jacques, "and, by a circuitous route, from England, Sierra Leone, Nigeria, French Equatorial Africa, and the Belgian Congo."

"When were you in England?" asked Harker.

"About six months ago," said Jacques.

The two officers had many questions. Just what kind of damage had been done by the blitz? Was it true that entire blocks of London had been destroyed by fire? Jacques gave them many of the details they wanted to hear. Yes, practically everything around St. Paul's Cathedral had been gutted or leveled. Newgate Street, Paternoster Row. Tooley Street, and the whole area around London Bridge Station were all entirely gone.

"With all this censorship," said Captain Wilson, "we know nothing of what's happening. When we meet someone like you, who's just been there, we get an idea of what has taken place."

After breakfast Jacques made his reservation on the wood-fueled paddle steamer which would take him to Kosti. His funds were running low, as the Belgians had blocked withdrawal of six hundred dollars which had been cabled from the U.S. to Barclay's Bank in Leopoldville. When he arrived in Juba, he was down to his last reserve in travelers' checks. He cabled that fact to the Ministry of Information in London: "Proceeding to Khartoum under own steam; pressure falling rapidly."

The cable intrigued the censor, a Pole who had fled his country during the German invasion. His knowledge of English was good, but limited. He was convinced the cable had a hidden meaning; however, after a detailed explanation and the reassuring prospect that the cable was directed to the Ministry of Information, he allowed it to proceed without change.

In the meantime he challenged Jacques to a game of chess, as he did every traveler passing through Juba. He was angered when Jacques won the first game, but the cable to the Ministry of Information was already on its way.

There was little to do in Juba except listen to the censored news, play chess, rest, and wait for the boat, which was scheduled to leave in four days.

On the day before he boarded the river boat, Jacques was seated in the hotel dining room, having a lemon juice soda before lunch, when a door at the opposite end of the room opened suddenly. A disheveled, dust-covered individual came to a sudden halt, appearing petrified. Only his eyes were free from the red dust of the African dirt track. His eyebrows, hair, and beard were caked in a thick coat of fine, reddish sand. After a moment of hesitation, he moved forward as one who has seen a ghost. "My God," Bigley said breathlessly, "it's not possible! This must be a hallucination. It can't be him. It just can't be! Jacques, is it you?"

"Yes, I am Jacques. You are not under an illusion."

"How on earth?" said Bigley. "What did you do? You were trapped, and here you are. I just can't believe it. How did you get here?"

"I rented a bicycle and pedaled all the way," said Jacques.

"Oh, come on!" said Bigley. "Don't give me that shit! I know you didn't come by plane, because there were no flights. I tried to get one rather than come on the Interfina. Look at me! I've absorbed as much dirt through my nose and mouth as you can see on the outside of me."

"If you've swallowed as much dirt as there is on your face, in your hair, head, and clothes, you'll certainly get a pretty bad indigestion." said Jacques, laughing.

"Let me tell you, Jacques," Bigley insisted, "you are mighty lucky to he here. I don't know exactly what they had against you, but they were absolutely determined to get hold of you. You should have heard the gossip. After we signed the statement that you hadn't taken photographs of military objectives, they had to find another excuse. That meant contacting Leopoldville because you're a British subject. I think they wanted to catch you to send you back to Brazzaville. The way they talked, it was a must, a do or die situation. There must have been hell to pay when they found you were out of their reach. I'd hate to be in the shoes of that police commissioner or that district commissioner. They watched the cars before we left Stanleyville, and they were still there when we pulled out. I can tell you, we were really worried about you. Now it's their turn to worry."

"They've probably spent a few sleepless nights," said Jacques, "and may have a lot of explaining to do. I'd like to hear more about it later."

"You can hear more now.' said Bigley.

"That's rather cryptic. What's the story?"

"I'll explain when I've had a shower and get rid of this dust."

When Bigley returned, he looked more like a human being. He and Jacques sat down at a table for two in a corner of the dining room. Bigley relaxed in his chair, ordered dinner, and lit his pipe.

He then looked at Jacques intensely, "Say, before I tell you what happened, I have one question: are you a pilot?"

"Of sorts, yes. When I was in the U.S., I joined a flyers club and got my pilot's license. Why do you ask?"

"I'll get to that later. Now let me start from the beginning. We left Stanleyville at ten-thirty on Tuesday morning. There were only two cars in the caravan, and I was in the second one. We'd been underway for about two hours when the engine died. The driver had no idea why, and he didn't know what to do. There was nothing around but the dense forest. We had no means of communicating with the other vehicle and had begun to think that we'd have to spend the night where we were when a cloud of dust on the track before us signaled the presence of another vehicle. It was the other car. The driver guessed we'd broken down."

"Then you went back to Stanleyville?"

"Yes. It was slow going. He towed us into town and dropped all the passengers off at the Hotel des Chutes."

"Of course. It was too late then to start off that evening."

"Right. We were in the lobby registering for rooms when the chief of police, the district commissioner, and another fellow I'd never seen before barreled in and frantically started questioning all of us, 'Have any of you seen the journalist? He's disappeared. Did he manage to get into either of your cars?'"

"That was a pretty desperate question," said Jacques.

Bigley just laughed and shook his head. He started eating his first decent meal since he'd left Stanleyville and launched into his story.

One of the travelers reminded the police chief that he had been there when the caravan left and should know that the journalist wasn't with them.

At dinner that evening, a mix of fact, speculation, and rumor deepened the mystery and enlivened the conversation among the delayed travelers, one of whose brother-in-law was member of the police force and the driver for the police chief. He delighted in relating that day's activity of the police.

Chief of Police van der Meer and District Commissioner Velmeire arrived at the Hotel des Chutes shortly after three in the afternoon, arrest warrant in hand. Only a flimsy excuse supported their warrant. Jacques hadn't registered nor had he obtained a new identity card within the twenty-four hour limit. His boat had arrived in Stanleyville on Monday at 2:00 P.M. and it was now 3:15 P.M. on Tuesday.

After waiting a while, the chief asked the desk clerk to ring Jacques' room. There was no answer. They knocked at the door of the room and there was still no answer. Returning to the clerk, they requested a key, but the desk clerk could not find it and the passkey would not open that door.

By the time the local locksmith, summoned by the chief, arrived and opened the door, it was past 4:00 P.M. The room was empty. There was a canteen on the luggage rack, and the toothbrush and toothpaste were there on the washstand. The bed had been slept in. Just where was the man?

This absence started a frantic search throughout the city—in every cafe, every *pension de famille*, and every hotel or private house catering to the public—but the elusive journalist was nowhere to be found.

"How about the airport?" Velmeire asked van der Meer.

"There were no departures today," said the chief, "only one arrival and departure, but that was a plane absolutely full with British servicemen bound for Alexandria. But if you insist, as a matter of course we can go out there to eliminate all improbabilities."

When they arrived at the terminal, they found the desk closed for the day; the clerk, an employee of Sabena, the Belgian airline, was on his way out.

"Albert," said van der Meer, "was there anything unusual at the airport today?"

"No, sir," said the clerk, "except that the Lockheed that refueled here had a sick man on board. So we took him off and sent him to the hospital. He looked pretty bad, too."

"So the plane took off with a vacant seat'?" said van der Meer.

"No, sir." said the clerk, "just as it was about to leave, a military man arrived and boarded the plane."

"What was his name?" asked the chief.

"I don't remember," said the clerk. "He had a British passport, and he just boarded the plane like any other military man."

"What did he look like?" asked the chief.

"He was of medium height, rather slim, wearing military clothes, dark glasses, and a pith helmet."

"Did he have any luggage?"

"Yes, sir, a couple of military canteens. I put them on the plane. He was a military man, all right."

"Do you know when this plane is coming back?"

"Yes, sir. It should arrive here tomorrow morning about eleven o'clock. We received word at four-thirty this afternoon that it landed in Juba."

"Thank you, Albert," said the chief.

When the clerk left, the chief turned to Velmeire. "That might describe our man, but I never got more than a glimpse of him. He came twice to my office to register and get an identity card. My wife talked with him for quite a while, but a description like that is too vague to conclude that the journalist is the one who boarded the plane. The man who got on that plane had a military requisition. I don't know how the journalist could have obtained one."

179

"Let me tell you, van der Meer,' said the district commissioner. "If he has escaped, there will be hell to pay for both of us. Leopoldville called me this morning, just before lunch, warning me that under no conditions should the man be allowed to escape. He is believed to he a most dangerous and able British agent masquerading as an American journalist. I do want to make sure, however, that he is the one who got off before I inform Leopoldville. I'll wait until we talk to the pilots tomorrow."

Bigley looked at his cup of after-dinner coffee and his dessert. "It's wonderful to eat and drink without the crunch of grit between my teeth." After a moment of silence, he continued, "These are the facts, as close as I could get them. Now for the rumors. The lieutenant governor's small plane was under repair at the Stanleyville airport. A stranger got into conversation with the mechanic and gave a hand when help was needed. When the mechanic went to his car in the hangar, the stranger jumped into the plane and took off for parts unknown."

Jacques put down his coffee and broke into laughter, "A fine cock and bull story. Of course they'll accuse me of stealing the plane. Do you think the chief of police cooked that one up to explain my disappearance? Karl, they'll have to find a better excuse than that." After a minute to recover, he said, "I assume you're going to Khartoum."

"Yes," Bigley said. "When does the boat leave?"

'Tomorrow at ten. I have a fairly decent cabin. You'd better choose yours before everyone else rushes for a ticket."

Chapter XV

Juba, at the southern tip of the Sudan, is about eight hundred miles from Khartoum as the crow flies. In 1942, however, the average traveler could not travel the way of the crow. He had to take a riverboat and a train. The boat could go no farther than Kosti, where rapids broke the White Nile. From there, passengers continued their journey on a train that meandered through the parched land, detouring east through Sennar, then heading north to Khartoum. All told, crossing the eight hundred-mile stretch took twelve days.

There wasn't a cloud in the sky when Jacques boarded the riverboat at the wharf in Juba. Already, at ten in the morning, the fierce sun baked the earth, and Jacques could feel it burning his feet through the soles of his shoes. His cabin was amidships, about three feet above water level, and seemed delightfully cool compared to the outside temperature of 114°.

With a blast of the hooter, the riverboat got underway. For miles downstream after Juba, the White Nile flowed through low, arid sandbanks, and wound through sloping hills. There were no trees or bushes in sight on this parched, undulated desert land—not a sign of life anywhere.

Gradually sandbanks and hills disappeared, and the boat entered a vast expanse of water almost five times the size of New Jersey, a part of the Sudan called the Sudd, an English word derived from the Arabic *sadd*. It was a shallow, marshy swamp, fed by the waters of the White Nile, which spread over the shapeless land. Water depth seldom exceeded six feet and often was no more than two feet. The riverboat—a wood-burning paddle steamer—was built for this environment and had a very shallow draft.

Even so it had to follow the narrow, winding channel, marked only by the absence of vegetation, to avoid landing smoothly on a half-submerged sandbank and be stuck there for hours. When not stuck, the boat wound along its corkscrew path at a comfortable pace—about one hundred miles in twenty-four hours.

The riverboat was a world of its own. It had no communication with the outside world. It could not call for help. It had to be self-sufficient. It carried a specially designed anchor and was equipped with a winch to pull itself off any unwelcome sandbank, but it had no protection against fire. On the wood boat there were no extinguishers, no lifeboats. There was no land in sight. There was nowhere to go in case of fire, except into a swamp teeming with crocodiles. That worried Jacques when he went to bed at night. His reason told him he could do nothing about it except trust to luck, although there was one plus on board and it reassured him: the entire crew was Moslem, so there was no drinking, and each one of these primitive people performed his job responsibly.

Every morning after breakfast Jacques would go up on deck. The view was always the same: In all directions to the horizon, the brilliant green of papyrus, emerging two or three feet from the water, mixed here and there with sword grass, when the mud of the swamp came to the surface, a stunted mimosa tree would provide a welcome landmark. Some would call this monotonous view depressing, but for Jacques it was a soothing rest after the turmoil of the past months.

His real worry came from what he'd learnt about the Nazi penetration of Africa: the airfields they'd ordered built, the Heinkel bombers they were bringing in, and the bombing Fort Lamy he'd witnessed first hand.

How and when could he get all the vital information he'd gathered to the decision makers in Cairo—or preferably, in London—in time to thwart Attila and Felix? That was his gnawing concern.

After a week in the Sudd, the riverbanks emerged. So did human life, clinging precariously to the arid, hostile land. Incredibly primitive life, no doubt, where human beings had no needs other than food. The tall, slender men wore no clothes whatever, but they carried a metal spear at the end of a long wooden shaft. The women wore a few dirty rags around their loins, barely distinguishable from their black, parched skin. The meager economy of these primitive human beings depended largely on the stops of riverboats, where endless chains of natives, like ants, brought the wood to fuel the boiler's tire.

It took the boat about twelve days to reach Kosti. Jacques boarded the train for its equally circuitous route to Khartoum. Departure was scheduled for 4:00 P.M. The cars had been standing all day with the windows open in the fierce summer sun. The compartments were like ovens. Jacques' portable thermometer indicated 112°.

Jacques was lucky. He had a compartment to himself—but not for long. Just as the train started, there was a knock at the door and an English officer stepped in.

"Sir," he said to Jacques, "there is a sick private on this train. It seems like an acute case of malaria, and I have given him my bunk. May I join you in your compartment for the journey?"

"By all means, captain. My name is de Thoranne."

"Thank you, sir. My name is Wetherill. I'm on my way to Khartoum and from there probably to Egypt with the eighth Army. The situation seems fairly serious. Rommel's Afrika Korps has advanced dangerously close to the Egyptian border."

The conversation centered on the war, the situation in England, and the prospects peace, but the officer was most interested in America's role in the fight and how long it would take to mobilize its industrial power.

Two more British officers joined Jacques and Wetherill for dinner in the dining car and later for a game of bridge. A few minutes before ten o'clock, the headwaiter warned the players, "Gentlemen, we close up at ten sharp, please be prepared to leave exactly on time."

"Just a minute," said Wetherill, "please let us finish this game. It will take only five minutes."

"Five African minutes," added one of the officers.

"No, sir!" said the waiter. "Five English minutes."

When the train pulled into the station at Khartoum around nine o'clock the next morning, a great throng of Europeans—military men, women, children, and natives—was waiting on the platform. As Jacques threaded his way through the crowd, a British officer came up to him.

"Mr. de Thoranne?" he said.

"Yes, sir," said Jacques, "but you have the advantage of me."

"My name is Cunning," said the officer.

"Just the right name for a man in British Intelligence," said Jacques.

"Never mind about that," said Cunning. "The chief wants to see you, as soon as possible. I have a car waiting. Let's pick up your luggage, and we'll drive over to his office."

"Who is the chief?" Jacques asked.

"His name is Sweeting, but in this country we take the local titles. For everyone here his name is Kaimakam Sweeting."

"What does he want?" said Jacques.

"He'll tell you himself," Cunning said.

After retrieving the luggage, both men got into the small khaki-colored car. Cunning drove rapidly through Khartoum's busy streets, finally stopping on the outskirts of town before a stone building, protected on all sides by a web of barbed wire and guarded by sentries with submachine guns at the ready. After inspecting the occupants of the car, the soldier opened the gate, saluted, and waved them through.

"You may leave your belongings in the car," Cunning told Jacques. "Just follow me."

The two men entered through a small door into a narrow, winding corridor and finally stopped at a desk where a sergeant examined them. "You may go in, sir," the sergeant told Jacques. "The Kaimakam will see you."

A man of medium height, with very dark, wavy hair, sitting behind a wooden desk, watched Jacques with a slight grin. When he finally spoke, he said, "You are not the type of chap I was expecting to see here; what do you have to say?"

"Kaimakarn, you summoned me here; what can I do for you?" Jacques asked.

"Perhaps my question has already crossed your mind," said Sweeting.

"Maybe my answer has already crossed yours." Jacques replied.

"Why do you think the British are, a bunch of fools?" Sweeting asked.

"I don't think it. I know it," said Jacques.

"Well, sir, you will have to prove that, or you will be in serious trouble. Why are they a bunch of fools?" he queried.

"Simply for one reason," said Jacques. "They are losing the war through their own stupidity."

"Give me the proof of what you say," said Sweeting.

"No problem, but I need a map," said Jacques.

"What kind of a map?" Sweeting asked.

"A world map, or half of it." Jacques said. "The Eastern Hemisphere will do."

"Let's go into the next room." said Sweeting, rising from his chair.

"Kaimakam," Jacques said as they walked to the map room, "I need not tell you that the British Army in Egypt has its back to the wall. It cannot be supplied through the Mediterranean, which is controlled by the Axis. All essential war materials must take the long route around South Africa."

"That is not in dispute," said Sweeting, "but I cannot see—."

"Please, Kaimakam, let me finish," said Jacques. "My whole reasoning is based on one premise, on which we must agree before I present my case."

"What's that?" said Sweeting.

"There are only three freighters in Britain's merchant navy which can travel from Liverpool to Capetown without refueling, *Tyndareus*, *Hephaestus*, and *Orion.*"

"1 don't know that. How do you?"

"I make it my business to find things out," said Jacques. "If you don't believe me, just check it out."

"All right. I'll take your word for it."

"All other ships must stop on their way to refuel. Most of them are coal-fired, and bunkers won't hold enough coal to cover the distance between Liverpool and Capetown. As the crow flies it's about seventy-five hundred miles: but as ships must travel in wartime, it can be anywhere from ten to twelve thousand miles. That means that practically all freighters carrying war materials and most of their escorts must refuel on the way. Now look at this map: There's one decent harbour in West Africa, Dakar, and that's in the hands of the Vichy French, which means that it's controlled by the Germans. What's left?"

"Freetown."

"That's right. Have you been there?"

"No."

"If you had," said Jacques, "you'd be just as horrified as I was. I spent more than a month there. There's no antiaircraft defense. There's no arsenal. There are no facilities for any major repairs, and only small jobs can be done on the Vindictive, an old aircraft carrier which has been converted into a repair ship. It has a couple of Bofors pom-poms and two four-inch guns, and that's it.

"Of course the British had counted on Dakar. But with the collapse of France—"

"Freetown had to serve as a substitute," said Jacques. "So everything there is makeshift: the fuel dumps, the coal piles, the bunker oil storage tanks. The town is built of wood and harbors a population of lazy, disgruntled natives. Fifty German planes, maybe only twenty, carrying high explosives and incendiaries, could level the place in one strike, especially on a windy day. Then what would we do?"

"There's no way the Germans could do that." said Sweeting. "That would require major preparation and basing planes in Vichy French territory."

"That's what you think. Earlier this month I talked to some pilots who landed at the airport near Bamako. They both told me that there were German planes there. They were camouflaged, and the pilots were not allowed near them. They did, however, talk to some local employees who confirmed their observations."

"Rubbish!"

"Kaimakam," said Jacques, "I can't understand you people. Why not look at the facts and at least accept them, even if you don't want to believe in their implications."

"All right. Just continue if you have any other so-called facts."

"I don't see the point in telling you what other reports I've gathered from escapees, said Jacques. "All I can say is that new landing strips are being, or have been, built in Senegal, Guinea, Mali, and Niger—even in Dahomey. These reports came from different sources, but all of them are from people who have seen the facilities or who worked on them, and these people did not know each other."

"There may be some work going on, but we do know there are no German planes," Sweeting insisted.

"Who gave you get that information?"

"We get reports from various sources."

'Kaimakam, your sources don't seem very trustworthy." said Jacques. "Did they tell you that Fort Lamy was bombed?"

"We heard some rumor to that effect," Sweeting said.

"Who do you think carried out the bombing?"

"Probably the Germans," Sweeting said.

"From where?" Jacques asked.

"They have bases in Libya, which is controlled by the Italians," said Sweeting.

"That's true. Tell me, Kaimakam, which base is closest to Fort Lamy?"

"Let's look at the map. Obviously, it's Murzuk, in the part of Libya called the Fazzan. Now, Mr. Cocksure, where does that leave your theory that the Germans have bases in French territory?"

"One question, Kaimakam," said Jacques. "How far is Murzuk from Fort Lamy?"

"Measure it on the map. It's just about nine hundred miles, a round trip of about eighteen hundred miles."

"Kaimakam, to my knowledge, there's only one plane in the whole German air force which could make the round trip from Murzuk to Fort Lamy with a bomb load, the Focke Wulf 200C, which has a range of twenty-two hundred miles."

"Well, what's wrong with that?" said Sweeting.

"The only thing wrong with that is that the planes which bombed Fort Lamy were not Focke Wulfs," Jacques told him.

"How do you know that?' Sweeting asked.

"I was there when Fort Lamy was bombed, and I saw the bombers. They were not Focke Wulfs."

"What were they?" Sweeting asked.

"Heinkels He 111 Ps."

"What does that tell you?" said Sweeting.

"With their range of about twelve hundred miles, the Heinkels came from a base much closer to Fort Lamy than Murzuk. I have good reason to believe that they came from Zinder. Let's look at the map again. Assuming they flew over the northern tip of Nigeria, a distance of about eight hundred miles round trip, my conclusion is plain: the Germans are gradually and systematically building a bomber force in Vichy-controlled Africa for several possible purposes—one of which can only be to destroy Freetown as a base."

Kaimakam Sweeting rose from his chair and shook Jacques de Thoranne's hand. I deliberately doubted all you were telling me to make sure you knew what you were saying. In fact, all the information you just gave me corroborates ours. It confirms it and completes it, especially your last observations about the Heinkels.

"I will send you to Cairo tomorrow to make a written report to the Director of Military Intelligence, the DMI. I have done all I can to make Military Intelligence understand the seriousness of the problem, but it just doesn't sink in. They know it all. I'm talking to you confidentially now, and I share and understand your frustration—but for heaven's sake, don't vent it publicly, or you'll end up in the jug. There's only one plane a day for Cairo, and every one is booked solid for the next month. Tomorrow I'll put you on the Canopus, a Sunderland flying boat. You'll bump a general, but he won't know who's bumping him.

"I'll contact the chief. You go directly from the plane to his office and be emphatic about the firsthand information you have."

"I have to retrieve my diaries to make a complete report," said Jacques.

"Where are they?" asked Sweeting.

"In the Congo. I left them in the hands of the British Consul in Leopoldville. I knew the police were after me, and I got out of the Congo by the skin of my teeth, with the help of Weiland. Had I not been successful and the police arrested me, I didn't want them to find any tangible evidence of what I knew."

"What's the rest of the story?"

"The vital part deals with a possible attack against Freetown. The rest is significant and concerns shipments of black diamond and gold to the Germans by the Free French in French Equatorial Africa and by the Belgians in the Congo. I know the routes they follow, where they are delivered, and how they reach Germany."

"Do you have precise, detailed information?"

"Yes, but that is also in my diaries, together with a sample of the rough diamond."

"You were wise to entrust your documents and samples to our consul in Leopoldville."

"If the police had laid their hands on my diary, my career would certainly have come to an abrupt end.'

"I'm sure you will cause a ripple in Cairo. You're a fresh source. Tell the general what you have told me. When I contact him, I will insist on the importance of your observations and the need for competent secretarial help. If he assigns his administrative assistant to this job, you'll know my cable has been successful. She is an extraordinarily efficient woman; she entire office strictly and methodically. She is beautiful and very intelligent, a real brain. Everyone in the office respects her, but no one likes her. Some say she's a real bitch. She's commonly called 'the untouchable.'"

"Maybe that's why they call her a 'real bitch.'"

"If the general does entrust her to you, handle her with kid gloves," said Sweeting.

"I'll do my best, but I didn't come on this trip to seduce women. I came in the hopes of contributing, in a small way, to get rid of Hitler."

"You may find it difficult to understand why the people in Cairo arc so smug," Sweeting said. "The attitude pervades the whole military bureaucracy, even more so here, where they are so far from the war. You've been through it, both on land and sea, and you sense its reality and the possibility of what an imaginative enemy may do."

"I try constantly to put myself in the shoes of the *Oberkommando der Wehrmacht*," said Jacques. "If I had the power of Hitler, this is just what I'd do."

"Precisely," said Sweeting. "That's why you are so convincing. In the meantime you have half a day left here. What would you like to do?"

"I'd like to have a look at Khartoum, and of course, see Omdurman and the site of Kitchener's famous battle with the Whirling Dervishes."

"That's a good way to spend the afternoon," said Sweeting. "Cunning will be your guide. You may take your cameras and photograph anything you like. I'm sure he'll take you to a local show tonight. There are some Armenian girls who are real experts at belly dancing.

"Be up no later than five. The plane leaves at six. You'll need a good breakfast before the flight. You probably won't be allowed off when the plane refuels at Wadi Halfa, so don't expect another decent meal until you reach Cairo around four. When you get there, go straight to the DMI's office and insist on seeing the general personally. I feel quite sure he will receive you."

Sweeting stood up and shook Jacques' hand warmly. "Good luck. I have a feeling you will stir up enough controversy to crack the apathy of this bureaucracy."

Both men walked to Cunning's office.

"Cunning," Sweeting said to his aide, "I'm entrusting our war correspondent to you until you deliver him to the departure of the Canopus tomorrow. Please make sure he has boarded the plane. In the meantime find him a comfortable room at the Grand, and be his guide and mentor for the rest of the day."

When Sir Alan McMillan, the Director of Military Intelligence in Cairo, returned to his office that afternoon, his administrative assistant, Irene Simms, handed him a high-priority cable deciphered from the super-secret H code. The general read it in silence.

"Miss Simms, will you ask Jefferies to come in?"

"Yes, sir."

Sir Alan handed the script to the ADC. Another one of these cranks, Jefferies, I'm afraid. When he arrives here tomorrow, listen to what he has to say and get rid of him as soon as possible."

The ADC read Sweeting's priority cable rapidly.

"What's the matter, Jefferies?" said the general. "You seem hypnotized by Sweeting's message."

'No, sir, I'm not, but I know this fellow Sweeting is sending us. He's no crank. Sweeting must really have been impressed to send such a forceful message."

The general looked astonished. "You say you know this man, Jefferies?

"Yes, sir, I know him well. I might even say I know him *very* well. I met him when I was deputy administrator to the High Commissioner in Palestine. I had many dealings with him. He used to be the attaché at the French Consulate in Jerusalem. I can assure you, sir, this man is no crank. I've seen him at work. As a matter of fact, I recall an incident in which he put his career on the line, paid us back in our own coin, and made our bureaucracy red-faced."

"What was the incident?"

"Four years ago the French Consul General in Jerusalem was transferred to New York, and the consulate was left in the hands of the vice-consul, an elderly man, who was taking care of all routine affairs when the new attaché, Jacques de Thoranne, arrived. He'd been there for about three months, barely long enough to get his feet wet, when the vice-consul was stricken with a rare tropical disease and had to return to France for prolonged treatment."

"So the new attaché was left in charge of the consulate?"

"Right. A greenhorn, fresh from the very competitive exam of the French Foreign Service, was left in charge of France's most important diplomatic post in the Near East. Someone in our administration thought this was a great chance to increase our local revenues. The British mandate in the Near East included Palestine and Transjordan. Normally one visa, costing sixty piastres, was given to travelers for both territories. Now we decided to charge a second visa, costing sixty piastres, for travelers bound for Transjordan—of course this applied to foreigners, not to British subjects.

"Naturally French citizens were angry to have to pay for two visas and took their complaints to their consular representative. He came to see me about it. I told him this was due to new regulations. He said this was not acceptable and promptly sent a cable to the Quai d'Orsay, asking for instructions. Knowing the French bureaucracy, we felt sure nothing would happen. We had deciphered the French X code and were quite amused by the attaché's repeated attempts to obtain some sort of answer from the French Foreign Office. No such luck. We were enjoying the situation until...."

"Until?"

"Until the morning I got an angry call from the head of CID, informing me that he sent his sergeant to get a visa for Syria and the French Consulate had charged three hundred piastres. We had two mandated territories, Palestine and Transjordan, but the French had five mandated territories, Syria, Lebanon, Sandjak, Alawites, and Djebel Druse. So the consulate was charging 60 *piastres* for each territory."

General McMillan burst out laughing. "Then what happened?"

"The attaché had not received a single answer to his cables about this action. We knew he was acting on his own. It took a greenhorn, and a greenhorn with guts, to take such action. No senior diplomat would have dared do it. He was challenging two bureaucracies, his own and ours, at the risk of his diplomatic career."

"What was the outcome?" asked the general.

"We decided to let him stew in his own juice. We hinted at an international incident. We believed the pressure would build up and become too great and felt sure he would back down after a while. Don't believe it. He stood by his guns! Finally His Majesty's Secretary, Battershill, called him in and settled the matter, ascribing the whole incident to the 'bungling of one individual.' I've heard since that the incident created much mirth at the French Foreign Office and that de Thoranne's cables dealing with the incident were circulated to all departments, where they were on a 'first reading' basis."

"What did they think of it in London?" the general asked.

"Not much,' said the ADC. "It brought some wry smiles, but no laughter. After that the French appointed a new consul general to Jerusalem and transferred de Thoranne to Philadelphia, where he served until the collapse of France. After France surrendered, the government issued new directives to French diplomats throughout the world. De Thoranne left the service, saying he wouldn't take orders from Hitler. So far he's been the only one in the whole service to do so."

"You mean to say that he's the fellow who resigned from the French Diplomatic Service last year?"

"Yes sir."

"From what you've told me, he was certainly running true to form. Jefferies, go to your tennis match tomorrow. I will receive this man."

"Yes, sir, and what do you intend to do about secretarial help?" the ADC asked.

"I'll talk to him first. Maybe I'll let him have Miss Simms. She's been moody lately and getting on my nerves. The office isn't very busy right now. Miss Adair can take over. Miss Simms and de Thoranne may use the building behind here with the entrance through the compound on the Sharia el Tolumbat. No one will interfere with them there. Have a typewriter taken over, and tell Miss Simms that she may be put on special assignment for a while."

"Sir, if you don't mind, I'd sooner you did that. I'll make arrangements for the typewriter, the supplies, and the other details."

The general smiled. "All right," he said at last.

In the meantime Jacques enjoyed the visit to a land he had never before seen.

"Well," said Lieutenant Cunning to Jacques, "let's get a bite to eat, and then we'll go across the Nile to the scene of the historic battle Kitchener fought with the Whirling Dervishes."

They ate at the hotel where Jacques was going to spend the night.

"You don't seem particularly disturbed by our Sudanese summer temperatures," said Cunning to his new acquaintance.

"I'm not," said Jacques. "On the contrary the air is so dry that it feels almost comfortable compared with the depressing sweat bath of Equatorial Africa."

"You'll probably feel the heat more when we get to Omdurman. It's just across the river, on the West Bank of the Nile, and only about five miles away."

Cunning commented as the two walked to the car, "You must have impressed the Kaimakam very favorably. I have yet to see him give anyone, outside of the military, the kind of treatment you're getting today."

"I really appreciate everything he's doing for me," said Jacques.

"The Kaimakam is very anxious about the future of the war in Africa," said Cunning, "but I think he overdoes it just a little."

"I don't agree," said Jacques. "I am sure he judges the situation very realistically: any external threat should be taken most seriously. I wish more people shared his anxiety. I do, I can assure you."

"I can understand why you two got on so well together," said Cunning. "His thinking isn't orthodox. He believes that well-planned *coups de main*, or penetrating observations gathered by one imaginative individual, can yield better results than complex military operations. Most people to whom he expresses his thoughts think he's nuts."

"The trouble with most people," said Jacques, "is that they don't think ahead, they don't think something can happen until it does happen."

"Maybe we are overconfident," Cunning said.

Jacques could see why. Everything looked so peaceful as the car rolled over the Nile on the long bridge connecting Khartoum to Omdurman.

In Omdurman, most of the natives rested in the shade of their huts on mats made of leaves and leaf stems. The few who did move walked lazily, protected by their long white robes, and the donkeys they guided seemed oblivious of the heat. In this environment who could feel any threat of enemy attack?

Cunning took Jacques to visit the Mahdi's tomb, the house of the Khalife, and what remained of the old slave market.

They stopped before a marble obelisk which marked the spot where the Twenty-first Lancers made their charge. "One of the men in the charge of the Lancers is a very illustrious citizen," Cunning said.

"You've got me on that," said Jacques. "Who was it?'

"None other than our present prime minister," said Cunning, "Mr. Winston Churchill himself!

Early the next morning, Jacques was shaved and dressed when there was a rap at the door.

"I expected to find you still in bed," said Cunning, "but since you are ready, let's go down and have a leisurely breakfast. The plane is on schedule. It is being fueled now. You will board at five-thirty."

There weren't many patrons at that early hour in the breakfast room of the hotel. Breakfast was served quickly, fried eggs on juicy slices of tomato, bacon (wherever that came from), toast, butter, typical English marmalade, and tea. There was no shortage of butter here, nor of sugar, nor of tea. There were no power failures and no lack of water or of any of the essentials of everyday life. Little wonder the war seemed remote to those military and civil servants stationed in this warm and peaceful city. The only symptom of war in Khartoum in mid-1942 was the relatively high proportion of military uniforms.

"Mr. de Thoranne, let's collect your belongings, and I'll take you down to the plane. I've been ordered by the chief to see you on board and to witness the plane's departure."

Canopus, a huge four-engine flying boat, floated lazily on the warm waters of the Nile. Dawn broke as Jacques walked up the gangplank to enter the ship. He handed his requisition to the steward at the entrance of the plane, went in, and took a window seat. A few minutes after 6:00 A.M. the crew started the engines, warmed them up, and the huge flying boat taxied sluggishly. It gathered speed as the engines roared into full power. It seemed glued to the river but finally broke loose from the water's grasp, and slowly became airborne. Even then it took forever to gain height—its load seemed too great for the engines. There was no wind, and the flight was very smooth as the great plane droned above the ruins of ancient civilizations, never far from the meandering river.

Four hours into the flight it landed at Wadi Halfa to refuel.

Six hours later it landed in Cairo.

It was just about 5:00 P.M. when Jacques alighted from the taxi and entered the courtyard of the building housing the DMI.

"What do you want?" asked the sentry at the gate.

"I came to see General McMillan," said Jacques.

"The general himself?" asked the sentry.

"Yes."

If the guard at the gate was surprised, he didn't show it. "Please write your name on this form and the object of your visit," he said.

"The general knows that. I'll just enter my name."

A few moments later, a sergeant appeared at the gate. "Please follow me, sir."

He led Jacques through a corridor, up a flight of stairs, and opened the door of the DMI's office.

"Sir, here is the gentleman you are expecting."

The general, a tall man with short-cut greying hair, aquiline features, and a wisp of moustache, rose to greet him. "Mr. de Thoranne," he said affably, shaking hands with his visitor, "take a seat. You are among your own here."

"Sir Alan," said Jacques, "there is no greeting I could appreciate more. Most of my colleagues think I am a traitor. I'm here because I don't think we are fully aware of what Hitler is attempting, but I heard him when he screamed he'd unite Europe under German hegemony."

"I've never been to Germany," said the general. "What convinced you that his words were more than the rantings of a madman'?"

"In the mid-thirties, I lived in Germany on several occasions as a student to learn German. I saw things that were not obvious to people on brief visits. I was impressed by the drive Hitler had infused into so many of his country-men. The purpose was clear: to rip off the shackles of the Versailles Treaty—peacefully, if possible, and by war, if necessary. I saw how that necessity was addressed, psychologically and militarily, with most of the government's ener-gy directed toward preparations for war."

Was it so obvious then?" said the general.

"It was when you lived there, but trying to convey that to people living beyond Germany's borders was another matter. For instance, in 1936 the Students' Association asked me to describe my experience in Germany. I did and told them that Hitler's Germany was a police state where there was no constitution, no citizens' rights, only the raw power of those in control. I told them how that power was channeled into preparations for war. I was booed out and called a warmonger. Now they're an occupied country."

"We came close to being one ourselves. If it hadn't been for the chan-nel….Mr. de Thoranne, I am most interested in your observations. I understand you went to America after your visit to Austria. What did you find there?"

"Sir Alan, I found exactly the same skepticism as had prevailed in France and England before the war. I sense it here today in many circles concerning the immense threat England faces in Africa."

"What major threat do you see?"

"Many of the facts I have gathered in my journey through African territo-ries point to one conclusion: Nazi planners are preparing a knock-out blow against Freetown that would sever England's supply lines to Egypt. I have col-lected numerous details and some hard evidence, all of which points in the same direction. It was not easy to detach absolutely reliable facts from the con-fusion and contradictions inherent to hearsay and to determine what valid inferences may he drawn. I heard repeatedly from different men that the Vichy government was building runways in strategic locations in the territories they control. Escapees who did not know each other brought the same story of German planes being stationed in the territory where they had worked. This, I agree, was hearsay."

"What convinced you that these stories were plausible?" said the general.

"When I was in Fort Lamy," said Jacques. "I witnessed an air raid on military objectives in that city. Fuel depots, ammunition dumps, and air hangers were bombed. The bombings were carried out with German planes, which I recognized as Heinkels He 111 Ps."

The general seemed surprised. "Did you see that yourself?"

"Yes, sir, I did," said Jacques. "I was close enough to feel the blast of a bomb aimed at supply ships stranded in the Chari River due to low water."

"What other hard evidence do you have?" asked the general.

"Soon after I arrived in Leopoldville, I learned from a reliable source that gold and black diamonds were smuggled to the Germans from the Congo. I stayed at a *pension de famille* called La Rotonde. Its café was a center of local gossip and beer drinking. While I played chess, all I had to do was listen. I gained valuable information and managed to get a sample of the diamonds."

"Do you have this sample with you?"

"No, I don't," said Jacques. "When I sensed that the Belgian police were hot on my trail, I gave it to the British Consul, along with my diaries, and left Leopoldville."

"We will have him send them here," said the general.

"Thank you, Sir Alan. In connection with that, there is another incident I would like to mention. I went out in company of the local photographer to get some pictures of native rituals. While in the forest, we encountered what may have been a group of diamond carriers. There were several natives accompanied by a few whites. What struck me there was not what I saw, but what I heard."

"I'm sure they weren't broadcasting the object of their mission for all to hear," said the general.

"No sir, they were not," said Jacques. "Some of the men were humming and whistling a tune which I hardly expected to hear in the depths of the Congo."

"What did you hear?" asked the general.

"A tune which provided a missing link: '*Auf einem Seemann's Grab da blühen keine Rosen*,' 'No roses bloom over a seaman's grave.' That's no landlubber's song. It's a German sailors' song. Were the men humming it German sailors? Probably. From where could they have come? A Nazi submarine waiting in the waters at the mouth of the Congo to transport the gold and diamonds? Probably."

"It is interesting, very interesting indeed," said the general. "Not many people would have been aware of what you have just stated. I know of no one on my staff who could have drawn such an inference. Do you have any other similar observations?"

"Yes, sir, I do, again in my diaries. I would like to present all the pertinent facts to you in a carefully prepared report. It would save much time if you could provide me with secretarial help."

The general pressed a button and an orderly entered, "Jacobs, will you ask Miss Simms to come in?"

"She's getting ready to leave, sir, but I'll try and catch her."

Obviously ruffled, the lady came in and stood before the general without a word. He sensed the heat behind the silence, and so, in his blandest voice, said, "Miss Simms, I'd like you to meet Mr. de Thoranne, the only member of the French Diplomatic Service to resign rather than serve the Vichy government and Hitler, and who sided with us when all seemed lost."

"I am glad to meet you, sir," she said, turning to de Thoranne.

The general seemed to discern a touch of mellowness in her usually harsh voice. *Maybe this will work,* he thought to himself.

"Miss Simms," he said, "Mr. de Thoranne has made important observations for the conduct of the war. Taken separately, by themselves, the facts might seem relatively unimportant, but when viewed together, especially in the light of information which only Mr. de Thoranne has obtained so far, they present a picture which could change the whole strategic situation and the outcome of the war in Africa. As such, it is highly confidential, and it would be disastrous if any of it got out. That is why I would like you, alone, to help Mr. de Thoranne put his observations together for our consideration and eventual action, if need be."

"Sir, I will be pleased to help him," she said.

"Very well, I will assign the guest house in the compound on the Sharia el Tolumbat to you both for your exclusive use. There will be no disturbance, and only you will have the keys. You may use the safe to lock up all confidential material. Of course Mr. de Thoranne will require a special pass. Mr. de Thoranne, may I have your passport?"

He examined it carefully and said, "Miss Simms, will you make up a temporary pass, and tomorrow we'll provide a permanent one."

"Yes, sir."

After she left the room, the general turned to Jacques. "Miss Simms is an extraordinarily efficient woman and is truly my right hand. She has only one failing. Some people find her hard to get along with, and she is extremely wary and circumspect with men. Some believe she's a man hater. Concerning her personal affairs, she's a closed book and is very discreet concerning the affairs of this office, which is, of course, exactly what we need."

"I'll have no trouble," said Jacques. "I'm sure she'll be very interested in the material I shall present to you."

The general rose and shook his visitor's hand. "Good luck. I shall read your report with great interest."

Jacques waited in an outer room until the orderly returned with his passport and temporary pass. "Miss Simms asks you to be at the office at 9:00 A.M. tomorrow, and the general wants you to stay at the Grand Hotel. When you register, ask to see the manager and tell him the general sent you."

At the hotel Jacques found many British officers and a room which provided all the comfort anyone could ask for in wartime. What a change from a month before when he was wondering how, if ever, he would escape from the Congo.

Chapter XVI

The compound on Sharia el Tolumbat was not far from Jacques' hotel. After a good English-style breakfast with an Egyptian touch—freshly pressed orange juice, hot-from-the-oven bread, croissants, fried eggs with bacon, marmalade, tea or coffee, and plentiful butter and sugar—Jacques walked briskly to the office.

The streets were cluttered with traffic, military and otherwise—erratic bicycle riders, burro-drawn two-wheel carts, and pedestrians overflowing from the sidewalks, walking, running, and chattering loudly.

Night had barely cooled the thick walls of the buildings along the streets. The hot July sun was turning the concrete of the sidewalks and the bricks of buildings into ovens. They exuded a subdued, aromatic oily smell with an occasional whiff of something cooking on a charcoal fire.

Not knowing what to expect from Miss Simms, Jacques left his shorts at the hotel and wore his war correspondent's uniform.

After inspecting Jacques' temporary pass, the sentry at the gate directed him to a building in what seemed to be a long courtyard. "The offices are not marked, sir," he said, "but it's the last building before the wall topped by barbed wire."

"I have an appointment with Miss Simms," said Jacques.

"You'll find her there," said the guard. "She's been here a while."

Miss Simms greeted Jacques formally but also, he felt, somewhat cordially. "Good morning, sir. I remember reading about your resignation and refusal to serve the Vichy government. I was in London."

"Most of my former colleagues called me a traitor," said Jacques. "My former chief in Jerusalem was then the consul general in New York. When he was criticized for receiving me in his office, he gave a classic answer: Remember, the British have not yet lost the war."

She smiled, but said nothing.

"First, said Jacques, "I need my diaries. They are in the safekeeping of the British Consul General in Leopoldville. I couldn't take a chance of having them on my person if I were arrested."

"What?" she said. "Arrested?"

"Oh yes. The police in the Congo had a warrant out for me. Fortunately, it was flawed. While they were trying to find a legal basis for it, I escaped."

"What did they have against you?"

"You'll see when we write the report, but I think the reason can be summed up in one sentence. They were afraid I knew too much."

"That can be fatal in this business."

"Miss Simms, I'm anxious to get started. Can you tell me where to get a good book on the geography of Africa?"

"Why do you need that?" she asked.

'My travels through Africa reminded me of the words of Bismarck: Among all the variables which produce history, geography is the only one that never changes.' In Africa, more so than in Europe, geography governs strategy."

"What is your conception of strategy?"

"Strategy is the art of planning and projecting a military move," said Jacques.

"That's an excellent definition," she said. "Where did you study strategy?"

"I took lessons with a Professor Jarré while preparing for the Diplomatic Service exam. He had me read Clausewitz and Sun Tzu."

"I'm familiar with Clausewitz," she said, "but I never heard of Sun Tzu."

"Sun Tzu was Chinese. Around five hundred B.C., he wrote a book on the art of war. A French Jesuit translated it into French and the King of France had it published in Paris in the late seventeen hundreds. Professor Jarré obtained a copy of the original work. It stressed the strategic importance of several factors, particularly psychological preparedness, military discipline, weather, and terrain, among others."

"Mr. de Thoranne," she said, "you'll be a fresh wind blowing into this stale office. There's a good English bookshop on Suleiman Pasha Road. They should have what you need. It will do me a lot of good to refresh my memory on these subjects. In the meantime I'll prepare instructions and a schedule for the woman who will replace me while I work with you. Here's your permanent pass."

After leaving the office, Jacques stopped at several bookshops and found the geography book he sought at one of them.

In Egypt before the war, there was poverty, hardship, and scarcity; in England, there was well being, comfort, and abundance. Now that was reversed. Three years of war had put the boot on the other foot. In England there was scarcity of almost everything and rationing of almost everything that was scarce: food, heat, water, gas, and electricity, not to mention clothes, shoes, or glass for shattered windows—through which poured rain and cold.

In Cairo, Egypt, life went on as usual. Abundance of food of all kinds, with little rationing, many manufactured articles from Hong Kong, no lack of water, and no air raids There was a sense of comfort and well being and little concern about the war—a lack of concern which made Jacques anxious. *Just what the Germans want for the success of Attila and Felix,* he thought.

The next morning Jacques sensed that something was amiss. Miss Simms seemed cold and sharp. She answered his greeting tersely. What had he done to irritate this moody woman?

He was about to show her the book he had found on the geography of Africa when she turned to him in a seemingly detached way. "Mr. de Thoranne, there's a big rat in the storage room behind the kitchen."

"Does it have two legs or four?" Jacques asked, smiling.

"Please, sir, don't try to be funny," she snapped angrily. "I loathe these creatures. I cannot stand them. I experience a profound physical revulsion at having one so near."

"Sorry, Miss Simms. Let's see what I can do about it."

He entered the kitchen, closed the door, seized the lid of one of the large copper saucepans by its long handle, and went into the storage room. The rat was still there, enormous, but quite sluggish. Beating it with the lid, he put an end to its activity. He lifted it on the lid of the saucepan and carried it at arm's length through the office to the courtyard. Miss Simms shrank from it in horror.

"Mac," he said to the guard at the gate, "where can I put this cadaver?"

The soldier started laughing. "Did Miss Simms see that? Did she run?"

"No, why?" said Jacques.

"You should see her when there's a rat around." said the soldier. "The fuss she makes. 'Can't you get rid of these creatures?' Her tantrums are a standard joke, but we have to be careful. She's very powerful. Thank God she's not the boss of Buildings and Grounds. No one likes her. She treads on too many toes."

"The rat was pretty sluggish," said Jacques. "Are you using poison?"

"Yes, sir, but it doesn't kill them outright. Give it to me, I'll get rid of it."

"When you've done that," said Jacques, "would you please wash the lid in some potent disinfectant. Rinse it well and hang it out in the sun to dry. I'll come back later to pick it up."

"The rat won't bother us anymore," Jacques told Miss Simms. "Where can I find a bucket, a few tools, some discarded bottles, and some cement?"

"The small office of Buildings and Grounds at the other end of the compound should have all that," she said.

Jacques broke a couple of bottles, stuffed the rat hole with broken glass, sealed it with cement, and took the tools back to the office.

When he returned to the private office, he found a much assuaged Miss Simms.

"Mr. de Thoranne, I sincerely apologize for having been so impolite earlier this morning. My horror of rats got the better of me. Every time I ask Buildings and Grounds to deal with the problem, I get the runaround. You solved the problem quickly. I thank you."

"Miss Simms, don't thank me. I don't like rats, either, but I must say that I owe a great deal to them as a species. I owe them something that has colored my entire life."

She looked at Jacques curiously and intensely with her big lavender-blue eyes.

"When I was a student in a university in the west of France," Jacques said, "I had an unusual professor of biology—the kind you get once in a lifetime. Some called him a crackpot, others said he was a nut. For me he was a real teacher, a nonconformist, and a true thinker. He was of medium height, a vegetarian, thin, with a pink complexion, blue eyes, white hair, crew cut, and an ardent cyclist.

"Sometimes before or after classes, he would talk about the trips he had made on his bicycle. He seldom failed to taunt the students, one at a time. 'See,' he'd say, 'what a diet and a healthy life will do for a man. You young people have yet to learn this. I'm sixty-eight, and I have yet to find among you nineteen or twenty year olds anyone who can keep up with me. Frequently I ride sixty to eighty kilometers on my bicycle before my 8:00 AM. class.'

"As one of his new students, I felt sure that some day he would challenge me. I admired the man, and I wanted to show him that at least one nineteen year old in his class could keep up with him. I said nothing but quietly started training, riding my bicycle twenty to thirty kilometers twice a week. One day it happened. Mr. de Thoranne, would you like to accompany me on my bicycle ride tomorrow morning?'

"I replied, 'I'd like to, Professor, and I will try to keep up with you.'

"Very well,' he said. 'Be at my house tomorrow morning at five-thirty sharp. If you are not there, I will not wait.'

"At five twenty-five the next morning, I arrived quietly before the grey stone house in the Rue La Fontaine in Angers and waited in such a position that I could not be seen by the professor when he opened the door. Two minutes later, the door swung open and the professor cast an angry glance at what appeared to be an empty street. He slammed the door shut behind him.

"Good morning, Professor Fabrel.'

"As he turned around, somewhat startled, the look of irritation on his face gave way to a smile. 'Mr. de Thoranne, I did not see you. You should have rung the bell. Have you been waiting long?'

"No sir, just a few minutes. I would not think of waking your household up at this time of the morning.' I could tell he appreciated my courtesy.

"Well,' he said, 'since you are here, I'll change my plans. Do you think you could ride some fifty kilometers this morning?'

"'I'll try, sir.'

"I was amazed at the resilience and stamina of the old man. When we returned, he was just as alert and almost as fresh as when we started, but my legs had all they could take. I was also surprised and moved by his consideration and the care he took of me. Gruff and sharp as he was, he would not allow me on the center of the road when we rode abreast, and he told me so in no uncertain terms.

"That first ride started a unique relationship. The professor was a generalist in the true sense of the word, and I was an avid learner. His knowledge of local history was unsurpassed, and I came back enriched from every ride.

"One day he told me, 'This morning we go to Champtocé to visit the castle of Gilles de Rais, otherwise known as Bluebeard.'

"It was a beautiful, cloudless morning in late March. The fresh smell of spring was everywhere in the air. There was practically no traffic on the Route Nationale. The professor turned to me as we passed a small lake.

"Mr. de Thoranne, what will happen to the fish if the lake dries up?'

"'They will all die.'

"'Why?' asked the professor.

"'Because their lungs are not adapted to draw oxygen from the air. They can absorb only from water.'

"'That is correct, but that is not what I wanted you to say.'

"A few kilometers further, the Route Nationale passed through some scraggly woods of oaks and pines.

"Mr. de Thoranne, what will happen to the squirrels if man cuts these woods and transforms the area into fields?'

"'They will all perish.'

"'Correct,' said the professor. 'Why?'

"'Because, with no trees to climb they will be caught by foxes, dogs, and perhaps even cats.'

"'What you say is true, but that is not what I wanted you to say,' said the professor.

"From then on, our attention turned to other things, to the One Hundred Year War and to the somber castle where Gilles de Rais carried out his alchemy, black magic, and torture. I still could not dismiss the professor's questions from my mind. What was wrong with my answers? What *did* he expect me to say? Could you guess, Miss Simms?"

"No, I could not," she said.

"I knew that if I were to ask the professor he would not tell me and that I might never know what he had in mind. He made his students think for themselves.

"A couple of months later, some time before exams, on my very last trip with the professor, we were pedaling painfully uphill, over cobblestones, through a squalid area on the outskirts of town. Suddenly a huge rat darted out of a hovel, crossed the street in front of us, and vanished into an alley.

"Mr. de Thoranne, what will happen to that rat if man cleans up these slums?' said the professor.

"That won't disturb him at all,' I said. 'He will go and live in the sewers. He can adapt anywhere, in any environment.'

"Ah!' said the professor. 'Now you have given me the answer I wanted from you. The rat is a generalist. He can live in the city, in the desert, in the woods, in the swamps, in the mountains, on a ship—almost anywhere, in fact.

"The fish and the squirrel are specialists. They are prisoners of their environment. they cannot adapt. Destroy that environment, and they perish. That is the fundamental lesson of biology. That lesson applies to you—now. In the kind of world in which we live, with that insane man in full control of our neighbors across the Rhine, anything can happen.

"There is no security anywhere in this world. Take the Confederation Générale du Travail, the biggest union in the country. The workmen who join it think they are secure. They are not! Their only true security is their capacity for adaptation.

"Organize your life accordingly, before it's too late.'

"That was my last ride with the professor. It left a deep mark and influenced my life. He convinced me to use my hands, as well as my brain, and preferably to combine both. I have always been fascinated with machinery, so during a vacation I went to help a friend of my father who had an auto repair shop. I worked without pay, just for the privilege of learning. I bought books on the internal combustion engine and studied them. I felt more secure as I was acquiring an extra skill.

"When Hitler conquered France, the specialists in the Diplomatic Service were prisoners of their environment. They did not dare forego their salaries, so they submitted to the orders of a government which was a vassal of Berlin."

"Mr. de Thoranne," said Miss Simms, "you have given me much to think about. However much I dislike rats, I appreciate the lesson. In some ways I, too, am a prisoner of my environment."

"Miss Simms." said Jacques, "now you're being cryptic. You are not execrated by your colleagues, or former colleagues, denounced as a traitor to your government, condemned to death in absentia…."

"That's true, but I have my problems, too. They have little to do with the present environment. It's something else I never mention it to anyone, but someday…maybe…one never knows…."

While waiting for the diaries to arrive, he worked with Miss Simms on the background of the report he was planning: the factors relating to military strategy in Africa, communications, storage facilities, rail and river transportation, location of airfields, fuel depots, and the like.

Jacques enjoyed working with Miss Simms. She was thorough, precise, and reliable. In the absence of his diaries, he worked very much from memory. Time and again she brought documented facts to fill the gap. Soon, wary as he was, Jacques decided he could trust her. Certainly she was sharp and standoffish, but her ambition was the same as his: to destroy Hitler and all he stood for and to dismantle his organization and crush the power of his military machine. As the days went by, he felt more attracted to her, more at ease in her presence. He admired her intellect, the sharpness of her brain. Also, she had a beautiful body which showed through even the crude military uniform.

One morning he said to her, "Miss Simms, we've worked together for five weeks now, and I understand a very complex picture a lot better. Would you listen while I sum up the facts as I see them? When I lectured in the States, I found few things were more helpful than stating my case to other people.'

"I shall listen with much attention," she said.

"The occupation of French territory gave the Germans deep water ports on the Atlantic Ocean. Three of these ports, Cherbourg, Brest, and Lorient, had well-equipped, modern arsenals, practically unscathed by war. This greatly increased the offensive capacity of Germany's submarine navy.

"U-boats operating in the Atlantic can reach any of these ports in relative safety, following routes patrolled by the Nazi air force, saving great amounts of time and fuel, besides markedly reducing crew fatigue. They don't have to return to German ports for repairs and refueling, using the long and dangerous route north of Scotland or the much shorter, semi-suicidal route through the Straits of Dover."

"I agree with that assessment," she said.

"The armistice terms between the Vichy government of Marshall Pétain and Hitler have neutralized the French navy and confined it to the southern port of Toulon. The Mediterranean is now a closed lake, controlled by the Italian navy and the German air force. This has severed the short route to Egypt. The supplying of Malta is precarious and extremely costly. Submarines have been used to bring in essential materials.

"The British merchant fleet, depleted by the thousands of tons of shipping lost to the U-boats since the start of the war, is stretched to the limit to supply Egypt. It must sail the long route from Liverpool to Freetown, to Capetown, then to Aden or Suez or Port Said. At convoy speed on wartime routes, that's an eight to twelve week trip to bring war materials to Egypt, compared to an eight to ten day trip through the Mediterranean."

"All your statements are perfectly correct," she said. "My figures show that we've lost over eight million tons of shipping since the start of the war."

"Now let's use a little imagination," Jacques said. 'Let me put myself for a moment in Nazi planners' shoes. What would I do? I would neutralize Freetown. How? I would prepare and supply enough air bases in territories controlled by the Vichy government to assemble a fleet of, say, fifty to seventy planes. In one raid, during the dry season and on a windy day, I would set fire to that wooden city and to its fuel depots with incendiary bombs. I'd immediately follow that up with a few planes carrying high explosives that would spread fire, destruction, and panic over the entire area."

"What you suggest is devastating," she said.

"All I'm saying, Miss Simms, is what I'd do if I were Hitler; in fact, I would already have made that move, but Hitler is a land man who's never been to sea and probably doesn't project the long-range consequences such a move would have."

"Why would you project them better than he would?" she said.

"I've spent months at sea. I know what a journey like that involves: the time, the fuel, the ceaseless battering of the ships by the ocean, the breakdowns, the change of routes to avoid U-boats, the stress on the crews. I know another important fact, probably unknown to Hitler. There are only three ships in the entire British merchant fleet that can travel from Liverpool to Capetown under convoy conditions without refueling: *Tyizdareus*, *Hephaestus*, and *Orion*."

"How do you know that?" she asked.

"I traveled on Tyndareus from New York to Halifax, where I boarded a corvette for the remainder of my voyage to England. During that trip I learned some important facts about these ships. They are the largest freighters afloat at the present time, twenty-two thousand tons. I've seen the engine room, the cargo space, and the controls. Their range would probably allow them to make the trip from Liverpool to Capetown without refueling. The naval bureaucracy knows their value and assigns them a place of choice in the center front row of convoys. That reduces their chances of being hit. I'm sure you know that subs usually attack convoys at night and from behind."

"It's a good thing you're not a German spy," she said smiling.

"If Freetown were destroyed, we'd have only three freighters to carry supplies from England to Egypt. What would happen to the war in Africa then?"

"Egypt would fall, but the people here don't think of the war in those terms."

"They should," said Jacques. "The Nazis have long been planning the occupation of Africa. Have you heard of Attila and Felix?"

"Yes, but I don't know the details,"

"The plan had top priority until Hitler's armies stalled in the Soviet Union. The first step was to occupy the whole of France, cross Spain, and seize Gibraltar. Franco thwarted the plan. He rejected Hitler's request to allow German armies through Spain. That's where the matter stood when I sailed from England last year."

"Where does that leave us now?"

"I've asked myself the same question," said Jacques. "The only rational assumption would be an air attack on Freetown. Is such a plan possible? I believe it is if the Germans can get the cooperation of the Vichy government, which controls most of the French Colonial Empire in Africa."

"Did you see any evidence of that cooperation?"

"I did," said Jacques. "Boisson, the French governor in Dakar, sent a navy reconnaissance plane to photograph harbor facilities and fuel depots in Freetown, confident that there was no air defense. The pilot brought the plane within the range of the camouflaged pom-poms of the old Vindictive. A burst of gunfire hit him and he crashed into the water. The crew was rescued and held prisoner on *Vindictive.*

"They were fishing off the side of the ship when I interviewed them. They didn't have much to say and mostly complained about the 'lousy' food they were served on the ship. W asked them what they were doing photographing Freetown's harbor facilities, they said they following orders."

"Boisson would never have ordered that reconnaissance mission on his own," said Miss Simms. "He must have received instructions from higher up."

"His orders could have come only from the government in Vichy."

"What other evidence do you have of cooperation between the Vichy government and the Germans?" she asked.

'It's hearsay and comes from the many Frenchmen who have escaped from Vichy controlled territory and have sought refuge in Freetown. I interviewed many of them and repeatedly heard the same story of new airfields being built in strategic areas."

"Did you have any other evidence than hearsay?" said Miss Simms.

"Not until after I left Freetown," said Jacques. "By then I knew how vulnerable the port was and how easy it would be to neutralize it."

"But you had no direct evidence that the Vichy government or the German air force would use any of these bases for anything other than air transport?" she said.

"Not until I got to Fort Lamy in Chad. The base's fuel and ammunition dumps were bombed and destroyed, and guess what planes did it, Heinkels He 111 Ps. I found out later that they came from Zinder, in territory controlled by the Vichy government."

"You told that to Sweeting."

"Yes, I did. He didn't know which planes had bombed Fort Lamy; but when I told him, he said it corroborated the data he had, and so he decided to send me to Cairo immediately to make a report."

"I must say," she said, "you've given me some pretty convincing facts."

"I'll outline a few more facts on Monday, when we meet again. I hope we'll have my diaries by then, so that we can start this report in earnest. I don't know when, or if, the Germans will be ready to strike, but I am anxious to produce the proof of it," he said.

"So am I."

"Miss Simms, could we have lunch here on Monday?"

She looked at him inquiringly, "What do you mean, Mr. de Thoranne?"

'There's a Nesco kerosene stove with an oven in the kitchen," said Jacques. "I could go to Spinney's, get some good food. and...."

"I am sorry," she said, "I don't know how to cook."

"Never mind. I do."

"You?" she said.

"Yes. Cooking is mainly the application of chemistry and some of the fundamental laws of physics. I looked into cooking when I was studying biochemistry and found it fascinating. When we went shooting the rapids in our kayaks, I was always the cook. The others pitched the tents and did the washing up. I don't think my menu will be worse than what you get in the mess hail. Is there anything you don't like or don't want?"

"No. Whatever you choose would be fine. What should I bring?"

"Not a thing."

Then," she said with a smile, "I'll do the washing up."

Jacques spent the weekend with a Commander Saunders who had never before been out of the United States. They visited Giza and climbed the great pyramid of Chcops.

On his way to the office Monday morning, Jacques stopped at Spinney's and bought a chicken, potatoes, tomatoes, onions, and squash. He also bought a bottle of white wine. At the native market, he got a bottle of virgin olive oil which was deep green and breathed the fragrance of olive blossoms. He packed all this carefully in a cardboard box which he carried under his arm as he entered the compound.

When he opened the door to the office, he could hardly believe his eyes. Miss Simms was dressed in civilian clothes. She wore a short white skirt with blue polka dots and a matching blue blouse with white dots. Hanging on a peg in the office was a jacket matching the skirt and he could not miss a trace of color on her lips. Lipstick! He had never seen her use it.

The woman's beauty was dazzling. Her deep lavender-blue eyes, her sensitive mouth, her dark, well-groomed hair, and above all, the refined distinguished and somewhat ethereal charm she exuded took all words out of his mouth.

He caught his breath and said, "Good morning, Miss Simms. I see you have adapted quickly to the hot air blowing in from the desert. That is a beautiful *ensemble, c'est de bon goût*. As you can see, I have done a little shopping and packed our noon meal in this boot box. At the gate, no one asked me what it contained."

She smiled, 'What do you have in there?"

"That is a surprise," he said. "You'll find out when the amateur cook serves your lunch."

"Well, I, too, have a surprise for the cook. Not a good one, however. The cook's diaries have not yet arrived."

"What can they be doing with them in Leopoldville?" Jacques asked.

"I don't know," she answered. "It may be procrastination, but it is more likely that they are trying to decipher the information the notes may contain."

"That leaves us no choice but to stick to our original plans," said Jacques. "We were going to work on the strategic importance of Mozambique for the Germans.

"The Gestapo has its headquarters in the vast Polana Hotel, located on high ground above the estuary of the Espiritu Santo River. The hotel dominates the port of Lourenço Marques, and the site provides an excellent view of allied shipping which stops there. From there the Gestapo distributes its agents throughout the southern part of Africa.

"I wanted to get a closer look at this operation, but the information I gathered in Leopoldville was so important, that I decided to proceed to British-controlled territory without delay.

"We can get to all that later, but in the meantime, I believe I should start cooking."

Miss Simms watched him prepare the chicken, wrap it in bacon slices, and place it previously heated oven over the two Nesco kerosene heating units. He heated a pan of olive oil and covered the bottom of the pan with sliced onions. When they were brown, he added potatoes, sliced French fried style. He then sliced and peeled the tomatoes and put them in a homemade Italian-style dressing. The whole meal was accompanied with white wine and followed by ice cream in dry ice.

"Mr. de Thoranne, I've eaten at least twice as much as I usually do. I can't recall eating such tasty food, except perhaps in the fanciest restaurants in Cairo. I want to do the washing up."

"Miss Simms, if I allow you to do the washing up, it will be against all my principles, but you may do so on one condition."

"Which it?" she said.

"Please do as we do in America. We know each other well enough now. Please call me by my first name, at least here in private."

She was standing next to him in the kitchen. A tinge of color flushed her face. Then she turned and looked at him. She whispered softly, "Jacques, I'm Irene."

He felt the warmth and abandon in that soft whisper. He seized her hand and brought it to his lips, slowly, gently. She yielded hesitantly, stiffly, almost reluctantly. Her hand quivered with inward emotion and excitement.

She said nothing for a moment and was breathing hard. Then, almost embarrassed, she said, "Let's do the washing up."

"I'll wash and you may wipe," said Jacques.

As he walked back to the hotel that evening, Jacques mind was on Irene. Why, he asked himself, had this graceful woman dressed in civilian clothes, which enhanced her stunning beauty? Her whole body trembled when he kissed her hand and yet, he surmised, she came a caste which would not show emotion lightly. He felt sure she was a woman of the aristocracy, bred to respect tradition and to practice self-control.

At dinner with the two British officers he frequently joined at table, the thoughts of the day surfaced once more.

"You must rate pretty high with the DMI," said Captain Fuller, "for the chief to have loaned the untouchable. This is the first time I have ever known him to assign her to an outside job."

"I'm sure," said Jacques, "he expects me to give her back to him as unblemished as when I got her."

"That won't be difficult, from the reports I've heard," Fuller laughed. "I hear she's as cold as the wind from the Arctic when she deals with men."

"I don't know." said Jacques. "She has always been courteous and businesslike with me. I have come here to bring what I believe to be important data to the DMI, and he probably considers that she is the best agent to correlate the different facts and present them to whom it may concern. I can tell you one thing about her. She's a highly intelligent and competent woman."

That, Jacques thought to himself, *should quell excessive speculation.*

Next morning at his usual time of 7:00 A.M., Jacques went down to breakfast and was surprised to find Captain Fuller already in the coffee shop.

"Good morning, Captain," said Jacques. "It's unusual to sec you here at this time."

"Yes," said Fuller, "I must go out of town and don't want to start too late." What's up?" said Jacques.

"Nothing in particular," said Fuller. "Although there is...I guess I can tell you. Jerry blew up an ammunition ship in the Gulf of Suez. I'm going to Alexandria to find out why they did not get the ship out of the way sooner."

"When ammunition is so badly needed," said Jacques.

"I know," said Fuller. "It's an absolute disaster. I'll have more information when I return."

Jacques went to the office in a somber mood. Irene was as inscrutable as ever. She wore her drab military uniform and seemed abrupt and despondent, very unlike the woman of the previous day. Was she, too, upset over the Suez affair? Before the end of the day, Jacques broke his self-imposed silence.

"Irene," he said, "when I went back to the hotel for lunch, a rumor was circulating about an ammunition ship which exploded off Suez."

"Jacques, it's true. I'm thoroughly disgusted with what's going on here. *Thistlegorm* made the run safely from England, only to be left at anchor in the Gulf of Suez for ten days. She finally received orders to proceed to Alexandria but was hit in the early hours of dawn with an oil bomb from a German plane and exploded with a terrible loss of life, and all because of the inefficiency of those miserable land-based bureaucrats."

"Irene," said Jacques, "was it inefficiency or treachery? They were saying at the hotel that only one plane came over and aimed only at that one ship. There must be spies at work among those bureaucrats."

"There are," said Irene tearfully. "I go to my office every morning before coming here and have warned them repeatedly and insisted that they get the ship out of the way fast. Nothing was done. That's why I've been so moody today. I can share my grief with you. If I were to vent it to the brass, I'd be told that these are some of the problems encountered war. It's awful to feel so powerless when you know what should be done."

"I'm beginning to wonder," said Jacques, "if we're ever going to win this war. This I don't give a damn attitude in the bureaucracy makes my blood boil. They should do everything they can to help the men who put their lives on the line twenty-four hours a day. This affair of *Thistlegorm* has made me sick. That and the underlying grief I live with has made this a miserable day."

"Underlying grief?" she said. "What underlying grief?"

"Oh, that's a personal matter," said Jacques. "It's this attitude of 'I don't care what happens to others as long as I'm comfortable and safe' that I saw all around me at Freetown. Just little things.

"For instance there are no launches there to go ashore from the ships at anchor in the bay, so the navy sends a launch to gather the skippers of merchant ships for a conference. When it's over, there is no launch to take them back. They are no longer needed. The navy's job is done. They must wait in the rain until some native with a boat is willing to ferry them out for an exorbitant price—of course, they can swim it."

"We're up against that mentality all the time. You know how badly we need all kinds of supplies. In Aden, the NCO's office is open from 10:00 A.M. to 1:00 P.M. and from 5:00 to 8:00 P.M. Skippers arrive there at one-fifteen for their routing instructions hut are faced sign: 'Office closed. Come back at 5:00 P.M. So the captain comes back at five is kept waiting, and then finds that it's too late to sail. A day has been wasted when ships are vitally needed. You have no idea how this angers me. Besides that, Jacques, like you. I am living with a deep affliction I've never mentioned to anyone, but sometimes I feel the need to share it with someone who will understand."

"Irene, anything you tell me will go with me to the grave."

"My life was ruined," she said, with a trace of a tear welling in her eyes. "My family had its sights set on the man I was to marry, the Earl of Dovercourt, a member of the British peerage. I never did care for him and didn't trust him, but my father, particularly, was adamant about it. I finally yielded. The man was uncouth, even during what I might call our courtship.

"The night of the wedding I realized the extent of the horror that had been thrust upon me. He got drunk, and his evil background came to the fore. His language was sickening. Before I even got into bed, I felt revolted at the idea that he would touch me. He pushed me into bed and started to pull my nightgown off. He then ordered me—I don't even dare tell you what—let me say, he ordered me as if I were a paid prostitute.

"Can you imagine what this did to me? I was brought up in a strict and straitlaced environment. So much as touching myself was taboo. I don't know how my mother even begot me.

"I was so revolted that I struggled out of the bed and ran to the bathroom to lock myself in. He got up to follow me, tripped over something, hit his head on the armchair, and was apparently knocked out.

"I dressed, took my belongings, and walked out, leaving the Do Not Disturb sign on the door. I called for a taxi and went to a nearby hotel, horrified by what I'd been through. I got a warm and comfortable room, took a bath, and lay sobbing in bed, wondering what to do. Then I made up my mind. Although it was past two o'clock in the morning, I called my aunt in Antibes, in the south of France, apologized for waking her up, and told her the whole horrible story. I had always been her trusted niece, and you cannot imagine how she consoled me.

"'Irene,' she said, 'come and stay with me on this beautiful blue Mediterranean, and we'll discuss the matter and decide what to do. In the meantime I'll serve as a buffer between you and your father. Get up early and take the boat train to Paris, and from there catch the night train for Nice, and I'll meet you at the Antibes station.' She asked me if I had any money, and I said I had about two hundred pounds and my passport.

"Jacques, you have no idea what that did for me. I was at a dead end. That removed a cloud—a cloud of despair. What could I do? Where would I go? When I boarded the train that morning, I felt sure that the Do Not Disturb sign was still on the apartment door. What would happen when that door was opened? Who would open it? I just did not know and did not care.

At the Gare de Lyon in Paris, I obtained a sleeper, and after a good dinner in the dining car—the first proper meal I had eaten since the ordeal—I slept until the train stopped in Toulon. I was still emotionally upset when I got off the train in Antibes. My aunt was there waiting for me. She hugged me affectionately. Her husband was there, too, and that affected me deeply. To me, his presence meant that if he did not approve, at least he understood.

"When we arrived at their beautiful villa, whose garden overlooked the sea, breakfast was served amid the orange trees, and my uncle discreetly disappeared as I told my aunt the awful tale. Then she telephoned my mother, who said the Earl was in the hospital with a concussion, and that's more or less where the matter stands. There's been no divorce. After a long stay in Antibes, my uncle entered me in a school for British Intelligence. I studied for three years. When I graduated, I was sent here—with a job, of course—but also with a wretched, lonely life. I, who wanted a family. I'm twenty-nine now and so lonely. Jacques, I know you understand the torment in my soul."

He took her in his arms, holding her tenderly. Her tears crept down his cheek. He felt her warmth and the distress in her trembling body. He felt her need for reassurance, for encouragement, for someone to tell her that her life was not ruined, not a failure but a triumph of steadfastness and dignity over submission to a life of indignity. He kissed her softly on her forehead, and she clasped him in her arms, against her breast. She said nothing, but her heavy breathing told more than a torrent of words.

After a while she said, "I feel so calm and rested, so reassured by your presence and your embrace. Selfishly, I've not pressed Leopoldville to send your diaries without delay because I wanted to spend more time with you and felt sure a few more days wouldn't make any difference to the war."

"Darling," said Jacques, "you are not alone with hidden distress. I've never told anyone about mine; I've never had anyone to tell it to. I know you will understand.

"I had a cousin, beautiful, intelligent, and loving—the only daughter of my mother's sister. We'd been brought up together; we went to the same school in England. When my family moved to France, she'd vacation with us, and I'd vacation with her family in England. We loved each other when we were children. Our love bloomed as we grew up, and our parents worried about it. They mentioned consanguinity, incest, and that marriage was out of the question.

"Then our careers took us apart. She worked in England; I went abroad. Hitler's dreams of conquest brought us together, after four years of separation, in a London at war. We were adults, now, alone, with all social restraints gone. Irene, you can imagine what that was like...."

"Perhaps I can," she said.

"I was ready to forget my trip to Africa and serve as war correspondent in England, close to Sheila. One morning I left London for a shakedown trip on a submarine based in Dundee. As I loaded my luggage in the taxi for Euston Station, the hall porter hurriedly gave me an envelope. I thrust it quickly in a pocket, thinking no more about it. In the train, as I sorted things out, I found it. The envelope had been sent by Sheila's brother. It contained a terse message: 'Sheila was killed in Monday night's raid. Her trolley received a direct hit.

Enough remains were found for identification. John.' Irene, I cried when I read that note. Thank God I was alone in the compartment. Those words drained every bit of energy from my body. I couldn't eat lunch. I arrived in Dundee limp and exhausted, thoroughly sick.

"A mechanical problem aborted the shakedown cruise. I returned to London depressed and disgusted—determined to do all I could to destroy those who'd killed my beloved. Irene, my heart has been bleeding ever since. Until now I've had no one to share my sorrow. I've never said a word to anyone. You don't know what telling you has done for me."

"Jacques, I do," she said softly.

They worked together in silence all afternoon.

"Irene," said Jacques, as they prepared to leave, "How about lunch here again tomorrow? I'll take the box and bring in the supplies unobtrusively."

"I would love that," she said. "I would like you to cook the potatoes as you did last time."

As Jacques was walking along Mohamed Mahmud Street on his way to Shepheard's Hotel, a man stopped him on the sidewalk.

"Excuse me, sir," said the man, "are you Mr. de Thoranne?"

"That's correct," said Jacques.

"My name is Trenet, and I am Gillard's copilot. We flew you out of the Congo."

"Of course," said Jacques, "I remember now. What happened when you returned **to** Stanleyville?"

"There was plenty of heat, and Gillard took it all."

"Where is he?" asked Jacques.

"He's sick with a violent migraine," said Trenet. "He's staying at the Heliopolis Hotel in Heliopolis. He has put a Do Not Disturb sign on the door of his room. He's nauseated and won't talk to anyone. We are returning to the Congo tomorrow, and he hates to fly when he is sick. That's why he is resting until tomorrow, but you can always try. He's in room twenty-three."

Jacques jumped on the next nonstop trolley connecting Cairo to Heliopolis; he had no difficulty finding the hotel. He climbed the stair and knocked carefully at the door of room twenty-three, which brought a terse, one word answer, "*Merde!*"

Jacques knocked again. "Who's there? Don't you see the sign? I refuse to be disturbed."

"When you open this door," said Jacques, "you will meet someone you have wanted to see for a long time and whom you may never see again."

"Who are you?" said the voice inside.

"Just take a look," said Jacques.

Mumbling and growling, Gillard opened the door a crack. "Oh no, you!" The scowl burst into a smile. "Do come in. I'm so pleased to see you. You don't know how pleased I am to see you. How did you know I was here?"

"I ran into Trenet on Mohamed Mahmud Street, as I was on my way to Shepheard's," said Jacques.

"Well, I say I'm pleased to see you," said Gillard, "but I shouldn't be. You have caused us more trouble than anyone I can remember."

"What do you mean?" said Jacques. "You didn't know me. I was nothing more than a passenger on your plane."

"That's true," said Gillard, "but you were a passenger who rocked the entire administration in the Congo. Now they have set up the most stringent passenger control system at all the airports. I've never seen security like it anywhere else. They even check us to make sure we are the real pilots.

"They were livid when we returned to Stanleyville. If I live to be a hundred, I'll never forget their faces. Velmeire and van der Meer were waiting for us. They cornered us almost before we got off the plane. Both were exhausted and shaken, and their haggard features and grim faces told of a sleepless night.

"Both asked the same question: 'Where is the journalist?'

"Knowing the story, I decided to have some fun at their expense. 'The journalist,' I told them, 'is staying at the Juba Hotel. He seems like a very nice person. In fact he asked our permission to join us for dinner at the hotel. Of course we were pleased to have him.'

"What did he say?' asked Velmeire.

"Do you want me to tell you exactly what he said?'

"Of course," said van der Meer.

"He said, I'm so glad to be here, out of the hands of those fools in the Congo."

"Well, we have to tell you,' said Velmeire, 'he is a very dangerous enemy agent. There will be hell to pay over his escape.'

"Escape? What do you mean?' I asked them.

"We had orders to arrest him and under no conditions to let him get out. Our careers are ruined. We are both finished. Did the man tell you about his plans'?' asked van der Meer.

"Yes, he did,' I told them. 'He said he'd take the river boat to get to Khartoum and from there go to Cairo. You gentlemen must have the wrong information. The man is a straightforward citizen. He is very nice, speaks French well, and is the bearer of a British passport. He lives in the United States and has recently been in London. He gave us a pretty good account of life in England. The man cannot possibly be a dangerous enemy agent. Far from it. He left us with the impression that he is a dedicated patriot, determined to do his share to help the Allies win the war.'

"What else did he tell you?' asked Velmeire.

"He described life at sea, and I sure prefer our life here. I cannot see how he can labeled a dangerous enemy agent."

"Of course, I never mentioned anything about the diamond traffic. Instead I asked them why they thought you were a dangerous enemy agent, and if they were sure of that, why they didn't cable to Khartoum and have the man arrested?"

"They were so frantic, they were not acting rationally and may well have done just that."

"That is a very interesting report," said Jacques.

"I'm so pleased you have come," said Gillard. "I never expected to see you again. Your visit has made me feel much better—in fact, well enough to go down to dinner. I would be most happy if you would join me. I'll take a hot bath while you read this latest issue of the *Bourse Egyptienne*, and we can talk over old times."

"I'll be glad to join you," said Jacques, "but we'll have to be careful when we discuss anything confidential. Egypt is full of spies. I've never seen a word of warning about that here, however. In France, the Germans have notices in all public places, *Der Feind hört immer zu.* The French Resistance has put up a sign of its own, *Silence des oreilles ennemies vous écoutent.*"

Jacques settled down in a comfortable armchair, perusing the drivel rampant in Cairo's daily newspaper.

"I have transmitted your request to whom it may concern in London, but I have no idea if it will be successful," Jacques told Gillard as they walked down the stairs to the dining room. "It went to someone with much power, and he will send it to the right authority. England is not as desperate for pilots as it was during the blitz. Besides, while you are still here, you may have access to important information."

"Yes," said Gillard, "I've just returned from Zinder for another prisoner exchange deal. They have built quite an airport there and are beginning to stock it."

"With what?" asked Jacques.

"I counted seven Heinkels," said Gillard.

"When was that?" said Jacques.

"Just a week ago today," said Gillard.

They sat down for a leisurely dinner. They discussed the war, the Nazi slowdown in the Soviet Union, the death of Heydrich and the reprisals which followed, but the conversation had a way of returning to the events that marked Jacques' escape from the Congo.

"You may recall my telling you that their first excuse for arresting me was that I had taken photographs of military objectives going up the Congo. When I got here, I had the pictures developed and chose a few photographs of buxom black women, had them enlarged, and sent them to van der Meer with a note which read:

> Dear Mr. van der Meer,
>
> I understand you were most interested in the photographs I took on my way up the Congo. Here are a few specimens of my work. May I thank you also for all the attention paid to me during my brief stay in the Congo. Warmest regards to you and Madame, who received me so courteously.

"You know, Gillard, that I had absolutely nothing against van der Meer. He was just doing his job."

'Yes," said Gillard, "but his failure to catch you has had major repercussions. Velmeire was demoted and sent to Matadi, the worst hellhole in the Congo. Van der Meer died under unexplained circumstances. I believe they killed him for his failure to capture you. No details have ever been released concerning the cause of his death."

"Gillard, I find that hard to believe," said Jacques. "It is horrible, if it's true. Assuming you are right, the matter would do little more than demonstrate the power of the Gestapo in the Congo."

Late that evening, when Jacques returned to the Grand Hotel, he stopped for a few words with the officers with whom he often played bridge after dinner.

"Missed you this evening," said his room neighbor. "What were you doing out so late? Dating the untouchable?"

There was a roar of laughter from the players.

"Would I be so lucky," said Jacques, smiling. "She's probably the best looking woman in Cairo."

"I was pretty sure you'd have no better luck than we do," added another member of the group. "She's what I call a real man hater."

Jacques saw no future in pursuing a conversation in that vein.

"I had dinner at the Heliopolis Hotel with the pilot of the plane which flew me out of the Congo," he told them. "The people down there are apparently just as neutral about the war as ever. Fine allies they are."

"Thank God Hitler was foolish enough to attack the Soviet Union," said one of the officers. "Had he not, we could never reconquer Europe, even with American help. In the meantime, let's finish this rubber."

Chapter XVII

When Jacques arrived at the office the next morning, Irene was wearing his favorite dress. He kissed her on the forehead, "I love that dress, Irene."

"That's why I wore it," she said. "Have you brought our lunch?"

'Yes, and something else interesting…."

"Oh?"

"After I left the office yesterday, I ran into the co-pilot of the plane which flew me from Stanleyville to Juba. I asked him what happened when he and his crew returned to the Congo. He sent me to the pilot, Gillard, who was staying at the Heliopolis Hotel. We had dinner together, and he gave me valuable information."

"What's that?"

"Last week Gillard flew to Niamey and Zinder for an exchange of prisoners and saw seven Heinkels at Zinder airport. In the report you and I are writing, I surmise that the planes which bombed Fort Lamy may have come from there. This information may provide a missing link; it confirms that Zinder is an active, hostile base. Obviously the Germans are distributing their older Heinkels, the original He 111 Ps, over bases in Vichy territory and, when the time comes, will assemble them at different points within striking distance of Freetown."

'What else did he tell you?" she asked.

"Gillard told me about the reception he got when the plane returned to Stanleyville. The district commissioner and the chief of police were frantic because they had failed to capture the dangerous enemy agent who knew too much. So Gillard, knowing the story, suggested that they send a cable warning the British in Khartoum, but he doesn't know if they followed his advice."

"They did follow it, and the Kaimakam thought it was hilarious."

"Does that explain why he was so interested in questioning me?" said Jacques.

"If he hadn't received the cable, you would probably have gone through Khartoum unnoticed."

"And I would never have seen the DMI—or you. See how things backfire?" said Jacques, laughing. "Because of my escape the district commissioner was demoted and sent to Matadi, the worst district in the Congo, and the chief of police disappeared mysteriously. Gillard thinks he has been liquidated. All that is pretty much in keeping with the normal practice of the Abwehr. I feel badly for the chief of police's poor wife. She was very courteous with me. Irene, I can't feel impersonal about war."

"Neither can I," she said.

Jacques went to her. "Irene, my self-control is weakening…."

"Jacques, the same is happening to me. You are threatening my virginity. What am I keeping it for anyway? For the man I have not found and am not likely to find? The man I know I won't find here, anyway. When the war is over, I'll still have to go through a divorce. How old will I be then? Too old to have children? Look at what life has done to me, partly through my fault and my own weakness, I must say…."

"Darling," Jacques said to her, "we are both trapped by our religions, our social conceptions, and our loyalties."

He sat in the armchair and took her on his lap. They remained silent for a while. He felt the warmth of her body through her thin dress. He drew her closer to him. He took her right hand in his and caressed it lightly, feeling her fingers and delicate skin, gliding his hand slowly over her wrist and forearm. She remained silent, her eyes closed, yielding to the soft caress. She seemed limp and helpless in his embrace.

Her dress had crept up, baring her knees and shapely thighs. Jacques was admiring their beauty when she opened her eyes.

"Jacques," she said after their long, quiet embrace, "you don't know what you're doing to me."

"If it's anything like what you're doing to me, I do know," he said. "But, darling, we can't let these lovely moments interfere with our determination to get that report out as soon as we can."

"Jacques, let's finish our day's work and think of ourselves afterwards."

"Another exercise in self-discipline," Jacques said, "then we'll have no regrets. In the meantime I'll fix lunch."

He cooked the quail he'd purchased at the local native market and made Creole rice and a salad of tomatoes and string beans accompanied by a few glasses of fragrant white wine.

It was an oppressively hot day, and the heat in the room was further increased by the kerosene stove.

"Jacques." Irene said, "I've eaten too much again and have probably had too much wine. That, and this heat, have made me terribly sleepy. Suppose we do as all the others, take a short nap now, and work later into the evening."

"I agree," said Jacques, "you take the bed, and I'll doze in the armchair."

"Don't do that, we can share the bed. I'll remove my skirt and my blouse and keep my slip and bra on," she said with a faint smile.

The silence in the hot afternoon was so profound that, despite their desire for other things, they both fell asleep.

Jacques was awakened by a gentle kiss.

"Jacques, it's already two-thirty. We must get back to work. I feel guilty when I think of those who are battling the Germans, in constant danger on the seas and in the air, not to mention those who are living under the bombs in London and elsewhere," she said, as she put on her summer uniform. "Why don't you dictate your comments on Angola. That will wake me up."

They'd just begun dictation when the telephone rang.

"All right," she said coldly, "tell her to come in. It's my temporary replacement, Miss Adair," she said to Jacques. "There's a problem and she doesn't know what to do."

Miss Adair entered, "May I speak before this gentleman?"

"You may," said Irene.

"The general is not here," said Miss Adair, "and I've just been informed that there's been another setback in Alexandria. The battleship *Valiant* was refloated, but there appears to have been another attack by frogmen. A mine was exploded under the ship and it has sunk and is resting on the shallow bottom. What should I do? Whom should I notify?"

"Find the general," said Irene, "and ask him what he wants to do. It's up to the navy to inform the admiralty."

"He told me to consult you when I didn't know what to do," Miss Adair said.

"I've told you what to do, Miss Adair," said Irene. "Find General McMillan and follow his instructions."

"Yes, Miss Simms."

"See what goes on here," Irene said to Jacques after the girl had closed the door. "I have repeatedly warned the navy to expect another attack by frogmen."

"I knew that *Valiant* and *The Queen Elizabeth* had been sent to the bottom of Alexandria Bay last December by Italian frogmen," said Jacques.

"Both battleships have been out of commission since then," said Irene. "Inactive crews become cynical, lackadaisical, and careless. I've warned the navy repeatedly. So now we still have no battleship at the eastern end of the Mediterranean. And see that girl! She has no idea where the general is, and she's supposed to know where to find him at all times. That's why I was so curt with her. Do you see why I get so frustrated?"

"I certainly do," said Jacques. "We seem to be suffering from a failure of purpose.'

"We are," said Irene. "We'll have to write an awfully convincing report to shake these people out of their lethargy."

"Let's get on with it, beautiful," said Jacques. "In the meantime I have a suggestion about our schedule. By starting earlier in the morning, we can still take a short nap after lunch and stop work at 5:00 P.M., or later if we have not finished by then."

"Approved," she said. "Jacques, tomorrow is Friday. Do you have any plans for the weekend?"

"None," he said. "Do you?"

"I have none either."

"I would like to take you out," said Jacques, "but...."

"Don't worry about that," she said. "I won't. Almost everyone leaves Cairo for the weekend. They go to the shore or to Alexandria, and I don't care who we see anyway. Tomorrow I'd like to go to the cinema."

"On Saturday we might rent a sailboat and have a trip on the Nile."

"Let's do that," she said. "I haven't touched a boat since I left Antibes, when I was staying with my aunt."

"We'll have to find a decent boat," said Jacques. "We don't want to get dumped into the Nile. I don't know if there are many crocodiles in the river at Cairo, but the water is filthy and full of parasites, which cause what the English call bilharziasis—we call it schistosomiasis."

"What's that?" she asked.

"A parasitic infection for which there is no good cure," said Jacques.

They started work early the next morning just after seven o'clock, when most foreign residents in Cairo were getting up.

That morning they compared information provided by British Intelligence with bits and pieces Jacques had gathered first hand from aviators and escapees from Vichy territory. They dwelt particularly on airport facilities within striking distance of Freetown—Guinea, Ivory Coast, and Mali, in particular.

The work progressed slowly. There was not a breath of air in the guesthouse; there was no relief from the torrid 100° heat. Lunchtime brought a welcome interlude.

Jacques had bought a fresh fish from the Mediterranean at the native market and cooked it when he first arrived at the office. He placed it in the refrigerator to serve cold with homemade mayonnaise and a salad of tomatoes and cucumbers. Ice cream for dessert and iced coffee helped them cool off.

After lunch they lay down for a rest. "We can take a nap now," said Jacques, "without feeling guilty. Why don't you lie down on your stomach, and I will quietly put you to sleep. Then I'll sleep, too.'

Irene removed her skirt and blouse and stretched out on the bed.

"Just raise your hips, beautiful, so I can put this pillow under you to relieve the strain on your lower back; you'll feel much more comfortable. Now I'll caress you from head to foot."

Starting from her shoulders and down her arms, Jacques massaged her. His fingers slid softly down her back to her hips. Through his light touch, he felt her smooth delicate skin, her goose pimples, her abandon, her savoring the pleasure his fingers brought to her entire being. While one hand caressed her back, the other undid her bra, which fell to either side of her body. Now nothing remained between his fingers and her sensual delight.

His fingers traveled deftly over her hips and down her legs to the tips of her toes, smoothly and lightly, only to start again from shoulders to toes.

When her skin and her breathing told him she was completely relaxed, he lay down next to her, caressing her lightly, until he, too, fell asleep.

At the movie that evening, they held hands for the length of the film. He felt her hand speaking in its own silent, subtle language, telling him "I love you." It spoke silently of that love all the way back to her hotel. He kissed her good night as they parted.

"Wouldn't it be nice...," she said.

"...if we could share the same room," he finished.

"You took the words out of my mouth," she said, "but they are so sticky around here about that kind of thing, and especially for me. To a large extent, I am a prisoner of this social/military environment. Jacques, dear, let's meet at nine tomorrow at the marina."

The marina, in a creek a couple of hundred yards wide, consisted of three wooden piers, jutting into the water like the fingers of a hand. Each pier had perhaps a dozen boats moored on each side. From the top of the sandbank overlooking the creek, Jacques could see the fleet of sailboats, motor boats, and rowboats.

When Irene arrived at the marina, she was surprised to see Jacques in a neat blue and white sailboat. The heat was already oppressive. The *khamsin*, the fifty-day east wind, was blowing hot, sand-laden air in from the desert. Irene wore a bandanna, dark glasses, a light blue jacket, and long pants. Despite her disguise, Jacques recognized her. A casual observer would never have recognized the brain behind the DMI's office.

"Let's go upstream," she said to Jacques. "We're already at the edge of town here, will be much more peaceful there than in the city. Besides, we'll have more privacy."

"There's another advantage to that," said Jacques. "If the wind dies down this evening, as it often does, the current will help bring us back to the marina."

When they were underway, she said, "Jacques, this is a dream come true. You have added a new dimension to my life. The pure sensual pleasure you gave me with your light, delicate touch over my back and legs gave me a feeling I have never had. Add to that the relief I felt when I shared my secret sorrow with you…. I have never tasted such inner peace since the day of that horrible ordeal. Just going out with you alone on this wide river, away from Cairo's crowds, is all I want. But everything within me is not tranquil. My soul may be at rest, but my body is seething with desire."

"You're not the only one,' said Jacques. "Irene, I want to kiss you so much, but I can't leave the tiller. It's the gusts we must watch. At sea you can tell when they are coming from far away, but here they are on you before you know it, and I don't want to put us both in this dirty Nile water. Look at the waves there. You're a sea girl, aren't you? Do you want to take the tiller?"

"I will, as soon as we are completely out of the city, and you can relax."

"I'll sit down near the mast and watch you," said Jacques. "That will be a real pleasure. The water splashed on your blouse and made it transparent. A good thing you have no bra on. They are beautiful."

"Jacques, stop it," she said, looking at the result of the drenching she had received when the boat hit a particularly heavy wave. The material of the blouse clung to her skin and outlined every curve of her shapely breasts.

"I'm glad we're practically out of the city now," she said smiling. "I would really be embarrassed to let anyone but you see them. The water has cooled me off, but if I had to put my jacket on, I'd stifle in this heat."

"As soon as you take the tiller, I'll record some of this pretty landscape for posterity, especially what's in the foreground," Jacques said, as he pulled his camera out of its waterproof pouch.

"Jacques, don't do that. I won't take the tiller until you promise not to photograph me in this condition. I mean it, I really do. I don't mind you looking at them, but I do not want them photographed."

"Darling," said Jacques, "the French were right. *Ce que femme veut, Dieu le veut*. I have no choice but to comply. Hurry up and take the tiller before your blouse dries."

"Jacques, stop it, or I'll put my jacket on, and then I will really suffer from the heat. Jacques, we were brought up differently. You have no idea of the straitlaced environment I lived in during my youth. Any comments about sex were unheard of in my family, and as for touching…I'll never forget the fuss my mother made when she thought…."

"I know what you mean," said Jacques. "Irene, you know I would never do anything you don't like or don't want. I was just a nasty tease."

"Jacques," she said, "you don't know what a change you have brought about in me. I'm alone with you, there are things I shouldn't want, but I do."

"Darling," he said, "it's the same with me. It's a good thing we are in the middle of Nile, where no one can hear us."

"How do you know?" she asked.

"I don't," he said, "but I have done what I could to insure our privacy."

"What do you mean?" she asked.

"I'll explain that to you in a minute, but I have been looking at the scenery beyond foreground. I see a cove on the west bank of the river with a few trees which could provide some shade."

She was obviously skilled at handling a sailboat and without hesitation brought it into the solitude of the deserted cove. As Jacques took the sandwiches from the knapsack, she asked again, "What did you mean when you said you did what you could to insure our privacy?"

"I arrived at the marina before you," he said. "I had reserved the boat by phone last night, and the manager chose a boat for me. When I arrived here this morning, he showed me the boat he'd picked out. But his sales talk was overdone, and I suspected he was giving me a bugged boat, so I examined it. I found no evidence of bugging, but I looked at other boats and chose the one we now have. It's not as nice as the one I refused to take, but it is acceptable. I have always been a little leery about our office, but you are in control there, and I have full faith in your judgment."

Irene laughed, "Jacques, we are two of a kind. I love this. You don't know how I appreciate you. Look at what I have here."

"What's that?" he said.

"It's a jamming device; it will jam any bugging ear within a few feet. I would have turned it on if our conversation had become more compromising. See, it's running now. You are something. I love you. We are really made to work together, maybe in more ways than one."

"There's no doubt about that," said Jacques, smiling. "But tell me, beloved, do you suspect our office might be bugged?"

"I don't think so," she said. "The general would never allow it, but Cunningham, the communications officer, hates me and is quite capable of doing it, although I control every means of listening device available to Intelligence here. I have a good agent on his staff. She is on my payroll and is very reliable. She has warned me to be careful. So I've had my radio frequency audio jammer at the office operating whenever we were engaged in any other activity than work. My uncle got it for me, and to my knowledge it is the only one in Egypt."

"I'm glad you are wary of Cunningham," said Jacques. "I know why he hates you."

"Yes," she said. "He propositioned me so crudely, so insistently, so boorishly, that I told him in no uncertain terms to stay out of my path. I told him to go and satisfy his lust with the prostitutes which roam Cairo's streets, but not to come to me with his offers. I told the general about it, and he understands why we are at daggers' point. I think he's wondering how you and I get along together."

"Do you think he suspects we are getting along too well?" said Jacques.

"I don't know," said Irene. "He may. I go to his office every morning before coming to ours and review what has been done the day before. The general is usually not there yet, but on Wednesday he came in early and asked me how our work was progressing. I outlined what we had done and told him I had received only one of your diaries and that we were waiting for number two. He said, 'Be patient. I talked on the telephone with Black yesterday, and he'll send it in the near future.'

"I think they are learning much from your work. They need someone they can trust, with a good knowledge of French and the ability to read your handwriting and interpret some or abbreviations, such as those I've come across in diary number one. That delay suits me perfectly. The longer it lasts, the more time we'll have together.

"The general also mentioned that I often miss meals at the mess hall. I told him we sometimes eat at the office and that you are the cook. Then I outlined our program and told him that for the next week or two we would work on the key to the control of Africa: communications. He seems to be ever more interested in our work, and I'm sure it will receive full consideration."

Jacques unwrapped the lunch. "Which do you prefer? The egg or the ham sandwich?"

"I'll have one of each," she said.

"We can rest here after lunch," Jacques said, "but I think we should be on our way back no later than three. If the wind dies down, we'll get back to Cairo quite late."

It was dark by the time they moored the sailboat at the marina.

"Jacques, we've had a wonderful breath of fresh air. How about a quiet day at the office tomorrow, with lunch there?"

"That's an excellent idea."

On his way to the office the next morning, Jacques stopped at a gift shop. He chose a purple scarab, with a gold chain, and had it wrapped by the store. There was very little gift wrapping paper left, but the employee did a good job with what she had.

Irene was already at the office when he arrived. "What do you have there?"

"Our usual assortment of vegetables," said Jacques, "and I found some nice lamb chops to go with them. I also stopped at the French patisserie for *babas au rhum*. I had thought of making some pancakes, but it's so hot today that the *babas* will have to serve as a substitute."

After lunch Jacques handed her the small package from the gift shop. "Irene, I thought you would like this small souvenir."

She opened the package carefully. "Oh, Jacques what have you done? This is beautiful," she exclaimed, admiring the violet amethyst scarab. "I've wanted one of these for a long time. I love you." She kissed him passionately.

When they had finished washing up, she said coaxingly, "I think we should take a nap. It was so lovely and calming when you caressed my back the other day."

"Let's do it again," said Jacques.

"Of course. I'll take my blouse and skirt off and put this pillow under my tummy as I did the other day. Jacques, this is so relaxing. I've never felt so comfortable and so distant from the outside world, so far away from the war and so content."

When her back was satisfied, she rolled over and her bra, which had been undone, fell off. She did nothing to put it back. She lay there, completely at ease, as Jacques admired the beauty of her body, her delicate features, her smooth skin, her obvious abandon of inhibitions. What a change, he thought, since the day he had first met this untouchable.

He kissed her affectionately and felt the lure of her femininity. He sensed, too, the intensity of her desire, the inside fire that embraced her. "I'm sure that I cannot leave the front to be jealous of the back," he said, as he caressed her forehead, her face, her neck.

She smiled and closed her eyes.

He continued the light, gentle touch down the body, over the slip, on the thighs, down to the toes. He felt her goose pimples, the electricity of her body communing with his, the excitement of her breathing.

"Jacques," she whispered, "I don't feel you properly when your hand passes over my tummy. Please pull my slip, everything, off and continue where you have touched through the material. I want to feel your hands on my skin."

He passed his hands lightly, ever so lightly, around her breasts, then over her tummy, between her thighs, and down her legs to her toes. Around them, in the warm room, there was silence, absolute stillness, no sound at all, except for her quiet breathing.

"Jacques," she said passionately, "I can't stand it any more. Please stop it now, before it's too late. I love you and I want you, but I don't want to get pregnant, and this is not a good time. I want you to take me, but I want to feel you, not a piece of rubber. You don't know what you have done to me. The pleasure I get from the touch of your hands is new for me. Let me try my hands on you."

He shared her eagerness and respected her restraint. Her hands, gliding over his shoulders and down his back, told him to be patient, and they quietly put him into the land of dreams.

Those dreams followed him all the way to the hotel that evening and into his bed. The reality of the present, the extraordinary relationship which had come about between him and his beautiful colleague, had brought a new perspective to his life—one he never expected.

Of course, she was married—legally, if not physically or emotionally. That was one major obstacle. She was a member of the British armed forces in a responsible position. That had to be considered, but he'd fallen in love with her, as she had with him. He was living in daily temptation, and so was she. Any other woman would leave him indifferent. He would not care about her or want her. But this one!

He had never been promiscuous. Even in his student days he was terribly discriminating. When he had his first taste of a woman, he'd been awfully choosy. She was a prostitute it is true, but he knew her quite well and liked her. He could not just pick up any woman off the street, one he did not know, get it done, and go his way. That was not his concept of love, nor even of sexual satisfaction. As for love, true love, he'd never given it to anyone except his beloved Sheila, and now, she was gone...forever.

He went to work early the next day. Irene was already there.

"Jacques, yesterday filled me with fresh enthusiasm for the report we're writing. But it did something else, too: it awakened the woman in me. Jacques, I love you."

He took her hands in his, "I know how wide awake that woman is. She's giving me an awfully hard time. I'm living in a temptation that grows fiercer every day."

"Jacques," she said, "I know how you feel. I have guarded my virginity—through my puritan background, my social upbringing, through my belief in God and also, to a large extent because I wanted to bring all of me, unblemished, to the man I hoped to find. For him I preserved myself, only to suffer that bitter disillusionment, that horrible deception of my awful wedding night. That night still haunts me like a dreadful dream; that night damped the desires of my flesh and left my hopes and self-denial in ashes. Then you came and stirred the ashes. Under them you found the embers and fanned them into flame. You set me ablaze with a passion I never believed I had, or could have. See what you have done."

"Irene, I feel the same."

When Jacques returned to his hotel that evening, he felt trapped. He and Irene were in a job together until it was finished, and he had still not received his second diary. He did not know how to control the love and desire he felt for Irene. They had so much in common. He could not dismiss the thought that haunted him persistently: Were they not made for one another? How long could they remain apart physically when their souls were already bound?

The more they worked together, the more he appreciated her understanding, her femininity, her refinement, her cultured mind, her physical beauty, and above all, the warm glow of her soul.

After lunch she'd sit on his lap, locked in loving embrace, his arm around her body, hand holding her just below the breast. The other hand would gently caress her legs, above the knees, up to the hip, ever closer to what she had denied to everyone that she had known before they fell in love.

Their romance did not impede their work. As they assembled ever more of the puzzle's skeptics in MI would dismiss as fantasy any prediction concerning Attila and Felix, and they both agreed to mention the plan only in passing. That did not, however, affect what Jacques considered his most important contribution to the war effort: alerting Cairo and London to the Nazis' plan to obliterate Freetown and cut off supplies to Egypt, leaving the eighth army to die on the vine.

One morning Irene said to Jacques, 'The general told me that he has heard from Leopoldville. Your second diary will come in next week's diplomatic pouch. It should arrive Thursday. I'm glad we've advanced our presentation showing that communications are the key to controlling Africa.'

"We still have much to do before that part is finished," said Jacques.

"We could work on it this weekend, Jacques, provided you have no other plans."

"No, I haven't."

"We'll have the whole compound to ourselves," said Irene. "With this hot weather, there will be no one left in Cairo after three this afternoon. Everyone will be out of town until Monday."

They started work early that Saturday morning, in silence, before the heat of the day became too oppressive. Irene reviewed the data compiled by MI on communications in Dahomey, while Jacques consulted his notes on river crossings. Irene seemed tense, perhaps repressing an inner emotion. He said nothing but sensed a strange uneasiness and feeling of subdued excitement in the air. He noticed, too, that she wore no bra, and that her thin white blouse was awfully transparent. He, too, was lightly dressed, with a shirt and pair of army shorts.

When she sat on his lap after lunch, he felt the electricity of her body, the passion of her kisses. He felt, too, that her entire being was trembling softly, like an aspen in a gentle breeze, telling him, "Jacques, I love you."

As his hand glided over her legs, between her thighs, it found no flimsy garment protecting untouched territory. Her breathing was heavy and fast. He said nothing; he just held her gently, affectionately.

"Jacques," she said after a while, "don't you think we'd be more comfortable on the bed?"

"I do," he said, "let's go over there."

She lay down uneasily, tense from excitement. What she needed, Jacques thought, was quiet and reassurance. So he lay down beside her unhurriedly and took her gently into his arms.

"Lovely," he said, "I know how you feel. Your soul is full of love and so is mine. Your body thirsts to fulfill that love and so does mine. We have plenty of time to enjoy each other's love and desires."

He caressed her gently, stroking her hair, her forehead, nibbling her ear, first with his lips, then lightly with his teeth. He kissed her neck, her shoulders, her chest. He unbuttoned her blouse, caressing her softly between her breasts, then on them. Gradually he felt her yield to abandon, and her tension disappeared.

"Jacques," she said, almost in a whisper, looking at him lovingly, "please remove my slip."

She was lying next to him, completely relaxed in body and soul. He ran his hands down her thighs and between them to the tips of her toes. He covered her with dainty kisses, on almost every part of her body. She lay there, eyes closed, motionless, except for her heavy breathing.

Finally, turning to him, she whispered, "Jacques, please touch me." Slowly and lightly, he let his fingers wander over her sensitive body and come to rest on her quivering femininity.

"Jacques," she said softly, "it's not right for me to want it, but I love you, and I do want it. Please go on."

"Darling," he said, "there's another one who wants it just as much."

"Until you touched me there," she whispered, "I didn't know how wet I was."

He kissed her lips lovingly. The lay in silence, enjoying each other.

"Jacques," she said softly, "I want to touch you."

She clasped him ever so gently, exploring with her fingers a part of the male body she had never held. Then she looked at him, "Jacques, I want to see it."

"Of course, darling," he said, as he continued his gentle caressing.

"Jacques, I want you. You've excited me beyond anything I've ever imagined. I can't stand it any more. I'll get my period in a day or two, and you can come in me safely. I want you to take my virginity. I want to feel you, your body, your sex against mine, with nothing in between."

"Darling," he said, "you can't stand it anymore? Neither can I, beautiful love. Just lift your knee, and I will come to you very gently."

They lay there, locked together, for a time that seemed so short, yet which lasted so long.

"Jacques," she said, "everyone has left Cairo for the weekend. Let's sleep here tonight, together."

"Irene, I'd love to, but your reputation...."

"On Saturdays the guard at the gate leaves at six. The next shift is always late and gets here around seven. We can both leave now, and I'll go to the office. If you come back shortly after six, you can probably get in unnoticed."

"All right," said Jacques. "I'll get some food, something to drink, and a few toiletries, and come back around six-fifteen."

There was no one at the gate when he returned. He'd brought enough food for the next day, including everything needed to prepare a good English breakfast: marmalade, eggs, bacon, etc. There was no one else anywhere in the compound. With the windows darkened for blackout and dimout in the city, they could look forward to a peaceful honeymoon in complete privacy.

"Jacques, you'll never know what you've done for me. You've transformed me entirely. Before we met, I had nothing but contempt for sex. I was asexual and satisfied with my frigidity. I had never tasted sex, even by myself. The experience of that awful night increased my contempt for what the man in the street calls love. The calls I've had from all these boors bent on satisfying their lust with me, their crude jokes, their uncouth manners, reminded me of that night and strengthened my resolve to have nothing to do with that unclean subject—sex.

"Then you entered my life. Somehow you seemed different. That day you joked about the rat. I was very unpleasant with you, but it didn't upset you."

"I understood how you felt," he said.

"I felt guilty for being so harsh, almost rude," she said. "All the more that you did what you could to solve the problem. Already then I had a secret admiration for what you'd done when you resigned. You threw away a good career rather than be a slave. Then came the day you asked me to call you by your first name, and the dainty kiss on my hand. Jacques, when I went back that night to my drab bedroom, I couldn't sleep. I lay tossing in bed with a vague feeling of hope. Already I knew I loved you."

"Irene, darling, I felt the same and couldn't sleep either. In my heart I knew I loved you. See what has happened now. After our minds and souls communed, so have our bodies. You did not even wince when I took your hymen."

"Jacques, I barely knew it. My joy was so intense I nearly fainted. I never dreamed of anything like that, that love could be so sweet—real love; when body and soul commune. Jacques, I want more."

"Irene, dear, we have all night and most of tomorrow."

"Jacques," she said, "until now, no man has ever seen me naked. Look at me now, lying here with nothing on, as though I'd done this all my life. I don't feel the slightest bit shy. I love you so."

"Darling, there's not much shyness left, after what we've done, but the loss of your shyness has brought one problem."

"What's that?" she said.

"I just can't keep my eyes on what I'm trying to do—prepare something to eat."

She smiled, "I want to ask you questions about things I've never asked anyone. Questions I would never have dared ask my parents. Questions about sex.

Asking my father was unthinkable. My mother would probably not have known the answer, anyway. Even if she had, she would have dismissed my question as unhealthy curiosity."

As they shared their evening meal, Jacques said, "I'm really hungry, but you seem to meet the definition the French give to their great lovers of the gentle sex—*elle vit d'arnour et d'eau fraiche*, she survives on love and fresh water."

"Jacques, I'll be hungry after a good night's rest, too." she said.

"Do you think you'll get much rest tonight?" he asked.

She looked at him coaxingly. "I don't know. Some of the questions I want to ask you may seem naive and silly to you, but...."

"They won't, darling," he said. "I'll do my best to answer them. Come and sit on my lap."

"Jacques, I'm curious to know exactly what are lesbians and how they do things."

"Don't be embarrassed," he said. "That's a question I had a few years ago and got an unexpected answer."

"Tell me about it," she said.

"It happened when I got a summer job."

"Where?" she asked.

"At the Colonial Exhibition in Paris in the mid-thirties. I was a student at the time and decided to make a little money during the summer vacation. Recruitment for the exhibition had not been well managed, and there was an acute shortage of English-speaking guides. I applied for the job, and when the manager heard my answers to his questions in broken English, he hired me instantly, gave me a blue and red armband, a map of the exhibits, and turned me loose without instructions or training. He thrust two English tourists, a husband and wife, on me without further comment. Both were very understanding when I explained my predicament, commenting, 'Well, let's explore the place together.'

"I picked up some pamphlets at each exhibit, studied them on the long way home at night, and a few days later found myself very much in demand at fifteen francs an hour. Not a bad salary at the height of the depression.

"I soon learned how to spot the right customers and quickly found that many wanted to see more of Paris than just the Colonial Exhibition. My fluency in German came in handy, too.

"Two German girls asked me in thick English how much I charged. When I answered in German, they hired me for the day. Before paying me they asked for the address of a nice lesbian establishment, information I could not provide.

"At the time I had much to learn about the ways of the world and did not know that such establishments existed, much less what went on in there. The time had come to broaden my knowledge. Newsstands in the Paris Metro displayed a recently published book with an intriguing title, *De Cythère à Lesbos*.

"I thought this might help. So on my way home one day, I bought a copy for eighteen francs. The book provided much of the background anyone might want, but none of the practical information I needed. That had to come from other sources which were readily available at my place of work."

"The guides who hung around the main entrance to the Exhibition were a motley lot, with strong representation from the underworld. I had helped some of them in their difficulties with English, and they were glad to return the favor whenever they could. From them I received some addresses of these dens of perversion but felt compelled to see things for myself. The directions had come from shady characters, and I had no intention of sending women who trusted my judgment to any cutthroat joint."

"Jacques," Irene said, "that's just like you. You already had the sense of responsibility that you have now. Tell me the rest of the story."

"I selected three addresses from among the establishments indicated by the cognoscenti of the underworld.

"My first call was not one I would easily forget. I went to the door and rang the bell. 'Get out of here,' the Madam yelled at me. 'This is no place for men. Don't argue. Get out! she insisted, slamming the door in my face.

"The next address gave me the creeps. Its dirty shutters, with peeling paint, its decrepit walls were enough to give the shakes to a clothing store mannequin. I couldn't imagine even the most dedicated disciples of Sappho going in there. I didn't ring the bell. I went my way. I learning, too, that these establishments had no façade, just a Street number.

"The next morning, at the Colonial Exhibition, I told one of the guides, a fellow everyone called Fifi, about my troubles. He laughed. 'Go to number four Rue Caulaincourt,' he said, 'and ask for Madame Simone. Tell them I sent you. Command with authority! Don't take no for an answer.'

"That establishment was located in Montmartre, a stone's throw from the cemetery. I rang the bell. The receptionist opened the door, "Men have no business here. Get out!"

"Fifi sent me here,' I told the receptionist. 'I want to see Madame Simone.'

"She is not up.'

"Tell her to come down. I'll wait.'

"Fifi must have been a wheel in the underworld. Some ten minutes later, bleary-eyed, an unkempt, bristling Madame Simone appeared. 'What do you want?' she asked sharply.

"Madame,' I said politely, 'I am a guide at the Colonial Exhibition, and some of my female clients want the address of a reputable house providing services like yours. I have come to make sure that any clients I may bring will be well treated.'

"Certainly, they will be,' she said indignantly, adding, 'Of course, you will get a commission for each client.'

"Madame, I do not need that. All I want is to make sure that my clients are well entertained and are not overcharged, particularly when they do not speak much French.'

"Madame Simone's bad humor seemed to waver. 'Monsieur, bring them here yourself, and I, personally, will make sure they are well received.'

"Madame Simone was obviously a good judge of people. She sensed immediately that I was not one of the usual species that hang around these haunts.

"You must be a student,' she said as I was leaving.

"Madame, you are right. I am spending my summer vacation making a little money and having an interesting time.'

"Some time later, when I brought three Dutch girls to her establishment, Madame Simone cornered me, 'Monsieur, we really appreciate the clientele you bring us, and you never ask for anything. I have already told you that you can always get a free meal in the restaurant up the street. Chez Emile is a very good restaurant, but you do not appear to have been there. Is there anything we can do for you?'

"Madame, I have not seen very much of the outside world, and you will think I am naive. I would like to know just how you entertain the lady clients I bring you.'

"Certainly, *monsieur*,' she said, 'that can be arranged. I am sure that Janine and Georgette, to whom I often assign your clients, will be pleased to show you how we entertain the ladies you bring.'

"They did! But, Irene, I was always a little uneasy about this aspect of the guide service. I never encouraged that kind of entertainment, but I did show my clients where to go when asked. In a foreign land, women can easily fall into wrong hands. I felt sure that at Rue Caulaincourt they would not be robbed or hurt. The reputation of the establishment was at stake, and my clients knew where to find me if they had any complaints. None did, although some returned later for further guide services. Besides, Madame Simone did not want to lose a source of profitable clientele. So the arrangement worked well for all concerned."

"Jacques, that's an interesting story," Irene said, "but it has not answered my question."

"It will, very soon," said Jacques.

The day seemed so short. They spent it loving each other and barely noticed how fast time was robbing them of what Irene called the most fulfilling day of her life. Outside, the shadows disappeared as day dissolved into dusk.

"Jacques," she said, "I have brought this candle lantern some friends gave me when England. I have a few spare candles. I have painted the glass blue, and it will give off a very subdued light which will be quite invisible from the outside."

"Irene, that's romantic. Love in the warmth, in this soft blue light, and the presence of your beautiful body is enough to drive any man out of his senses—which is just about what you have done to me. Do you think you can stand another session of massage?"

"Of course, I can," she said. "When you start with the back first, it's almost too soothing, but it's also terribly arousing. I feel as though I'm dozing off but want you ever more. Jacques, I need your love so intensely. I have given you all I have—my body, my virginity, and my soul. I love your gentleness, your sweet caresses, and everything you do to me, especially what you are doing to my sides now. You haven't touched me there before, but your hands are so light, your fingers so persuasive, that I feel them saying, 'Darling, I love you.'"

While his hands still caressed her sensuously, his lips covered her with dainty kisses—her ears, her neck, her breasts, and beyond.

"Oh, Jacques. What are you doing? Oh, I love it. Oh, Jacques, I want more. Please, go on."

She lay there, moaning softly, "Oh, Jacques. What have you done to me? Oh, come, Jacques, please come in me."

The candle in the lantern had long since burnt itself out. They did not need its light, anyway. They did not have to see. All they had to do was to feel each other's presence, each other's body, each other's love. They lay there, relaxed and spent.

It was broad daylight when they awoke, or rather when Jacques awoke. Irene was barely emerging from her deep slumber. She finally opened her eyes. "Jacques, what are you doing there?"

"Preparing breakfast before you faint from lack of food, after what you did not eat yesterday for supper, and what you did during the night. Here's a big glass of orange juice the eggs will soon be ready. The French bread has been warmed in the oven, and coffee's ready when you want it. Lovely, beautiful maiden, now woman, should I serve you breakfast in bed?"

"It's time I got up," she said, "and I'd better put something on, just in case someone should come by."

No one did. They had a quiet, leisurely breakfast, relaxed and content. They talked about the days of their youth, the strict ethics of the times, and how the war had shattered so many accepted norms.

"By the way, Jacques," she said, "you still did not answer my question about the lesbians."

"I did, darling, but not in words. I just showed you how they perform. If I had been a woman and both of us lesbians, you would have done to me what I did to you."

"I loved it," she said.

"Lovely, one must really love a woman to do that, to her."

"Jacques," she said, "I want it again. I could not think of doing that with another woman, but our love is so intense, so violent, yet so sweet, that I want it again."

The day went by before they knew it. When it came to a close, they put the house in order, leaving no signs of their weekend paradise.

As they were about to leave, Irene said, "Jacques, I'm concerned because my period has not yet appeared. It should have started yesterday, or today at the latest. There's still no sign. What does that mean?"

'It means that your body has responded to your changed state, from maiden to woman. I'm sure it's a perfectly normal physiological reaction and that your normal cycle will soon reappear. Don't worry and get a good night's sleep. I'm sure you'll sleep very well, and so will I.

"I will stop at the office before returning to the hotel," she said. "Let's start work as usual, early tomorrow morning. Let's have our report—see, Jacques, what I'm saying. I'm calling it 'our' report, when it's really your report—ready to be finished by the time we receive diary number two."

"Of course it's our report, sweetheart. Let me give you a long hug and a big kiss before we part."

As he walked back to the hotel that night, Jacques relived the events in his life during the past two years: the brutal conquest of his homeland and the silence of those he loved; his refusal to submit to Hitler; his departure from the United States to do his part to help Britain in her death struggle against the conqueror foreseen by Jules Verne in his great novel, *Les 500 Millions de la Begum*; his interview with Sir James; his acceptance of the dangerous job to judge the worth of Britain's allies in Africa; the byproduct of that quest, more important than the quest itself; the facts he uncovered about the threat to Freetown; his escape from the dangers foreseen by Sir James; the wealth of information he'd gathered—information which required sifting, analysis, and selection of the important facts; the presentation of these facts in a clear, convincing report, a report which brought another change in his life—an untouched, untouchable woman with whom he worked and fell in love, a love which both felt should not be, but which was....

Chapter XVIII

Irene was already in the private office when Jacques arrived the next morning. She wore a short-sleeved silk dress with a low-cut back and wide shoulder straps.

"It fits you beautifully," Jacques said, admiring the English garden floral print on the soft white background of the thin dress. "It couldn't be more exquisitely tailored."

"I've never before worn it. It came with a shipment of dresses from Hong Kong; I fell in love with it and bought it, although it wasn't my size."

"I don't see how you could have a better fit," Jacques said.

"I had it adjusted by an Egyptian seamstress who does the work by hand."

"It's pretty provocative," Jacques said, fascinated by Irene's well-proportioned body. Her slender waist and softly curved bosom were complemented by the tight-fitting dress, and her graceful arms and sleek legs only enhanced the lovely effect. "Your seamstress is a creative artist. What she has done with the dress—Irene! I can't get over it."

"Jacques. I wouldn't dare wear it on the street, with this lace-up front and tight fit, but I felt this was the day to put it on in the office. Besides my period came this morning. I feel so calm and relaxed and so different from the moody woman I used to be."

"You didn't have to wait long to know you're not pregnant."

Irene smiled and softly kissed Jacques. She shook her head as if to break a spell. "There's another happy thought. They've finally heeded my warnings about spies in Alexandria."

"What a shame it took the destruction of *Thistlegorm* to prod them into action," Jacques said.

"Let's hope Freetown isn't destroyed before we complete our report," Irene said.

"All we need," said Jacques, "is diary number two. It contains clear evidence that the Nazis are preparing to use Vichy-controlled territories to destroy Freetown. If they can manage that, a major offensive of the Afrika Korps will surely follow. It will probably be combined with the uprising of Hitler's allies in Egypt. Remember a couple of weeks ago, Cairo University students marched in a huge rally, chanting 'We want Rommel.'"

"Yes," she said. "Britain's situation is terribly precarious.'

Several considerations dominated the report, but both authors agreed that geography was the cornerstone; boundary lines and political loyalties were secondary.

In 1939, when World War II started, most of Africa was divided among six European powers: Britain, France, Portugal, Italy, Belgium, and Spain. France had the lion's share: some four million square miles, about one-third of African territory, and strategic ports in North and West Africa, which controlled the sea lanes and were vital for allied prosecution of the war. When France collapsed and Europe was occupied by German armies, most of the French African colonies rallied to the Vichy government and their vital ports fell under Nazi domination.

Britain stood alone, her lifelines in critical danger.

These political changes did not alter the geography of Africa. Control of the land depended then, as before, on communications. In the past penetration of this vast land depended entirely on communications. In 1941, to a large extent, its strategy still did. The means of communication with Africa was by sea. Ports were mere watering places, with little, if any, hinterland.

Rivers were the first practical means of access beyond the coast. Railroads followed; then came roads, most of them dirt tracks. Finally the plane radically altered the strategic aspect of the continent. To a large extent, mastery of the air was the key to the domination of Africa. It implied the use of previous land means of communication. Materials to set up air bases had to be brought from industrialized countries overseas and unloaded in African ports—many of them inadequate and ill equipped. They were then reloaded and hauled inland by river, rail, or road. These operations required a network of ancillary services, technicians, maintenance personnel, and laborers. Above all, these operations required time—an essential component not to be ignored or underestimated.

These considerations formed the framework of the report, and the diaries were to provide the missing links.

The second diary arrived on schedule from Leopoldville. Five pages had been torn out, but the remainder was intact.

"Jacques, I think we can complete our work within three weeks. We can combine work and love without neglecting our obligations. Now that I've tasted the forbidden fruit, I want more. I want you to show me more of it. Jacques, you are so good at making love. Where did you learn it all?"

"I learnt the little I know from various sources—some from biology, some from books. The East is quite prolific in this field; their literature runs the whole gamut from spiritual control in Swami Vivekananda's *Raja Yoga* to the satisfaction of carnal pleasures described at length in the *Kama Sutra*."

"They aren't the kind of books I ever saw in my parents' library," said Irene.

"Nor in mine," said Jacques.

Receipt of the second diary put the work in high gear. Irene hammered away on the old Remington typewriter, and Jacques reviewed the text before the final draft was typed. Irene handed the final version of the report to General McMillan early on a Monday morning. "Sir Alan," she said, "after receiving the second diary, Mr. de Thoranne and I worked two full weekends to get this to you without delay. The data in it were needed to complete the work."

"I understand that, Miss Simms," said the general. "The consul in Leopoldville found the contents of the diary very useful. He did say that parts of the work were cryptic, and he and the translator spent a lot of time deciphering the more obscure parts."

"Sir Alan, is that why five pages were torn from the diary and are still missing?"

"I didn't know that, Miss Simms."

"Yes, sir," she said. "Mr. de Thoranne tells me the missing pages contain precise data concerning the gold and black diamonds traffic. If you want more information on that traffic, we will need those pages. The report deals primarily with the Nazi plan to cut supply lines to Egypt, but it gives only a few details about the diamond traffic."

"Miss Simms, we may need more information about this. The next time I talk with Black, I will ask him for the missing pages. He also said that the money Mr. de Thoranne had received from America, which the Belgian authorities froze in Leopoldville, has been transferred to Barclays Bank in Cairo. It should be available to him now. In the meantime I won't close your temporary office in the compound. There may be more to do."

"Very well, sir."

After Irene left his office, General McMillan sat down in his comfortable armchair and read the twelve-page summary, which condensed the detailed study Jacques and Irene had prepared.

He gave the summary report a second look, rose, and compared its findings with the large map of Africa on the office wall.

He rang the bell. The orderly entered and saluted. "Jacobs, will you ask Jefferies to come in?"

"Yes, sir."

"Jefferies," said the general, "your opinion of de Thoranne has proven very discerning. The report he has prepared is lucid and disturbing. If all the facts it states are correct—and I know many are—the conclusions it draws are inescapable. Action against Africa appears to be high on the list of the OKW's projects. Whether the plan will be implemented or not is hard to tell, but preparations are too advanced for us to ignore them. The report leaves little doubt about the threat to Freetown and the menace to our supply lines. De Thoranne and Miss Simms have assembled a wealth of information in a short time. I understand they started work early in the morning and frequently left late at night."

"That's correct, sir," said the ADC. "They've been arriving at the office around seven every morning."

"Jefferies, take a look at this summary and tell me what you think of it. Of course, it's confidential," said the general. "Convene a meeting of the staff by Wednesday, if possible. Sweeting should attend. If he can't get here in time, postpone the meeting until Thursday or Friday, but no later."

When the ADC left the room, General McMillan pored over the lengthy report. It contained every piece of information an army strategist could want: analysis of barriers presented by distance in this vast land; distances to be covered to supply a moving expeditionary force; practicability of terrain according to temperature or humidity; navigability of rivers according to depth and season; crossing points of rivers; bridges, their length, capacity, and state of repair; bridges under construction; river crossings by barges and ferries and time required, maximum weights, etc.; lengthy reviews of airports built and under construction; population statistics with percentage of local populations versus Europeans, etc.

This, thought the general, *is by far the best piece of work to come across my desk. Considering its contents, it has been produced very fast. While I am sure de Thoranne is the main architect, I detect in subtle ways the hand of that brilliant woman who assists me with her razor-sharp brain The time may have come to turn that brain into a human being.*

In the meantime that brain returned to the office, where Jacques was reading the latest gossip in the *Bourse Egyptienne.*

"Jacques, I delivered the report to the general. He seemed quite satisfied, but I'll know more tomorrow. I must be in his office at nine-thirty. He told me that Black has instructed the bank in Leopoldville to transfer your money to Barclays Bank here in Cairo. You should be able to withdraw it today. The general didn't know that some pages of your diary were missing and will ask Black to send them. He also said he would keep this office open, as he may want a detailed account on the gold and black diamonds traffic—not to mention the agreement the Société Générale made with the Nazis. We'll have a little more time to spend together."

"Things are certainly going our way," said Jacques.

"One more thing," she said, "I sent a copy of the report to Sir James. There's a confidential pouch leaving today by air. Now I'm going to see that everything is in order in the office."

"I'll go and collect my money," said Jacques. "I'll be here tomorrow around ten."

When Jacques arrived at the office the next morning. Irene came into his arms as usual, but she was tense and excited.

"What's the matter, darling?" he asked.

"Jacques, she said, "you'll never guess what happened."

"No, what?"

"When I walked into the general's office this morning, he stood up, which he never does, and shook my hand. Then he told me to sit down, which he never does, either. Then he mentioned how pleased he was with the report. He said it was the most thorough piece or work on the strategy of Africa and on Attila and Felix to come across his desk. He was particularly impressed by the way we documented the threat to Freetown. He added that this work must have required very close cooperation between the two of us."

"Do you think he implied cooperation in any other field than work?"

"I don't think so. I told him that we had worked together very closely, that we understood each other, and that you were most anxious to provide all the data possible to help Britain in this struggle. I told him that, although we did not always see eye to eye, we always agreed to abide by the facts and not argue about their interpretation. 'Miss Simms,' he said, 'I am so pleased with this report that I suggest you take a couple of weeks of well-deserved vacation. That is a minimum your work merits. I know you have always wanted to go to Luxor, and I suggest that you take that trip at your convenience. I have only one reservation; I do not want you to go there alone. Whom would you like to have as a companion?'

"I told him Edith Stanfield and I have talked many times about taking that trip, but we've never been able to coordinate our time and that this is a wonderful opportunity.

"Yes,' he said, 'I agree. Unfortunately, it cannot be. Miss Stanfield was ordered back to England and left Egypt last Thursday. Can you think of anyone else?'

"No, sir,' I said.

"Then came the bombshell. 'Do you think,' he went on very blandly, 'that Mr. de Thoranne would be willing to accompany you? You surely know him well enough by now.'

"Jacques, I was stunned and felt myself blushing to the tip of my ears. My head swirled. Fortunately I was sitting down with my back to the light. The general looked the other way at that moment, but I was so taken aback that I could not find anything to say. Finally I said. Alan, I don't want to look as though I'm proposing, but I am not averse to going with him.' I was so embarrassed. He must know we spent the night here together. I'm sure he saw how flustered I was. Then he mentioned a few details about work and told me to stop at his office tomorrow in case I had any better ideas concerning a chaperone."

"I'm sure you don't," said Jacques, laughing.

"Now I've got over the shock, I think it's a wonderful idea. It is the last thing I would ever have expected," she said.

"And I've collected my six hundred dollars from the bank and changed most of the sum into travelers' checks and the rest into Egyptian pounds," said Jacques. "So we won't be paupers. I'm beginning to think your boss is a real human being. I wonder if he knows he's playing with fire."

"Jacques," she said, "I'll never get over this. It will be the best time in my life. You've no idea how I'm looking forward to it."

When Irene entered the DMI's office the next morning, the general told her that he had convened a meeting of the staff to decide what course to take, if any, in view of the findings of the report. He also said that the Kaimakam would attend and finally asked her if she had found a chaperone.

"Yes, sir, I have," she told him, "the one you suggested. We will leave Friday by train and spend a full week in Luxor. Then we will return by boat."

"There's no rush," said the general. "Resume your duties two weeks from Monday."

Irene returned to the private office. "Jacques, we have two weeks to ourselves. I told the general we would go to Luxor, and he wished us both a very pleasant vacation."

"Where would you like to stay?" Jacques asked.

"Edith and I discussed that many times and had decided to stay at the Winter Palace Hotel, on the corniche overlooking the Nile."

"All right," said Jacque "I'll make the reservations for the hotel and for the journey. We'll do what you had planned: go by train and return by boat."

August is hardly the time to visit Luxor—average daytime temperatures in the shade register 105°—but Irene and Jacques had no choice: it was now or never.

The railroad's first class compartments provided good sleeping accommodations. By taking the night train, travelers could sleep in comfort and have breakfast in the morning before the blazing summer sun transformed the ears into hothouses. While the train was moving, the heat seemed bearable; but when it stopped in Luxor, at the peak temperature of the day, the station felt like a blast furnace. Even the natives in their long white robes seemed subdued and listless.

Jacques and Irene went immediately to the hotel, where the thick walls offered some protection from the heat.

Luxor's Winter Palace Hotel was built in the nineteenth-century and included all the luxuries architects of the time could imagine. It was built for the affluent. In the mid-century Thomas Cook, of travel agency fame, inaugurated Luxor tours for wealthy British industrialists, in a day when England was the financial power in the world.

When Irene and Jacques arrived there a century later, it seemed there hadn't been much change since the days of Thomas Cook. The old British plumbing was still there, and so were the worn carpets. There was still the traditional luxury service and pampering of tourists. At dinner there was entertainment for the few guests in the vast dining room.

A male flutist in a long white robe wrested oriental tunes from a wooden flute while two girls in long black dresses beat rhythmically on tambourines of different sizes and shapes. When the tune was well under way a dancer of great beauty appeared on the floor.

She was barefoot and clad in a dazzling halter top of red and black silk, embroidered with gold thread, and a black, flowing silk dress, secured tightly around the pelvis below the navel. The dancer gyrated gracefully and lasciviously almost within reach of the guests.

She stopped repeatedly before Irene, unfurling a long green gauze veil, floating it through the air, rhythmically clicking the ivory castanets on her fingers to the beat. She looked steadily at Irene, rotating her pelvis, as much to say, 'Here, you newlywed, you lovely girl, are some tips from an expert to make your honeymoon more enjoyable."

After the beautiful performer left the floor, Irene turned to Jacques, "Edith and I heard so much about belly dancing when we got to Cairo, we thought it had been instituted for tourists. We were surprised to learn that the custom dates back thousands of years and is profoundly anchored in Egyptian society. Even today virtually all affluent Egyptian families hire a belly dancer for wedding parties."

"Where did you see belly dancers in Cairo?" Jacques asked.

"We didn't. We left that to the men. This is the first one I've seen."

"How did you like it?"

"Very much," said Irene blushing. "It fits my new frame of mind perfectly."

"Now that the performers have called it a day, supposing we do, too?" said Jacques.

"I was just going to tell you, I can't wait."

The room was hot and stuffy. A big fan over the bed silently breathed warm air upon them.

"Jacques, when I think of the Miss Simms of three months ago, I can hardly believe how uninhibited I've become. I would never have dared appear in the nude before any man, or even before any woman. And look at me now."

"I am, darling, and I love it."

After a good night's rest, they rose at dawn the next morning and went down for breakfast.

The breakfast room overlooked the Nile. Jacques said to the waiter, "What happened to the river during the night? It seems higher than yesterday and has a strange greenish color."

"You're right, sir," said the waiter. "We don't like this. There has probably been a heavy storm between here and Khartoum, and the force of the current has torn up hyacinths, water lilies, and many other aquatic plants. That's what's giving the river this greenish color."

"Does this happen often?" asked Irene.

"No, ma'am," said the waiter. "Local people consider it a bad omen, but you needn't worry, the river won't overflow."

The two lovers walked down the corniche along the Nile for their first visit to the Great Temple. There was no one at the ticket booth. Arm in arm, they walked through the monumental entrance adorned on both sides by great statues of Ramses II.

"Irene, when you and Edith were planning your trip to Luxor, I'm sure you refreshed your knowledge of Egyptian history. When did Ramses the Second reign?'

"Between thirteen and twelve hundred B.C.," she said. "There are two distinct eras in Egyptian history. One was a creative era, when imaginative leaders and hard-working peasants transformed the swamps of the lower Nile into productive land."

"If those swamps were anything like those I went through in the Sudan," said Jacques, "that civilization performed a titanic job."

"The second era," continued Irene, "marked the breakdown of the Egyptian civilization. Instead of using their power to improve the living conditions of their people, the kings of Egypt built the pyramids to achieve immortality for themselves, using sheer physical force."

"Which kings were they?"

"Kings Snefru, Cheops, and Chephren," replied Irene. "Building the pyramids broke back of the Egyptian peasantry and doomed Egyptian civilization."

"Irene, you've summed up in a few words the evolution of thousands of years of Egyptian history. Your capacity of synthesis is unmatched. Where are we now?'

"This is the precinct of the temple," she said. "Look at this magnificent piece of work. I can imagine this place, filled with hundreds of men toiling in the heat of the day to build this edifice by hand and under the whips of the overseers. Those poor people. Look at the place now. It's a skeleton with no flesh and no life. The dead silence within this empty shell is eerie."

"When I admire these remains," said Jacques, "and think of what you've just said about the misuse of power by the Egyptian Kings…isn't our civilization on the same path? Using its power to self-destroy? To ruin our social structure, as did the Egyptian kings?"

"As things stand now, that's an open question," said Irene.

On their way back to the hotel, they stopped at the animal market. "We've seen vestiges of the dead past," said Irene. "Now let's see the living past."

"The market doesn't seem to have changed much in thousands of years," said Jacques.

"With the same animals for sale," said Irene. "Donkeys, horses, mules, and, yes, I see even camels."

"The fellahin have continued to live on, poor as their ancestors, through wars, social upheavals, pyramid building, and disease," said Jacques. "And there's a living city, too. I thought there were only ruins here. How many people are there?"

"Thirty-five to forty thousand," said Irene.

"We've walked a lot this morning in this 100° heat. Are you ready for lunch?" asked Jacques.

"I am," she said, "and a nap afterwards."

They were both hungry, and the meal was welcome. Fresh fish from the Nile, lamb chops with fried potatoes, and a delicious platter of sliced eggplant, fried and seasoned in a tasty tomato sauce, aroused their appetites for a desert of flambéed bananas, broiled in a potent liqueur, followed by a cup of French/Egyptian coffee.

The shades had been drawn in their room, mellowing the harsh outside light. Irene shed her clothes and lay on the bed. Jacques lay next to her and took her hand.

"Beautiful, lovely woman, every moment I spend with you lets me know you better and love you more. When I first met you, I was enthralled by your intellect and the sharpness of your brain; then by the beauty of your body; and now by the compassion and sensitivity which well from the depths of your heart—of your feel for the enslaved workers of Egypt—and for your comments after that terrible tragedy of *Thistlegorrn* about all the grieving families. Lovely beautiful, you have every wonderful quality a woman can have—intelligence, beauty, and heart. Darling, I want you to be my wife."

She looked at him lovingly and drew his head to her lips. She squeezed him tightly in her arms; they remained there for a while, feeling each other, without a word. Finally Jacques looked into her eyes and said softly, "Darling, beloved, there remains only one problem to solve!"

"What is that?" she said.

"Your divorce must be settled before we can make this official. What formalities must be undertaken?"

"Jacques, there's no problem. The day we left Cairo, I received several letters in the diplomatic pouch, including papers legalizing my divorce. The Earl took care of the proceedings."

"Sweetheart, why didn't you tell me?" Jacques asked.

"I didn't want you to think I was pressing you," she said.

"Irene," said Jacques, "you're too discreet. You should know me better than that. I've been worrying about the divorce since we left Cairo. I'm so happy. This solves our problem. What more do you want?"

"Only one thing," she said.

"What's that?" Jacques asked.

She hesitated for a moment and whispered, "I want your baby—now."

Two days later they were legally husband and wife. They visited and explored Karnak, Thebes, Denderah, Abydos, and Deizel Bahari, the valley of the kings and queens. On the day their riverboat was scheduled to leave for Cairo, Jacques stopped at the desk to settle their account.

"Sir," said the cashier, "there's nothing due on this account."

Jacques returned to the room. "Irene, when I went to pay the bill the cashier told me there was no money due. He assured me there was no mistake."

"No, there wasn't," said Irene. "I went down earlier this morning and settled the account."

"Darling, I don't want you to do that," said Jacques.

"Jacques, I do want to do it. I'm on a regular salary and you've been putting all your time into the report. Besides this was money I had put aside long ago for this trip, which out somewhat differently than I had ever expected."

"You are so thoughtful," said Jacques, kissing her. "A good thing I've paid for the boat tickets."

When Irene entered the general's office on the following Monday morning, she said, "Good morning, Sir Alan. Your administrative assistant is now a married woman."

"Madame de Thoranne, that was not entirely unexpected," said the general. "I'm sure both of you have made an excellent choice. You have shown that you know how to work together, and I am sure you will know how to live together. I know that you both wish to go to the United States, but I need your husband's help for the next two or three months."

"I'm sure he'll be willing to give you any help he can," said Irene. "He's waiting outside. Shall I ask him to come in?"

"Please do."

When Jacques had been shown in, the general said to him, "I have told your wife that you have both made an excellent choice. Although no one told me so, I sense that you both will want to go to the United States. Before that, however, I have need for your services."

"How can I help?" said Jacques.

The general thought for a moment, then said, "Your broadcasts from the BBC in London to the French in France and those from Freetown and Lagos to Vichy-controlled colonies in Africa were excellent. Here and now, we need a man we can trust to broadcast a message in French two or three times a week to the general population of Morocco, Algeria, and Tunisia. Would you be willing to undertake this job?"

"What kind of message, sir?" asked Jacques.

"A message to convey to the inhabitants there that they have more to expect from allies than from the Germans," said the general.

"That sounds to me like the prelude to an Allied invasion of North Africa."

"Mr. de Thoranne," said the general, "you may draw any inference you wish from my request. I cannot confirm or deny anything of what you may be thinking, but you may prepare your broadcasts with that possibility in mind."

"Sir Alan, my broadcasts from London to France attempted to sustain hope in a helpless, occupied populace, a populace crushed in an overwhelming defeat, absolutely convinced that Germany had won the war. My broadcasts from Freetown and Lagos had a different objective."

"What was it? I'm not familiar with your African broadcasts."

"That message suggested," said Jacques, "that the time might come when they could take up arms to expel the invader from the fatherland. Since I gave those broadcasts, the situation has changed and America is in the war, German armies have been mauled in the Soviet Union, and a German victory is no longer certain—in fact, it is improbable."

"That is precisely the information I want you to convey." said the general.

"I would be careful," said Jacques, "not to leave the impression to suggest a revolt against the army, the navy or the French colonial administration. That would certainly backfire. The French army believes the British betrayed them at Dunkerque, and the French navy is traditionally anti-British. That resentment was fanned into flame by the affairs of Mers el Kebir and Dakar. The French colonial administration is anti-de Gaulle.

"I would dwell mainly on how the Nazis are treating the conquered population of France with a daily levy of three hundred million francs a day, shortages of food, heavy rationing, arrests without charges, shooting of hostages, et cetera. Then I could create the hope that American might will turn the tide. After that, I would have to play it by ear."

"Mr. de Thoranne," said the general, "I trust your judgment. Your scripts should be passed by censor but as a mere formality. In addition I would like you to provide all the information you gathered about the gold and black diamond traffic. Leopoldville has sent the missing pages of your diary. You may continue to use the guesthouse as your office, not to mention, of course," he added with a smile, "the help of the newly-married woman."

"Thank you, sir," said Jacques. "I will plan on three five-minute broadcasts per week. I cannot forecast what success, if any, these broadcasts may have. I can only hope for the best. Please provide me with any pertinent information which can be disclosed safely."

"You will get our confidential daily report," said the general.

At 6:00 P.M. on Sunday, November 8, 1942, the telephone in Jacques' bedroom rang. "Mr. de Thoranne," said the voice of the ADC, "General McMillan wants to see you immediately. This is an emergency."

"All right, sir," said Jacques, "I'll be in his office in a few minutes."

When Jacques arrived, the general said to him, "Mr. de Thoranne, an Anglo-American task force is landing in Morocco and Algeria at this very moment. The British landing parties are wearing American uniforms because it is believed that only Americans will be welcome. Unfortunately the invading force is meeting resistance in several sectors. French officers are complying with Marshal Pétain's standing orders to resist invasion from wherever it may come. After months of broadcasting to North Africa, your voice is well known, and the information you provide is trusted. Get on the air to reassure the population that a friendly American task force has come to prevent occupation of North Africa by the Nazis. Go to the studio immediately."

"All right, sir," said Jacques, "but I need a few minutes to collect my thoughts to deliver a coherent and inspiring message."

"Mr. de Thoranne," said the general, "the population knows you. Go on the air extemporaneously. This is urgent. We are all losing good men. Time is of the essence."

"Sir," said Jacques, "I will not talk of surrender or yielding or laying down of arms. I will stress cooperation with friends who have come from America to rid France of the invader."

Later in the day, Jacques returned to the general's office. "Sir Alan, I have improved the hasty broadcast of this morning. While the new one has the same general theme, I have added two extra thoughts: First I said it is rumored that the Nazis are about to invade the unoccupied part of France; second I said the loss of lives of good people on both sides can be avoided by acting logically and helping friends, rather than obeying orders which are no longer relevant. Sir Alan, I don't know what effect that last statement will have."

"Events will probably bear you out on both counts," said the general.

Three days later Hitler's armed forces entered the unoccupied part of France and imposed the conqueror's rule on the entire country, from the English Channel to the Mediterranean Sea. That occupation, in violation of the armistice, brought French armed forces in the colonies back into the war on the Allies' side.

There was only one holdout: Pierre Boisson, Governor General of the French colonies in Africa, who still felt bound by Marshal Pétain's orders. The port of Dakar, where Boisson had his headquarters, was badly needed by the Allies. General Eisenhower insisted on obtaining Boisson's cooperation and sent an emissary, General Bergeret, to Dakar for that purpose. Fearing a trap the wary governor sent his own trusted emissaries to Algiers to discuss the matter with General Eisenhower. Only then did he agree to cooperate with the Allies.

General McMillan called Jacques into his office.

"Mr. de Thoranne, your broadcasts are the only obstacle to a formal agreement between General Eisenhower and Governor Boisson. The governor has agreed to put the port of Dakar at the disposal of the Allies, provided these broadcasts cease immediately."

"I have no objection whatever," said Jacques smiling. "Do you, Sir Alan?"

"No," said the general. "We have learnt something, Mr. de Thoranne. You expressed doubts about the effectiveness of your broadcasts. Now do you have the answer?"

"I certainly do, straight from the horse's mouth."

"Now that your special job is finished," said the general, "I know you want to return to the United States. I will make arrangements with the navy to provide passage for you and your wife on a warship going to the U.S. for refitting."

"Where will we embark?"

"I don't know yet. It could be Gibraltar or Freetown or perhaps even Lagos. I will try and obtain a berth on a cruiser, which, at this time of the year, will be more comfortable than a destroyer."

"Thank you, Sir Alan," said Jacques. "My wife is a good sailor, but she is pregnant, and I'm sure she will appreciate that."

"As soon as you arrive," said the general, "go to New York and call on Mr. Stevenson, who coordinates American and British Intelligence Services. Your help is needed at the Office of Strategic Services. Your knowledge of the Moslem world and your expertise and fluency in French will fill a gap there. American coverage of French African colonies is rudimentary. In 1940 the United States had only five consulates and twenty employees in that vast area, which has become so important now."

Late in the afternoon, a few days before Christmas, the eight thousand-ton British cruiser *Shropshire* docked at the Philadelphia arsenal. Dusk was settling on the waterfront. A cold, biting wind, driving a thin, drizzly snow, deepened the gloom hanging like a shroud over the dimmed lights of the great city.

Irene and Jacques secured their greatcoats as they walked down the gang-plank to a van sent by the Immigration and Customs office. Formalities did not

take long; uniformed personnel were whisked through rapidly. The two boarded a taxi for Jacques' apartment on Spruce Street.

His landlady, a wealthy widow, had kept the apartment exactly as Jacques had
left it. She had even kept the telephone connected. She greeted Jacques warmly,
"I'm so glad to see you back safe and sound, and what is this? Do I see a wife?"

"You do, Mrs. Nicols, a wonderful wife."

"I'm delighted to meet you, Mrs. de Thoranne," she said to Irene. "You'll find
the apartment ready to welcome you. Just turn up the thermostat, and you will be
warm and comfortable. I've kept the temperature at fifty-five degrees to save fuel."

Jacques had just turned the thermostat up when the telephone rang.

"Now no one can know I'm back in the apartment. There must be an error
or a call from someone who just found my name in the phone book. Holloa!"
he said, lifting the receiver.

"Are you standing up, or sitting down?" a voice asked.

"I'm standing up," said Jacques, "but who is this?"

"Well, you'd better sit down, because you're going to be floored. This is
Hanson."

"Oh no, George. I recognize your voice. How are you? How's *Burdock?*
Where are you?"

"I'm in Philly at the Navy Yard. I came to get a new corvette. *Burdock* took
such a beating on our last convoy to Malta that they decided to scrap her."

"Get a taxi, and I'll meet you in half an hour at Bookbinder's for dinner,
and I'll bring my wife. I'll call now to make reservations."

"I didn't know you were married," said George.

"I wasn't, but I am now."

Jacques introduced Irene to Hanson as they sat down for dinner. Over dinner George and Jacques discussed their experiences and the trip on *Burdock*
from Freetown to Lagos. George told them about *Burdock's* last trip when she
was part of a large force escorting six freighters to Malta. Four freighters were
sunk, but two got through, saving Malta; however, the *Burdock* just about made
it back to Gibraltar.

George described another harrowing experience when a whole convoy was
lost. *Burdock* and a destroyer were escorting a five-ship convoy south of
Gibraltar when they were attacked by a wolf-pack of seven subs. They lost the
five ships, but one sub was sunk, and most of the crew captured and stuffed into
the lobby of Burdock's magazine, which was empty by then. They were left in
there for two days, packed like sardines without once being let out. Hanson
caught hell from Admiral-Gibraltar for mistreating prisoners of war.

"What did he want me to do? Give them the run of the ship?"

"George, who was that idiotic admiral in charge of Gibraltar? How can we
expect to win a war with fools like that in control? Do you think that fellow has
ever seen naval combat?"

247

"Jacques, we may still win the war in spite of them. Listen to this. Both of you work in intelligence, so I'll give you a piece of news that's been kept ultra secret. As far as I know, it's still super confidential, so you just don't know anything about it.

"This happened some time before I was sent to Philadelphia. The Germans had assembled a fleet of Heinkels in Vichy-French territory, with the obvious purpose of destroying Freetown as a base, and you know what that would have done.

"Well, someone must have got wind of it in the War Office. A secret air base was set up in the backwoods of Sierra Leone, with a hidden wing of old Hurricanes and a few modern Spitfires. The place had invisible radars, and shortly after the German bombers got off the ground to attack Freetown, the English fighters took to the air and picked them off. Only three Heinkels got through. One was shot down over the water, and the other two dropped the bombs on target, but the fires were quickly put out.

"What do you think of that, Jacques? After all this time, maybe we've learnt something. For once, we were not caught napping."

Irene and Jacques smiled at each other

In the taxi on the way home, Jacques said to Irene, "We would never have known about this, if it hadn't been for the news from George."

"I'm not surprised," said Irene. "In school I learned how Intelligence operates."